WHAT PEOPLE ARE SAY

TIME SPHERE

A rip-roaring adventure that takes the reader on a dizzying journey from suburban England to ancient Egypt. Wild chases, mortal danger, mystical intrigue, unlikely heroes. This book has it all.

A young English schoolboy, naïve and thinking little beyond what is for dinner, is swept up in an adventure that, unbelievably, takes him from his staid suburban home to an ancient druidic ceremony and finally to Ancient Egypt. Along the way he falls in with a beautiful Egyptian priestess and a student of Pythagoras, and together the three of them battle the mysterious Society of Secrets for control of the ultimate prize, Time itself. This novel, comparable to Time Bandits, will enchant the reader. Warning: make sure you have enough time to read it in one sitting, because you won't want to put it down once you've started.

Philip Duke, author of *A Terrible Unrest.*

A spectacular adventure where ancient and modern combine, where good and evil are challenged and where fantasy fiction reaches a clever, hilarious and wonderfully engaging level – gripping!

M.C. Morison takes the reader through time's doorways and corridors. His story is filled with secrecy, exotic locations, dark characters and wonderful imagination. In Time Sphere we hear an authentic voice which makes the impossible possible when characters from the past and present entwine to counteract evil.

Marie Quirk-Smith, author of *A Place in the Choir*

This is an exciting book with something important to say. I read it on the train on the way to and from a meeting and was so engrossed I almost missed my stop.

Rhory is a lovely character – a perfect mix of a highly intelligent lad with all the normal adolescent angst. We care about him and Natasha and my heart banged in fear in places. M. C. Morison has brought alive four worlds in this unusual time slip story – the

Egyptian world, the Greek, the Druids of Albion and the modern world. Rhory's world is our world and what kept me turning the pages was the unravelling of how these worlds are inextricably linked in a way we had not realised. For this book is about how our era is living in darkness – that our time has forgotten or been separated from a knowledge held by those in ancient times.

This book is full of all the best ingredients – character, adventure, mystery, history and the ultimate quest for meaning and truth.
E. J. Bousfield, author of *The Jewel Keepers*

This tale of a teenager, mysteriously embroiled with the Egyptian past is a compelling and painstaking encounter with the classic concept of good and evil. Rhory is borne from the predictable present to contend with black arts and the riddle of the Time Sphere which if solved will prevent the Society of Secrets from controlling time for their own dark ends.

The plot moves between present and past with atmospheric conviction. The mundane and mysterious are skilfully combined to create a magical dimension of time travel with a wealth of well-crafted perils and revelations.
Linda Talbot, former arts editor, *Hampstead and Highgate Express*, London

Time Sphere is an exciting YA novel that is sophisticated enough to appeal to adults too. When Rhory visits the British Museum he unwittingly begins an adventure that will keep the reader guessing what will happen next. As his dreams turn into time travel he is connected with a teenage priestess from ancient Egypt and a teenage boy whose sister marries Pythagoras. Much to his surprise, he discovers that he has been chosen to work with them to save Time from the control of nefarious characters from the past and present.

This action-packed story is sure to keep you reading and by the conclusion of the story it will have you questioning the relationship between the past, present and future.
Jan Krause Greene, author of *I Call Myself Earth Girl*

Time Sphere

Time Sphere

M. C. Morison

Winchester, UK
Washington, USA

First published by Lodestone Books, 2014
Lodestone Books is an imprint of John Hunt Publishing Ltd., Laurel House, Station Approach, Alresford, Hants, SO24 9JH, UK
office1@jhpbooks.net
www.johnhuntpublishing.com

For distributor details and how to order please visit the 'Ordering' section on our website.

ISBN: 978 1 78279 330 4

A CIP catalogue record for this book is available from the British Library.

Design: Stuart Davies

Printed in the USA by Edwards Brothers Malloy

We operate a distinctive and ethical publishing philosophy in all areas of our business, from our global network of authors to production and worldwide distribution.

For Heather and Roxy
who both like a good tale

Acknowledgements

The creative springs behind Time Sphere are several and those who have helped along the way are many. I hope I can do them all justice here. Bob Zablok founded our writers' group in Crete and offered nothing but encouragement. Marie Smith and Linda Talbot have provided valuable feedback and Phil Duke has helped at every stage, not least with a careful edit. My old school friend John Grzegorzek heard about Time Sphere on Facebook and offered his exceptional copy editing skills just when they were needed most. He, more than most, could appreciate the presentation of Scrivener's, which drew on our own schooldays in Collyer's.

Many friends on JustWriteOn gave helpful feedback for the earliest version of Rhory's adventures. Later, the inestimable Scribophile community provided detailed critiques, always constructive, as Time Sphere unfolded chapter by chapter. In particular I am deeply indebted to Nessie Strange, A. K. Fotinos-Hoyer, Alice Grace, Jennifer Rowan, Adam Richardson, Sylvia Stone, Amy Rose, Irene Carney and Kirsty Anderson. Douglas Foote believed in this project at its inception and my brother, Ian Morison provided a crucial input about the balance of dark and light in the book.

Elizabeth Michaels whom I know best as Elizabeth Luffy, gave exceptional support in our Inkpop days, as did Liese Pfeuffer Semans.

My wife Heather listened attentively and always supportively to the chapters after they had been tapped out on my iPad. For her encouragement and patience all the way through I am most grateful.

This book would never have come into being without the ideas seeded by the work of the Fintry Trust. Those who would like to know more about the Hermetic tradition and the perennial philosophy it embraces are encouraged to visit www.thefintry trust.org.uk

For more information about the background to this book and the next two volumes of Rhory's adventures please visit www.timepathway.com

Chapter 1

A Stranger Calls

England – about now

"Ouch … stop! Stop it, you furry monster!"

I sat cross-legged on my bed, having finished with homework. Jester, intrigued by the 10 little grey mice at the end of my feet, pounced. His claws went right through my socks.

"Ow."

I pushed the cat onto the floor but he jumped straight back and started washing himself. I continued sorting out my notes for my English project.

The doorbell rang. "Mum! Mum!" No reply, so taking a deep breath, I shouted, "Muuum … it's the door."

I waited. The doorbell rang again and echoed through the silent house. Actually, I could hear something; faint strains of violins wailed classical something or others from Juliette's bedroom. Why my sister didn't just wear earphones remained a mystery. The loud music gave her the perfect excuse for not answering the door though.

"Mum!" I tried again, shouting even louder, before remembering that she had gone across to the library. *Bother, I don't need this.* I padded down the stairs, jumped the last four steps and landed more noisily and painfully than I'd intended. I yanked on the front door, as it always stuck.

"Good evening, my friend!"

A young man stood there. He'd spiky dark hair, a little moustache painted on his face, and a black jacket with bits hanging down to the back of his knees, like someone at a posh wedding. He wore white gloves and ridiculously shiny shoes.

"Er, hello."

"May I enquire, is the lady of the house at home, or indeed your esteemed pater?"

He didn't look dangerous to me, but you never knew. Whatever they were that began with the syllable 'pea', and threatened children, came in all shapes and sizes; though I admitted, I never imagined one with a little black moustache – unless it was Hitler of course.

"No, um that is, they'll be back any moment. Can I help you?"

"That's very kind of you. I am collecting signatures, but they have to be from the householder. We are trying to save the local bandstand. The council wants to bulldoze it and put some awful leisure centre there. It's historic and, as I suppose you know, young sir, we do little entertainments under its ancient roof, throughout the summer. Here's my card."

He slowly held up his empty-gloved hand. He showed it on both sides and then proceeded to produce a business card out of thin air. He held it out to me.

"Wow!" I reached for it a little gingerly. "Are you a magician, then?"

"Not really," he replied, flicking the card up in the air, where it promptly vanished and appeared in his other hand. He held it out again.

I took it, thanked him, and put it in my trouser pocket.

"How'd you do that?" I asked, my voice sounding a bit loud in my head.

"Ah, now, that would be telling wouldn't it?" He held up a clipboard. "It's quite tiring walking the streets, though I've a goodly number of signatures."

He swayed a bit and his eyes lost focus. I was about to ask if he wanted a glass of water, when a long, straight walking stick appeared in his hand. He leant on it.

"That's better." He smiled at me and I noticed how blue his eyes were: bluer even than Mum's. He flourished his stick and it turned into a snake that disappeared slowly up his sleeve. I'd never seen that trick before and could feel giggles developing inside. My shoulders crept up towards my ears.

Perhaps he sensed my discomfort because he stepped back until he reached the gate to our tiny front garden.

"Have you noticed?" he said. He pointed up the street towards the railway line at the end. There above the trees hung a huge, yellow full moon.

"People say when it looks that big, it's an illusion, but I don't know. It looks real to me! Thank you anyway, young man. I might come back to see your parents later, if that would be all right with you?"

I didn't answer, because the moon was, well, actually … enormous. I'd never seen it so big. I stared up our road at it for a moment or two before I remembered my manners. I turned to answer the strangely dressed guy, but he wasn't there.

I couldn't believe my eyes. He'd just gone. Even if he'd run, he would've barely made the corner as I turned.

A little way down the pavement, a small black and white dog scrabbled about chasing its tail. It stopped. It looked at me, or possibly the moon, barked a couple of times, then ran down the road towards the park and disappeared around the corner. I'd no idea where it had come from or if it belonged to the strange man who seemed to have just vanished.

Moments later, Mum appeared at the same corner.

"I thought you were doing your coursework, Rhory. Remember, we are off to London tomorrow. Why are you out on the street, and why aren't you wearing shoes?"

"Someone rang the doorbell. You must've seen him. He was dressed like … well like someone at a wedding. You must've passed him coming back from the library, didn't you? And there was a small dog."

"I don't think so, dear. No, I'd have noticed a man in a morning suit with a dog, I'm sure. Goodness, you look pale, Rhory. Are you okay?"

"You must have. He was right here." I nearly stamped my foot.

Mum smiled her, you're-having-me-on-again-Rhory smile.

"He gave me a card, actually," I said, a little too loud, and reached into my trouser pocket, where I found only a broken pencil. I tried the other pocket. The card took a bit of extracting as it had fused to a half-sucked boiled sweet, wrapped in a bit of Kleenex that had in turn welded itself to my pocket.

Finally, I retrieved it.

"Look, Mum," I said, waving the card. But Mum had also disappeared and I could hear her calling up to Juliette inside the house. I read the card. On one side it said simply,

Caduceus Productions

On the other it said,

Magic, Mystery and Illusion
we are at your service

There was no name or phone number.

Chapter 2

The Egyptian Room

The following day a London taxi whisked Mum and me past cafes, newsagents – with tempting displays of crisps and sweets – and little shops offering Chinese prints, obscure books and small statues. A window with chipped paintwork displayed posters of Tutankhamen. Finally, I saw one place that might be worth visiting, a shop with a huge collection of comic books.

"Hey, Mum! I could wait in there, couldn't I?" It looked more fun than the museum.

"Where, darling?"

"The comic shop … back there."

"We might go after I meet up with you, dear. I think you'll find there's more to see in the museum."

The taxi drew to a halt.

"Okay then, I'll pick you up in about an hour and a half, when I've got the tickets. Make sure your mobile's on."

Mum leaned over and buttoned up my jacket. I grimaced. Once out of the taxi I undid them again.

"And, Rhory, wait in the foyer, in case the…" My mum's voice floated out of the departing taxi's window but the whole message didn't. I assumed she was worried the mobile might not work inside the huge building that housed the British Museum.

I strode up the entrance steps narrowly avoiding a school party coming in the other direction. Excited voices shared intense experiences, and dark eyes sparkled with pleasure. I didn't understand a word, as they chattered to each other in Chinese.

The chilly wind found its way inside my open jacket as I reached the top of the stairs.

"Your bag, please."

A burly man in uniform protected the main doors. He pointed at my little rucksack, the one with the picture of the skateboarder doing a somersault.

"I need it with me," I said.

"I'm not going to take it. I already have that one in my collection." His grimace, an attempt at a smile, revealed a missing front tooth. He had the look of a boxer. "I just need to check inside," he said.

He rummaged about, finding a pack of chewing gum and examining two sandwiches made by my mum. ("Just in case, dear.") My book about the history of dragons appeared briefly and then slipped back inside. Apparently none of these things caused alarm. There would be no headline tomorrow saying, "British Museum demolished by a prawn, lettuce and mayo sandwich."

"Enjoy your visit, sonny," he said as I made my way to the huge doors.

Sonny! I resisted the urge to be cheeky and entered the enormous foyer. It was full of noises, echoes and people.

The entrance doors swung open letting in a cold blast of air. Something moved in the breeze by my feet. A feather hovered and twisted on the ground. I picked it up. The colours were various greys with more than a hint of very dark green. It looked a little longer and wider than a pigeon's feather, and appeared too exotic for a standard London bird.

A group of kids chatted noisily in French in front of the signboard that showed where to go for the different exhibitions. One girl, with her hair in a high ponytail, wore a long white padded parka and short red boots. She turned her freckly face and looked at me standing there with the feather in my hand. I slipped it into my jacket pocket, feeling slightly silly.

She gave me a grin highlighted by a flash of braces and went back to chewing. A bubble of gum expanded out of her mouth and popped on her lips. It confirmed my opinion that the French are not as cool as they sound.

Where should I go first? A large poster advertised the Chinese Vase exhibition with the title 'Porcelain and Plunder'. Even that catchy description couldn't disguise the fact it would be a room full of old pottery. 'Coins Through the Ages', declared the next poster. My heart sank.

The French children left and I watched Miss Red Boots moving her arms about as she chatted to one of her friends. It proved she could walk, talk and chew at the same time, which impressed me. Where they had been standing, a display showed two bronzed men fighting with each other. I moved closer and read, 'The Battle of the Gods'. Now that showed distinct promise. A special exhibition in the Egypt Room explored the never-ending fight between a dude in bandages and one with a head like an outraged anteater. *Just my sort of thing.* I might not have to visit the comic shop after all.

On the landing above the stone steps descending into the Egypt Room, a black woman with a lioness's head sat on a cold stone throne. Her bare breasts were at eye level and I tried hard not to stare. According to the little printed sign, she went by the name Sekhmet and had been worshipped as an Egyptian goddess. Some hard-working sculptor in ancient times had carved her out of one piece of black basalt. Below her, the exhibition hall could have comfortably housed two basketball courts. Way up above, the glass roof cast a cold light on rows of statues so huge that the visitors wandering around looked a like a race of pigmies on a Sunday outing.

I went in and skimmed stuff about the Rosetta Stone, and a Frenchman with a long name who had cracked the code of the Egyptian language. Further down on the left, two huge cardboard cut-outs stood on either side of a doorway. One showed the bandaged man wearing a tall white hat with a feather on either side; he looked a bit like an overdressed extra from *The Return of the Mummy*. His face had a sickly blue colour. The other man stared at him with reptilian eyes. His large square ears and coal black face, sporting a huge snout, didn't make him very cuddly. His body would have impressed the girls on any sun-lit beach though. He had the distinct advantage over his murdered brother, of being alive.

I passed between the two effigies and entered a dark corridor. It opened into a room that glowed with three-dimensional and coloured holograms. My heart beat a little faster as I moved between transparent Egyptian gods hovering in space, their ghostly eyes watching me.

Immediately on my left, the creepy god with big ears invited his handsome brother to get into a coffin. The coffin maker went by the name of Set, according to the sign. He was tricking his brother Osiris to try the coffin out for size. At this stage Osiris displayed a handsome tanned face and clearly enjoyed life.

"Amazing aren't they," said a tall man. He bumped into me as he passed. The man didn't apologise and continued his loud conversation with a woman in a close-fitting dress, who had to be way younger than him. She hung onto his arm and clacked through the room on startlingly high platform heels.

As I walked around the exhibits, I learned how the clever god Set chopped up his brother and scattered him all over Egypt. It was cool though, because Isis, his sister-wife, gathered all of his bits and stuck them together again. Well, one embarrassing bit was lost, eaten by a fish, but somehow Osiris managed to become the father of a child. I allowed myself to think for a millisecond, about marrying Juliette, my older sister. I decided I'd prefer to be chopped up into small pieces.

The next exhibit showed Isis. She looked very content hovering on a throne in the air, her little baby on her lap, with his hair in a rather neat top knot. The chair was covered with tiny golden hieroglyphic carvings. I walked around it and looked up as the French kids came into the room filling it with what sounded like *'Ooh La Las'* and *'Mon Dieus'*. I couldn't see Freckles with the bubble gum and white parka.

To keep away from their continuous babble, I moved swiftly towards the next room. The description at the entranceway told how the priests of Egypt had battled against each other in support of their various gods. They backed pharaohs they liked and murdered those they didn't. *A bit violent for priests.* Under the text, a picture of a pharaoh embalmed as a mummy, emphasised the same point.

I passed through an unlit tunnel that opened into a darkened space.

"Gosh," said a woman's silky voice, "but it's sooo real."

The young woman with the tight skirt, stood next to the man who had bumped into me earlier. An olive skinned head of a queen, complete with blue and gold crown, floated in front of them – the best hologram I'd ever seen. The woman laughed as the man passed his hand through the coloured light that made the queen's face. As he did so the laser beams flashed on his ring, producing lightning strikes of bright purple light. I blinked and moved.

The rainbow colours from the hovering bust of Nefertiti played on his face and made the man look somewhat grotesque. Dark shadows replaced his eyes and in the gloom, his skin looked scaly. He stared right at me. The ring on his hand continued to glow with a purple light all of its own. I swallowed and decided the noisy French kids were preferable to a ghoul, and walked back the way I had come.

Chapter 3

The Feather

My hands shook a little. The man in the dark room had unnerved me.

I crossed the huge exhibition hall, between assorted gods and pharaohs. On a stand in front of me a statuette of a temple cat sat motionless. The French girl with freckles was looking at it. She turned and caught my eye and I won another metallic smile. I smiled back, grateful that her natural warmth made me feel a bit less spooked.

I walked past her, trying not to grin and feeling completely tongue-tied. A doorway just beyond the stationary cat gave on to a long narrow room. It had soft lighting and the exhibits were arranged in little niches all the way down. My heart began to return to its normal rhythm as the atmosphere felt safe and comforting, like being in a small church.

I wandered slowly past displays of pictures, jewellery and statues. Set back, almost in a room of its own, was a huge stone chair. Although somewhat damaged, with small chunks missing, it still looked very impressive. The legs were carved like lions paws, and the arms ended with the heads of lionesses. I wondered what it would be like to sit in it, but it was protected by a red velvet cord suspended between two brass poles. Even though no one else could see me at that moment, I resisted the urge to step over and try it out.

The plaque said that the chair had been carved in an early dynasty before the time of the pyramids. No one knew its exact purpose.

I moved back towards the glass cabinet opposite the chair. This display had one large chunk of plaster from a mural, held in place with metal brackets and brightly illumined by a spotlight. It showed a woman's face and shoulders from a side view. Her dark hair was bound with a circlet of braided blue cloth supporting one green-coloured feather, pointing upright. The woman's deep blue eye was picked out with black lines of make-up.

According to the label, the mural showed a portrait of a young priestess of Maat, the goddess of truth and justice. I looked again at the painted feather and reached towards the one in my pocket. I froze. The glass of the display reflected the big chair behind me, with someone sitting in it! A figure dressed in white. A jolt of excitement passed through me at the thought of being followed. *It must be the French girl.* She'd get in so much trouble if an attendant saw her. Despite the braces on her teeth I found her quite pretty.

I turned slowly, practising *bonjour* in my mind. The chair was empty. She couldn't have just vanished. There was nowhere for her to hide. I looked down the hallway of exhibits. No one. *I'm imagining things.*

I turned back to the portrait of the woman. The label stated the priestesses had been called the Sisterhood of the Feather. At different times in Egypt's history they had been revered almost as gods themselves, because of their magical abilities.

Once more my eyes focused on the reflection of the chair. The girl had returned. *It must be an optical illusion.* I looked carefully. It wasn't the French girl but a tall young woman with long dark hair, braided with beads. Her eyes had make-up exactly like the painting in front of me. Her feet weren't covered with short red boots, but dark gold sandals.

"Wow," I said to myself. This was the coolest hologram I'd ever seen. I'd no idea how the museum could do it, and swung round quickly.

No one sat in the chair. Closer inspection showed no laser lights here. Anyway, the room wasn't dark enough for a hologram like the ones I'd seen earlier. I felt a little giddy.

I turned back to the mural of the priestess, trying to catch my breath. Carefully I drew out the feather I'd found in the entranceway to the museum. It virtually matched the one painted about 5,000 years ago.

My heart thumped away as I registered the young woman had returned to the chair. Holding my breath, I resisted turning this time and studied the reflection. The woman smiled, her face changing into that of a pretty girl about my age. She held my eyes with hers.

Inside my chest, somewhere near my heart an idea quietly settled, followed by the words, "At last."

Another idea followed the first producing the words, "Now I can see you properly."

The girl or priestess or whatever she was, shifted slightly in the chair. "My name is Shoshan."

These words blossomed within me like a smile and I had the distinct image of a lotus flower floating on the water. I didn't know how to communicate back, and tried thinking the words, "My name is Rhory."

I could see her frown, and inside I heard, "Red King?"

She waited. I nodded and said, "Rhory."

She smiled again for a moment before shifting in the chair as though someone had spoken sharply to her. She looked to the side. I felt a wave of sadness pass through me that I knew came directly from her. She vanished as though a light had been switched off.

I looked round. The man and his young girlfriend stood in the entranceway and were staring right at me. He no longer looked reptilian, rather he reminded me of one of those people you see on television who explain how fox hunting is actually kind to foxes.

Stifling the urge to run, I left the long narrow room by the second exit, as far away from the man with the flashing ring as possible. I felt as if I'd been swimming under water for too long and couldn't get enough oxygen. The statues of dead pharaohs were all around me and I needed space to breathe. I mounted the stairs at the far end of the hall, slipped past Sekhmet the black lioness, and found a big leather bench. I eased myself down onto its cool softness.

Had I just hallucinated? I didn't think so. I'd seen someone real, a girl about my own age. I'd heard her thoughts. I couldn't explain it any other way; her thoughts had just sort of popped into my mind. She ... Shoshan she said she was called ... she felt familiar; like seeing a good friend who has been away from your school for a year or two, and comes back for a visit.

From my leather bench, I could still observe the busy exhibition hall with all the Egyptian statues. At the far end, the man with the ring stood with the young woman, looking around carefully. I'd a nasty suspicion he was looking for me. Watching him as he systematically checked the room, I knew he'd broken the communication with the girl from ancient Egypt. For just a moment I wanted to do to him what Set had done to Osiris.

Instead, I decided to go in search of the canteen. I could feel a big empty space where my stomach should be. I waited for some people to pass by and tagged along with a couple of English families heading in the right direction, keeping them between the man with his girlfriend and me.

I couldn't see an empty table when I entered the canteen, so I joined the queue to get a drink. I had to hold on to the counter for a moment to avoid falling over as a wave of dizziness swept over me. A slice of carrot cake and a can of fizzy fruit juice looked attractive sitting on the chilled display unit. After paying, I scanned the tables to see if Amethyst Man had arrived with his popsy or topsy or whatever girlfriends who are way too young are called.

I chose a table tucked in the corner. The sensation of chilled fizziness at the back of my throat felt great. I drank, keeping an eye on the entrance to the canteen. Mum's sandwiches looked inviting and I quickly overcame the guilt twinges that I shouldn't be eating something I hadn't bought in the canteen. Biting into the brown bread sandwich provided the familiar taste of home.

All around the buzz of voices suggested that young and old were enjoying their visit. Gradually I felt less like I'd been dismembered like poor old Osiris. I still couldn't explain what had just occurred, but deep inside I knew. I'd somehow sneaked a view of a time different to my own, a time where a priestess from long past had found a way to speak to me.

Her face lingered clear in my memory and if I directed my attention deep, deep inside, something of the girl remained in contact. Her words echoed inside my mind – a voice shouting from far away. I shivered even though I felt hot.

My hands still shook as I moved on from the prawn sandwiches to the carrot cake. I fished out my book on dragons and flipped through a few pages.

A stab of fear in my tummy reminded me to check around the canteen. Everyone looked friendly, normal and definitely twenty-first century. My mobile remained entirely silent. *Mum surely must have bought the theatre tickets by now.*

I pulled out the feather and I ran my finger down the soft edge. It soothed my jangled nerves. An image of Shoshan holding a feather just like mine, floated into my mind.

I looked up to see the freckly French girl heading in my direction with another girl. She was smiling and talking. They both looked across at me.

At that moment Mum rang my mobile.

*

The man with the amethyst ring surveyed the foyer to the British Museum. He tapped a number on his mobile.

"Our vocalist has proved accurate once again," he said softly. Indistinct noises came from the other end of the line.

Meanwhile, his girlfriend tutted at a ladder that had started in her tights. She balanced on one high-heeled shoe and peered over her shoulder at her leg. Her hand rested on the man's arm.

"No, he was there all right," continued the man, "just as she'd said he'd be. I couldn't get a good look at his face but I saw how he was dressed. He had a distinctive bag… No don't do that…" said the man as the girl pulled at his arm with an 'I'm sooo bored' expression on her face. "No, not you, someone at the museum," he continued into the mouthpiece. "I'm waiting in the foyer to get a good view as he comes out."

He listened for a bit and mouthed, "In a minute," to the girl.

"Yes, yes, I agree," he continued quietly into the mobile. "Another meeting is essential, just as soon as we can get the girl out into the countryside again." He listened some more and then said, "Okay, I'll make it happen. There may be no need though. I'll follow him when he comes out. Accidents happen in this part of London all the time."

He hung up and suggested to the girl that she should go to the canteen and wait for him there.

She pouted.

*

"Well done, Rhory," said my mum, as I clambered into the taxi.

"Why didn't you come to the front, Mum?" I asked, pulling down one of the seats that promptly snapped up again.

"Come and sit next to me, silly," said Mum patting the seat next to her. "The taxi driver said it's easier to wait around the side of the museum. The police move you on at the front, something to do with terrorism. Did you find the side exit okay?"

I wasn't able to answer as the taxi driver launched into complaints about both the police and the foreign terrorists who were taking all the jobs. He pulled out into the busy London traffic, still wittering on, while Mum proudly showed me the bunch of tickets for a ballet called *The Nutcracker*. That produced all sorts of imagery in my head that I kept to myself. I crossed my legs.

Chapter 4

Netherworld

Egypt – the dawn of time

The priestess entered the subterranean room where Shoshan sat alone, her slim figure and white robes dominated by the bulk of the stone chair. Her eyes were closed and her dark hair spilled over her shoulders.

"We must stop at once," Hasina announced.

"But why?" said the girl, full of excitement. "We have finally made a contact."

"I know," said the older priestess. "You've done amazingly well, Shoshan, better than we could have hoped over such a short time..." Hasina trailed off. Tension and fear clogged her usually clear mind.

The pretty face of the young priestess turned towards her.

"Come," Hasina said, gesturing to the doorway.

Shoshan walked across the stone floor, her face radiant with success.

"I actually saw him. It wasn't easy, but I found him."

"I know," responded the older woman, her chest tight with concern.

They mounted the stone steps together and entered the Temple of Protection. Twelve wooden chairs were arranged in a large square around a simple altar adorned with flowers. Incense burned in copper dishes on raised wooden posts.

The other priestesses crowded around a figure lying on the floor.

"Merit, is it Merit?" Shoshan asked, stopping at the top of the stairs, worried sick about her closest friend.

"Give her room to breathe," Hasina said, and gently moved two of the older sisters from where they knelt leaning over the unconscious girl.

They chose the weakest link, Hasina thought to herself. *I should have foreseen this possibility.* Not for the first time this day, she regretted that the head of their Order had had to leave so suddenly for the south of the kingdom.

"What happened?" said Shoshan, her voice now shaking.

Hasina looked up from where she had squatted down by the prone girl, and saw Shoshan had turned milky pale. "We're not sure," she said. "When she fell, she said something about a cat..."

"A silvery cat it was, I heard her distinctly," said one of the two older priestesses.

"We must get her to the infirmary," said Hasina, "and ensure she has complete rest." She gave a series of instructions concerning herbs and medications. She knew that the holy oil they had immediately administered had probably saved the girl's life. This type of attack had never taken place before in this temple. It provided further evidence, if any were needed, that the servants of chaos were practising their poisonous arts.

When the wounded priestess had been safely carried out of the temple on a litter, Hasina told the other priestesses to go and rest, for they'd be needed again soon.

"Walk with me," she said to Shoshan.

The temple was set within a colonnade, which kept it cool in the punishing heat of the summer. They crossed the spacious courtyard beyond the colonnade, and on this cooler day, Hasina enjoyed the cleansing warmth of the sun as it radiated fiery heat over her skin. Even this close to the equinox, the daytime sun could be too powerful to be exposed to for very long. They found a cypress wood bench in the shade of some trees.

"Tell me what you experienced, Shoshan, and then we will talk of what must happen next."

"At first it was hard for me to really concentrate," she began. "I needed to line up all the Doorways, just as you've taught me, and found I couldn't hold them all clear in my mind. After a while, your chanting came very close and I could move through the bands of mist. As I did so, I had a waking dream." The excitement of the experience animated her face and hands once again.

"A feather ... a feather like our holy feather fluttered in front of me. I picked it up and used it to guide me through the mistiness. I can't tell you exactly how, but the feather seemed to show the true way."

Shoshan stopped and her eyes became wistful.

"And what happened then?" Hasina asked, touching the young priestess's hand.

"For a moment I found myself somewhere entirely strange. It must have been a temple. It appeared truly enormous, bigger than any temple in Ta-Opet. I could hear noise everywhere but nothing made any sense. Then I saw the feather once more at my feet ... except they were not my feet..." She stopped and looked across at the older priestess. "Do you understand me?"

"Yes, I do, dear, maybe more than you know. Just go on and explain what you saw."

"I couldn't find my way. Everything had become dark. I could sense a part of myself a long, long way away, as though at the far end of a very long journey... I don't know how to explain it better."

Hasina, squeezed her hand. "I'm following. Keep going."

"This other part that was me, yet wasn't me all at the same time, searched ... but didn't know what it was searching for. And then it all became clear. That's the amazing thing – I could see the picture of Katesch."

"What picture?"

"The one in our refectory, where all the portraits of the High Mothers are painted."

"You mean the one of Katesch, painted when she was anointed as leader?"

"I didn't know when it was done, but yes that one. That image dissolved and I could see a different temple, with cabinets made of clear crystal. A boy stood in front of one of these glowing cabinets, the one with Katesch's picture, a boy who knew me even as I know him. He's the link we have been seeking. He even proved clever enough to tell me his name. I think he is a Hearer, like you and me. The sound of his name is really strange, you know. It's something like Ro-Ree."

Hasina frowned; this wasn't an Egyptian name.

"But," her young friend continued, "I heard what the name means, it means Red King. I think he's actually a king, isn't that remarkable?"

"Indeed." Hasina grasped her hands together. "Remarkable." She paused and looked at the younger girl. "What you've done, Shoshan, is also remarkable and perhaps much more significant than you currently realise. You've forged a powerful link with another Seed of Life. We are all proud of you."

The younger girl smiled at her friend, and then a cloud passed over her features. "What caused Merit to collapse?" she asked.

"We can't be sure," the older priestess replied, thinking Shoshan deserved the truth. "Remember, treasure, that the work we are doing takes us into the borderland of Amenti, the netherworld. It is here that Time is coiled like a great snake, and can be traversed. Those who master Time's mysteries become guardians of the ages yet to come and – some say – of the ages that have passed. It is the deepest purpose of our blessed Order."

"Why are some trying to stop us then? Surely we all serve the same Gods, the same truth?"

"Others seek to gain control of time for their own reasons, wishing for personal power rather than service to the holy Gods."

Shoshan stopped, and turned to the older priestess. "Will Merit be all right?"

Hasina wondered how much to explain, for she didn't know for sure if Merit would fully recover. "The aspect of Set in the netherworlds that seeks personal power beyond all things, can appear as a cat, silvery and persuasive, but also deceitful and deadly. I believe this force may have attacked Merit. The Sisters acted quickly and we must pray to the Gods they acted in time."

Hasina put her arm around the other girl's shoulders and gave her a squeeze. "Go and rest, treasure. You will need all your strength again tomorrow. Now you've found another of the Seeds of Life, far away in time, we must work to protect him, for he'll know little or nothing of his true purpose. He lives an age of great spiritual darkness as you know."

The next day the priestesses gathered in the Temple of Protection once more. Merit's place was taken by another experienced priestess, and all wore protective amulets around their necks, according to their name and status in the Order.

Hasina and Shoshan descended into the room beneath and Shoshan eased herself back into the stone chair. Her graceful hands rested on the two lions' heads carved into the chair arms. The room carried the faint fragrance of kyphi incense used in the simple ceremony of preparation.

"Remember, Sister," said Hasina, "just forge the bond with our Red King. It is he who has to awaken to his true purpose. It is there deep inside him as it is deep inside us all. Let Anubis be the guide. You are just the messenger."

Each wall of the small room displayed a painting of one major deity. The chair faced a larger than life-size view of the jackal-headed god, Anubis, the guide of souls. Like all the walls in this crypt, it had a light of its own. The tiny crystals in the stone walls scintillated with a brightness that healed as well as revealed.

The light gently illumined Shoshan's features. The girl prepared to take the image of Anubis deep within herself and send it through the shifting corridors of time, to awaken and guide the boy.

The science behind these glowing walls would eventually be lost, Hasina knew. In her own explorations through time, she'd seen ages where darkness, not light, held sway and the purity of their fair

Egypt would also be lost as though it had never been.

Much of the deepest knowledge of their Order would be withdrawn in the centuries to come, so that its power could not be abused. Set's Children would inherit the earth and lose the heavens. Their reign wouldn't be forever, not if Shoshan's work proved fruitful. Her task, with the other Seeds of Life, would be to shift the flow of Time itself.

Looking back once more at the youngest of their Order, thin as a graceful reed in the stone chair, Hasina climbed the stairs to join the Sisters in the room above, murmuring a quiet prayer.

Chapter 5

Paralysis

England – about now

I woke up and found I couldn't move. My eyes wouldn't open, my muscles wouldn't obey me. This had happened once or twice before and I'd managed to shake myself awake.

I could sense a presence in the room. I had to sit up and see what was there. An icy emptiness opened up inside me.

I tried to kick my legs, but nothing happened. I lay there, unable even to raise an eyebrow, alone with my thoughts my fear and this thing in the room. I tried to move again and failed. I'd never felt someone else there before. Whoever it was waited patiently but that didn't stop me from drowning in my own fear.

Then from some inner recess of mind, I remembered there was a way out of this state. I'd used it before. It would take an enormous effort of will. I had to disregard whatever stood watching me. Instead I focused on my toes. The toes had a slight immunity.

I tried to get a tiny bit of movement in the little toe of my left foot. With a huge effort of will, I managed to flex the whole foot. That did it. I straightened my leg and shifted my whole torso with a violent twitch. Finally, I opened my eyes, sucked in a huge breath and searched unsuccessfully for the light switch.

Scrabbling to get clear of the bedclothes, I stood up. A glowing eye watched me. All the rest of the person had been rubbed out. I shouted. It continued to glow in the dark, suspended in space. After a few more heart-stopping moments, it gradually faded. It vanished entirely when Juliette came in and flipped the lights on.

"Bloody hell, Rhory," said my sister, "I thought you were being murdered. Just as well Mum and Dad sleep with earplugs in."

I sat back down on the bed and mumbled something.

"You're too bloody old for nightmares." She came and sat next to me.

"It wasn't really a nightmare."

Juliette put her arm around my shoulders. My older sister could be a royal pain, but she was essentially kind.

"Never mind, Rhory, I'll tuck you up. Do you want some milk?"

Feeling more like six years old than twelve, I got back into bed. "No thanks," I said, swallowing and shivering.

Juliette kissed my forehead, something she'd not done for ages. I eased my way down the bed with my heart hammering away.

Juliette turned at the door and whispered, "That was a hell of a shout you let out. I'm surprised the neighbours haven't called the police. Go back to sleep now, Rhory, it's three in the morning."

The door quietly closed and the house subsided into total silence.

I must have just been dreaming. That's what I thought until I noticed Jester, lit by the light of the street lamps and crouching in the corner of the room. The cat's eyes stared at the point where the floating eye had been. All his fur was on end.

The next morning, I sat cross-legged on my sister's bed. I often did this at weekends, when we surfaced long before our parents, chatting about this and that.

"What do you reckon, Jules, was it just a dream?"

Juliette sipped her tea, from a huge mug with a picture of a cow, and looked at me through its vapours. She had the duvet wrapped around her, so only her head and arms emerged from a soft cocoon of feathery comfort.

"Well, Rhory, that's the simplest explanation, Occam's Razor and all that."

"Oakham Raise her?" I asked. "Who or what is that?"

"Not Oakham, turnip ears, *Occam*. He was the guy who

suggested when there are two explanations, the simplest one is most likely to be true. In this case, the simplest one is that you were dreaming."

"But why couldn't I move, Jules? I didn't like it at all."

Juliette put down her cup and composed her face into that 'now I'm going to lecture little brother' look.

"Did you know that in Soviet Russia they used to drive people mad like that?"

"Like what? Like forcing them to experience strange visions?"

"No, dear boy," she said in her smoothest sisterly voice. "By preventing them from moving."

"How on earth did they do that?" I asked, feeling faintly alarmed.

"Well, when they had locked up a dissident…" She paused and arched her eyebrows to see if I knew the word. I wasn't going to let on if I did or not, so I just looked back at her, all wide-eyed and innocent. "That's someone who had upset the regime," continued she-who-must-explain. "…Then such a political prisoner would be wrapped in a wet sheet. When it dried they couldn't move at all. It's like being buried alive. It would soon drive people mad."

"Well I'd be pretty mad if someone did that to me."

"Yes, Rhory, you would I'm sure," said Juliette with mock condescension. "But they went stark, raving bonkers."

"Thanks, Sis, that makes me feel a lot better."

"In your case, insanity came first!" she said. "What it is, Rhory, is part of your brain wakes up and part doesn't. You are aware you are awake. The bit that moves your body is still in blissful slumber. So you can dream and be awake at the same time."

"Sounds like being at school, Jules."

Juliette smiled at that.

I went on, "But I sensed a presence in the room and when I sat up and could look, there was an eye, glowing and watching me. How does Mr Oakham explain that?"

Juliette turned her high octane IQ onto the puzzle of the eye. "I don't know, Rhory. If you really were awake, then you would have been having an hallucination. I suppose that's like a dream but worse," she offered, turning the sisterly screw another ratchet.

"What about religious people?" I asked. "You know when they have visions of angels or what-have-you."

"Well you know me, Rhory, I'm agnostic to my core, and I don't have much time for the idea of angels. I'd expect that they are also hallucinations brought on by fasting and wanting to see one so very, very much."

At that point Dad walked past the door, with a cheery, "Morning, Kidiwinks, come down for breakfast or you'll be late for school." That put an end to exploring the stranger corners of my mind, at least for the moment.

That night, I lay in bed in the dark, Jester curled up on my pillow, his whiskers dangerously angled towards the most ticklish part of my ears, and reviewed what Juliette had said. Unlike me, she essentially believed what she could touch. I didn't agree with her that science had all the answers, or the Amazing Mr Occam for that matter. I had had too many experiences that did not fit into her simple common-sense universe.

I hadn't let on to Juliette about my flying dreams. To the rest of my family dreams remained dreams – sometimes fun but definitely not real.

My nocturnal trips seemed very real indeed. The vivid landscapes I soared over didn't appear to be of this time, containing as they did strange monuments, temples and castles. After arriving back in bed from my flights (or when I'd woken up, Juliette would maintain), the experiences seemed as vivid as my memories of being at school or going on holiday.

I lay there thinking about that and watched the eye that in return watched me.

I sat up with a cry. A person stood in the room. He had a black dog's head with enormous ears. A startlingly blue-black eye watched me steadily. He held a golden stick of some sort. His muscular arm sported a solid gold bracelet on the biceps. He glowed with an inner light. I could see every detail clearly. I jumped out of bed.

My heart beat so hard, it thundered in my ears and behind my eyes. My chest ached as I held my breath. The man or beast had an extraordinary blue collar. From its glittering edge a golden pendant hung onto his green leather vest.

I expected the apparition just to vanish as I woke up more, but it remained, hovering. My feet seemed stuck to the carpet; my visitor's reddish legs were suspended about half a metre off the ground. The blue eye continued to watch me.

I heard someone or something calling, and calling from a great distance, too far away to be heard. I listened hard, but couldn't really catch any words. The voice might be that of the girl in the museum. For a moment I thought I could hear her, but the sounds coiled back into distant silence. The figure in the room, like illumined powdered glass, slowly faded, while the eye hovered for a while longer in the darkness and abruptly vanished.

My nails bit into the skin of my forearms where I hugged myself. I wiped the dampness off my forehead and sat down heavily on the bed. My mouth tasted sour. The house remained as still as a deserted grave. At least I hadn't shouted.

I put on the light and checked the clock. The hands once more showed exactly three in the morning. So I must've been sleeping after all? I'd no memory of settling down to sleep. A long time passed before I felt confident enough to turn off the bedside lamp.

Chapter 6

A Journey

Egypt – the dawn of time

Shoshan sat once more in the warmth of the late afternoon sun, resting after her studies and the successful work of the previous evening. Hasina walked over to her.

"The pharaoh has been murdered." Hasina watched shock spread across Shoshan's face.

"How ... how did it happen?"

"Both the pharaoh and his queen have died. We will hear in time that the deaths were through illness; but Katesch is sure they were poisoned."

Shoshan sat upright on the cedar bench and closed her eyes; she took deep, slow breaths. Gradually she brought her shaking under control and sat as motionless as a statue.

"Shoshan, treasure," said the young woman, "there's no point. You will not be able to connect with Katesch from here. We're too close to the priests of Set and she'll hide herself from both them and us for a few days."

"But you spoke to her, Hasina, you just said so. What's to stop me?"

"She connected with me only for a few moments. I mostly saw her message as pictures rather than words. She informed me of all I needed to know, then she drew the veil around herself."

Shoshan wiped a tear from her eye with a brisk movement. "Will she be safe?"

"She is the head of our Sisterhood. Those who know us little, but fear us much, are convinced we are magicians. You know we are not and never could be, but someone like Katesch can hide in time's doorways and move through time's corridors. Even the most powerful of her enemies won't find her if she decides to remain hidden."

"Is she coming back?"

"The whole of Egypt is at risk, and Katesch is one of the few who have the power to ensure the Dynasties unfold as has been foretold. She'll do what needs to be done."

The younger priestess nodded, the shadows from the leaves on trees across the courtyard playing on her face. She wore no ceremonial make-up today but her eyes could still be startling in their directness. She looked at Hasina and said, "There's something you haven't told me."

Hasina nodded. Not much could be hidden from a Hearer, even by someone as gifted as herself.

"You'll need to leave at once, sweet sister. It's no longer safe for you here. Soldiers are marching. We can hear the blood lust in their minds. Our skills are no match for a direct assault at this time. Something happened when you found the boy, something or someone broke in, wounding little Merit. They discovered we'd forged a connection with the End Times. You are the first link in that chain of gold and the Red King is the last. We must get you to safety. And for him, we must offer prayer."

The young priestess nodded, and half closed her eyes to look towards the red disk of the setting sun. Shoshan had only seen thirteen summers and remained far more a young girl than a young priestess. Yet her slight shoulders now carried a great responsibility. Like most of the Sisters of the Feather she could 'hear'. Like her sisters, this had drawn her to the service of the Goddess Maat. But Shoshan alone could navigate these doorways of time from first to last. Even Hasina lacked this ability.

"I will need the chair," said Shoshan. "Without it I cannot move my mind down the rivers of time. I just lose myself."

"I know, sweet one," said Hasina. "The chair is very special, but it is not unique. Two were made, and a third that is no chair, but is Osiris's own sarcophagus."

Shoshan frowned. "I thought only one chair had been made and that it needed to be here, in Ta-Opet."

"That's what most priests believe also," said Hasina. "There's another chair carved from different rock. It's kept safe at the Hall of Records."

"I didn't know," said Shoshan.

"It is a secret well-kept from those who would seek to control the destiny of Egypt and the times beyond our time," said Hasina, moving over to her young friend. She placed her hands on Shoshan's shoulders. "Sho-sho, these times were foreseen. We are moving from the age of Garden of the Gods to the dark time of the desert of men. It has to be so. We are at that moment when time itself changes."

Shoshan stood and walked around under the trees, circling the bench and her friend. "Changes from what?"

"From the rule of Osiris to the misrule of Set. It is the way of things. Even our pharaohs foresaw that they might die, but couldn't use that knowledge to avoid their destiny. That is the reason Katesch travelled to the south of Egypt last month. She urgently needed the counsel of her king and queen and she wanted to see for herself what the Brotherhood of Set had planned. She found out more abruptly than she expected."

"What is she going to do now?"

"She'll travel north, Shoshan, and so must you. She'll find out if it is safe for you to go to The Hall of Records or whether the hand of Set has reached into that sacred ground as well."

Shoshan frowned again, as she absorbed how her life would now change. "And if the Hall is not safe?"

"We believe it will be, but not all of the area around. You need to be close to its influence to speak inwardly to Katesch. The dark brethren will be watching out for you. They know now what you can do."

"How do they know? We have kept all of this secret."

"Yes, but not secret across all time. As soon as you sail the waves of time, others can see what you do and try to stop you. One such stood near your Red King. We don't know how he found out, but he did. That was why we broke the communication so he couldn't trap the boy and locate you."

Hasina stood up and put her arms around the younger girl. "Come on, my little lotus flower, we need to get you ready for your journey."

The small, dirty craft bumped against the quay. Shoshan grimaced as she surveyed the cramped boat. She placed her belongings with care, avoiding the water sloshing around the bottom of the hull. Dressed as a boy, with a loose fitting cotton top and a crude kilt of coarse material, her long dark hair had been well hidden under a grimy headscarf.

The boat bobbed up and down on the canal, the flickering light of the torches barely reaching the top of the mast. Shoshan and Hasina awaited the setting of the sun, so the boat could slip out from this underground waterway and join the other traffic on the river.

"It's time," said Hasina, hugging Shoshan again. "May Maat watch over you on this and all your journeys."

Shoshan looked up at her friend. "You can travel time, Hasina. Have you seen how this works out?"

"I've walked beneath the stars on the Plain of Time, little one, it's true. But some things are veiled and some things are like the tumbling of a rock down the hillside, they can go this way or that. I pray for your safe arrival, because that is what I believe it will be." She smiled with much more confidence than she felt.

The sailor called from the boat, "Everything is stowed; we must go."

"Yes, Captain," said Hasina.

The round-shouldered man, whose physical bulk dominated the slim boat, beckoned to Shoshan. His craggy face remained unsmiling. Hasina turned back to the young priestess.

"Here," she said. "I've a gift for you."

She gave the girl a package wrapped in cloth. Shoshan opened it with care and studied the embroidered feather of a priestess of Maat, picked out in dark green against the dove grey of a cloak. She looked up at the young woman and made to give it back.

"This is your cloak, the cloak of a full priestess," Shoshan said.

"It's my cloak, you're right. But it's going to one who has earned the right to wear it. It will keep you warm in the chill of the desert and its blessings may keep you safe." She gently pushed the package back towards Shoshan. "Put it safely in the boat and wear it when you travel on your own. There will be no value in disguise at that point."

Shoshan wobbled on the small gangplank before stepping into the boat. "Careful, girl, careful," said the captain, as Shoshan stumbled and nearly lost her balance.

The boat eased out from the dock and Hasina admired the skill of the captain, pushing the large paddle at the back, and propelling them towards the great river. They disappeared into the gloom, as they moved out into the current of the river. Hasina knew they'd be safe for a while, on this overcast night. If the captain could not get Shoshan to safety then no one could.

She shivered as she remembered a vision of Shoshan transfixed by a spear, pinning her to the wood of a temple door. She murmured a prayer of hope that this future wouldn't come to pass.

Shoshan is not a mere rock on a hillside. She is wise beyond her years. May Maat watch over her.

Chapter 7

Dream Diary

England – about now

The alarm clock had rung and still feeling somewhat shaky, I got up. I'd achieved teenage status. I'd no idea who or what it was that had appeared in my bedroom the previous night. I guessed it had something to do with the girl I'd seen in the museum.

"You can come down now," Mum called out. On birthdays in our home, you have to wait until the table is prepared. Birthdays came with presents. I loved presents. I'd that sense of pleasant expectation and inhaled the aroma of fresh toast wafting its way up the stairs. I went downstairs to join the family. Music played – something classical and twangy.

"Morning, Rhory," and "Happy Birthday, darling," and "Well, look at him. Oh my God! Spot the difference! Now he's a teenager!"

That last comment came from my sister Juliette, of course.

"Wow, Mum, that looks nice," I said. As always, the big chair and the place setting were decorated with flowers. Perhaps it was a Norwegian tradition – I am half-Norwegian after all – but it was one we always followed. And the pile of presents looked suitably glittery and interesting.

In my family the years are 'bumped in'. So I had my dad at my feet and Mum and Jules with an arm and shoulder each. I got raised and bumped a full 13 times, with my backside hitting the floor repeatedly. How they managed, when even at my coming-of-age I was taller than most adults, I don't know. But they did.

It was official. I was no longer a child. I'd achieved that in-between zone between child and adult. Great, I thought. Maybe.

After a bowl of cereal and a piece of that lovely toast, with mountains of marmalade, I turned to the high point of the day: the presents.

There were the usual cards and quite acceptable gifts from my aunts – who always remembered – and acted on behalf of three uncles – who never remembered. A large parcel from Mum and Dad looked intriguing.

"Boom boom," said Dad.

I ripped off the paper and revealed bongo-drums in red wood.

"You can tune them," said Mum.

I grinned from ear to ear.

"My present is boring in comparison," said Juliette. "A book!"

I opened it. Juliette smiled her winning, beauty pageant smile; she was clearly pleased with herself. I saw the word 'dream' on the cover.

I often had vivid dreams, ever since I can remember. Sometimes I described these dreams over breakfast. Mum would say something like, "That's interesting, Rhory, did you have cheese on toast last night?"

Dad would be a little less random. "It's all symbolic you, know," he'd say.

Juliette would baffle me with some insight from her A Level Psychology course. Perhaps this was the reason for her birthday gift.

"It's a dream diary, Rhory," she said, "and it's got this cool dictionary part, so you can look up what your dreams mean." In rather lurid writing, across a picture of a fantastic sky above a dramatic ravine, it indeed said, 'Your Dream Diary'. It was written by a lady with the extraordinary name of Celeste Starwalker.

"Thanks, Jules, it looks really great," I enthused. And it did. *A very timely present.*

"Look at the front, Rhory," she said tapping the cover, "it has a really good guide. Now if you dream of penguins you can look up 'penguin', and see its meaning. It even has an entry called 'sister' –

see, it says 'Sisters represent your Wise Being and their every suggestion should be followed without question'. It seems quite comprehensive and surprisingly accurate."

She was right. Well, not right about the sister bit, but many of the things I remembered dreaming about were covered. Now I might actually have a way of making sense of my night-time visions. I wanted to explore the dictionary part, but that would have to wait until I'd returned from school.

The day at school proved totally predictable – boring, boring and tedious. The final bell of the school day rang and I headed for my form room. My mobile whined like an approaching police car: quite realistically, judging by the looks I got from the Year Sevens in the corridor.

"Hello, Dad!"

"I'm outside the school in the side road," said a tinny replica of my dad's voice, sounding much more Scottish than normal. Phones do that I've found.

"Uh, okay. Why?"

"We're going out. It's your birthday, remember!"

Of course it was, as if I'd have forgotten. My heart sank however, because I shared a birthday with my Uncle Andrew. He's one of the four Scots 'As', as Jules and I call them – my dad and his three brothers. I guessed this might be connected with Dad's surprising arrival.

At home, Mum gave me a cup of tea and a slice of cake "for the birthday boy" and told me to get on with my homework! That done, I changed rapidly, and then we were back in the car, Jules, Mum and me, with Dad driving, to go the mile or so to Hammerford's foremost hotel, the King's Head. Oh drat. Oh squashed hedgehogs. A family dinner party!

Chapter 8

The Kings Head

The King's Head in Hammerford had once used as the setting for a Dicken's story in a TV production. They displayed pictures in the lobby, celebrating their five minutes of fame. The hotel still had a coach-gate with a room above and a cobbled courtyard beyond. All very atmospheric, with beams and plaster and copper utensils everywhere. It provided the backdrop for my birthday bash, or rather for my Uncle Andrew. I suspected I came as a package deal.

Andrew, the youngest of my uncles, had achieved thirty. Apparently, this constituted a big enough deal for the whole Bruce clan to gather. He'd married Auntie Evette from Geneva. Just as well she hadn't married Dad's brother Adam. My family had enough claim to weirdness, without having Adam and Eve as an uncle and auntie!

As we came in, I spotted Uncle Adam, talking to the receptionist in the hotel lobby. He always appeared tanned (he spent a lot of time in Egypt) and remote (he spent a lot of time in the Egyptian section of the British Museum). I didn't like Adam that much. Too semi-detached and up himself.

"Don't tell me the twins are coming!" I whispered to Juliette. My young, identical cousins, are a royal pain in the nether regions.

"I hope not," she murmured. "I can see Aida though and no twins! So we may be safe!"

Aida was Adam's wife. He never tired of saying, "I unearthed her in Egypt." A joke I suppose. Ho, ho. Aida's Egyptian. Aida's nice.

The evening started with drinks in the bar. Dad presented me with an alcohol free cocktail. The glass, dramatic in shape and colour, had minty crystallised something around the rim, and a large orange plastic stirrer. A sharp orangy zest filled my nostrils. I saw various relatives wishing they'd gone this route, rather than the boring wines or whiskies they chose instead.

I gathered various cards and gifts in addition to those I'd garnered at breakfast. *Perhaps a joint birthday party is a good idea after all.*

Aunt Sofia must have returned from Eastern Europe. I looked around for my cousin, but couldn't see her. Sofia came over and gave me a package beautifully wrapped in gold paper.

"I didn't know you were back, Auntie."

"Yes, Rhory, we came back a while ago. We've been quite busy opening up our house again. And we had to fix Natasha's school. Unfortunately Natasha isn't going to be here tonight."

"Oh!" I said. I'd rather hoped I'd see my annoying but fascinating cousin.

"Yes, her school had a theatre visit to Brighton and she really had to go." Aunt Sofia looked away as she said this, and her eyes clouded over.

"Ah," I said, discovering that being officially a teenager didn't result in greater conversational skills with aunts.

"We must invite you round sometime soon! Uncle Arthur and I would love to see you." I noticed she didn't mention Natasha. Oh well, it seemed I was still in the doghouse with my cousin.

"Yes, Aunt Sofia." I drew breath to ask what school Natasha now went to, but my aunt had already turned, and was saying in her in wonderful Eastern European accent, "Evette, darling, it's been ages and ages."

My polyglot family, four Scots brothers with names beginning with 'A' and assorted foreign brides, sat down to the birthday feast. I nearly fell off my chair when I saw that Natasha's dad, my rather serious Uncle Arthur, had his head entirely shaved. He just wasn't the sort of guy to do that kind of thing.

As I received some wine from the waiters who didn't know any better, I forgot about Uncle Arthur's somewhat dramatic fashion statement. I didn't find out why he'd done it for some weeks, while I recovered from the attack in Hammerford Park.

Chapter 9

The Jackal

Egypt – the dawn of time

Chilly droplets of water speckled her arm, as Shoshan trailed her hand in the river. The small boat ran with the current. The palm trees on the banks slowly appeared, passed by and gradually fell away behind them. Their progress over the past few days had been so slow.

Captain Gruff managed the boat with ease, barking directions at her and uttering salty oaths when she messed up. She messed up frequently at first, but soon learned, and now the atmosphere on the boat had become one of truce rather than harmony. Shoshan didn't actually call her boat captain 'Gruff', but she'd awarded him this title in her head, as he'd yet to say a kind word to her, never smiled and hadn't told her his name. His lined face and crinkled eyes, narrowed against the sun, suggested he was much older than her father.

Hours and hours passed with little happening. Above her head the sail flapped and snapped as the captain allowed the wind and current to carry them down the wide river. They stopped near small villages and bought fresh food. They never took the local water. When a villager had offered them some, Gruff had rudely ordered him away. He'd frowned at Shoshan and said, "I don't want to deliver you with the squits." Shoshan could imagine what having the 'squits' would feel like and was glad they had several casks of the safe, sweet water from Ta-Opet.

One day had merged into the next. At night they'd tie up at the bank, and make a camp a little way inland. Gruff would direct Shoshan to collect driftwood and palm fronds for a fire. With sunset, the night-time chill soon had them both wrapping themselves in their cloaks. Gruff dozed sitting with his back against a tree. He kept a spear close at hand. Shoshan chose not to ask why; her stomach frequently turned over with anxiety anyway.

A movement by the boat startled Shoshan from her reverie. The hot sun burned down on her bare skin, skin that had been a pleasant olive colour and now was the dark reddish brown of field workers. She splashed some water on her face. Dipping her hand back in the water, she enjoyed its coolness and dreamt of swimming, to wash away the stale sweaty smell that now assaulted her nostrils.

The boat tipped sharply to one side so far that her hand jerked out of the water, and then the other way, plunging it back in. She gripped her wooden seat with her other hand, expecting to fall into the river any moment. A shadow passed between her and the sun and something flashed in the sunlight. The captain stood astride her and beat at the water with an oar as he shouted, "Pull yer arm in, lad!"

She obeyed and saw – just a cubit away – the cold eyes of a crocodile above the surface of the water. It had been moving towards the boat and now veered away from the splashing made by the oar.

Captain Gruff cursed under his breath as he righted the boat and put them once more before the wind. They'd come quite close to the shore. "Keep your eyes on me, lad," he hissed at her. "Don't look to the shore."

But Shoshan had already seen the two men, dressed like priests, standing close by on the bank. Had they heard the captain shout? She couldn't be sure, but if they were watching out for a fleeing priestess, they might now be alerted.

Gruff moved the boat into the centre of the river and set the fullest sail, giving up all pretence of being a fishing boat or local craft trading at the riverside villages. They moved on much faster now and passed by several small hamlets, where curious children watched them go swiftly by. Some called out, but the boat sailed too far away to hear their words clearly enough.

For the first time they noticed soldiers; a group of men sat in the shade of a clump of palms by the water's edge and the sun sparkled on the spears they had leant against the trees. The captain looked at Shoshan and grimaced. Shoshan guessed he didn't know whether they were servants of Osiris or of the rebellious priests of Set. They weren't about to stop and ask, and risk being caught.

That night, they pulled into shore, out of sight of any village. Earlier in the day, a trailing line and hook had taken a couple of river fish. These were soon cooking in the glowing embers of a fire.

The fishes tasted delicious and both Gruff and Shoshan washed down the welcome white flesh and crispy skin with weak beer. Gruff threw away the bones and burped into his fist. He wiped his mouth with the back of his hand and burped again.

"I need to leave you for a bit, boy," he said softly. His eyes caught the firelight. Shoshan saw anxiety reflected back in them and possibly fear. *Does he know I'm a priestess?* She wondered if he'd now betray her, and resolutely pushed the thought out of her mind.

"There's a village an hour's walk from here, on the river's edge. It's near a small temple. The priests we saw earlier may have come from there. I do not know if it has stayed loyal to..." He didn't finish the sentence but looked out over the dark waters of the river. After a moment he continued, "It's not late. I will go and see if it is safe for us to pass. You sleep, child, and I will be back long before dawn." Without waiting for Shoshan to protest or ask any questions, he stood, took his spear and walked off into the night.

Rivulets of fear spread through Shoshan's limbs. Shivering, she moved closer to the light and warmth of the fire, adding a few twigs and the final large, water-smoothed piece of driftwood. Its twisted shape was soon ablaze and the light provided a little comfort. The moon had just emerged above the palm tops, and over her head, she could see the familiar constellations that Hasina often spoke about. The stars flickered their cold light across the black sky.

Around her the landscape brooded, with a deeper darkness than the sky, and no stars to give it definition. Acrid wood smoke caused her eyes to smart. The river swished and gurgled, as it made its way towards the distant sea. On the riverbank, just beyond the weak glow cast by the fire, two red stars did not flicker. They watched Shoshan – unblinking.

Chapter 10

The Desert

Shoshan stifled the urge to scream, and glanced around to see if there was a second spear. The eyes could be the crocodile returning for the meal he had been cheated of earlier, or his cousin deciding to brave the light of the fire.

She scooped up a handful of sand, ready to throw at the eyes of the creature, before making a dash for the possible safety of the boat and its heavy oars. The thing moved closer, and for a moment Shoshan thought she recognised the familiar shape of a village dog. Something about the ears looked wrong to her: they were too big, and stood up proud of the head. The snout seemed longer than that of a dog. The animal turned away from the fire and walked a little distance towards the desert, before looking back at her.

Shoshan breathed out, releasing the pressure on her lungs, and clutching the sand tight in her hands. Perhaps it would just walk away. It didn't and came back towards the fire. Shoshan reached for the driftwood in the fire, but its whole length glowed with hot flames. Once more, the animal turned and walked towards the desert. It stopped and looked back at her.

Deep within, almost hidden under the sludge of her fear, Shoshan found the thought that this beast might be a sign. *Anubis carries a jackal's head and guides souls.* Dropping the sand from her hands, Shoshan stood and walked a few steps towards the jackal. *Perhaps the Gods are guiding me.* It trotted ahead and then stopped and glanced back. Shoshan followed slowly, as the dim light from the rising moon and the stars meant she had to pick her way with caution.

A few days in the boat had left Shoshan unused to walking on land, and she wobbled a bit as she felt the sharp stones through the thin leather of her sandals. Occasionally she tripped and nearly fell. The jackal, if jackal it was, waited patiently and then padded on a few cubits in front of her. With its dark pelt it almost vanished but the white fur on its chest glowed in the moonlight when it faced Shoshan.

The jackal knew where it wanted to go. Shoshan followed as her guide wove between small sand dunes and past cultivated fields. Gradually they climbed and the deeper darkness in front of them revealed the dark humps of low hills. The climb began to make her leg muscles ache and her breathing became laboured. The jackal stayed just far enough ahead to be out of reach but not so far that it went beyond her vision.

Shoshan glanced back, and her stomach clenched as she realised how far she'd walked from the river. A distant pinhead of light might be her fire; she couldn't be sure. Beyond, the river cut across the desert like a long, black ribbon stretching as far as her eye could see. She looked in the direction Gruff had walked and wondered if she could see torchlights or just the phantom lights that flickered when her own eyes were pressed tight shut. She shook her head, blinked a few times and looked again.

The animal snorted.

"Sorry," Shoshan murmured, her voice sounding very lonely on the hillside. The path climbed more steeply, and her breathing became harsher. Above, the moon sat like a segment of white fruit and painted the rocks surrounding her with cold light. She had to pick her way more carefully now, and the jackal allowed her to come closer. They followed a definite path and Shoshan wondered if it had been flattened by hungry goats or by priests approaching a mountain temple.

The chill in the air seared her nostrils. A faint aroma of some herb rose when her foot crunched on a small bush. A light passed across the sky, leaving a luminous gash that faded as quickly as it had appeared. Shoshan had never seen a shooting star as bright before and stopped to see if there would be another. The stars winked back at her from their icy depths.

She looked around to discover where her guide would lead her next. He had vanished. She shut her eyes tight, in case the falling star had blinded her for a moment. Searching again, she could see nothing but boulders and sand. *I've been abandoned.* Some dark spirit sent by Set had led her far into the desert to perish.

Various paths led to this point. Which one had she been following? She'd no idea. All around her boulders reached up towards the sky as the stars looked down, entirely unconcerned.

Shoshan breathed a rude word she'd learned from Gruff. She didn't exactly know what it meant, but it seemed to help a bit. She moved over to a ledge of rock to take the weight off her complaining legs.

Rather than swear again she whispered out loud to herself, "Breathe to connect to Spirit." Katesch had taught her this when she had first met the Reverend Mother. She took a slow breath and held it awhile, before allowing the air to slip past her lips. She remembered to pray, a quick prayer to Isis – who never abandons her children.

She leaned her back against the boulder – her eyes closed. The emptiness in the pit of her stomach lessened and her heart gradually stopped racing. When she opened her eyes, the moon had shifted just enough to reveal markings on the rock face in front of her. Curious, she crossed the open space and examined a picture etched into the stone.

It showed a woman in side view, with her body closely covered in netting. Her right hand held the loop of an ankh, with its cross piece below her fingers. Her left hand pointed with a staff, adorned with a lotus bud.

Shoshan drew in a sharp breath. Her own name meant *lotus. This is a sign from Isis.*

Picking her steps with care she walked in the direction of the staff. A moment later she saw the slight glimmer of light on the rocks ahead.

Chapter 11

Beware the Children of Set

England – about now

I woke with a start. Sitting up, I looked around the room. Outside the wind moaned softly. The shadow play of the leaves on my bedroom wall provided the only drama in an otherwise still room. No strangers with dog's heads stood observing me.

I couldn't find my dream diary on the bedside table. Bit by bit, I recalled I'd woken earlier. Fragments of a dream began to float back. In particular, I could still hear the fearful whines and shouts filling the forest, as the flare of the torches moved closer to where I hid.

I put on my bedside light. The diary lay open lower down the bed. I attempted to focus on the handwriting that covered the page but the letters floated around in a blur. My eyes weren't yet awake. I rubbed them and blinked a few times. Gradually I could read my writing and, piece by piece, the dream came back to me.

The girl sees two red eyes. She leaves the safety of the fireside and follows a great dog up into the hills. Everywhere the rocks look silvery in the moonlight. The dog just vanishes leaving the girl abandoned. Something or some people are searching for her. They want to stop her or worse.

At this point my spidery scrawl finished. I'd no memory of what happened next. But there was more writing below. It was in an entirely different hand.

Just five words were written beautifully:

"Beware the Children of Set."

I'd no idea what that meant but it sounded vaguely ominous. I'd have to do some research in the school library.

There was nothing free about free periods. We only had two during the week, and they were generally used to catch up on homework lost or forgotten. I had a science test rapidly approaching. The strip lighting in the library hummed and buzzed overhead. One distant lamp had started to flicker on and off. A faint whiff of polish hovered above the library desks.

I couldn't think about photosynthesis. Even with the exam looming, I wanted to find out more about the god 'Set'. I remembered I'd seen his picture at the British Museum and how he had chopped up his brother, but I couldn't remember anything about his children. I'd begun by looking up the word 'set', but 'setting a table' or 'arranging a piece of music' or 'hardening like concrete', didn't meet my particular need.

I went to the large book section and found a heavy encyclopaedia of World Mythology. Conveniently, pictures and descriptions of the Egyptian gods were located near the beginning of the tome. Set was easy to find. Known also as Seth, he controlled darkness and chaos. A troublemaker, he picked fights with both his brother Osiris and his nephew Horus.

The diary entry had said to beware the Children of Set, but apparently he didn't have any. He loved war and would change himself into a wild boar when he felt brassed off. He tried to murder his nephew just like he had his own brother, but he didn't succeed. Horus and Set had many battles and in the end the other gods told them that they had to learn to get on together.

A sharp pain in the back of my ear was accompanied by a wet pellet of balled up paper landing on the picture of an Egyptian god. I turned to see my least favourite classmate sneering at me over the carols in the library. Calvin removed the empty ballpoint pen tube from his mouth.

"You're just looking at pictures, Brucie baby. Not got work to do?"

"This is work," I hissed back. "It's called research."

Calvin shrugged and we both noticed that Miss Griffiths was looking across at us. No one really feared her but equally no one really tested out what would happen if you defied her.

I looked at Calvin who smirked and shrugged. I didn't like Roger Calvin. He liked to pick fights and although short, he often won. The idea of fair play wasn't one he recognised.

I brushed the tiny wet ball of paper away from the picture. It showed the Egyptian god, Anubis. I stared at the man with a dog's head, my stomach doing little somersaults. He stood there in the image just like he had in my bedroom. I didn't feel overjoyed to discover he had the dubious distinction of guiding the dead.

I read the description and found his head came from a jackal and not a dog. Jackals also took care of the dead. As the book pointed out, they ate them. I felt hot and cold at the same time and rubbed my palms together, a nervous habit of mine, which Mum told me I should stop.

The bell rang for change of classes.

"I hope you got some useful work done, Rhory," said Miss Griffiths brightly as I walked towards the bookshelves.

"Yes, ma'am," I lied.

The Encyclopaedia glistened with the sweat from my palms when I returned it to the shelf.

Chapter 12

The Cave

Egypt – the dawn of time

Shoshan edged her way across the rock-strewn sand and realised the light came from a cave, partially hidden by one of the boulders. *Perhaps this is where the jackal went.* She hovered at the edge of the light and then went in. After a narrow entrance, the cave opened out quickly and rose so high she could hardly make out the roof in the darkness above. Rush matting lay on the floor and both light and warmth radiated from various braziers. Enjoying the soothing feeling of the rushes under her tired feet, Shoshan edged forward until she saw something moving.

A woman worked at a loom. A brown ribbon encircled her jet-black hair. Her long linen skirt had a covering of pale netting extending over her otherwise bare breasts. She turned towards Shoshan, her eyes glittering with reflected firelight as she raised her finger to her lips. A dreamy calmness spread through Shoshan. The unsmiling woman went back to her work, and her shuttle flashed back and forth across the tapestry.

On the wall above the loom, a bow and quiver of arrows rested on hooks. The new tapestry appeared at bewildering speed from multiple spinning spools of coloured threads. The walls of the cave, which extended deep into the hillside, held tapestries as far as the eye could see.

Making her way further into the cave, Shoshan studied the woman's work. In one picture, an enormous lioness watched a rising sun across the dazzling waters of a great river. The lioness had a headdress and Shoshan heard the word 'Sphinx' sound somewhere within herself. *This must be the Plain of the Lion that her teacher Katesch had spoken about.*

Something shimmered deeper in the cave on the far side. Shoshan wandered over, soothed by the swish of the woman's shuttle, speeding back and forth. The image of a house had been captured in delicate threads, surrounded by trees in bloom. Shoshan drew a sharp breath and tears sprang to her eyes. Her family home, built of wood and cool mud bricks, lay before her. So real, she could almost make out the expressions of their faces – her mother and older brother looked out at her. Walking with his soldiers, her father looked grand in his regalia, as he returned from the Meeting Hall for his province.

On her departure with Katesch, so many months ago, she'd seen him cry. The only time she could remember him, a ruler of a mighty province, looking vulnerable. Yet he'd wanted her to go and fulfil her destiny. Shoshan had the gift to 'hear' within. He'd told her she must use it to serve the Sisterhood of the Feather.

Firelight flared from a brazier even deeper in the cave. Another tapestry close by danced and shimmered in the warm light. It revealed a face woven in fine threads, with dark hair and deep blue eyes. Shoshan moved closer, smiling as she recognised the priestess by the green feather gracing her headband.

Tall and commanding, even in a picture, Katesch looked right at her.

Tears again blurred Shoshan's eyes for a moment. "Mother," she murmured, even though her actual mother stood revealed in kindly threads, a few paces away. A wind stirred all the flames in the braziers and the rush mats on the floor. With the wind, came images and ideas forming themselves into words.

"Go deeper, my child; beware the boar and seek the fire that warms your body, and in your seeing, trust your heart and not your eyes. Backwards will be forwards when you dress in priestly raiment once again, the time for disguise has passed. The Hall is safe and I will see you once more before you

reach its sanctuary. Fear not."

The eyes on the tapestry still watched her, but no further words sounded in her heart. She knew, without doubt that Katesch remained safe.

Go deeper. Shoshan moved on into the cave. She found it more difficult to study the tapestries, as fewer braziers cast their shimmering light. Looking for a boar, Shoshan wandered further from the entrance. The tang of smoke from the torches combined with the dry dust of ages past.

No longer did the swish and click of the shuttle soothe her. Strange armies marched over burning landscapes. Buildings more vast than any she had seen, and craft for road and water, stranger than those she knew, appeared and faded with the movement of the flames. Stopping at one point she noticed a boy, much of her age, dressed in a pale tunic, with a pattern of squares along its hem. He stood near a finely built temple, unlike those of her Egypt but beautiful in a different way. He listened to an elderly man clothed in white speaking to students gathered close by. At the grey-haired man's side stood a much younger woman, with dark, curly hair. Shoshan knew in a way she could not explain that this woman was the boy's sister. The names 'Theano' and 'Dimitris' sounded inside her.

Shoshan couldn't find any pictures of a boar. Deeper and deeper she went, feeling her way carefully in places that remained too dimly lit to discern anything that she could understand.

Great chariots of metal squirted fire at one another in some dreadful corner of Amenti, the underworld for tortured souls. Cold, damp thoughts swirled around Shoshan, and she could see nothing that made much sense. *Godless and hopeless.* Peoples teemed in cities too large to be believed. This world, caught in drab grey threads, had the quality of a nightmare.

As she pulled her eyes from scenes of fear and misery, she realised the cave divided into two. A small tapestry hung on its own and she walked over to study it. Here stood a boy and behind him a man wrestling with a bull, in a subterranean chamber. Shoshan looked closer. High above him grew a tree the like of which she'd never seen before, with a thick trunk and hefty branches. Near the tree, a small-pillared house glowed with a blue fire.

A further picture depicted three children in a stone temple. The children stood in circles carved on the floor. Priestesses danced around them. Shoshan examined the children and her breath caught in her throat. The girl looking out of the picture could be no one else but her, as she knew her face from a copper mirror. To one side of her stood the boy Dimitris, still in a tunic. To the other side the pale boy from a time far, far away. She'd seen this boy in the odd temple, the last time she'd sat in the Stone Chair: the 'Red King'.

Something nagged in a corner of her mind and she finally looked away from the tapestry with the children. She searched around her but could no longer see the way back to the cave entrance. Passageways extended all around her, some lit and some dark. One brazier remained nearby, flickering warm light on a small loom, which held an incomplete tapestry.

A detailed scene moved with the flames. Men, carrying torches, walked along a riverside. Captain Gruff led them. The path wound along low hills and by tall palms. Near the bottom of the tapestry, a boy, or perhaps a girl dressed as a boy, lay close to a fire. The men marching towards the clearing would soon arrive. Shoshan ground her teeth and shivered, as fear and panic sapped the strength from her legs and arms. Gruff had betrayed her. The false priests of Set, would soon bring her to a painful death. She didn't know which way to run. The small fire at the bottom of the tapestry grew in size.

Chapter 13

Hammerford Park

England – about now

I was born in Hammerford.

It was one of those towns everyone had heard of but no one could quite place. Signposted from the motorway that ended up in Brighton, it was also mentioned on many of the A roads that criss-cross the south of England. Unless you tried very hard, you didn't ever go through it.

Other towns grew, flourished and lost all their large houses, so that gardens could be infilled, with small housing estates. Hammerford, with its ring road, had remained so much the same that to drive into it, could you find the way, was like a return to a bygone era.

At Scrivener's we referred to it as 'the town which time forgot'. This was because it had only a few measly coffee bars, shops with names no one had heard of outside Hammerford. It had no McDonald's.

But it did have a park, a swimming pool (unheated), and the bandstand where a brass band played on sunny Sunday afternoons and actors occasionally performed. This was the bandstand the funny young man, with the fake moustache, was trying to save.

The park had acres of grass where football and cricket matches were played, and picnics enjoyed. It had the oldest oak tree in the south of England: a tree with a monstrous trunk and huge limbs. As the park was only a five-minute walk from our house, we spent a lot of time there.

The weekend after my birthday, walking through the park with Juliette, she said out of the blue, "You know, statistically, Rhory, there is a good chance you are gay."

"Bog off, Jules," I responded, feeling just a bit outraged. "I know I'm not."

"No, Rhory, don't get touchy with me, I'm talking science here. We learned in psychology that second born children are more likely to be gay than first born, that's all."

"So are you saying Mum and Dad are gay then?"

Juliette paused while her super octane IQ computed the ramifications of this remark. "Well," she said, "they're both second born, that's true..." She squeezed my arm.

"Ouch! What's that for?"

"Well I've seen how you look at some of my girlfriends from school, so I know you are *not* gay! But it's interesting what you say about our parents."

She walked on in silence for a moment, her brain whirring, no doubt. "They are both second born. You're right. And so were their parents. And I think, our great-grandparents were as well. How odd," she conceded. "You know Dad and I are drawing up a genealogy of the Bruce family?"

"Yeah, Jules, I'd noticed."

Juliette and Dad used one of those ancestry web sites. They were constructing a family tree to see if we could trace our descent from the old kings of Scotland, Robert the Bruce and such. Juliette would like it if she was an actual princess, even from a defunct Scottish line.

My sister was a prodigy. If you look up prodigy you will find something about brilliance, unusual talents and so forth; if you are the younger brother of a prodigy, then you know the definition is,

"Irritatingly able to remember all facts, even if only read once; unusual capacity to learn the piano aged four and the violin, aged five; and the skill to take your school entrance exams, two years earlier than is actually decent".

People referred to me, with a slight frown, as 'Juliette's younger brother'. I was measured by the mould used to make Juliette. And of course, I was found wanting.

That night, I asked Dad some questions and found that I was descended from 'second-borns', as far back as we could trace. That seemed bizarre. Some of them had done great things.

One had held high office in India about two hundred years ago, and had been involved with the discovery of some famous cave temples or other. So perhaps, even though the second born receive the scrapings from the pot of talents, those scrapings might, just might, be of value.

Mine appeared to be playing bongo-drums and the ability to contact people from other times. Unfortunately, that kind of talent often resulted in visits from flapping white coats and doses of medication.

Chapter 14

Nick Hillman

School had run its weary course. As usual, Nick and I walked back together across the park, braving the autumnal winds. We headed for the footpath under North Road, a tunnel of moss, mystery and old stone walls. Even as a kid, I'd been able to get into the park on my own using this tunnel, safely avoiding the traffic.

The path down from the busy thoroughfare divided into two worlds. Turn sharp left and you went through the tunnel and into the park. Go straight on and you passed under the railway lines and emerged quite literally, on the other side of the tracks. Houses were smaller, less well built and people were supposedly poorer and stingier.

My experience of life, suggested the poorer were often more generous with tea and cake than those in the huge houses of Weald Road or Twisted Lane. The rich looked down their well-powdered noses at scruffy Rhory from Suffolk Road. They would think that a glass of water on a hot day showed too much generosity.

Nick lived in the poor but generous streets, which summed up both him and his parents. He was a good mate, one of my closest friends since we joined the school. I decided to tell him about the vision I'd had, but not the messages that were appearing in the diary.

"I had a truly weird dream a few nights back," I said.

"Tell me something that would surprise me," Nick responded, with a laugh in his voice.

I ignored his teasing and went on, telling him about waking up paralysed and how that had led later to my seeing the vision of an

Egyptian god. Nick looked at me as if weighing something up.

"Apart from this, things are normal, right?"

"Yes. Don't worry, I'm not going mad."

Nick stopped and looked at me. "You know, Rhory, let's assume you're not nuts. That can be our going in position."

"You're too generous."

"No wait. There was a guy I read about once who could hear the radio in his head, right? They found his fillings picked up the signal from Crystal Palace radio mast or something."

"Okay," I said, not sure where this was heading.

"And psy-ops people, you know the army clever-clogs types, have tried to send messages straight into people's heads. It must be true, it was on the History Channel." He grinned.

"Oh, right."

"Well let's say it may be true. What if someone is actually trying to send you a message and the picture of Anu, Annie..."

"Anubis."

"Anubis, thank you. This jackal-headed god is like the calling signal. All you've to do is to indicate you've received it."

I bit my lip.

"Don't make monkey faces, Rhory, the wind might change."

"No, I think you might be right. Along with the picture, I really did sense a presence in the room. You know, something intelligent. And once I stopped being scared shitless, I didn't believe it was from the dark side or whatever. In fact it felt sort of ... well, kind, I suppose."

We reached the bandstand and dropped our bags at the top of the stairs. I walked over to the far side and looked out at the sky. Using a dampened finger, I tested the wind direction.

"I think we're okay, the sky is lighter where the wind is coming from. We should escape the rain." In the distance I could see two other boys from school heading across the grass.

"The challenge is to find a way of sending a message back, I think," I said, wandering around the stage area. "The whole idea is a bit freaky, because either it's a message from people in the present, which is, well, freaky, or it's people in the past, which is, frankly, freakier."

"Yeah, I agree, but I don't think we've really got a handle on time yet." Nick came over and leaned on the rail, next to me. "Last week I read about some research a Russian scientist had done about time." He tapped the railing and frowned. "Bylinkin, that's his name. Bylinkin says time goes in seven huge spirals before it starts again with a new aeon."

"He's called Blinkin? Just as well he doesn't go to Scrivener's, he'd have a tough time."

"Not Blinkin, Stanislav Bylinkin." Nick spelt the name out. "The interesting bit was that the loops of time that are above each other, well, he thinks they're sort of connected and that's why you get certain patterns repeating in history."

And that might be why I was linking up with ancient Egypt. I said as much to Nick, without mentioning seeing the girl reflected at the British Museum; even Nick might balk at that.

He looked up towards the council buildings. "Trust the council to give themselves the best offices in Hammerford," he said. "They have a view right across the park."

"They're not stupid are they!" I looked over the railing. There was a small door about a metre and a half high set into the brickwork. The paint was peeling but it looked sturdy.

"What do you think is through that door, Nick?"

"I've never seen it open," said Nick. "But there must be some place the parkie stores the deck chairs, you know, the ones they put out on the only fine day of the year."

"I hope you didn't say, 'Paki'. That would be racist wouldn't it?"

"No, I didn't, Rhory, you cloth-eared git. I said 'parkie'."

"And if the parkie was a Paki?"

We both swung round at the sound of our school bags crashing onto the tarmac.

Chapter 15

Backwards is Forwards

Egypt – the dawn of time

Shoshan sat up and nearly screamed. Caught by the wind, the fire had flared up and woken her from some nightmare in a cave. The clothes on her back were damp with the chill of the night. Nearby, the Nile swept on, like time itself, toward an uncertain future. Shoshan stood and thought she heard the sound of a voice, on the northern wind.

Danger approached. The vision of the lady and the tapestries … or dream … or whatever, tumbled back into her mind. She looked down to where the boat had been tied up for the night, and knew what she had to do.

The boat had been made fast, front and back, next to a flat, rocky promontory that broke some of the force of the current. Shoshan picked her way down and collected the cloak Hasina had given her, and the package containing her priestess robes. She'd noticed an irrigation well when she followed the jackal earlier. She carried her clothes there. If she'd only had a dream it proved accurate; she stripped off the smelly ship-hand's garments by the well and gasped as she washed much of the grime from her sunburnt skin. The cold water on her head brought her fully awake and she thought about Captain Gruff.

If the vision could be trusted then he'd betrayed her to her enemies. Otherwise why would he be leading priests and soldiers back down the path? What had Katesch said in the cave? Trust her heart rather than her eyes. Pulling on her dress over her damp skin proved a bit difficult; she didn't want to tear the fine linen. She quickly bound her wet hair with a blue ribbon as she walked back towards the faint glow of the campfire. No sounds came from further north and she judged she'd a few minutes before the men arrived.

In her heart she knew Captain Gruff was loyal. Crusty, awkward and grumpy, but nevertheless loyal to the priestesses whom he served. It occurred to Shoshan he'd been captured as he reconnoitred, and the false priests were forcing him to lead them back to the boat.

"Backwards is forwards."

The priests expected to find a sleeping girl unaware she'd been discovered. If she wasn't there, they'd look for a boat travelling down the Nile. Perhaps their spies had already said she might be disguised as a boy.

"Backwards is forwards."

Shoshan fixed her cloak around her shoulders with a clasp, pulled the cowl over her head. She threw the ragged clothes onto the fire, which sputtered with a hiss of steam and smoke. The air stank of damp, dirty cotton.

Moving purposefully down to the boat, she released the hitches on the painters as she'd done so many times before. She stepped onto the decking, rocking it crazily for a moment or two, until she pushed away from the small wharf made by the flat rock. The current took hold of the light craft and Shoshan thrust back and forth with the paddle on the stern, easing it further out into the river. Once clear of the bank, she hauled up the sail as she'd been shown. Gruff's voice sounded in her ears, "Careful, careful."

She offered a prayer of thanks to the gods of weather and river that the wind had remained westerly. *I can use it to run against the flow of the current.* Water slapped noisily against the side of the boat as she turned the prow southward. With a crack the wind caught the sail, and she tacked up stream. For a while, Shoshan felt stuck, as though Tawaret, the Hippo goddess of the Nile, held her back. A gust of wind changed that, and soon she could see again the distant glow of the final embers of her fire. Her wet clothes had not extinguished it and one or two small flames licked the air.

Ducking under the sail, Shoshan tacked to the East and sailed far out into the river. When she next turned to tack westward, torches moved everywhere around the camp. The faint sounds of men shouting floated over the river. Captain Gruff stood with his back to the little quay as men went down to the water's edge and called out, pointing north.

Shoshan guessed they thought she'd sailed with the current, not believing a girl would know how to take a boat against the flow of the river. The moon had long since vanished behind a bank of clouds and she doubted she was visible from the land; anyway, they were looking the wrong way.

Shoshan considered what to do next. *I can't just leave Captain Gruff to fate. He is a servant of the Order of the Feather. Does he have the gift to hear inwardly?* Despite the cold wind, Shoshan blushed to think he might have been listening to her thoughts as they had sailed north. Easing the sail so it spilled wind, she held the boat southward but hardly moving. Carefully, she projected what she intended to do, in image and word, directly to him. If he could hear, then perhaps he'd act as she intended. For just a moment she could see his blue eyes looking deeply into her own and knew he'd heard.

Ducking once more under the boom, she used the paddle as a rudder and swung the prow northward, allowing the wind to fill the sail. The boat leapt forward and sped towards the camp. Shoshan had helped dock the evening before and knew the water near the flat rock remained deep. She sailed close to the shoreline on her left. The captain had moved down to the water's edge and she could just recognise him by the light of the torches and the sputtering firelight.

Shoshan stood, shook the cowl of her cloak from her hair. The mass of dark curls streamed across her shoulder. The wind caught the cloak and revealed her white priestly robes just as the moon emerged from the cloud. As she sped towards the quay she shouted, "Captain."

With an agility and speed she'd not seen before, Captain Gruff pivoted and ran to the flat rock, leaping gracefully above the river water. He landed on the prow, pushing it for a moment beneath the surface before it bounced up. He shifted his weight, preventing the boat from tipping completely over.

"Duck down, girl," he shouted.

Shoshan did, and the thrum of arrows passed overhead. Moments later a spear splashed in the water at her side. Then they were out of range. Angry shouts carried on the wind, but they had no boats with which to give chase.

Gruff knows I'm a girl. Shoshan wondered what that might imply.

"Head towards Sothis," he yelled, pointing to the Dog Star, "and only turn at the far bank." He made no move to take the rudder, showing how completely he trusted Shoshan.

"Most priests and soldiers came south to capture you, and only a few boats are waiting in case you'd already sailed," he explained, once they were beyond earshot. "They won't be expecting us, but they are armed and will try to stop us if they see us."

When Shoshan finally tacked back toward the western bank, the captain took over. Shoshan decided he looked taller and younger. His stoop had gone and his shoulders appeared broader. The lines were less noticeable on his face, which had become good-looking. He caught her staring at him and smiled for the first time.

"It is not just the priestesses who are masters of disguise."

"Who *are* you?"

If he heard her question, he didn't respond. The wind had picked up and the small craft sped toward a string of lights that spanned the river ahead.

"Sit at the back," he ordered, his crabby nature reasserting itself.

The lights came closer and Shoshan could discern figures standing on large boats moored across the river. To her left a village appeared, with lamps lit in many of the houses. Further back from the bank, the mud walls of a temple rose, picked out faintly by the moonlight. Shouted orders showed they'd been seen, their sail glowing in the pallid moonlight. Lamplight reflected off armour and the boats moved to block their passage. The rhythmic splash of oars sounded in the distance.

Chapter 16

The Grenade

England – about now

Facing us and blocking our exit were two of Scrivener's bullies. They'd just tossed our school bags onto the ground below the bandstand. My knees threatened to quiver.

"You knobheads," said Nick. "What d'yer do that for? I might have had a computer in my bag."

"Well, if you did, it would be a broken computer now, know what I mean?" said Stratford. "And who you callin' knobhead?"

I knew Gary Stratford. He sometimes helped set up the lights for the school plays. Unlike Muffit, he didn't resemble the shape of a brick-house toilet. He had more of a lean basketball player's build, and he also had a mean streak. It was Stratford who'd just kicked our bags off the stage of the bandstand.

"Keep cool, Gary," said Muffit, sauntering over. His coat was open and his shirttails showed below his pullover. The school tie had vanished.

Muffit looked almost as broad as he was tall, with a neck that would do justice to a wrestler. I didn't know his first name but had seen him knock the stuffing out of someone in the year above me. I didn't know why and certainly didn't enquire. Up to now I'd avoided him.

"We're figuring you might want to help in our business venture," said Muffit.

By now he stood close enough for us to hear the slight wheezing as he breathed. His face was blotchy – the effects of the cold wind playing out on his pale skin. His washed-out blond hair stood up at odd angles. He dropped his own school bag on the floor and put his hands in the pockets of his coat.

"It works like this. You give us money. We give you the ecky or skunk and tell you who to get it to. You get paid by them. Simple."

"I'm not really interested, Muffit. Even if I could work out what you meant," I said. "Though it's kind of you to think of us with your business venture."

Stratford moved behind me. "Don't get cute with us, skinny boy."

"No, that's right," Muffit continued. "Let me spell it out to this long streak of piss." He looked at me as he spoke. It didn't sound complimentary.

"You collect and deliver the e-tablets and the funk."

He must have seen incomprehension spreading over my face.

"Marijuana, you pin brains!"

"No, I'm definitely not really interested," I said, my mouth completely dry.

"This isn't an invitation you can turn down." This came from Stratford.

"Oh, I think it is," said Nick, finding courage from somewhere. "It's against the law and could get us expelled."

"Nah," said Stratford. "It's as easy as falling off a bandstand! You won't get caught. You'll only have the gear for a few minutes. The punters know where to wait in the school, and where they can hide stuff."

"And it's not a choice, mule-features." Muffit moved a little closer to Nick, pinning him to the railing around the bandstand.

I looked around to see if there was anyone we could shout to in the park, but the heavy grey sky had deterred dog-walkers. In the dim light, I could barely spot someone, far beyond the distant rugby pitches.

"No, we've got to shift drugs around and we want … rather, we demand, that you help us do it. If you've got lingering doubts, I'll quite happily work you over. There'll be no marks but you'll be real sore for weeks." Muffit offered a wheezy grin.

"And I'll—" Nick started to shout back; whatever bravado Nick was going to show, we didn't learn. Muffit hit him in his belly and he doubled over, struggling to breath. I tried to step back but my vision vanished and a shock went right through my head when Stratford rabbit-chopped my neck. I caught the railing to keep my balance.

"You'll do what we say, and if you do it properly for two weeks, then we'll let you keep ten per cent. And don't say we ain't generous. You just have to be turning over two hundred quid a week and then you're dealt in."

I didn't totally get what they needed us to do, but wasn't about to suggest a tutorial. I felt I might throw up any moment.

Muffit slowly drew his hand out from his pocket and thrust its contents under Nick's face. Momentarily I thought he held a small tortoise. It filled his palm and had raised square shapes on its surface.

"You're crazy, Muffit," I shouted. "That's a grenade."

"Isn't it just."

"You're a lunatic," muttered Nick, who was still struggling to get his wind back.

Muffit slipped his finger through the ring on the grenade.

"Yeah, maybe I am and maybe I ain't. But in case you think this is a repro, remember my dad came back from his second tour in Afghanistan a few weeks back."

I'd no idea his dad was in the army, but the grenade looked real enough. I couldn't stop myself shaking.

"So," said Muffit deliberately. "We'll enrol you tomorrow. Don't even dream about going to the police. We don't ever have drugs on us and we'll deny it all. And," he said suddenly swinging the grenade over towards me, "we'll make it really nasty for you if you—"

As Muffit turned, his foot caught on the edge of his own school bag. He stumbled and put out a hand to stop his fall. He jerked the ring at the same time. The sound of the ring hitting the bandstand stage surface had Muffit looking around desperately.

Stratford jumped back, staggered and yelped something unintelligible. He ran, leaping down the steps from the bandstand and falling hard at the bottom.

Muffit was half-sitting and half-crouching with both hands squeezing the grenade. The pasty colour of his face convinced me it wasn't a reproduction. Whether it was charged or not was not something I wanted to find out. I glanced over to see Stratford's gangly form legging it across the park.

Nick bent down and picked up something from under his foot. He walked steadily to the stairs. He turned at the top, took a deep breath, and said, "Here's the thing, Martin. I can just walk home or to the police station..." He caught his breath again. "The choice is yours. I could let you have this or ... or drop it down a drain. As I say, the choice is yours."

Muffit sat very still.

"I'm going to need your help," he said. "I'm holding it closed but my hands are slipping. I need you to just put the safety pin back."

"And the drug dealing?" I asked, pleased my voice was not quivering too much but feeling everything had gone very unreal.

"It's an opportunity..." Muffit squinted up at me, his bulky frame beginning to shake. "But you don't have... Oh for the love of God just put the pin back in!"

He worked his way onto his knees and looked like he was going to try to get up.

"Just stay there, Martin," said Nick. "Tell us really clearly that you don't need us for your drug scams."

"Okay, Nick. I'll let you off this time."

"This time or any time," said Nick, not moving from his place by the bandstand steps.

"Not any time. Not ever. Just give me that bloody pin."

"I've not got my glasses on me. They may have been broken in the bag you knocked off. Rhory's got good sight. Here Rhory..." He made as though he was going to throw the pin to me.

"No, bloody hell ... we might lose it, it's getting dark," said Muffit.

I walked over to Nick. "How do you know his first name?" I asked quietly. Nick kept his eyes on the kneeling figure wheezing loudly behind me.

"We're both in the Rugby Club, remember?" he said, smiling, but up close I could see his hands shaking.

I nodded, took the pin and walked slowly back to Muffit.

A flash made us all jump. Nick had taken a picture on his mobile. "Insurance," he said.

Slipping the pin through the small hole would be relatively easy with a steady hand. Mine wobbled all over the place and it took two or three goes. Finally, it clicked home. Even in the cold I could see the sheen of sweat on Muffit's face as he scowled at me.

We left him leaning against the balustrade, dragging hard on a cigarette. Collecting our bags, we walked swiftly towards the park tunnel. We didn't say goodbye to the quivering Muffit.

Chapter 17

The Plain of the Lion

Egypt – the dawn of time

"Now is the time to call on Katesch!" The captain steered straight at the boats ahead. For a moment Shoshan had no idea what he meant. Then she concentrated on her breathing and inner focus.

Not knowing what to say to the Reverend Mother or whether she would even hear her, Shoshan simply asked for help. Katesch had told her once that she shared the eyes of all the priestesses who were close to her. If invited, she could see even as they saw. Shoshan stood up, spreading her feet to keep her balance; once more she revealed her priestly robes as the wind spread her cloak like a pennant.

"We need you," she thought, holding her image of the Mother of her Order clearly in her mind.

The sail blocked most of her line of sight, but the shouts of men and the clanking of boats and oars told her that they were close to their enemies. The boat dipped and she flexed her knees and grasped the side to keep her balance. Spume stung her eyes. Ahead, she heard cries of alarm and fear. They raced towards the noise. The captain tacked and the sail snapped to the western side. Shoshan raised her head after avoiding the boom.

Katesch stood tall in the prow of the boat, facing her enemies and holding the lotus staff of her office. She appeared magnificent in her full regalia and wore the ceremonial crown. Whether the torchlight and the moon provided the illumination, Shoshan couldn't decide. Katesch's robes shimmered and glowed, blue as a kingfisher's wing. Shoshan had heard of solar-boats and seen paintings in the temple.

Now their little craft became one, radiating fiery light.

Soldiers were trained to fight and oarsmen to row, but few were brave enough to attack a goddess standing astride a boat of dazzling light. In moments they passed between two vessels, and Shoshan saw men standing with bow and spear, immobilised. The smell of sweat and bilge water assailed her. By the time a priest had shouted something about trickery, they had put the distance of two bowshots between them and the closest craft.

Wood cracked and splintered, as oars became entangled between the boats behind them. *We're safe for a while.*

When Shoshan looked forward again, the sail reflected the light of the moon, and the prow of the boat was empty. The fiery light had extinguished and Shoshan wondered if she'd imagined it all.

She looked to the captain for an explanation. He smiled as he wiped spray from his face and broke off an arrow lodged in the boat's side.

"Masters of disguise, the servants of the Goddess Maat, true masters of disguise."

That doesn't really explain anything. Perhaps my fear affected my vision. She drew the cloak around her as the wind had taken all the warmth from her limbs and a shiver went right through her body.

Her companion rested his hand on her arm.

"You never know your true power until it is called forth. You did all that you know. Without you that couldn't have happened. That's why the misguided servants of the Hippo want you stopped."

"Servants of the Hippo?"

"That's our name for the Children of Set, the ones who follow the murderous God of the desert. He has the viciousness of a hippopotamus, when it attacks a small boat like ours."

The captain held a steady course. Shoshan sat once more, her skills with the ropes and sail not required. Her heart still raced and she felt cold and shaky now the immediate danger had passed.

For a long time neither of them spoke. Whenever she glanced at the captain, weakly lit by the moon and stars, she couldn't understand how he looked so much younger. His dark hair, now released from his turban, fell to his shoulders in the traditional style of a judge or prince. Her father wore his the same way. His eyes, searching the river ahead, had a depth and wisdom she hadn't noticed when they first set sail. *Is he a master of disguise? If so, who is he?*

As that thought crossed her mind, he looked at her. "Soon we will reach the Plain of the Lion. There may be sentinels placed who will be looking out for you. The night will be dark, but you can always see the face of the Sphinx. It is never completely overcome by night. Guide yourself by that. Keep close to the shadows. They will not have expected you to get this far, and hallowed ground is not safe for Set's minions. But look well and listen even better and you will reach your sanctuary."

Shoshan nodded, a surprising wave of sadness moving up from her heart to her throat.

"Who are you? What is your name, sir?"

The captain didn't answer, choosing that moment to bring the boat about on a different tack, in response to a shift in the wind. Shoshan had to duck to avoid the heavy boom swinging close by her head.

"My name is not important. I am known by many names and not all of them complimentary. To some I am a thief, to others a knave of trickery. I have had the honour to serve our blessed Egypt for more years than you might imagine, and I am known by those who truly know me as the Messenger and also the Keeper of Time. Yet this tells you little, I think."

He looked over at Shoshan, and she could feel his eyes seeing in, through and around her. He smiled, and just for a moment, all her fear and shivering vanished.

"You might better ask what is your own name? And why were you named as the lotus? You, Shoshan, are both seed and flower. You live in both mud and air."

She'd no idea what he meant and nearly fell over into the water sloshing about in the bottom of the boat, as the prow mounted a low sandbank and the boat came to an abrupt halt.

At the captain's murmured request, she pulled down the sail. Ahead, she saw for the first time in her life the distant face of the Sphinx. The light of the setting moon reflected from the ceramic face, and the extraordinary eyes of the Lioness looked straight at her.

"Go," said her companion, resting his hands briefly on her shoulders. "Head for the Sphinx and seek the lights of the Hall of Records. Not all can see them. Watch keenly."

Shoshan jumped down onto the sand and climbed the bank. The Lioness loomed huge in the distance, watching her every move. She'd never seen a statue so big and wondered who could have carved it from the living rock. Around the Sphinx, lay desert wrapped in darkness. Nearby, she could just make out dunes. She listened but could hear nothing except the sound of the river behind her. There were no lights.

Turning to speak to the captain, she found his boat already under sail, pulling steadily from the shore. The man at the tiller raised his hand. At least she thought he did; she wasn't sure, as the darkness of the river swallowed the boat. She hadn't even thanked him and realised she still had no idea who he was.

Somewhere far away and deep inside, words rumbled. They echoed in her mind before she could make any sense out of them. As unchangeable as hieroglyphs carved into rock, Shoshan heard the meaning clearly. The eyes of the captain watched her.

"I closed the gates of Time Past that Egypt could be. You will see me again when the Path of Time Yet to Come, is chosen."

She could see nothing of the boat but stood a long time staring into the darkness. Only the sound of oars splashing far to the south reminded her she'd not yet reached safety. She turned and walked towards the silent Sphinx.

Chapter 18

Javelin Hunt

The ground rose steadily from the river's edge, and as she climbed, Shoshan could just see the head of the Sphinx in the distance, the body still hidden by the bank. After a while, the ground began to level out; she pulled her cloak more tightly around her shoulders, slipping the cowl over her head and making sure the white of her robes remained hidden. The moon had set some time back and the desert lay in front of her in various shades of dark grey and black. The sound of oars became more distinct, but looking south, she couldn't see any lights.

No path offered itself and Shoshan's sandals sank into the softness of the low sand dunes. The great statue lay ahead and a little to her right. A deeper darkness to her left suggested some higher sand dunes. She decided to take the slightly longer but more sheltered route in case unfriendly eyes were watching the approach from the river.

The wind dropped and Shoshan became aware of the sound of her own breathing. She stopped and held her breath and listened. The silence near her in the desert seemed complete. Behind her the sounds from the boats increased. She breathed out slowly and took another deep breath. Shock jolted through her as she heard the sound of whispering. It came from so close by. Nudging into the soft sand of the dune on her left, she looked up. Silhouetted against the night sky she thought she could just make out a man's head. Luckily he was looking in the opposite direction, towards the river and the now distinct noise from the approaching boats.

She could hear two voices; the men spoke softly but with a strong southern accent. Shoshan couldn't make out what they said at first. As the words became clearer, she realised the men didn't know who manned the boats; they feared they might be caught between the followers of Osiris coming up the river and those who controlled the plain.

Someone on the boats knew the men were there and shouted for them to look for the witch who had just broken through their barricade.

"Blast," said a voice just above her. "We'll be up to our ears in it if we let her slip through."

They stood up from a crouching position. Shoshan knew she'd be discovered if they walked down past her. She froze, biting hard on her lower lip.

They headed towards the river and she started to creep in the other direction towards the Sphinx. Her heart beat so loud she felt sure it would be heard. She had covered half the ground towards the statue when slightly further to the right, lights appeared, floating above the desert. *The Hall of Records!*

She breathed a prayer of thanks to Isis. Shoshan didn't know if only she could see the lights and quickened her pace. A man shouted for her to stop. Glancing back she discovered a third man had stayed behind. She sensed rather than saw him run down the soft sand towards her and she sprinted in the direction of the lights. Shoshan hoped she could outrun him, but the fragility of the cloth protecting her back made her pray he didn't have a javelin.

She glanced at the impassive face of the lioness high above her, as she raced close by. The lights from the Hall of Records beckoned about one hundred cubits away. She could run that in a few heart-beats. Shoshan heard herself scream as she caught sight of the man close behind her, loping along the ridge of the dune, his javelin poised for a throw.

Her legs could hardly move and she had little breath left. Her feet kept sinking in the soft sand. Panic swept through her when the lights vanished; but climbing a low dune revealed them again and she confirmed she was running in the right direction. She could now distinguish the lights in brackets, on either side of the huge doors to the Hall.

If she could reach those doors, they'd open to the safety of the corridors below. Her legs had no strength left and only fear kept them moving, that and the laboured panting of the man closing in behind her.

She pulled hard on the giant rings on the doors. They did not budge at all and she screamed as she banged the door furiously. Her shouts and fists produced empty echoes and the doors remained shut against her. Behind her the man took aim with the javelin.

Chapter 19

Blow Pipes at Two Paces

England – about now

The lessons at school passed in a bit of a blur and I didn't have much of a chance to work out what the implications of the confrontation involving the grenade, the previous night. I met up with Nick again, to walk back home.

"Did you see Muffit today?" I asked.

"No, I'm not even sure he was in school. I did see Stratford scowling in the distance. He was with Hacker, but I was nowhere near them for him to take revenge."

"Hacker's a nasty piece of work," I said. "Worse than Muffit even. I've always kept out of his way. I don't think he even knows my name and I'm happy to leave it that way."

"Remember, I've got that picture of Muffit as a gibbering wreck holding the grenade. It would look just fine on YouTube. I think they'll leave us and our friends alone."

"Nick, you've got your blow pipe, right?" I asked.

"Of course, Kimosabe," he replied. Quite why he called me that was a question for Nick, not me. He came up with random names every now and again. We prepared to engage with the great sport of invisibly 'pinging' the passers-by. We knew Hammerford Park really well and it had certain unexpected qualities.

"So where's the new shooting range, Gunga Din?"

"It's over there just to the right of those horse chestnut trees." I pointed to a place beyond some rhododendron bushes. We pushed through and clambered over the knobbly roots. No one would easily see us from the driveway that ran past the council buildings, behind us.

"You are really well-hidden by the trees when you peek over the wall. It's brilliant," I added.

"Okay," said Nick. "We'll give it a go, Gunga. Get those poisoned darts damp, and we're all set." We both popped little rolled up bits of paper, from our store in our pockets, into our mouths.

I placed a hand on the cool smoothness of the capping stone of the wall. Under my feet the leaf mulch had become so deep over the years that on this side if I stood up straight I could see over. I avoided leaning into the wall as the stones left a grey-brown deposit on the dark material of my school jacket. Resting my elbows on the wall I leaned over. The wide pavement passed by on the other side at least two metres down, giving us a distinct advantage. I couldn't see anyone coming in either direction and eased myself back. A cursory inspection showed green moss stains on the upper arms of my jacket that smeared as I tried to brush them off.

We both started preparing our deadly Amazon-style blowpipes. I took a ballpoint pen from my inky jacket inside pocket and bit down on the little plastic stopper at the end, and removed it. The thin tube of ink had nearly run out so I dropped it.

I now had a mini-version of a blowpipe. Some might call it a peashooter. However, when I'd tried in the past to shoot a pea down the plastic tube, I just got a green clump stuck halfway. That rendered it useless and me, a twit. Little paper balls, carefully chewed, worked perfectly in it.

Nick and I had introduced this weapon into class. Calvin, as he'd demonstrated a few days before, had copied us.

Being more careful with my jacket arms this time, I peeked over the wall again. Someone in a hat was walking up towards the station on our side of the road. He had an 'I'm an important adult, and in a hurry' expression on his face. His dark green jacket, with leather shoulder patches, indicated he shot birds for sport. He had the sort of dog that would fetch any dead waterfowl he'd killed. He looked vaguely familiar.

"Him," Nick whispered.

"I'll go for him, you get the dog," I replied, still struggling to remember where I'd seen this guy before.

We each fired a wet sting of paper with deadly effect, just ducking down after the shot, as the man went past. We heard a satisfying "ow" from him and "arf" from the dog. Bullseye! He clearly wondered if he'd been stung by a stray wasp. He would look around in angry bemusement! Served him right for killing sweet little ducks.

We heard his footsteps stop. Nobody had done that before. I held my breath and looked at Nick, whose scrunched up features only just held in nervous giggles. To date no one had ever realised the cause of their woe was crouching a few feet away, cunningly hidden behind a wall of imposing height. The silence continued punctuated by my racing heart.

The footsteps started again, quicker than before. I looked across at Nick and shrugged.

"Do you think he sussed us?"

"Naw," said Nick. "How could he?"

I peeked over the wall to see the man leading his dog purposefully towards the station. He turned and I ducked.

"Jeez! I hope he didn't see me."

Nick pulled a 'so what if he did, face'. Nick had been my good mate since primary school days. He nodded in the direction of the main road.

I looked again. The man and his dog had gone. There was a lull in hostilities while an elderly lady walked along, talking out loud to herself. She seemed an unfair choice of target.

The barking dog from the other side of the rhododendrons made me quite literally jump. I looked across at Nick, who turned the colour of old putty.

"Come out," said a voice, smooth and authoritative enough to belong to the man with the hat and hunting jacket. I grabbed Nick's arm with one hand and my school bag with the other and ducked below the curling branches of the bushes. Perhaps as an adult he'd forget that copses like the one that ran along the park wall had tunnels made of bushes and tree trunks.

We wiggled along, ignoring the muddy dampness on our knees. The man continued to stand still, expecting us to come out meekly. The racket made by the dog covered any noise we were producing. About ten metres of crawling later, the trees and bushes thinned out a bit, although I could just see the man's brown shoes.

The dog went apoplectic as he spotted us.

"Quick," said Nick and vaulted himself onto the wall. I followed, glad that I'd paid attention in gym classes. We landed in a heap on the far side of the wall and sprinted off in different directions. I raced across the road and up by the carpet emporium. Our back wall backed onto scrubland that surrounded the old cinema building, now filled with rugs from goodness knows where.

As I climbed into our garden, I remembered where I'd seen the man before. Something clamped in my guts and my arms went weak. I stood for some moments under our cooking-apple tree listening for sounds of pursuit. The man, once I took his hat off in my mind, became the man I'd seen at the British Museum, with the flashing purple ring. *Not cool,* I thought, *not cool at all.*

Chapter 20

The Hall of Records

Egypt – the dawn of time

The man grinned as he drew back the javelin. Shoshan held her breath, pressing her back against the unyielding doors. The man remained still, only his eyes grew wider. The spear fell from his grasp. He slowly reached for his throat and let out a gurgling cry. Dropping to his knees and looking hard at Shoshan with unseeing eyes, he pitched forward on his face.

Mmm, silly man, to think the Lioness doesn't protect her own.

These words sounded clear inside her and Shoshan looked around wildly. A discreet cough showed one of the Keepers of the Hall of Records standing, dressed entirely in black, in the shadow of the great pylons that were on either side of the doors. He raised his arm revealing a long knife and pointed to the statue of the Lioness. There stood one of his brothers, identical in every way, feet astride on the great left paw and holding a bow high above his head.

An easy shot; he stood so still.

Once more the words crystallised within her, for the three Keepers, with their jug like ears and permanent grins, never, ever, spoke aloud. Katesch had told her that a long, long time ago.

Light flooded the sands as the doors swung open and a friendly hand took her arm. She turned to see the third of the triplets, identical to the two outside with their bow and sword. Before closing the mighty doors and returning the sands to darkness, he smiled grimly and pointed to the men carrying torches and searching for her.

They've walked right into a trap. You are safe now, Shoshan and can continue your work. Drink this and you will feel refreshed. We were expecting you and the rooms are prepared.

His kindly green eyes held hers, and his jug like ears wiggled. His mouth didn't open but held the warmest of smiles. Shoshan drank her fill, and enjoyed the strength returning to her muscles. The great doors closed with a gentle thud. Enormous locks slid into place.

"Katesch?" Shoshan asked, her voice booming in the silent corridor. The priest grimaced, as though she'd just screamed in his ear.

Sorry, she formed the word in her heart, remembering her manners.

He smiled back at her, and his ears moved forward and back, the torchlight producing patterns of light and shade on his completely bald head.

She is safe ... but the war we have all feared for so long is now underway. The Children of Set, of now and of future epochs, have co-ordinated. This is the moment of greatest peril, but it is also the moment when their fearsome schemes can be unravelled, for they are showing their faces in all the provinces of time.

Shoshan's legs wobbled. She leant back against the great doors drawing comfort from their thickness and weight. Outside she thought she heard some men scream. She looked sharply across at her companion, but he just smiled and nodded, repeating his brother's thoughts, *the lioness protects her own.*

They walked deeper into the Halls, and through three doorways guarded by jet-black Nubian soldiers, dedicated to the service of Osiris. She followed the priest, her eyes jumping to his prominent ears; she struggled to keep her mind blank as she knew he'd pick up every thought.

These are the Chambers of the Pathways of Time, my dear.

The priest's ears distinctly wiggled as he smiled. *He must have heard me.* The priest indicated she should enter on her own.

Shoshan breathed more easily. Now no soldiers were needed. Katesch had taught her that the uninitiated couldn't long survive here, even if they could find their way through the identical corridors and their apparently endless turns.

Light softly flowed from the walls themselves. No torches were needed. In a room nearby she'd soon sit on another great throne of stone, also carved it was whispered, by the one who had taught Katesch all she knew, so very long ago.

That's right, Shoshan.

Shoshan spun round to find the priest had left and in his place stood her teacher. Katesch.

"How … but … you were—"

Katesch held her finger to her lips.

Sorry, Shoshan formed again in her mind, as her previous words still echoed around them both.

Come, there is much we need to accomplish this night. It is a turning point and you are needed, my lotus flower. I will explain as best I can shortly, but for now people are awaiting us.

Katesch walked ahead, her considerable height assisted by the ceremonial dark wig. Shoshan followed, noticing her teacher's burnished sandals and an anklet of gold she'd never seen before.

They entered a large room that held some chairs and a huge shallow basin of carved stone sitting on four substantial wooden stands, each shaped like a lion's paw.

Four priestesses stood in the room, making calm preparations for a ritual. The seven chairs were arranged in a way Shoshan had never seen before. One, bigger than the rest, had lions' feet. Three other chairs, slightly smaller and less ornate, were arranged to form a cross with the master chair, with the large shallow bowl between them. The chair opposite, the one with lions' feet, had lying on its seat, a perfect lotus flower. This chair had further chairs on either side and one behind.

Now your training really begins, my lotus flower. We do not have much time and there is much to learn if you are to become a real Mistress of the

Bowl of Time.

Shoshan looked at Katesch, who smiled and pointed to the seat with the flower. Shoshan walked over and carefully gathered up the fragrant bloom. She sat in the seat with the flower held on her lap. The other priestesses took their places. Katesch sat behind her. The bigger seat, directly opposite her, with the stone bowl between remained empty. The priestesses began to sing softly.

Chapter 21

The Oak Tree

England – about now

My feet began to fizz and the fizziness spread up my legs and with a sort of 'pop' swept over the rest of me. I couldn't see anything but I had the sensation of floating along a bit like a bubble. I'd never experienced anything like this before and far from being scary, I enjoyed it. For a while I bobbed along in a warm, dark sea just relishing the experience.

As I looked around me the darkness began to disappear like wood smoke in a breeze, and I could make out my bedroom, distant below me. *Surely I must be hovering many metres above the roof*? The roof promptly appeared and my bedroom vanished.

I'd had flying dreams before but nothing like this. I looked towards the tall trees just beyond the back wall of our garden and immediately I found myself near their highest branches. The leaves moved gently in the slight breeze reflecting the streetlights on the main road.

I soared higher and viewed the roof of the old cinema, now the carpet place. Someone had left a plastic chair out which lay on its side. Going higher still, I could see across North Road to the council offices and the park beyond. I wondered if I could fly as far as the bandstand.

Moments later I could feel the cold stone of the raised platform of the bandstand beneath my bare feet. I could even sense the sharpness of some grit. I thought for a moment I could hear singing. I looked out into the park but could distinguish very little in the darkness.

I ran my hands over the roughness of the wooden railings and tingled all over. This had to be the best dream ever. It was totally real. There, I could hear something again. Like a church in the distance when the choir gets underway. Even in a dream this deserved investigating.

I walked down the stone steps and made my way towards the tall oak tree that dominated the centre of Hammerford Park. The rough grass underfoot proved wet and a bit chilly on my bare feet. It looked more like a meadow than the park, with tussocks and small bushes; I had to pick my way with care, until I found a track worn smooth by other people walking in the same direction. Why had I never noticed this track before?

The oak tree towered above me blotting out the stars. Behind it I could see many more. Somehow the park had filled up with oak trees. The path continued into what now looked like a wood of considerable size. I hesitated at the edge unsure what to do. When I looked back across to the bandstand, all I could see was the track I'd followed leading up towards two large standing stones with some steps between them.

I turned back and noticed a distant glow between the trunks of the trees. It became darker as I entered the wood, and I stubbed my toe on a root. I concentrated on moving more carefully. The path curved a little to the left, and I could see light flickering on the trunks of the trees. I stepped into a clearing that had a considerable fire burning in the centre, with sparks going straight up towards the pale stars above. I thought that the park keeper would be furious to have his grass destroyed by a bonfire, but realised he'd be more troubled by the sudden appearance of the wood.

I looked around and thought I could hear some people singing much closer now. I should have been terrified, but instead calmness descended like a warm cloak around me. That was just as well, as when I looked down, I saw I was standing there in my pyjamas.

In front of the trees, as though caught in the firelight, I could see something like smoke rising from the ground – not smoke but a mist. The mist separated into shapes, catching the glow from the fire as the voices came closer.

Behind me, and to my right a voice distinctly said, "Salutation."

I turned around. A man with white hair and a trim beard looked at me, his eyes twinkling in the firelight. The flickering light made it difficult to tell the colour of the clothing he wore. He had a pale robe with a darker blue cloak and something shiny and metallic around his neck. He held a staff.

My God, a wizard.

The man smiled.

"No, there is no wizardry here, though there are wonders as you can see."

He spoke more in my mind that out loud, but I could see his lips move and heard his actual voice as though it came from far, far away.

"You've found your way here," the man continued. "It is well, and it is timely."

The music or singing now came from all around me. The patches of mist looked more like people, I could make out faces and some clothing, but nothing remained very long in focus. Looking back at the grey-haired man I saw he'd become more sharply defined, and could make out a chain of gold around his neck, glinting in the firelight.

"Who are you?" I asked out loud.

The man looked puzzled for a moment, as though trying to catch what I was actually saying. I remembered the girl at the museum, the one I'd seen reflected in the glass had heard me when I formed the words inside my head. I did so now, and thought the words, *Who are you, sir?*

"I am Abaris. I have been expecting you. We have long known about the Red King!"

He smiled at that, and I wondered what he meant. The girl in the museum had said something similar, but I thought I might have misheard, as I was not used to voices popping up inside me.

He raised his staff and pointed to the far side of the fire, indicating I should walk round. I did so, seeing the figures standing in a circle as though through falling water. They were real but not completely there.

The boy standing on the far side of the fire had dark, curly hair that was longer than most girls. He stood there, sharp and clear. He didn't smile. He also had a cloak and the sort of dress worn by Brownies. His muscular legs had straps on them and sandals. I realised that if he looked strange, then I probably looked ridiculous in my pyjamas.

Abaris moved nearer to us both. I couldn't be sure if he was walking or gliding; in fact he seemed to stand still while the clearing, the fire and me and the boy in the tunic, revolved. He looked at us both from under his bushy grey eyebrows.

"The work you are to do is of utmost importance. No one else can do it for you. You," he said looking at the other boy. "You are an earth protector. It is written in your name. And you," he said to me, "carry the blood of a king."

Well, that's news to me.

I remembered the research Juliette and Dad were doing. Juliette believed that our family name, Bruce, might be traced back to Robert of that name, a king in Scotland way back when. The one who didn't like spiders or something.

Once more Abaris changed his position without really moving. I arrived somewhere else in the circle of firelight, and he raised his staff to point out the moon that now peeked above the branches of the trees.

"The time is now. The meeting is now. We can protect you. Here, Dimitris." He turned and retrieved something from the gloom behind him. Turning back he gave the boy something made of leather.

"Go together," said the grey-haired man. "A chain of darkness must be broken tonight. That is your task." He looked at my new-found companion as he said this. Then he faced me, and his eyes flashed in the firelight.

"You, stay with him until it is done and then you will return here."

Chapter 22

The Black Dog and the Silver Cat

Dimitris moved to the edge of the circle and took what looked like a large stick. He held it in the fire for a few moments. The head of the stick must have had some special material on it, as it sprung alight. He bowed to Abaris, and nodded at me before he turned and set off between the trees. I realised I'd become entirely disorientated as the direction he took wasn't the one I remembered coming down.

I had to walk quickly to keep up, as the boy moved quite fast. He held the torch up high, and the branches and leaves above his head appeared and disappeared as he walked under them. I'd no idea we'd come so far into the forest; with so little light I had to be careful not to trip. My feet were now sore and I rubbed my arms to combat the chilliness.

The trees began to thin out and I could see a large clearing ahead with the path crossing over the meadow, toward two dim shapes that must the great stones I'd seen earlier. Dimitris paused, and I heard the words, "We must not delay; Abaris told me before you arrived that there are those who will tamper with the tracks of time and trap us here if we aren't careful. We need to get to the sacred circle."

He pointed up ahead to where the tall stones stood like great, grey pillars. I heard something moving in the undergrowth behind me and looked back into the forest. I could faintly make out the barest glimmer of the distant fire and thought I could still catch the sound of chanting. Once more I heard something in the bushes but couldn't see what made the sounds. I turned and found that Dimitris had moved a considerable way up the path. I started to walk swiftly after him; he held the burning torch up high, but the light hardly reached me anymore. I nearly lost my balance and kicked my foot against a stone, stubbing my toe for a second time. I worked my way along the path placing each foot with care.

When I looked up again, Dimitris had stopped. He held the firebrand to one side and moved his head as though searching for something. The light dimmed and brightened and I wondered why he appeared so indistinct when I could see the grass around him quite clearly. One moment he was there and the next I could barely make out his outline. He stood just in front of the two great stones, which reflected back the light of the torch. These also became transparent and foggy as I watched them.

I could hear a voice faintly calling from a long way off. I turned to look back at the forest, but could only make out the one familiar oak tree. Again the voice sounded, far away but somewhere inside me. I couldn't hear what it said but I did catch the fearful tone. When I looked back, Dimitris had gone; the two stones had also disappeared and now I could see the bandstand quite clearly.

I didn't know what to do. I'd completely lost contact with Dimitris. He had just gone from sight. I stood once more in Hammerford Park; the council offices loomed beyond the bandstand.

Something furry brushed my leg, and I jumped and shouted at the same time. A white shape ran off and then returned slowly. I could now see a cat; not just any cat, for I saw that Jester had found me, somehow, in the park. He turned and faced towards the council buildings and hissed. Darkness rolled down the hill towards me, swallowing the last remnants of colour from the grass. A liquid fog of blackness, it flowed towards me accompanied by a stench of something rotten. I thought I could hear screaming but when I held my breath the only sound I could make out, came from a distant car.

Icy rivulets of fear trickled down my arms and legs. At this rate I might be the next one to scream. I decided to walk swiftly the remaining distance to the bandstand. Dimitris had said something about the Sacred Circle, and the only circular shape nearby was the stage where the band would sit. My legs had become heavy and incredibly tired. My feet hurt. I hardly had the energy to move at all.

I spotted a huge dog and my stomach knotted in fear. It moved slowly at the front of the menacing dark shadows flowing towards me, misshapen and of a blackness that came from a total absence of colour. Its eyes glowed a dull red, the sort of red you see when you kick a large fungus off a rotting tree. I didn't hear it growl, rather I felt the anger of the dog thrusting right through me. The rancid smell of decay became far worse. Everything inside me said 'run' but my legs were now so cold and leaden they wouldn't move.

"Laugh!"

Someone had spoken. The furry shape rubbed against my leg and Jester looked up at me.

"Laugh; you know it makes sense."

Even wrapped in chilly fear, I registered that my cat could talk. As I watched him in total surprise, I'd swear he winked. I laughed out loud. Jester winked again!

"That's, m'boy."

Immediately, the warmth returned to my legs and the putrid black mist started to recede. I could make out the dog's eyes, little pinpricks of malevolence, but the way to the bandstand had cleared.

I giggled.

"You can talk, Jester," I said, but realised he was off chasing a moth or something, and looking just like a normal cat. The pinpricks of red light went out as the dog completely disappeared. I reached the tarmac that surrounded the bandstand, when a soft voice caressed the air behind me.

"Rhory, no need for that. You are a king remember? You've king's blood in you and you are destined to rule."

I looked around and at the edge of the tarmac a slinky, silvery shape moved. If someone had made a large cat of solid silver and then breathed life into it, it would have been like the creature that stood just where the grass met the tarmac.

"Stay here, my fine young man," said the silvery voice. "You know you are special. Who else could travel the corridors of time? No one that you know. Your gifts set you apart. Only someone destined to be a king again, could do what you do. Just follow me and I will show you what to do. You can have anything you desire. Anything at all."

Images of food, and boats and holidays on golden sands came to mind, as well as the strength to beat the stuffing out of ten Muffits all at the same time. And big houses, lots of them, as well as designer clothes, plus the pick of all the pretty girls in the soaps on TV.

Now cosy warmth surrounded me. I could just curl up and go to sleep. This silvery cat would caress me with wonderful words, and I'd drift into beautiful dreams. And I was drifting away when sharp pinpricks tore into my legs.

"No," shouted Jester, as he hung on to my bare legs through the thin cloth of my pyjamas. I'd wandered onto the grass and the silvery cat stared at me with ice cold eyes, blocking the way back to the bandstand.

Jester dropped to the ground between me and this cat whose shape rippled and flowed. I couldn't move my eyes from the glassy pools that were looking into mine. Words flowed into my mind, about kingdoms and power, money and fame. Anything could be mine.

The silvery cat sprang with a dreadful shriek. Somehow Jester had lunged at the same moment and the screeching, hissing shape missed its mark, almost. A searing pain went through my left arm.

"Run, run, Rhory," I heard and loped towards the bandstand, staggering up the steps. I looked back and saw Jester lying on the bottom step, entirely still. Of the silvery creature there was no sign. Far in the distance a mobile phone rang, but it faded away as darkness gathered all around me.

Chapter 23

Return

I couldn't quite wake up. My left arm had gone to sleep numbed by the weight of my body. My right hand and my feet felt icy. Jester stretched out immobile at the bottom of the bed. I moved my left arm but it felt swollen and fuzzy, with no real definition. In the night the duvet had fallen entirely onto the floor. I moved my numb arm and wiggled my fingers. As feeling gradually returned I realised that the outside of my biceps (perhaps my triceps, but I never paid much attention in Human Biology) hurt, and the events of the night before flooded back into my mind.

Something red lay on the bed-sheet. I rubbed my eyes to get them to focus and studied the blood on the sheet. Blood had collected there in a pool of silver. I blinked and worked out my mistake. Now I could see the earphones for my iPod that I'd left in my bed when I settled down for the night. They had made a distinct impression on my arm.

Jester stretched, and mewed mournfully. He started licking furiously on his right side. There was a whole tuft of fur missing revealing an angry graze. He hissed when I tried to get a better look at it.

"Jester must have been on one of his all night jaunts again," said Mum, over breakfast. "He's had a run in with the tomcat from Number Seven."

She could have been right. The vicious tomcat should have been neutered years ago in my opinion, or drowned at birth. I'd just had an amazingly vivid dream then?

"Come on, dear, eat up, you will be late for school, Juliette has already left you know."

I looked at my watch. "Heck, Mum," I said. "Why did you let me sleep in? I am going to have to run all the way."

I arrived at school with about a minute to spare. Nick was in the classroom, sorting out books for the first lesson and kit for PE, which followed.

"Have you been in the wars, Gunga Din?" he asked. "Did the man with the dog find you?" He grinned at me. "You've got a really nasty scratch on your neck, unless it's a love bite, you crafty devil."

I felt my neck, and the pain and the scab told me he was right, at least about the scratch bit.

"I've so much to tell you, Nick," I said, "but it'll have to wait until break."

When I changed for PE the boy next to me, one Fred Perkins, said, "Bloody hell, Bruce, who did that?" I looked at my arm and saw two livid scratches. I hadn't noticed them earlier. I realised that the numbness in my shoulder still extended around that part of my arm. Cold fear crept through all my limbs. What had happened in the park had apparently been real, or real enough to leave marks.

I gave Nick an overview of what had occurred last night after we'd each drunk a small carton of chocolate milk, at break.

"That's awesome, Rhory," he said. "Those wounds of yours, unless you did them yourself, or your cat got the better of you, are a kind of evidence aren't they?"

"But was I actually there, Nick, or did I just have such a vivid dream the marks appeared by themselves?"

"I don't know, mate, but it seems you need to be careful where you fly in future. You do have an interesting life that's for sure."

At that point the bell rang and we had separate lessons to go to.

I arrived home that afternoon to find Jester was really very ill. This raised all sorts of questions that I hadn't settled in my quick chat with Nick. I lay on my bed and thought about it.

Had I actually been there, right in the park? If so, how? Did I go back through time, far enough back to meet an actual druid?

Even as I thought the thought, I imagined being sent to see a doctor at a funny farm. Time travel couldn't be discussed in the same way as a trip to London. So who could I tell?

Certainly not my mum, she was much too down to earth. And not my dad. He was perhaps more open to the idea that the world is not all it appears to be. But he'd also converted to atheism. In other words he'd consciously chosen to reject any beliefs that smacked of spirituality, afterlife, religion, reincarnation, angels, Atlantis, or Masters of Wisdom.

Now Juliette, paradoxically, would listen and really weigh up the evidence. She'd do so because I was her baby brother and therefore adored. She'd think it all possible. But it would all, finally, have a rational explanation. A bit of physics, chemistry and psychology would explain it all. *There isn't strictly a mind*, she'd say, *just a brain burbling away*.

I knew that what I'd experienced went beyond a feverish brain. How? Well, I just knew. In fact when I thought about it, I'd always known.

Life is more, much more than it appears, and Atlantis is a reality, and there are angels and there is a kind God that watches over us all.

Had I learned this in Sunday School? Absolutely not. There I learned that God often smote those who displeased him, and those who fell a bit short might well end up in a hell that lasts forever. And that I also knew was incorrect.

So I just knew. Full stop.

I woke up in the morning with my head pounding and my whole body aching. Jester stared with glazed eyes and didn't move. His breaths came rapidly and his body trembled all over. My eyes teared up as I thought he might die.

Chapter 24

Dog Days

The man drew strongly on his cigarette, the silver holder held between the third and fourth fingers of his left hand. He blew the smoke out through half-closed teeth, narrowing his eyes against the washed out October sun. His brown brogues crunched against the gravel on the path between the rows of raspberry bushes. A few feet behind, his dog scratched hopefully at a possible flea.

He put his hand cautiously up to his ear, to avoid burning it with the cigarette. He'd no idea what had hit him a few days before, but suspected a pellet from an air gun. "Bloody hooligans," he said to the dog. "Terrorist hoodies."

It hadn't hurt that much, but no one had made fun of him for years and got away with it, and he didn't expect it in his own town. "Dammit, I'm Chairman of the bloody council."

He'd guessed they were concealed on the other side of the wall, having climbed a tree or something. When he'd reached the place where he thought the yobs were hiding, he'd been tempted to release the dog. But spaniels are not Rottweilers and he didn't want his dog kicked by some thug. The bushes had been too thick to march into, without doing potential damage to his Burberry jacket. He thought they'd run out when he shouted and he would catch them. They didn't, and somehow had wriggled away and must have climbed over the wall. He hoped they had twisted their ankles dropping down to the pavement below.

He kicked at the gravel in annoyance. He felt ... no, he knew ... something odd had gone on. He'd the same feeling he'd had in the

British Museum. The one they were looking for, the one the Irish girl had told them about from her trance state, had crossed his path twice now.

He drew again on the cigarette, the amethyst ring catching the sunlight this time. He wasn't psychic. Not like the girl, anyway. "She's a freak of nature," he said, pulling out a lone bamboo cane not attached to a raspberry bush. The dog looked up at him with limpid eyes. He wasn't psychic, but since he'd started this work with the Society, he'd come to realise that such things not only had a reality, they held the key to real power.

As he walked across his lawn, near a bed of tall flowers still in bloom, he realised his mistake. "Not twice, you mangy cur, thrice. He's crossed my path three times." The dog wagged his tail. The man slashed a head off a convenient flower with the cane.

If his wife had seen him beheading her hydrangea, she didn't say. He gave her a sour look anyway, as he stomped through the kitchen. Once upstairs he unlocked his study and sat down at the desk overlooking the long, neat garden. There on the lawn lay a large flower head and the bamboo cane.

The leather-bound book on the desk creaked as he opened it, the pages releasing the smell of ancient dust. On the frontispiece, a device in smudgy black print showed a shield with a black dog on one side and a white feline creature on the other. "Fat lot of good you were," said the man. Underneath this picture in blocky antique print, were the words '*Articles of the S.O.S*'.

He opened the book about a third of the way in, putting on his reading glasses, to cope with the tiny print. The section called Summoning and Sealing, involved doing eight things in precisely the right order. He checked again. Yes, he'd carried out all of these, including dribbling the disgusting mixture of liquids all around the bandstand. He'd even waited in his office in the council building until the stroke of midnight, to burn the rice paper with the phrase handwritten in Latin.

Well, something had happened that night. He'd looked out the window into the park. The darkness had been deepest near the ancient oak. In fact for a little while he would've sworn that whole part of the park had been invaded by trees. Some sort of trick of the light or the moon. He even thought he'd seen lights moving, but they vanished when he blinked. But something had been down there.

The bloody Steward, or whatever the Irish girl called him, had been there too. The 'Red King'. A blooming stupid name in his view. How could he track down someone called Red King? Frankly the girl exasperated him most of the time.

He opened a small wooden box on the desk and took out the mobile. "Designed to deceive," his associate Emerald had said, when she gave it to him. "No one would steal that model. It was old hat six years ago. If anyone sees you with it, you'll just look sad," she'd added somewhat acidly.

In fact the phone in his hand couldn't be bought in any shop. The hardware inside apparently transcended 'Top Secret'. If he did lose the mobile, only a cryptological expert would be able to reverse engineer it. Most casual thieves would just throw it away concluding it was broken.

He squeezed the phone in the way she'd demonstrated. After pausing for a count of 'four bananas' he squeezed it in a different way. The small screen lit up. He used the keyboard to enter a particular phrase. The phone hummed. After a brief wait, a mechanical voice said, "You have dialled a wrong number, please dial again." Instead he entered another word, a string of five numbers and a further word. He held the phone to his ear. Silence. He waited, and then... "Yes?"

"Amethyst," he said.

"I know," the woman responded, adding, "enter your code."

He did so, typing in a further phrase and initiating the simultaneous encryption. After the beep, he murmured, "We need a meeting in the west." A pause and a click.

"So soon after the last one?" He could sense the frigidity even after de-encryption.

"Time is of the essence." Pause, click.

"Indeed," said the female voice at the other end. "I'll speak to Diamond and get back to you."

The line went dead.

Chapter 25

Recovery

I remember only a little of what happened after I fell ill. Various things seemed to repeat. I'd be aware of Mum feeding me soup and applying a little ointment to my arm. She'd also give me some disgusting medicine with a teaspoon. And then I'd experience the whole thing again, in exact detail, right down to the disgusting taste.

My temperature could dry out a damp, chilled flannel laid on my forehead, in just a few minutes. Then it would do it all over again.

I know, because Juliette helpfully told me, that at first the doctor even feared for my life. It was Mum's insistence that I stay at home in my familiar bedroom that got me through.

She didn't want me going to hospital and catching some awful disease from the hospital itself. She somehow knew I needed Jester near to me. Even enlightened Hammerford Hospital didn't allow sick cats at the bedside.

Jester lay very still at the bottom of my bed. I could feel him there almost as a dead weight. Occasionally he'd lick his wound slowly. His fur looked all wrong.

I heard Mum say outside my door, "Poor Jester's very ill, I think we need to take him to the vet."

"I'll do it," said Dad.

I was aware of my parents creeping in and putting Jester in his plastic carrying box. He looked like a limp rag doll.

I cried a little when they left the room. *He's going to be put down.*

That night I ran a high fever. At one point I woke, and saw the dog sitting near the door. I recognised it by its smouldering eyes. I heard a strange sound, something between a snigger and a mew. On the mantelpiece above the fire, perched the silvery cat, looking at me.

A voice said quite distinctly, "We'll find you." I screamed.

They were gone by the time Dad came into the room a few moments later. He stayed and kept the light on, while I blubbered. Dad must have assumed I'd had a nightmare. I knew I'd been tracked down. I didn't know what had tracked me down.

Jester returned three days later, much perkier. After straightening my pillows and easing me up, Mum sat on the end of the bed, gently stroking Jester. He had a bandage on his wound and looked ridiculous.

"The vet put him on a drip, darling," she said. "He didn't hold out much hope, but the drip worked wonders. The vet said he could come home. We have a whole bunch of medicines for him!"

Jester improved but remained weak. He no longer had a one-way ticket to the River Styx. But the wound refused to heal. Apart from feeds and brief visits to the garden, he never left my feet. We convalesced, together.

During this time I had one dream so vivid it could have been real.

I am sitting by a river. It is very wide, and on the far shore I can see distant palm trees. I sit there for a long time just watching the river flow. I am waiting but not with any impatience. I am waiting for something important but I do not know what it is, only that I must wait.

I become aware of a bird by the water's edge. It has a black head with a long curved black beak, and white feathers for the rest of its substantial body. It is wading through the water on its long black legs and seems to be searching for something. It emerges with a snake in its beak. It takes off and I see its wings are tipped with black feathers. It soars right over my head and seems to circle, but the sun is above me and I cannot see it clearly because of the dazzling light.

When I look down, the sun has temporarily blinded me. As my vision clears I see a man standing between me and the river. He is dressed in a white linen kilt and his back is bare. There is a circlet of jewellery around his neck of blue and gold and it is two or three inches wide. He is facing away from me and I am aware that he is unusually tall, with hair of such blackness it is almost blue. He watches the river for some time. I know he is aware of me and I feel very calm.

I checked my dream diary when I felt strong enough, but I'd no written messages. The dream didn't involve Shoshan. I knew the man was important though.

Chapter 26

Shelley Takes a Train

Paddington station hummed with humanity as the young Irish woman wove her way through the bustle, towards the newsagent. Shelley checked her watch – a good 15 minutes before her train left. As always, the ticket had been delivered by courier. As always, she'd no idea which of her employers paid, and didn't much care.

Something to read on the journey to the West Country. Shelley worked her way down the women's magazines looking but not looking, just seeing what jumped out at her. That always worked best. *Ha! 'How to hold a pyjama party'. That looks fun.* She took the magazine off the shelf and flipped to the relevant article.

Kids jumped up and down on beds, wearing pyjamas with a variety of patterns. One stood with his hands on his hips, dressed in a traditional striped jacket and pyjama bottoms, a dressing gown draped over his shoulders. Shelley froze.

Just like the boy in the dream. Exactly the same outfit, surely? Not really a dream, more like my vision thing. Not the same face, too young, but the pyjamas are spot on.

She closed her eyes for a moment.

Two boys, one in a tunic of some sort, carried a torch and the other wore these bizarre nightclothes, out in an old oak forest. The boy with the tunic hurried along purposefully but the other one, looked around, and then stopped and looked back … towards where the sound of singing could be heard. This boy was important.

Shelley rubbed the edge of her nose; something she did when the second sight bobbed in and out of consciousness. A few butterflies took off in her stomach. Something strange had happened, if she could just remember.

The first boy, rather dashing with his long, curly dark hair, made it to the temple or whatever. The other one, barefoot and tall, with a pale face…

"Excuse me, are you going to buy that?" said a voice with more than a hint of irritation. A shop assistant stared at Shelley and pointed to the magazine which now hung by one cover from her hand.

"Oh," said Shelley. "Er, no, it's not the one I want." She put it back and grabbed a pocket edition of a magazine, with a grinning celebrity on the front, and beat a quick retreat towards the PAY HERE sign.

As she queued, she felt her attention tugged by something outside the shop. A woman in a cream suit – bought somewhere near Harrods, surely – clicked passed in rather nice Jimmy Choo shoes, with impossibly high heels. Shelley leaned back so a man in jeans and a leather jacket hid her from the woman, whom she knew only as 'Onyx'.

Frightening bitch. So much power and control in her aura colours – all sharp angles and red tinged hues.

Onyx hadn't learned to screen her aura from Shelley, unlike the other Stones. Shelley watched as she made her way to a coffee kiosk. Shelley paid for her magazine and slipped it into her handbag. She wheeled her overnight bag towards the doorway of the newsagent, and hovered just inside. Onyx said something to the girl at the kiosk and walked off towards the train, her heels clacking the rhythm of a slow motion machine gun.

When Shelley reached the kiosk herself, she saw at once that Onyx hadn't been pleased with the Asian-looking shop assistant. She ordered a tea and a blueberry muffin, and tuned in to the girl's energy field. There, right in the centre of her chest, her aura had a rent. Her face had drained of colour.

"Are you okay?" asked Shelley, knowing the answer already, and fishing in her handbag.

"I feel quite ill all of a sudden. The previous customer, she got annoyed 'cos I didn't know what a dry cappuccino was. I did my best but she ... I don't know, she just seemed so angry."

"Here," said Shelley giving the right money and a little bottle in a yellow box. "Take a drop now, and every five minutes till you feel better. It's Rescue Remedy. It'll do the trick."

Juggling the hot tea, muffin and her two bags, she made her way to the economy class area of the train, keeping her head down as she passed the first-class carriages towards economy class, jumping in taking the first available seat.

People didn't scare Shelley very easily, but the butterflies in her tummy were now a swarm. What had seemed a nice little earner in the ad in the Evening Standard – only four months ago – had become something she couldn't really control. She should have walked right out after seeing the eye thingy at her interview in the Savoy Hotel.

She leaned back, as far as her seat and two children arguing opposite her would allow. The day of the interview returned in all its grim fascination.

"Are you Prendergast?" the overweight woman had said.

"I'm Shelley Prendergast, yes," she had responded.

"Okay, follow me."

They had sat down near one another in the plush seats in the lounge area, and Shelley had looked at the stout woman, with her rather severe hair-do. *Fifty-five, if she's a day,* she had thought. Even though they were well into May, and the sun sat in a clear blue sky above the Thames, the woman had been wearing a two-piece suit of some tweedy material. Her brooch had caught the hotel lights, releasing green flashes the colour of mould on old cheese.

The first questions had been what Shelley expected, allowing her to explain her background as a secretary and the sort of jobs she'd held. Then they moved on to her 'gift'.

"So, you're a psychic then, are you?"

"Well, I've got the second sight, certainly."

"Have you done trance work before?"

"I've danced to trance music… No, not really. I tried channelling and automatic writing a few times, but just produced gibber."

"You've been hypnotised?"

"People have tried, but not succeeded."

The woman looked at her over her chunky glasses. Her eyes, dark as a lake on a winter's day, brooded on Shelley.

"Yes, I can see that." The woman reached into a large handbag on the floor at her side and took out a coppery object with a handle. She held it so that Shelley could see the Savoy ceiling lights reflected in its polished surface.

At first the lights bobbed around and Shelley wondered about the age of the mirror. It looked seriously antique. She switched into her soft focus and breathed out through her mouth. A cloud passed across the mirror from a sky far, far away and very long ago. Not a cloud, smoke … smoke from a brazier. Men were gathered around it, men in white robes of some fine material, with partially bare chests and arms. The fire flared and the smoke became whiter.

When she realised an eye filled the mirror, she'd no idea how long it had been staring at her. Something sticky slid slowly over her abdomen. The Eye, coal black, had the sort of heat you get from touching something very, very cold. Shelley jerked her head back.

"So?"

"What on earth was that?" said Shelley, failing to keep a tremor out of her voice.

"You saw then?"

"If seeing means a…" she checked herself from saying the 'F' word, "a blooming, great eye, then yes, I saw. What on earth was it?" Shelley didn't look at the mirror as the woman slid it back in her bag.

"I only need to know that you saw." The woman snapped her handbag closed. "The job is yours. We can work with you. You will tell no one about this interview. You will sincerely regret it if you do. Your money will be paid into your bank account on the first of the month. You will travel when we need you to. Generally you will work monthly, but more frequently if we request it. You can do temp work as a secretary, but our needs come first, is that understood?"

Shelley nodded. "What do you want me to do?"

The woman stood up, and stared for a moment at Shelley. "You'll learn that at The House. All you've to do is to travel to the town named on your train ticket, and arrive at the time stated. We'll do the rest."

With that the interview had ended.

Shelley remembered squinting in the sunlight outside the Savoy realising she'd had no idea of the stout woman's name. The lady had not introduced herself or shaken her hand. The fat cow had masked her aura though. Shelley had been unable to read anything, and realised now that she hadn't even thought about it. She had known one thing though, the woman with the green brooch had some real occult power. That eye thingy had been alive – was alive now – but also had been looking at her from long, long ago. She'd shivered.

The money's good though. More than I make in a month working full time, and I'll only be doing four days a month, max. For that, I'll look at a few putrid eyes, she had thought.

But another shiver had shot through her, and she had touched the crucifix at her neck.

Chapter 27

The West Country

"Tickets please!"

The conductor passed down the aisle between the crowded seats. Shelley gave him her ticket and he scribbled something indecipherable on it. Her station would be a few stops before the train terminated in Bristol. Always the same station. Always the same procedure. She'd be met at the station by Joe the Killer. She wondered if today she'd have to travel in the car, with Onyx of the icy heart. She hoped not.

She replaced her ticket carefully, with the return portion, in her handbag. Leaning back she mused about the first time she'd arrived at the small country town station.

Emerging onto the station forecourt Shelley had looked around. She'd had no idea who would meet her here, nor what she'd do if no one had showed up. She hadn't even had a telephone number she could call. The few passengers from the London train had taken taxis or been picked up. For several minutes Shelley had stood alone not sure what to do next.

A large dark car, with slightly shaded windows had then pulled out from the car park and had crept towards where she stood. It had drawn up alongside and the driver had leant across and released the back door on her side. She'd wondered if he'd get out and help with her case but he hadn't, so she had heaved it onto the back seat and slid in.

Shelley started off chattering away about the journey, but the man didn't even grunt. He just said nothing at all. She looked at the solidity of the skull beneath his severely short haircut. His eyebrows, the colour of old straw, contrasted with the darkness of his slightly mirrored sunglasses. His ears bent back towards his head in a way that suggested his mother had stuck them there with sticking plaster when he was a tiny child. The pullover he wore had a ribbed design and epaulets with buttons. It looked military. He looked military. Shelley tuned in to his energy fields and then wished she hadn't.

This man has killed people. And he enjoyed it.

Shelley settled back into the seat of the car and watched the countryside flow past. A sign with the word *Stonehenge* caught her eye; she'd never seen that landmark and wondered if they'd go near to the old stone circle.

Twenty minutes later, the car slowed as they approached a gate set in a high wall. The driver must have pressed some button on a control in the car because the gate slowly slid open. The car moved through the gate. Shelley had no idea where they were. On their way here *Killer Joe,* as Shelley had named the driver, had followed a route of tiny country lanes for some miles, with high trees all around. He'd driven too fast for her to read most of the road signs, from the back seat.

Tall pines flanked the drive leaving a gash of sky above them. A couple of tracks led off to goodness knows what, in the grounds. After a minute or two they pulled up on front of a substantial house from some past century.

Her door opened and Shelley looked towards the driver to see what she should do next. He stared ahead.

"Shall I go in then?"

Killer Joe turned his blank mirrored lenses in her direction, shrugged and turned back. Shelley pulled her bags off the back seat and walked over towards the front door. The car's wheels crunched on the gravel as it pulled away from the house.

"Come on, girl, I haven't got all day."

Standing in the front door was a strikingly beautiful young

woman, with blonde hair arranged in a way that suggested she'd soon be attending a fashion parade.

"Sorry," said Shelley.

"I'm Onyx," said the blonde, somewhat disarmingly. She didn't offer to shake Shelley's hand.

"Sorry, you're who?"

"Onyx," the woman had said again looking at Shelley the way a society hostess looks at a sponge cake, where a fly has just landed. "We don't use our real names here, Shelley." Her hand had floated up towards her jet-black earrings. "Onyx," she had repeated.

That had been about four months ago, give or take. Shelley now stared out the train window watching the Gloucestershire scenery whip past. She'd seen Stonehenge once, when Killer Joe took a route close by. Her skin had goose-bumped all over. She could feel the vibes even in the car.

The boy came back into her mind. There had been more in her vision. Shelley rubbed her nose.

The firelight flickered and danced on the faces of the circle of priests and priestesses. They all looked at their leader, Abaris, as he led the chanting. He stopped and a powerful silence enveloped them. Slowly he pointed with a golden arrow at the fire. The wood settled, sending a shower of sparks soaring towards the stars above.

"The Red King does not know his destiny. Neither does Demeter's son. Tonight is their awakening. We can only stand and watch and pray. The path they walk is their own and no one can walk it for them. The followers of the Desert God know this too and will do everything to stop them. It is for us at this time, and all time, to ensure they fail."

Abaris had looked right where Shelley had stood in the circle, as he had said this.

Shelley stretched and watched the telephone wires appear to swoop up and down as the train sped past. *I was a priestess in a previous life? Or perhaps I've tuned into some ancient druid lady? OMG! And the boy in his ridiculous pyjamas is a king! Now that's seriously cool.*

Two little girls across from her were arguing about what crayons to use to colour in a fairy-godmother picture. One pinched the other.

Each time she'd taken the train, the pattern had been similar. Joe the Killer picked her up but didn't exercise his conversational skills. She'd wondered if the Stones had had his tongue cut out to ensure his silence, but that seemed too medieval, and anyway he could write she supposed. He always followed a slightly different route to the house, sometimes taking fifteen minutes longer. Shelley remained confused as to the exact location of where she did her work.

On her first visit, Onyx had shown her to her room, but not helped with her bags. Shelley was allowed to stay in her bedroom or come down the back stairs to a small lounge where she had her meals. She had always eaten on her own. In the corner of this room a TV, probably used by the Romans after they invaded, showed anything free to view in washed-out colours and with a persistent flicker.

"Don't wander around the house," Onyx had warned. "Be ready at 4pm for your first session."

The train lurched and orange juice spattered onto her jeans.

"Now look what you've made me do," said the older of the two kids, who'd just knocked their drink all over Cinderella's Coach. Rivulets of sticky orange liquid advanced towards Shelley. The mother, sitting across the aisle, looked across at her offspring and said, "Behave, or you'll be sorry." She didn't catch Shelley's eye.

Shelley fished in her handbag, looking for the pack of tissues she always carried. She pulled out the small aerosol of Glob-off, designed to deter attackers in city streets. It delivered sticky red goo all over the face that only came off with water. She wondered if she had the courage to use it to discipline the brats. Instead she mopped up the juice and smiled. The older of the two girls stuck out her tongue.

Shelley ignored her and speed dialled on her mobile. After hearing about her friend's latest crisis with her boyfriend, she decided to confide a little.

"I had this amazing dream the other night," she said. "I seemed to be in the country or maybe it was a park, I dunno, it doesn't really matter."

The voice at the other end said, "Go on, Shell, I love your dreams, what happened?"

"Well, I was sort of following this cat, a ginger and white cat. It seemed very purposeful. You know what I mean? Striding in a way that was not totally cat-like. It seemed to be on a mission."

"Yeah," said the voice at the other end, "and..."

"Well, then I got one of my chills, you know, like I do when I'm awake and something or someone rather nasty passes by."

"So, what happened then, Shell, don't be a tease?"

"I saw the dark side, Laila, it was quite creepy. A horrid black dog. I could sort of smell it. Not dog like. Just a minute Laila..." Shelley left her seat and walked to the relative privacy of the corridor. "Are you still there?"

"Yes, go on."

"You'll have to speak up Lay, I'm in the corridor. I was doing a Shelley broadcast, so I thought I better move! I was getting looks, know what I mean?" Shelley moved the phone to the other ear, as someone passed by. "Well, it had a smell like rotting things and sewage."

"What does? The train carriage?"

"No, you sausage, the dog."

"Oh, yeah,"

"It was evil, Lay, and I didn't like it. I knew it was something to do with this hush-hush work I'm doing. You know, the one that pays so well."

"In what way evil, Shell?"

"Well it didn't wish anyone any good. And I heard one of my voices. It said, *'The Destroyer'*."

"God, Shell, that's wicked," said Laila. "What do you think that meant?"

"I don't know, but when I saw the silvery cat, the voice said, *'The*

Deceiver'."

"What silver cat, Shell, now you've got me confused?"

"It was another beast, and I do mean beast. It smelled like cheap perfume. And then I saw the..."

"You're breaking up, Shell. What's that?"

"I saw the boy again, the tall thin boy."

"Can't hear you, Shell. What...?"

"The boy, in his pyjamas, in the park. His face was completely clear. I'd know him anywhere if..." At that point the train went into a tunnel and the connection was lost.

Chapter 28

Miranda

Jester lay at the end of the bed, still slightly the worse for wear. I rested against my pillows, not really reading a library book Juliette had found for me, when a woman came into the bedroom with Mum. She'd a lot of red hair, and a dress that seemed to float around her as she moved. It was all blues, and purples and shades of sea green. I noticed she had an incredible number of necklaces, made of wood, silver filigree, and stones with a deep amber colour. *How could she walk without a stoop*?

"This is a friend of Aunt Sofia's, dear," said Mum.

"Hello, Rhory, I'm Miranda," she said. Her voice had a rich depth. Not a voice suggesting the owner smoked too much, rather the voice of someone you might expect to be able to sing, with deep velvety notes. She laid her hand on my forehead. I sighed, relaxing into her cool and soft touch.

"Well," she said, "you're a poorly boy, I can see that. But I'm sure we can get you better in no time at all, and back to school where you ought to be!" The bit about school she said with a twinkle in her eyes.

Miranda asked Mum some very odd questions about me. What sort of food did I like? Was I keen on pickles? Did I prefer my milk warm or cold before going to bed at night? Was it better to sleep on my hurt arm or on the other side. Surprisingly, it worked better for me to sleep on my hurt arm.

"Mmm, a right-sided remedy then," Miranda murmured to no one in particular.

Even through my grogginess, I thought her questions and

comments seemed to have just a smidgen of the witch about them.

"I'm just going to explore your energy fields, dear," she said, in a matter of fact voice, as though we did that sort of thing in Hammerford. She moved her hands about six inches away from my body.

"Now just lie there, dear, you don't need to do anything. Imagine you are sort of floating in a warm sea..."

I could feel warmth where her hands passed, even though they were at a distance and over the duvet. After a few minutes, she stood back from the bed, and shook her hands swiftly, as though trying to rid them of honey or ants.

"Bring me some water, Kyrsten, with two teaspoons of salt mixed in, please."

Mum went off to do this.

"Well, Rhory dear, you've been through quite an experience. Your solar plexus chakra is really, really depleted. I've done a bit of balancing and sealing. You will need to sleep a bit soon, once I've had a look at this hero."

Miranda sat down at the very end of the bed and laid her hands on Jester. She sat with her eyes closed for a few moments. From inside her handbag, she extracted a little object on a thread.

"This is my wisdom on a string," she said, with a half-wink at me. She held a tiny carved ivory owl dangling at the end of the thread.

She suspended the owl over Jester, and seemed to be asking herself questions. Sometimes the owl hung immobile, sometimes it swung quite energetically back and forth, and sometimes it went in a circle. All this happened even though Miranda kept her hand perfectly still. The owl had a life of its own apparently. *Impressive witchcraft this.*

Mum came back with the bowl of salty water.

Miranda thanked her, dipped her hands in the water, and held them there for a few moments. Then she shook the drops into the corners of the room. Again, it looked as if she was trying to get something sticky off her hands.

The phone rang downstairs at that point and Mum went off to answer it. Miranda moved a chair closer to the bed.

"Rhory," she said, "you've been through a dreadful experience. I picked up a lot just reading your energy fields." I must have looked quizzical, because she continued, "Don't worry about that now. In brief, dear, you've been under an attack. You probably saw things…?" She raised her eyebrows.

"Yes," I mumbled, not sure how much of my experiences to share with this strange lady.

"I don't need the details, dear, they'll be different for each one of us. But you came up against forces that wished you no good at all." She looked at me with a smile more in her eyes that her face. Although she was saying scary things, I felt really calm.

"I've cleared this room and it is now protected. They've not established a true link. I could tell that when I worked on your solar plexus and heart chakras." She pointed her hand at my tummy and heart. "I'm sure you'll get better now. Take the remedies I'll suggest to your mum and plenty of rest. You'll be back at school in no time at all!"

Before I could thank her, Miranda had left the room, leaving a slight fragrance in the air like a rainbow that I could smell.

Chapter 29

Trance

Shelley returned to her seat in the train compartment where the older of the two little girls opposite had just pinched her younger sister. Shelley stared out the window again, ignoring World War III breaking out across the table, and remembering the first of her sessions.

"Ah, good day to you, young lady." A silver haired man had stood in the doorway of the small lounge of the house. "Have you had sufficient breakfast?"

She had nodded.

"I'm Sardius." The man had extended a manicured hand in her direction. His leathery skin had felt dry against her own, but the handshake had proven firm. "Follow me," he had said offering a smile that would do credit to game show host on afternoon TV. "You don't want to get lost in this house, I assure you."

Shelley followed him along the hallway.

"The Billiard Room," Sardius announced pointing his elegant hand towards a substantial oak door on the ground floor. "Here's where we will explore the unknown and conquer universes." He opened the door, and announced, "Miss Shelley Prendergast," to the half dozen or so people gathered within.

Shelley felt about as comfortable as one of Henry VIII's wives on execution day. Six pairs of eyes appraised her. She hoped the gap between her jeans and her top didn't reveal too much pale flesh, and she swallowed.

"Now let me introduce you," said Sardius, continuing with his game show smoothness. "You know our esteemed Emerald." It was the stout woman Shelley had met at the Savoy Hotel. *So that was her name.* She nodded at Shelley but didn't smile. "And this is Onyx of course." The blonde wore light tan trousers and a soft black leather jacket. She also nodded briefly before continuing a quiet conversation with Emerald.

"Amethyst, may I introduce Shelley? Shelley, this is Amethyst." A man about the age of her dad nodded at her from the other side of the billiards table. His broad shoulders and trim waist, suggested a man who worked out regularly. He had the good looks of a love-you-and-leave-you sort of man. She didn't trust him an inch.

The others were introduced with their semi-precious names. *Powerful men, rich ... but I wouldn't want to go out with any of them. Just look at their eyes.* Shelley didn't attempt to tune into their auras. Her nerves wouldn't allow it. Anyway, she didn't need second sight to pick up on Power, Money and Ego.

The huge billiards table had a futon or something laid on it, with a white sheet of slinky, silky material covering it. *That's the altar and I'm the sacrifice.* A large book lay at one end and three small crystal vases held salt, water and a pale blue liquid. A tall tripod of wood presided over the table, with a copper mirror like the one Emerald had used at the Savoy Hotel. The handle of the mirror fitted into a purpose made hole and in front, a blue candle flickered. The reflected light from the copper surface dazzled. Shelley avoided looking for the eye thingy.

A small set of dark wooden steps allowed Shelley to climb onto the adapted billiards table, where they actually used a compass to ensure her feet pointed to magnetic north. Other adjustments went on around her as Sardius spoke comfortingly from his seat somewhere near her head.

"Just relax now, Shelley," he said, as she strained her neck to see Emerald and Onyx consulting notebooks. Somebody fiddled with the volume of a recording system. "We're going to put this soft silk scarf over your eyes now, to help you tune in. Breathe normally.

Listen to my voice."

Shelley slowly drifted far away.

The desert sun pressed down on her head. The stonework of the ancient temple shimmered in the heat. Even the thick leather of her sandals could not entirely protect her from the hot stone slabs under her feet. She longed for shade. Somewhere cool. A voice said, "Enter," and hot air wrapped around her in the chamber of the temple. In front of her stood three jars, decorated with seated figures seen from the side, their knees drawn up to their heads. The voice said, "Listen," and then words in a strange tongue crept around her, sliding into her ears. "Speak," said the voice. "Speak over the desert wastes of time."

"Drink this, Shelley," said Sardius, as Shelley felt herself jolted back into the room. She took the glass of water and sipped away the dryness in her mouth. As she sat up, dizziness clouded her whole head. When her vision cleared, she looked around the Billiards Room. The men had left, leaving Onyx and Emerald. Onyx smiled at Shelley, whose arms felt achy and her left leg cramped slightly as she flexed it. Part of her still floated near a squat temple in a remote desert.

"Amazing, truly amazing. Do you remember anything?" asked Onyx, arching her eyebrows.

"A desert. A temple. The heat. And the voice, talking and talking. Was I out for long?"

The two women exchanged a glance. Shelley looked at her watch but her wrist was bare.

"We had to remove the watch, Shelley. Metal," said Sardius, as though that would be enough explanation. He retrieved the watch from a side table.

"Just long enough, Shelley," said Onyx. "You did really well." She tapped her notebook as she spoke. "Remarkable actually. Have you done past life regression?"

"No," said Shelley, and wondered again about the vision of being a druid priestess. "What are you researching if I may ask?"

"You mayn't," said Emerald.

"Oh don't be too harsh," said Sardius. "The girl deserves to know something."

"The girl only needs to know one thing – discretion," said Emerald.

"I'm sure you understand you cannot speak of what we are doing," said Onyx, giving a smile that added even more to her model good looks. Shelley's insides squirmed slightly. She wondered if they had hypnotised her after all. "We are researching time streams. You are one of those who can look down time's corridors as it were. We are linking to the past so we can make the future we need. Of course if you speak of this outside this room, we will know." She vaguely pointed in Emerald's direction.

"You've no idea who this is, but she knows pretty much everything about you."

Emerald narrowed her eyes slightly at this. She moved towards Shelley.

That green and yellow monstrous building on the Thames. MI5 or MI6 or whatever. God, she's a spook. The image of the Headquarters of British Intelligence had just popped into Shelley's mind.

"If you do tell anyone," said Emerald, "they'll think you are mad, talking of time travel and things like that. We know that you cannot do this work without picking up on some aspects. But these things are more secret than state secrets, believe me. We don't require you to sign the Official Secrets Act, although we could if we needed to, couldn't we, Sardius."

"That won't be necessary," Sardius had said, as he gathered up the various objects that had been laid out with such care on the billiards table.

"No, it won't be necessary because we never, ever forgive betrayal, and no one would believe that people like us use people like you," Onyx had added.

The train pulled into the little station some distance from Bristol. Shelley reached for her bag from the overhead rack. The two brats were now arguing over dividing up some sweets their mother had produced. The mother, all ample flesh and over-tight clothes, talked loud and long on her mobile, ignoring the children. The carton of orange, with a straw, lay on its side in a small puddle of stickiness. Shelley's case landed on the carton, sending a jet of orange juice over the front of the most annoying of the two children, staining a T-shirt that stated 'Mummy's Little Angel' in glitter.

"Oy," said the girl. "Oy, you."

The doors to the train beeped and swished open, and Shelley left the train smiling to herself.

"In you get," said Killer Joe, as the car door glided open.

"My God, you can speak," said Shelley.

The driver pushed his dark glasses up on his forehead for a moment and turned his pale grey eyes towards her. *He's in his forties, surely.* "Don't let that give you any ideas," he said, and the rest of the journey to the house occurred in customary silence.

There were a number of cars in the forecourt of the house when they pulled up. Killer Joe let them in at the front door with a key, and even carried Shelley's bag up to her bedroom on the third floor.

"Wait here till you're called."

"Okay, and thanks for the help," said Shelley to the door as it closed. For a moment she thought he might lock her in, but that didn't happen.

The train tickets had been delivered by courier yesterday, with a message saying simply, "Do not miss this appointment." *Charming.* Something had happened at the last session when she'd been summoned just over a week ago. She could tell when she'd woken up on the billiards table. There were fewer of the Stones there than usual. Onyx and Sardius of course, but not Emerald or the creepy Amethyst.

"Did you see anything?" Onyx had asked. Shelley wasn't sure. Sometimes the pictures came back afterwards, even days later. She always kept what she saw to herself.

"No, I don't think so."

"Who's the Red King?" had asked the oddly named Beryl, whom she thought looked like an ex-head boy from Harrow or Eton.

Onyx had flashed him a look of deep annoyance. He had persisted as though he'd not noticed her. "Did you see the Red King? Can you tell us who he might be? Are you sure he lives in Hammerford?"

Shelley always felt woozy after visiting the desert temple – she'd start there each time – and didn't at first understand what Beryl had meant. "I've no idea," she had lied.

Sitting on her bed now, awaiting developments, she could hear voices in the distance and a car door slamming. Perhaps all the Stones in their secret society would be meeting today. Her window rattled as a machine gun clattered away somewhere in the garden. She jumped off the bed and went to the window. *Machine gun?* Her view looked out at tall pines and not the lawn, with its Greek statues, in front of the Billiards Room. Her window quivered some more as a helicopter passed over the house.

After it landed, complete silence descended on the house. Shelley waited but no one called for her. She pondered the Red King. *He must be the boy. The one in pyjamas. So he lives in Hammerford.*

Shelley thought of herself as tough rather than kind, but something about the boy had touched her. Or rather she sensed she connected with him in some way. *The druids. My link with him is through the druids. I wonder if I can find him and warn him.*

Chapter 30

Dimitris and Rhory

Greece – in ancient times

The spume stung Dimitris's eyes, as he stared out across the endless waves. He rubbed at them angrily, annoyed at his own tears. The rhythmic splash and swash of the oars became the beat of his life. Crete and Delphi had gone, perhaps for ever. An uncertain future beckoned as he accompanied his sister to join the Old Man of Croton.

He turned his red-rimmed eyes and looked across at where his older sister sat on a stool, a warm woollen cloak wrapped close around her, its ends flapping in the sharp sea breeze. She smiled at him and beckoned.

"Dimitri," she said, looking steadily at him, "it's no shame to grieve for our mother. It's no shame to grieve for the life we're leaving behind. To be at the behest of a God is never easy. But the prophecy could not have been clearer and we are right to follow Apollo's shafts of light, when we are given them."

Dimitris kept his legs astride and his knees slightly bent to deal with the steady rise and fall of the deck. "I know, but her death was so sudden and the oracle so unexpected. It is hard to believe that only ten days have passed since we arrived at Delphi."

"Is it really so few?" Theano drew the cloak tighter as the wind picked up. "It's right to keep careful count, brother, as we must honour our mother's passing once more on the forty-ninth day. By then we should be where the world doesn't bob up and down and always taste of salt."

They fell silent once more, as the sound of the oars took over. Theano's eyes sought out the horizon and the life that now called to her. Dimitris watched his sister, her dark wavy hair not quite held in place by pins and ribbons. Her brown eyes remained steady in their gaze, even if screwed up slightly against the glare of the sun, as it began its descent towards the west. *She can see from this world and into the next,* thought Dimitris, not for the first time.

Theano had always been marked out as special. Even as a child she had prophesied and their father had spared nothing on her education. Theano's gifts had led the whole family to travel from Crete to Delphi. She'd come, aged seventeen, to the Temple of Apollo to seek guidance. They all assumed she'd remain as a priestess, perhaps becoming an Oracle herself. Dimitris's thoughts were interrupted by a high-pitched voice.

"There's land ahead!" Dimitris looked up to see his younger brother confidently limping towards them from the front of the ship.

"We're to take on water," said Sophos, grinning at the chance of a new adventure. He had been the first of them to get his sea legs. Even with his special sandal and twisted foot, Sophos had managed better than both Theano and Dimitris, and hadn't been sick even once. He proved to be a great favourite with the sailors, had mastered their knots quickly, and now spent his time at the front of the ship playing with twine and trying to invent a knot the sailors hadn't thought of.

"Castor and Pollux say we can land if we want to," Sophos whispered loudly into his sister's ear.

"That'll be up to the captain," said Theano. "And don't call them that where anyone can hear you. It might be taken as offensive."

Dimitris smiled. He doubted that anyone would be offended by his irrepressible brother. Castor and Pollux were their names for two of the sailors who appeared identical enough to be twins, right down to the way they walked, laughed and always knew what the other one would say next. They weren't even brothers as far as Dimitris knew, but always went around together. Dimitris wondered if perhaps you grew to be like the person you shared an oar with.

The isle had a small bay that gave protection against the worst of the waves and a tiny harbour where the ship could be safely moored. It also had a spring, which the sailors could use to top up their casks of water.

"Let's walk round the island," said Sophos.

"No," responded Theano, "we don't know how long we will rest here." She sat down on an upturned cask, in the shade of some wispy trees growing near the harbour wall.

"But there might be dragons and winged serpents," said Sophos, "and we'll miss them."

"All the more reason to stay put, I'd think," said Dimitris. But like his younger brother he wondered if this isle held more than just a fresh water spring. Some ruined houses clustered near the harbour, suggesting others had once made this their home.

"Only five years ago several families lived here," said the captain, as though reading Dimitris's thoughts. "We think pirates must've raided, for the houses are stripped bare, and burned. The water remains fresh however, and pirates would think twice before attacking our ship. We're well armed."

The captain, a weather beaten man with a waist as wide as his shoulders were broad, had taken them on board at Corinth. His reputation, and the size and quality of his ship, had convinced Dimitris's father that his children would be as safe as could be hoped in their travelling to the west.

This fitted with what the Oracle at Delphi had stated. Theano would be known till the end of time itself, if she chose to travel towards the setting sun and serve the Python's Child. They were now doing just that.

The sudden death of their mother had shocked them and for the two days dominated by the funeral, they could give the oracular verses no thought. Without Dimitris's love of stories, they might have still been languishing in Delphi, with its sad associations. But he had solved the meaning of the reference to the Python's Child.

"Ha!" said one of the sailors.

"Ha ha!" said another.

Dimitris looked up to see Castor, or perhaps Pollux, standing near them, each holding a snake by the tail.

"You see—" said one whirling the snake around his head,

"—they can fly," completed the other.

"Be careful," shouted the captain. "Some o' them snakes is really deadly."

"Oh they won't bite us, Captain."

"We're too salty!"

"Anyhow, they can't move their heads—"

"—close enough to bite."

The two men continued to spin the snakes just fast enough so their heads couldn't strike. The sailors were looking at Theano. Dimitris didn't like the way they were seeking to impress her.

"And so —" said the first.

"—it ends," said the second.

Castor and Pollux flicked the snakes as you would a whip, breaking their necks with an audible crack. For a moment the two reptiles hung loosely from their hands, the heads now reaching nearly to the ground. The sailors grinned at each other and pirouetted, spinning the two dead snakes right across the deck and into the sea beyond.

Theano looked at Dimitris, her eyes troubled. Before she could speak, a crash of thunder reminded them that the Mediterranean could produce storms just as easily as venomous snakes.

*

England, about now

Everyone expected me to go to school the next day. Miranda's visit had done me the world of good and I'd improved rapidly.

Consequently, I felt miserable and angry to find myself sick in the middle of the night. I thought I might puke up on the bed and got up to head for the loo. The whole room pitched and heaved. The floor rose and then fell. I staggered and put my hands out to grasp onto something. Stumbling towards the door, I ended up leaning against the cool wood of the huge wardrobe that filled one side of the bedroom. Even it moved, leaning in towards me and then falling away.

I found the doorknob and turned it. I had the weirdest sensation on the landing outside the bedroom that huge waves were moving towards me, invisible in the dark. Lurching forward, I caught the wooden knob at the top of the bannisters and just about negotiated the three steps down to the toilet, without falling down the stairs.

However hard I tried I couldn't throw up quietly, and kneeling before the oddly comforting coolness of the toilet bowl, I wondered why anyone would bother to write the word Shanks, just above the water line.

"Here's a flannel, dear," said Mum, kneeling behind me, her hand dry and gentle on my forehead. I wiped off what I could from my chin before producing another series of sounds, like the expletives in a fight in a *Batman* comic.

"I wonder what brought this on. You were doing so well."

I thought so too. I made my shaky way back into the bedroom.

Mum said, "Do you want a drink of water, darling?"

I don't know what I'd have answered as something struck me on the head at that point.

Later that night, when I woke, I saw a person sitting in a chair, in the corner of the room. At first I thought Shoshan, the Egyptian girl, had manifested there for some reason. I didn't have the energy to move, but kept my eyes open long enough to see this young woman was older and her dark hair longer and more curly. I blinked my eyes and the chair had no one sitting there, just Mum's pale dressing gown draped over the back.

In the morning everyone said the welt on my forehead had been where I'd hit it, falling against the wardrobe. I said nothing, but I knew I'd been hit in the middle of the room, as I crossed towards the bed.

*

Greece, in ancient times

Theano held Dimitris's hand.

"Are you feeling better, brother?"

"I'm not sure," he mumbled, raising his hand to the bandage on his head. "What in Hades' name happened?"

"It's never good to call on the Gods like that," said his sister, frowning. She sat opposite his little bunk, where a couple of cloaks provided bedding. All of Dimitris's clothes and the cloaks were damp from the storm. His sister touched his cheek.

"You took a great wallop on your head, Dimi. Some spar became loose in the storm and it hit you as you were making for the side."

Dimitris remembered the night before in confused bits and pieces. The dull ache of fear still lurked in his stomach. The boat had been tossed around like a toy as great waves rolled by and thunder and lightning seemed to surround them. He had never, ever, felt so ill and remembered standing at the rail for what seemed like hours, retching bile into the breakers as they crashed against the hull. Judging by the smell of his cloak, most of it had been blown back straight onto him.

"The captain himself caught you. You could have been washed overboard. You were completely unconscious when they brought you down here."

Dimitris gingerly put his hand to his head, and felt the lump underneath the strip of cloth.

"I don't remember," he said. "I just remember how huge the waves were." He paused for a bit as though listening. "It's calm again now, isn't it."

"We prayed to Poseidon himself," said Theano, "and he must have heard. The storm ended almost as abruptly as it began." Dimitris watched as a shadow passed over his sister's face. Fear clutched more sharply at his stomach. "Sophos," he said. "Sophos is all right isn't he?"

"Oh yes, he is fine. He used his new knot to lash himself close to the oarsmen for the worst of the storm. When it became calmer, he carried fresh water to those who continued rowing. We did lose two sailors though." She ran her fingers through her hair, easing out the rime-filled tangles. "Both Castor and Pollux were swept overboard shortly before the storm calmed down."

Dimitris looked hard at his sister and she shrugged.

"Storms claim lives, Dimitris. We are all lucky to be alive. I thought you might be dead. You were unconscious for some time when they put you here. I sat watching with only lamplight and you were so still. At one point you opened your eyes and stared right at me. But..." she ran her hands slowly through her hair once more, "but they were not your eyes. They were from far, far away and I thought you had crossed over to the land of the shades already. Then you closed your eyes and let out a mighty snore, and I knew you'd be all right. Shortly after that the waves subsided and the skies cleared."

Carefully, Dimitris eased his legs over the edge of his bunk, and attempted to sit up, as far as the deck above his head allowed.

"Somewhere in the night I had a dream. I stood right inside the dream, and watched as it happened all around me. A woman, Alkmene, swelled with child. A serving girl, swift as a weasel, ran around the room, making me dizzy, and confusing everyone. For a moment all the Gods held their breath, and then the child came forth. The child's name was Herakles."

Dimitris's voice took on a different note. No longer quivering with shock or weak with sickness, his words filled the space between them. He spoke of the birth of the hero Herakles, and how a trick by the Goddess Hera meant he would not rule the world as Zeus had intended.

"The Goddesses were in the dream, sister," Dimitris spoke without seeing. He felt back inside the dream once more. "Great Athena took the child who had been abandoned by his mother, to die on a desolate plain. She brought it to Hera, and persuaded the

Queen of the Gods to give the child the milk of her own breast. Hera did, but the baby drew so strongly that she flung it far from her. Later, back in his cradle, two massive serpents crept up on the child. Herakles clasped them with his hands and strangled them."

Theano knew parts of this story, which her nurse had shared with her, but she'd never heard it told with such authority.

"I saw it all," said Dimitris, his voice sounding wistful and more like that of his thirteen years, once more.

Theano looked at him for a long time after he finished. Dimitris's eyes were focused on the floor between them, and he remained wrapped in the glowing folds of the dream.

"The Oracle said more, Dimitris. I chose not to tell you until I was sure, until I'd had a sign."

Dimitris looked at her, screwing up his face in puzzlement, as though her words had not quite reached his ears.

"The Oracle said I'd be safe if I travelled with one who ran with heroes and one who had the Lame God's blessing."

"You didn't tell me," said Dimitris.

"No, I didn't. It appeared clear to me that Sophos is blessed by the Lame God. His mind is so clear and his hands so clever, he might have been fathered by the Hephaestus himself, were it not that he looks just like our father."

Dimitris nodded, a slight smile returning to lighten up his face. For the first time that morning, sunlight cut through the gloom of the cabin area.

"The one who runs with heroes is clearly you. I know it now. I spoke with the priest of Apollo before we left. He is a wise man, Dimitri, and he knows the power of stories. He says we live in the time when tales are being crafted, even as Sophos crafts his toys and knots. These tales will travel right down the corridors of time to the very end of all things. We hear the stories, but you see them as they are. He said to me that you will be a seer. My destiny is different. I'll be known in times to come. You, fair brother," and she smiled across at him, "will make stories that will be remembered for ever."

A silence descended as loud as an explosion.

"They've stopped rowing," said Dimitris.

The cry from the deck above told them why.

"Sail, ho!"

They rushed up on deck. The oarsmen sat with their blades raised above the waves. The captain stood leaning against the deck rail, staring at the distant ship that sailed parallel with their course.

"It's following us." The captain spoke to Theano as an equal. "It wants to see how we will react. If we run it will chase, I am sure."

"So it's a pirate."

"Undoubtedly," said the captain. "But they are not sure if we carry goods for trade and plunder, or soldiers."

"The Gods did not bring us through the storm to give us to barbarians," said Theano. "Do you have flour in your stores, Captain?"

He squinted at her. "Yes, of course."

"And do the soldiers have helms and spears?"

Dimitris had not spoken to the half dozen or so soldiers who were travelling with them to Crotona, and they stayed at the back of the ship playing dice most of the time, when the weather allowed.

"They do have helms," said the captain.

"Swiftly now, bring me a helm, well-polished, and with its horsehair rubbed with that red dye you carry. A spear and the great brass dish we eat off. And flour, Captain, a cup of flour."

Sophos understood more quickly than Dimitris, what Theano intended, and helped her cover her face with flour, till it appeared pure white. She slid off her cloak and the large golden clasp at her shoulder flashed in the sunlight.

"Dimitri wear a helm as well, but one without horsehair. Then stand with me and we will look, to superstitious eyes, like Athena travelling with Odysseus's son. While pirates may attack a merchantman with goods to steal, they'll think twice about attacking a Goddess."

Dimitris watched as Theano explained her stratagem to the

captain. He had taken her father's gold, but that didn't mean he had to follow her orders. Yet her words were so persuasive and her authority so complete that he agreed as though he was conversing with Athena herself.

The ship turned 40 degrees and began to sail directly at the other vessel that had drawn closer. Dimitris stood right at the front with his sister at his side. Her face, white with eyes picked out in black lines, became ageless and austere. The gold flashed on her shoulder and helm, and the spear seemed longer than any he'd seen before. Her hand angled the brass serving plate so it reflected sunlight straight at the other ship.

Had he not known he was standing next to his sister he'd have sworn she was a woman taller by a couple of spans, with fire playing in her eyes. She looked straight towards the vessel as they bore down on it, the painted eye on their warlike prow smashing through the waves. Now they were close enough to see the sailors on the other ship. They just stood staring, mouths agape. A man, possibly the captain of their craft, had his sword half drawn, but seemed frozen as though he'd just seen Perseus carrying Medusa's head.

They drew closer and seemed to increase speed. The distant captain shouted and their oars moved, drawing the boat backwards and out of their way. Neither Dimitris nor Theano turned to watch, but Sophos, kneeling at their side told how their wake rocked the other boat and all stopped rowing once more. Men were arguing and the captain appeared to be haranguing people on his crew. A sudden squall caught them unawares, and the ship pitched dangerously to one side. They seemed caught in a play of wind they could not master, and pulled down their sail. Not long after, Theano and Dimitris were able to sit down once more, and Theano giggled as though she were once more at school.

She turned to Dimitris and winked.

"Sister," he said. "What happened to you?"

Her brow creased a bit before she responded. "Sometimes the Gods are closer than we think, Dimitri. They come to you in dreams, but to me, it seems, they are sometimes…" Her voice fell silent. Both of them knew certain things, however true, were best left unspoken.

The next morning they arrived in the port of Crotona and sought out the Child of the Python.

Chapter 31

Natasha

England – about now

Walking on jelly legs proved bothersome. I looked in the mirror. *Hmm, gaunt, interesting but somewhat skeletal.* Just crossing the bedroom floor took most of my energy. Moments later I emerged from the bathroom having replenished my glass of water.

"Well, you're on the mend, Rhory," said Mum reaching the top of the stairs.

"Still a bit wobbly, but getting there." I knew that school could only be a day or two away now. *Will Muffit and Stratford seek revenge?*

I crashed out on my bed. I must have slept for a bit. The rumpled duvet provided the illusion of huge snowy mountain peaks to the vision from my left eye. Above these peaks a pirate with an angel's face appeared. I tried to focus and failed.

I'd become used to bizarre dreams. I thought this was another to add to the list and put in my dream diary, when my arm felt strong enough to write once more.

"How ya doing, Rhory?" said the pirate.

I moved my head so both eyes could focus, and there just inside the door stood a girl with red and blue bandana on her head. Her expression suggested she wasn't quite sure how she'd be received. My apparition, or angel, became just a girl of about my own age. A girl I knew, or had known, whose blonde hair was hidden under a silky turban.

"Oh, typical, Roaring Boy, you don't even recognise me."

Then I knew for sure. Natasha! At once my favourite cousin and also the most irritating person in the universe. Tough as a walnut shell and as stubborn as the proverbial mule, she could be really warm-hearted when she chose. I'd never actually seen her hold her breath until she fainted but I am quite clear that she could have done so if she chose.

Three years before, Natasha and I had argued about something and she'd said, "If you think like that I won't talk to you ever again." And she'd meant it.

Now, she appeared out of the blue, in my bedroom.

"Yes, I do recognise you, and I'm pleased to see you, Nat." I called her Nat – or Gnat – which is pronounced the same, but is a small and very irritating insect. It all depended on the context.

"Apparently you've been delirious, Rhory, and saying really strange things. Your mum and dad were really, really worried. Did a dog actually bite you? And did you sleep walk? They think you may have done because of the mark on your arm. Or did Jester scratch you? That's what Jules thinks. She thinks Jester scratched and bit you 'cos you're so annoying and then nearly died from the taste!"

She was grinning and poking the lump in the bed that connected to my knee.

"We were all so worried, Rhory. I wasn't allowed to come and see you for days and days. Mum'd said it was touch and go for a time and I even prayed, and you know I'm not at all sure there is a God, but I prayed anyway because I couldn't see it would do any harm. And then I heard you were getting better after lovely Miriam came to see you and I'd be able to visit, and here I am."

All this was said without Natasha appearing to draw breath. For the first time for what seemed an aeon, I began to feel more like normal.

"I'm pleased to see you," I repeated a bit lamely.

Looking at her grey-green eyes, full of such warmth, I felt tongue-tied. Nat had been an honorary boy last time I saw her and now, even in the bandana thing, 'tomboy' didn't really fit any more.

"Tell me what really happened, Rho."

"I don't know where to begin," I said. "It's all been so strange."

"Try starting at the beginning, and don't leave anything important out. I'm all ears."

So I did. I could always talk to Nat.

I brought her up to date on the visit to the Museum and seeing Shoshan, and finding myself at a druid ceremony in the park with a Greek boy. Natasha's mouth dropped as I described the eye in the bedroom and then how the jackal-headed man had tried to talk but couldn't.

"A sort of verbally constipated jackal!"

"Ho, ho, Nat. No, he actually glowed. He wasn't hairy and smelly like an actual jackal – but real, as though he'd made himself out of crystallised light."

"He had weight and I could see him both before and after opening my eyes. Well before opening them, I just knew he was there, but after I got them open he looked straight at me and I could nearly hear what he thought, if you get what I mean. He tried so hard to tell me something. I just know it. But he couldn't find the words."

"Goodness, Rhory, that's amazing," said Natasha, without a hint of sarcasm. "What do you think he wanted to tell you?"

"I just can't imagine. But I did find writing in my diary after my birthday. The writing said, "'*You must find us*'."

"Wow. Do you think the 'us' is this Egyptian girl and Dimitris? Are there more clues in your diary?"

I reached for my dairy as the bedroom door opened wider, and Aunt Sofia came in with Mum.

"Hello, my darling," said my aunt. "Your mum has been telling me all about your woes and travails. You've really been in the wars, but now you're a little better?"

"Yes, Auntie," I replied. "I think both Jester and I are a lot, lot better now thanks. I think I need to thank Miranda though. It seemed to be her that did the trick. I don't remember much about what happened before she came by."

"Miranda's one in a million," said Sofia. "She's amazing with that pendulum of hers you know. She can even ask questions about your ancestry and seems to be able to dig up really useful information from her owl!"

I love to listen to Sofia talk. She has an accent something between a Russian spy and a Transylvanian countess. Her English is excellent, but Macedonia's mountainous magic remains in the way she uses our language.

"I'd like you to tell me the whole story soon, darling." (The word 'darling' had just the hint of a 'k' at the end.) "But I expect you've done that already for Natasha and I don't want to overtire you. You must come over as soon as you are up to it, and then I want to hear all about what happened."

After Mum and Sofia left the room I looked at my cousin. She stared back.

"What's with the pirate fashion, Nat?"

Her mouth pulled slightly to the side, as she sighed.

"I've not been well. Actually I've been pretty ill. I got cancer."

She looked up at me and her eyes watered.

"It scared me, Rho, really scared me. I think that's why I was beginning to behave in funny ways, you know. And then when we went back to Macedonia, they diagnosed leukaemia. I'd something called CML. But they had great treatments. Only trouble was I lost much of my hair along the way. It's coming back now, but I promise you this bandana is better than me doing a slaphead impression."

"Is that why your dad shaved?"

"Yep, Dad shaved his head to give me support."

"Why didn't we know?"

"Oh, I think Auntie Kyrsten knew but the mums decided not to tell you or Jules or any of the other cousins, not until they were sure I'd be okay."

I swallowed. "And are you … okay I mean?"

"Yeah, I think so. Since I came back to England I've felt a lot better and my medical readings seem fine. I've even become captain of our girls' football team in the local league. You must come and watch me play."

"So you don't feel ill or anything?"

"No, not as long as I take my pillocks." Nat wiped a tear that had escaped onto her cheek and stood up. "Well Mum needs to get away I think, so I'll love you and leave you, Rhory. It's great to see you, cuz."

"You too, Nat," I said to the door as it closed.

A couple of days later I'd improved enough to return to school.

Chapter 32

Dimitris in Croton

Greece – in ancient times

The flash of movement caught Dimitris's attention as a flight of pigeons turned and wheeled in unison far out over the bay, the sunlight turning the undersides of their wings brilliant white. He nearly lost his balance on the rock where he stood, declaiming to an imaginary audience. Adjusting his stance, he spoke in as deep a voice as he could manage. "Clasping the trunk with his mighty, snake-crushing hands, the son of Zeus, his eyes afire, pulled, and in one mighty sweep, the tree was freed from rock and soil. Tearing the branches from the limb, Herakles made his club, the one famed for all time..."

The birds wheeled back again as Dimitris listened to the sound of his own voice echoing through the wooded hillside. Since he'd arrived in Croton, the dreams had come with greater frequency, dreams involving the Gods and their troublesome son, Herakles. Once dreamt, he didn't forget the details, and now struggled to find the words to do justice to his visions.

He took a deep breath, and raised his right arm once again, looking out to where the birds ignored him in their flight.

"It's a good tale that."

This time Dimitris did lose his balance and had to jump down off the rock, getting pine needles impressed into his bare knees. He looked up to see a man leaning on what might be a shepherd's crook, a wide-brimmed hat shading his face from the sun.

"I didn't mean to interrupt you," said the man walking over to

Dimitris. "It's good to hear the story of brave Herakles thundering through these trees. And you tell it well, young man, if you don't mind me saying so."

Dimitris looked at the stranger who sat down on a lower rock near the one he'd just tumbled from. His face, rimmed with grey hair, had the lines and creases of a seafarer or ageing shepherd. Tanned berry brown, he clearly worked on the estate as a gardener or watchman of some kind.

"I think you've only recently arrived, young sir," said the man, removing his hat, and scratching a surprisingly thick thatch of hair.

"Yes, we came into port last month. My sister has business with the school here."

The man looked at him but said nothing, so Dimitris continued, "We came from Delphi. My sister, Theano, received an oracle directing us here, so here we are."

"Well, it's a pretty place, surely," said the man. "What was it the oracle said, if I may ask? In my opinion, these oracles are often a little vague and can be interpreted in various ways."

"This one was clear," said Dimitris, surprised to feel a little defensive. "In fact I was the one who solved its mystery."

Again the man just looked at him, his eyes unblinking and observant. Dimitris pressed on. "You see, the oracle spoke of seeking the 'Python's Child'. After my mother's funeral, we needed to discover what that meant. We had been told to travel west, you see. I talked to one of the priests about the nature of Apollo, and why he was born on Delos and not on Crete, like his father Zeus. Anyway, he told me the answer to that question but also that he'd once met a child of a serpent."

"Did he, now?" The man raised his eyebrows.

"Yes, he solved the mystery. You see the child of the Python lives right here in Croton. His mother was a great priestess, known as the Pythais of Samos. He was raised by her…" Dimitris trailed off. "But you'll surely know that if you live here."

"You know," said the man, "stories have a way of growing and changing as they cross the seas. Tell me, what did the priest tell of this child of a snake?"

"Of a serpent ... or rather, the Python. Well, of course, once we knew it wasn't actually a python he was easier to trace. In fact his name says it all, for it is Pythagoras of Samos himself, the great teacher of Croton."

"And you've met this great teacher?" asked the man.

"Oh, no," said Dimitris. "Even my sister had to wait a month before she was allowed into his august presence. And then she wasn't allowed to speak, and that, for Theano, must have been really, really hard."

"Why is that?"

"Well, she knows so much, more than anyone I know. And she can explain it all so well." Dimitris kicked a stone, surprised to find himself extolling his sister's intellectual prowess quite so enthusiastically.

"You know, she even knew how to outwit pirates on the way here. We tricked them and sailed right past. They thought she was the Goddess Athena herself."

"Hmm, perhaps they did. She sounds an impressive young woman, your sister."

"No, the one who is really impressive is my younger brother, Sophos." Dimitris wondered why he was gabbling on like this to a passing shepherd.

"And what of you?" said the man, wrinkling his nose as though a fly had just landed on its tip. "What is your name, and did the Gods give you a gift or just your brother and sister?"

"I am Dimitris." He stood with his hands on his hips as though challenging the man to say otherwise. "My gift, if gift it is, is to see stories." He started to walk up and down, forgetting the presence of the old man for a moment.

"Apart from dreams of great Herakles, I've travelled far in my visions. While we journeyed from Crete, one night, staying near Corinth, I found myself in a wood way to the north of Greece. The trees were like none we find hereabouts. The land was cold and I met with a priest. He didn't worship our Gods, though he knew them all. He was dressed in woollen robes of white and blue and wore a circlet of pure gold around his neck. He carried an arrow made of gold, also."

"Did he?" said the man. "Did he tell you his name?"

"It's Abaris," said Dimitris. "He venerates the sacred fire, and also the wood that grows high up on trees, like the nest of some strange bird."

The old man chuckled, and murmured, "Abaris ... strange bird indeed, I wouldn't wonder." Raising his voice he continued, "And what did he want of you, a servant of our own great Demeter?"

Dimitris looked puzzled for a moment, and then smiled. "Oh, I see, my name. Yes it does mean Demeter's servant. I'm happy about that. I've always felt at home in the countryside. You know, what was really strange was the other boy."

"The other boy?"

"Yes, when I last saw Abaris, in his woods, there appeared another boy. He had strange striped garments that tied about the waist. I'd never seen anything like them before. And his feet were bare. I thought he might be a vision for a story, but he knew little and said less. Abaris told us to go together, but as I carried the flame and led him to the small temple at the edge of the woods, he disappeared. I went back to seek him out, but all I could see was a swirling mist, and moments later, I woke back in my bed, near Corinth."

"And who is this other boy, do you think?"

"I'm not sure. This vision with the boy and his strange clothes, is the one that has puzzled me most."

"Well," said the man, getting up off the stone, "perhaps you will find out how he fits into your story. Now I must be on my way, and leave you to your Hero and his Twelve Labours."

Once more he wrinkled his nose against the invisible fly, and winked at Dimitris.

"I think your stories will be remembered even as long as your sister is remembered."

He walked down the path faster than Dimitris expected, and soon disappeared around the curve of the hill. Only once he'd gone did Dimitris realise he'd not had the courtesy to ask the man's name or what he did in these parts. He wondered how the man had known the bit of the prophecy about Theano being remembered. Surely he'd not mentioned that.

*

"You talked with him!"

"Yes, Theano, why shouldn't I have talked to him? I thought he was a shepherd..."

"You thought he was a *what*?" Theano's eyes blazed at her brother. "You speak to the man we are not allowed to talk to for – for – for ages ... and you mistake him for a shepherd. And you tell him about your visions, and me and—"

"How was I meant to know this man is your precious Pythagoras. He looked more like the gardener."

"Dimitri, he is considered the wisest man ever to walk the earth, and you think he is a gardener?"

"No, I said he looked like a gardener. In fact he seemed kind and understanding. I just spoke to him like I might speak to you or to Sophos. He was the easiest man to talk to."

Sophos pushed himself between his brother and sister and looked from one to the other, with his eyebrows raised high and his eyes full of merriment. Theano gave in first and started giggling, followed by Dimitris, and soon all three were laughing.

Theano wiped tears from her eyes. "You know, Dimi, some of the Master's disciples have had to wait three years before they can even ask him a question. They are called the Akoustikoi, or the Ones Who Listen. They are meant to keep silent and just hear the teachings. You, who don't even belong to the Brotherhood, get to meet with Pythagoras face to face and explain his own birth to him..."

She started laughing again and then sighed. "It's really too much you know. He is the most remarkable man. He told us today about his time in Egypt. He travelled there for years and years, going from temple to temple. Do you remember Father telling us how secretive the Egyptian priests were? Everything had to be kept hidden? Well, they taught Pythagoras all they knew, he impressed them so much. And now he is teaching us."

Dimitris looked across at Theano, her head thrown back laughing again. Even with their mother's death so recent, she bubbled with joy. Every evening when she returned to their lodgings, her eyes sparkled as she spoke of what she'd learned. Dimitris knew he'd be able to leave soon and return to Crete with Sophos. He had no idea that Theano would be married in just a few short weeks changing all of their lives, forever.

Chapter 33

Scrivener's

England – about now

I shuddered as I approached the bandstand, on my way to school. Just a plain old bandstand, but the utter blackness of the dog and the sickly-sweet smell of the cat hovered in the air. I gave it a wide berth and stayed close to the old oak tree. Had the oak forest been real? And the druids? My legs only just about obeyed me and ached like I'd done a marathon the day before. My school bag cut into my shoulder, heavy with textbooks. Dad had taken the car in for a service and so getting a lift today had been out of the question.

Emerging onto Mercer Road, I looked at the Victorian pile that made up Scrivener's School for Boys. The red brick building, with its little towers and gothic-type windows would make a good setting for a TV murder mystery. A 'phut-phut' noise floated up from the playing fields. The groundsman rode on a rather fancy red tractor, pulling a huge grass cutter behind him. *'The Severed Schoolboy', that would be a good title for the drama! Notorious gang leader Hacker, found hacked to bits by grass-cutter… Rhory of the Yard is sent in to investigate, uncovering a plot of devastating…* A bell rang out. *Surely it's not assembly yet?*

I looked at my watch, as panic ascended like cold water when you walk down the steps into Hammerford swimming pool. *No, just a fire engine.*

The groundsman swung his tractor in a wide arc near the cricket pavilion. The building boasted a new coat of paint, no doubt to prevent it entirely falling over in the winter. A large sign had appeared near the main school gate. I investigated.

"Founded in 1542 by Sir Robert Scrivener..." blah, blah, "...purveyor of fine wines to the nobility... " Blah, "...originally called Hammerford House for Scholars." *Ah, there's the title for the drama, 'Hammerford House of Horrors!'* That would particularly apply to Year Sevens, a herd of whom were pushing past me, all eager to improve their minds.

Once inside, the old hall echoed with the slap of school shoes carrying their owners to their classrooms, to drop off their school bags. Indecipherable voices squeaked or growled depending on their age, and I made it into the uncharacteristic silence of the Year Eight and Nine cloakroom. A few boys hovered by the back playground door, looking past the hanging coats and kitbags. *Something's scaring them?* I heard a voice that sent an icy hand straight to my guts.

"Put it in your mouth."

That's Muffit surely? I looked around to see if there was a teacher or a prefect nearby. No of course not. They were respectively sipping tea or discussing last night's football, in their private rooms, before the school day started. I peeked around a grey overcoat, and down the row of anoraks and parkas, to where I could see Muffit, Stratford, and another goon, surrounding some poor sucker.

"Put it in your mouth."

"Get knotted, Muffit, you great baboon," said a voice I knew and liked. An unwise move to take on three older teenagers on your own, even if you've the nerve that my mate Dave clearly had. In spades.

"Don't make me ask you a third time," said Muffit, asking for a third time. A nonce when it came to maths, clearly.

Dave Milford had been forced into the softness of the coats behind him. Muffit stood with a large screwdriver in his hand, holding it just near Dave's mouth. Stratford and another git, stood behind him, grinning.

"Watch Out! I'm after you!" The voice sounded shrill and clear from just below my chin. Everyone turned and looked at me. My mobile continued to shout from my inside pocket.

Muffit looked over at me, puzzlement wrestling with annoyance on his face. He didn't see Dave's hand as he swung it, pivoting on his feet to deliver a resounding thump. Dave then used the advantage of being shorter to head charge Muffit in the stomach. The other boys, cowards that they were, leapt back. Dave ducked out of their grasp and dashed towards me.

"Run, Rhory!"

Stratford gave chase. I swung my school bag, making use of *Introductory Physics* and *Robert's Basics of Biology*, to deliver a blow to Stratford's knees. And, incidentally, a lesson in science. Perfect aim, luck and complete disregard for the consequences, laid Stratford sprawling on the floor. His head rested on muddy football boots. Neat.

"Watch Out! I'm after you!" shouted my pocket, no doubt in triumph.

I fled towards the relative safety of the classroom, fiddling with my mobile, and wondering if I'd make it home alive tonight.

Chapter 34

The Cricket Pavilion

"I won't forget that, mate" said David. "You came just in the nick of time. I thought I was pretty much screwed." He grinned at his own pun, intended or not. "Your fantastic mobile ringing just gave me the chance I needed to escape. Where on earth did you get that ringtone?"

I checked and found Juliette had called me. She'd no doubt set up my phone while I was ill, to ring with the shouting voice. It sounded very realistic and had certainly come in handy.

"It's my sister's little joke, Milford," I replied.

"Rhory, there's a handle to my name you know," said David.

I'd forgotten he was touchy on the subject of what he was called. Scrivener's is one of the last of the declining band of Grammar Schools surviving in England. Being a school with Tradition (with a definite capital 'T') staff often use the family surname when addressing students.

"You're right, Dave, there is," I admitted. Dave's eyes had their characteristic red rim. It sometimes looked like he'd been crying, although actually he had an allergy. In fact he was tough, as he'd shown.

"What do you think they'll do?" I asked Dave, my brief moment of courage rapidly disappearing with the adrenaline, and being replaced by a sense of dread. "They're not going to want to kiss and make up anytime soon," I added with a bravado I didn't feel at all.

"No, they'll get revenge if they can. The one we have to worry about is Hacker, not Muffit. He runs the gang, and is the only one with nous."

"What did they want, in the cloakroom?"

"Oh, to push their stupid drugs of course. That's why I know Hacker's behind this."

"And you didn't agree, so they were trying to punish you?"

"Exactly. And now we'll just have to use our brains. I've an idea that may work. I'd thought about it earlier this year, when I saw them make a monkey out of Landsman, forcing him to be one of their mules. No one was going to get me to do that. They told me enough this morning. They hide their stuff in the cricket pavilion. Stratford is a really good batsman and has kept a key from last summer. We'll make a well-timed visit to the Prefects' Room at break. Will you come with me, Rhory?"

"I guess it's the safest place for us, Dave, so yup. But what's your plan?"

David told me. It rested on the fact that his older sister had gone out with Bob Dyer, the deputy head prefect. She'd moved on to pastures new, but had kept a friendship going. Dyer had always liked David, whom he'd seen on many visits.

"I'm not a snitch, Rhory, but this is survival of the fittest and they are going to be delivered to a Darwinian backwater."

We put Dave's plan underway and made sure that we moved around the school with large numbers of other students at hand, and preferably with a teacher or two in shouting distance. We didn't see Hacker, Muffit or any of the others, but learned from a breathless classmate that Muffit now sported a noticeable black eye and had had to see the school nurse.

When lunch break started, we waited for five minutes after the bell had rung, and then sent one quick text message. When the reply came in, we set off for the cricket pavilion. To get to it meant going past the art hut and by the back of the gymnasium and fives court. Then we could see the end of the pavilion, presiding over the cricket pitch to our right. Some trees and a holly bush near the building, meant anyone watching us could be hidden.

"Into the dragon's den, Rhory," said Dave with his customary good humour.

"Yup," I mumbled, my mouth having gone extraordinarily dry. My legs had returned to the consistency of rubber.

We came closer to the pavilion and I still couldn't see anyone. Just at the point when I thought that Muffit's black eye might have changed the nature of the game, I heard a voice say, "Either you've got amazing nerve or you're incredibly stupid. Probably both." The voice came from behind, cutting off our retreat to the safety of the school. Muffit had been well hidden near the holly bush and had come out behind us. The blotch under his eyebrow shone a glorious purple. *Bullseye.*

Chapter 35

Deal Breaker

Feet crunched on gravel between us and the freshly painted cricket pavilion. We swung back to see Hacker and Stratford, plus the other oaf from the cloakroom this morning, approaching from the far end of the wooden hut. So four onto two. And they weighed twice as much. *Piece of cake*. My innards didn't agree, froze and sank towards my knees.

Dave spoke first. "We've come to do a deal."

Hacker glowered and said, "No deals, you little runts. Muffit lost an eye 'cos of you and you're going to suffer for that."

"Too bleedin' right," said Muffit behind us.

Hacker's gelled hair extended at odd angles. He kept flexing and clenching his hands. His lips settled into something between a sneer and a snarl. He reached into his jacket pocket. "Who needs a screw tightening first?"

"Well," said Dave, somehow managing to sound calm and confident, "of course you can beat us up, and no doubt in your twisted logic, that's justified. However, we're prepared to get involved in a business deal for you. I'd have told you that this morning if Cyclops there hadn't wanted to practise amateur dentistry." He pointed with his thumb at Muffit, who scowled behind us, but said nothing. "If you lay a hand on either of us, then there's no deal."

I could feel my knees beginning to shake. Dave stood with his legs planted astride, like a footballer before an important penalty shot. Hacker's brow definitely showed signs of puckering. Dave's nerve held for the moment. I swallowed.

"Look at it this way, if you beat us up, we'll go to the Head and tell the whole story. He might or might not believe us. However, we are business people."

I glanced sideways at Dave. He had his arms open, like a salesman offering double glazing.

"Provided we get a cut, we'll move your merchandise around. No one will suspect us, and both of us have older sisters. This means we know quite a lot of older students and can come and go without being suspected."

My legs gave way. Neither pure fear, nor my recent illness, had put me on the ground. Muffit had kicked me in the hollow of my leg behind the knee. He did it with speed and savagery to us both, bringing us to our knees.

The gravel bit into my skin. Hacker watched, impassively weighing up the advantages of using Dave's undoubted nerve and the gift of the gab, and his wish to take swift and painful revenge. He tapped the business end of a large screwdriver on the palm of his hand.

"Here's the thing," Dave continued, as though he chose being on his knees as a business stratagem. "You give us the supplies you want shifted at 8am. We deliver in the twenty minutes before school actually starts, using the chaos of everyone arriving and getting to class, to move around and make the deliveries. You collect the money. We take ten per cent of the profits. If in two weeks it has all gone successfully and we've increased your level of sales, our cut goes up to twenty per cent."

Hacker pouted up at the sky and beat time with the screwdriver. During this lull, Dave stood up.

"In fact, let's get underway straight away. I'm going to the rehearsal for the school play after school. Let me see what you can offer and I'll have a word with some of the Luvvies, I am sure there is a market for some 'e', black hollies and eggs and suchlike."

I didn't know what he was talking about, although I guessed 'e' was ecstasy. His sister must have more of a Technicolor life than I'd imagined. Or Dave had done this sort of thing before, which I doubted.

Hacker's jaw chewed imaginary gum as he calculated the joys of sadism now against profit tomorrow. A few more seconds passed, lasting like minutes.

"Gary, get the stuff."

Stratford said, "I'm not sure that's wise."

Hacker replied, "It's not your job to think, G, just get some samples. We'll see if this runt is all mouth." He jabbed the metal point at Dave and then at me. "You better get it all moved by tomorrow or you'll be well and truly screwed this time."

Stratford crossed to the pavilion. A key flashed in the sunlight. No doubt the drugs were hidden there. A safe spot in the football season, which is why the smokers in the school hid near there at break time. A minute or so later he returned, and managed to bump hard into my shoulder, twisting my knees further into the gravel.

He held the package out to Dave. "This is the 'e'," he said.

A creaking noise behind Hacker caused him and Stratford to swing round. A side window now stood open.

"I'll take that." The disembodied voice came from out of the gloom within.

The pavilion, which had a number of small rooms and places to hide in, had no windows at the back. The open side window faced towards the school. Just a black void one moment, the next it showcased the smiling features of Dyer, the rugby playing prefect.

Fear and fury passed in quick succession over Hacker's face. I stood up. Muffit went pale, making his black eye all the more visible, and Stratford, ever the hero, started edging his way back towards the school.

He stopped when Pete Sheldon, a prefect as well as an effective scrum half in the rugby team, stepped out from the bushes between the school and us.

"Ah, the wonders of science," Dyer said, as though to himself.

"You see, Hacker, not only have I recorded your delightful repartee, but I've transmitted it all from my trusty mobile, to another phone, and cunning recorder, located in the science lab." His face, framed in the small window, lit up with enthusiasm. Dyer had hidden in one of the back rooms, while we were all still in lessons. That had been Dave's brainwave.

"Just look above the trees here and you'll see that the chemistry room has a pretty good view of this spot. If you wave, they'll wave back ... ah yes, they are doing so. And they've used the good offices of the Physics Department. Did you know we have an astronomy speciality at this school? No? Ah well. They've used the Physics Department to supply a telescope and this little tête-à-tête has all been captured on a computer. Sound, vision and everything. We didn't even have to wire young David and young Rhory. Well done, lads, by the way."

While he'd been talking Richard Lawrence, the biggest guy in the school, had come from the front of the pavilion and closed off the other avenue for flight.

Ever the smoothy, Dyer carried on. "Just come with me to the Old Man and make a full and complete confession, and there's a chance, or at least the whisper of a chance, you'll get off with an immediate suspension. The school won't want police and a scandal, so I suggest you go with any deal the Old Man offers. He's expecting you."

So it was. By the start of afternoon classes, all four had been suspended and various younger students had been told to see the headmaster. Now. By 4pm, the drugs ring had been dismantled.

We'd achieved safety and I'd experienced what a clear head and steady nerve could accomplish. The Head, not anybody's fool, had said to the Gang of Four that if harm of any description whatsoever happened to Dave or myself, the rich evidence of drug dealing would be given to the police and the court case would probably land them all in detention for up to a year. "You better hope they don't even catch a cold over the coming months or you may regret it." The

Old Man told us himself that he'd said that, so we could sleep more easily at night. Clearly, he knew nothing of my nocturnal visits and visions.

"Well that was all a bit more exciting than expected!" I said to Dave as we walked along the path that bounded Hammerford Park.

"Yeah, well, he had it coming, didn't he! Now Hacker has his wings clipped. Mind you, I wouldn't want to bump into him on a dark night..."

"Or in broad daylight for that matter," I interrupted.

"I think he'll heed the Old Man's warning. He wants his GCSEs like the rest of us."

We were approaching that bit of the park where a high metal fence kept God-fearing folk away from a tangle of briars, old leaves, hawthorn bushes and two magnificent horse chestnut trees. My dad once called this out of bounds part of the park, the *Wild Wood*. The name had stuck.

"Wow, look at those," said Dave pointing to the trees, which were heavy with the spiky seeds encasing shiny brown conkers. With a bit of gymnastics that would have pleased the PE teacher, we swung ourselves over the fence and crunched through years of fallen leaves.

"Have you ever eaten these?" said Dave. He pulled a couple of leaves off a hawthorn bush and proceeded to chew them.

"Aren't they poisonous?" I asked.

"No, my nan calls them 'Bread and Butter' bushes. I won't say they're tasty, but they are entirely edible."

I tried some. They were, well ... leafy. I wouldn't be recommending Mum to add them to my salad.

"Hey, Rhory, look here." Dave held back one of the spiky branches of the hawthorn bush. Just visible underneath, stood an old circular structure made of bricks.

"Looks like a well," I said.

I searched around for a stone, and found one after scrabbling through layers of damp leaves. The top of the well had a wooden cover held in place by metal bands and some large screws. There were chinks in the wood, however. I dropped the stone through and listened. A few seconds later I heard a distinctly wet 'plop'.

"It's a well, all right."

"Strange place for one," said Dave, clambering onto it, holding a chunky stick. He took aim at the large horse chestnut tree and his first throw brought down a shower of conkers.

"I declare the conker season officially open," he said, from his elevated position. "Mind you, I don't think these are a patch on Midlea conkers. They're the best in the world." Dave, like Natasha, lived in Midlea.

Chapter 36

A Visit to Midlea

At the weekend, I cycled for the first time since my illness. Midlea village, my speedometer had told me many times, lay exactly three miles from my house. The '3' appeared as I passed the Lucky Dog pub that marked the beginning of the village boundary. This day I had to push my bike up the steep hill that led to the village. My legs remained weak, and believed they needed further convalescence. I remounted and cycled into the village. Someone shouted.

"Hey, Rhory."

I thought it might be Dave Milford and skidded my bike to a halt.

"Not seen yer about, mate, what's been goin' on?" said the voice.

I spotted Tony Barnard on the far side of the road. He was also in Year Eight, but in a different class to mine.

"I've been ill for a bit, Tony. How are you?"

"Yes, I heard. You were bitten by a dog or something. So was it rabies?"

"Yeah, something like that. Have you done your homework already?"

"Nah. I leave that to Sunday night. Got to go to the shops for her-who-must-be-obeyed. See yer 'round."

I assumed he meant his mum, said, "Cheerio," like some RAF chappie from a WWII movie and cycled on to Natasha's house.

"It's your lucky day, Rhory, I've just been baking," said Aunt Sofia, as I entered by the back door. "Are you feeling better, darling?"

"Yes, Auntie, much better, thanks, although Lucky Dog Hill was nearly the end of me!"

"It never gets any less steep, Rhory dear, or at least that's my experience when I take the dogs for a walk. That becomes my task when Uncle Arthur is away."

We'd never been allowed a dog, because both Juliette and Dad had asthma. Natasha's house had two wonderful Collie dogs that were very friendly, and great bouncy companions when you took them for walks.

"Is Nat in her room, Auntie? I'll go up and see her." Aunt Sofia nodded and I went up the stairs trailing the wonderful smell of fresh biscuits behind me.

"Uh oh, trouble," said Nat after I'd politely knocked and entered her bedroom. "How are you now, Rho?" she enquired.

"Much better, thanks," I said, settling myself on her bed. Natasha had a dark blue bandana tied around her head. She sat at her desk, which had a brilliant view over the smallish garden to the fields beyond, and a paddock that became a cricket ground in the summer. A wood dominated the far side.

This wood, known rather grandly as Midlea Forest, had been the setting for many of our imaginative games, especially in the ruined abbey on the far side. This was before Natasha imposed the Great Silence, and promptly went abroad. Her textbooks were open on her desk, but her iPod pumped out her favourite music, obliterating all possibility of clear thinking.

"I was waiting for you to come round. I've so many questions and I wasn't sure if you wanted to answer them with Mum or Auntie Kyrsten present. What you told me was amazing, but it leaves the mind reeling a bit, don't you think?"

"Well, it's hardly something I can tell everyone about or I think I might be on medication quicker than you can say 'school sucks'!"

"Did you bring your diary? Have you made any new entries? What do you think it all means? Have you flown again? Is your arm okay now? Do you—"

"Enough, Nat. One question at a time. And remember I don't have many answers."

Natasha turned down the volume on her speakers, and looked at me expectantly. I told the tale again, starting from the zombie state and the tongue-tied jackal, and going right through to confrontation with the dog and the cat in the park. I mentioned how my room had become a deck of a ship and how I'd been seasick in the upstairs toilet.

"I didn't actually see waves, but outside my room I could sense a huge storm going on. I couldn't even stand straight. After I'd been sick, I got a clonk walking in the middle of the bedroom." I pointed to the faint red mark on my forehead.

Natasha's mouth rose on one side only, a sort of lopsided question mark.

"There's more that I've not told anyone."

"Go on."

"After I went to bed, the floor eventually stopped heaving about and I stopped feeling pukey. As I lay there, a girl appeared in the room looking right at me. She sort of materialised, on the chair in the corner."

"Shoshan?"

"I thought so at first, but when her face came properly into focus, she was older, with much curlier hair. I could tell – now don't laugh – I could tell she cared about me. Except it wasn't me, it was her brother, the boy I saw in the oak forest. The one called Dimitris."

"How do you mean it wasn't you?"

"I mean I could tell she could see him *and* me in some weird way. Like our minds had melded together in the storm. I can't explain it any other way."

"Blimey."

"There's more." I took out the dream diary. "Look at the entry I made that night." I showed Natasha the writing.

"What on earth does that say, it's written in symbols."

"No, well, yes. It's written in Greek. I worked it out. It spells Theano."

"What's a *theano* when it's at home?"

"No, it's a name, Nat, a girl's name. The girl in my bedroom."

Natasha leaned back in her chair, her eyebrows arching up above her eyes. "What is it with you and girls turning up in your bedroom at night!"

"Nat, this is real," I said, my frustration giving my voice an edge.

Natasha smiled. "I know, Rhory, I know. It's just a little bit freaky." She raised her hand to where her long hair had once been, and rested it on the headscarf. "Do you think you're linking up with those times in some way?"

"More than that. I've done some research. Theano is not a very usual name. The most important one from ancient Greece..." I paused. "Well, the famous one became a disciple of Pythagoras."

"The triangle guy?"

"That's the one, the hypotenuse and all that. I'm pretty sure I'm right because I also researched the druid. I remembered his name eventually, after you visited. He's called ... was called, I suppose ... Abaris. He's one of the three most famous druids. And get this. He's supposed to have met Pythagoras. And there's more. He had a famous golden arrow."

"Mega cool."

"I know. That gave me dates to work with and that's how I'm pretty sure that the girl is Theano."

Aunt Sofia came in and delivered squash and some freshly baked biscuits. Afterwards, Natasha flipped through the pages of the diary stopping at the section headed, 'Miss Starwalker's Dictionary of Dream Symbols'.

"Oh, I love these definitions. Shall we look up Jackal?" She did so. "It says, *'A creature associated with the underworld. Wild unbridled passions. Cunning and patient, also, a guide for souls.'* I wonder if that is significant, Rho? I know you've 'wild unbridled passions' particularly if you don't get your own way!" Natasha grinned at me. "Perhaps that is why all these girls—"

"Enough already..."

"Okay, okay." She held up her hands and smiled her winning smile. "But let's see your other entries, are they at the back here?"

Natasha turned more pages and stopped. After a moment or two she said, "But you've put more things in here than you said, Rhory. Look, when did you draw this?"

Natasha brought the book over to the bed, and sat down with the book between us. A picture of a bird, and one of some circles, were on the left-hand page with really neat writing on the right-hand side.

Now I'm no great shakes as an artist. I've inherited nothing from my dad in that regard, he being really good at drawing. These pictures were cool.

"I think that may be a bird, called an Ibis. I searched the internet and that's the closest match. In fact that's how the ancient Egyptians drew it on their temple walls."

"It's a bird, certainly, Rho," Natasha responded. "The picture below looks like the Olympic symbol drawn into a circle – or perhaps it is a series of circus rings around a central ring. Did you really not know you'd drawn these circles?"

"Scouts' honour." I didn't think I'd done any more after the bird picture. "I was really ill, remember."

She looked at the picture below the bird.

"It seems to be like one circle connects the other six," offered Natalie. "But look, in this circle at the top, there is also a really small picture. I think it is the same bird again but drawn much smaller. Wow, that's quite an achievement for the middle of the night, when you were ill."

We both looked again at what I'd drawn.

"I can't read what you've written beneath it."

I stared at my untidy scrawl.

"It says, 'Aunt Charlie'." I got up from the bed, biscuit crumbs cascading to the floor. "Now what on earth could I have meant by that?"

"And who could she be?" said Natasha. "If she's your aunt then she's probably mine, unless you've an Aunt Charlie out in Norway somewhere. Shall we go and ask Mum?"

Chapter 37

Aunt Charlie?

The dogs bounded over as we came downstairs, making a fuss of both Natasha and me. A couple of minutes later they could be heard whining in the garden.

"No, I don't think you've an Aunt Charlotte," said Aunt Sofia. "Your real aunts are only your dad's brothers' wives, if you think about it. None of us are called Charlie, though I suspect most of us can be proper Charlies on occasions. Now your granny has a sister. Her name is ... let me think. Her name is Bridget isn't it? I am sure she's still alive, though she must be eighty if she's a day."

"But if her name isn't Charlie, then that's irrelevant, Mum," said Natasha in her usual in-your-face style.

Aunt Sofia paused for a bit, looking out the window into the garden. A smile started to play across her face. Her green eyes held more than a hint of merriment. "So, Rhory, this is something from your dream diary, is that right?"

"Yes, Auntie."

"And you're telling me that some of your entries are very neat, but this entry is in your usual schoolboy scribble."

"Yes, Auntie," I repeated, not sure where this was leading.

"So it's something you heard in a dream and then tried to write down... A sort of 'sounds like', as when you are playing charades."

"Oh, yes, I see what you mean, Mum," said Natasha who was clearly quicker on the uptake than me, and she tugged her ear and said, "Sounds like Charlie."

"That's right, dear, well done."

I couldn't see where this joint mother/daughter appreciation society was getting us. "And so Aunt…?" I asked.

"And so," said Aunt Sofia with just a little hint of Sherlock Holmes style triumph, "I think you meant *Chorley*." She emphasised the last word.

"But I don't have an Aunt Chorley either, do I?" I asked, genuinely perplexed.

"No you don't, dear, but your Aunt Bridget lives in Chorley Wood, which is just outside North London, off the M25 motorway. I think your dream was telling you to see your Aunt Bridget in Chorley Wood!"

Yes. I knew her. Jules and I liked to play in her garden and she made smashing lemonade.

But much would happen before I did see my Aunt Bridget. None of it nice.

Chapter 38

The Grim Reaper is No Laughing Matter

The weather was moving from the joys of an Indian summer to the chillier demands of autumn. On the Friday after our confrontation with The Hacker Mob – *another good title for my first gangster movie* – I walked across the park to school, picking up masses of wet grass on my shoes. Looking back I saw a distinct track in the dew laden grass. Only I had crossed this bit of the park today. The keen early morning runners seemed mesmerised by jogging around the path that circled the park, and never venturing onto its damp green perfection.

I knew that Dave Milford's bus dropped him off near the library at the south-east corner of the park, quite near our house. Not being girly, I didn't wait to meet him off the bus so we could walk in together, but I did decide this day, to leave him a dew drop message.

By walking in a clever way on one of the slight grassy rises, and jumping between letters, I spelt out his name 'Milford' in wet grass. My steps led to it and then away from it, but the name was dramatically readable. When I arrived at school, I discovered his dad had brought him in from Midlea by car. My creative efforts were wasted.

"Milford, what are you doing here?"

"I go to school here, Rhory, in case you've not noticed. And I've a handle to my name, remember?"

I started to explain my cleverness in leaving him a message, when the bell rang for assembly. Later that day I challenged Dave to a conker competition. At least in our school the Health and Safety Brigade hadn't banned conkers.

Our esteemed local council had discussed roping off the horse chestnut trees in the park in case some passing nipper looked up and caught a spiky seed in his eye. The local paper had great fun at the council's expense. Net result, the council backed down. Children could still throw sticks up to knock down the heaviest and shiniest conkers.

On my way home across the park I did just that, and stuffed the spiky seeds into my backpack. I'd ten potential winners. Too large and they'd break open easily. Too small, and they couldn't inflict damage. At home, I soaked them briefly in vinegar. Juliette had told me this worked and it wasn't cheating. We also borrowed Mum's oven for a little while and put all the conkers in at a very low heat for about half an hour.

"This toughens them up, Rhory, but still leaves them supple enough not to break apart through brittleness." We used a skewer to make holes in the exact centre of each of them and, having raided the laces from some shoes that we'd never seen Dad actually wear, we went into our yard and tested our product.

Juliette and I were fairly evenly matched in the sport of conkers. We were both accurate enough to avoid hitting each other's fingers. I felt I was well prepared for next Monday when, during break, I'd challenge all comers, but especially David.

On Sunday morning I heard a knock at our back door. Tony Barnard stood on the bottom step. This surprised me, as he and I aren't really mates. I wondered if he'd been crying. Behind him, his bike lay on its side, the back wheel slowly turning.

"Dave's dead," he said suddenly. "Died in hospital last night. I thought you'd want to know."

My face took on a life of its own. My mouth started grinning. Actually grinning. I laughed and converted it unsuccessfully into a cough. Tony looked small and far away. The angles of my house had changed and I nearly lost my way back to the dining room. "Come in, Tony," I said. "What do you mean he's dead?"

I walked across to the window and failed to see the garden

through blurry eyes. Tony Barnard hovered in the dining room doorway. His face elongated as his mouth opened. A convulsive wobble rose up through my body and I cried for real. I could hear Tony crying behind me and my mother came down from upstairs.

"What on earth's going on?" she said a bit too sharply, and then, recognising the tears as real, and not the result of some schoolboy tiff, asked, "Are you okay, both of you?"

"Dave Milford's died, Mrs Bruce," Tony said.

"Oh my goodness me!" said my mum. "You'd both better sit down, I'm going to call your dad, Rhory, and make a cup of tea."

Tony Barnard found his equilibrium quicker than I did. He explained that Dave Milford had been climbing up a conker tree in Midlea, and had fallen from a branch. He'd hit his head either on the way down or when he landed.

His parents had taken him to Hammerford Hospital at midday on Saturday. Various tests showed he had slight concussion. The doctors decided to keep him in one night for safety and observation. A blood clot found its way to an important part of his brain and he died in the night.

Of the rest of that awful day I've no memories. At school the next morning, the Head started assembly with the news of the death. I just stood and cried. I wasn't alone because it seemed that Dave Milford had been quite well known in school for the generosity of his nature and his courage in tackling Hacker's gang. That story had gone right through the school.

A week later he was buried after a service at Midlea Church. My parents went and apparently the church overflowed. They decided I shouldn't go, as it might prove too distressing. I think they were right. I grieved that I'd never see him again. But things turned out differently.

Chapter 39

Coffee in the Carfax

After David's death, getting to school and back, attending lessons, participating in rehearsals for the school play and doing homework filled a rather grey time. My dream diary lay unheeded in the drawer.

Whenever I thought of Dave, tears would well up with a feeling so wretched that in fact I kept him out of my mind when I could. I couldn't decide if something of his nature still survived, as more than just a memory, or if all he'd been, had just gone for good.

Juliette supported me. She might be annoying but she'd also been very upset by David's death. "You realise he can't suffer," she'd said when I felt really down in the dumps. "In fact in everyone's memory he'll be eternally young."

"I don't understand what you mean," I'd said.

"Well he'll never get old will he."

"No, he's dead, isn't he, so of course he can't get old."

Juliette had ignored the petulant tone in my voice. "And he'll be remembered by all who knew and loved him for all his very best qualities. That will be all he is for as long as people remember him,"

"I suppose so."

"Nothing of the consciousness can remain beyond death, Rhory, because the brain cannot function without oxygen," she'd continued. "So he can't suffer because there's nothing to suffer."

"What about his soul?"

"Well, that's a religious idea just to back up their 'behave to-day and you'll be rewarded tomorrow' form of social control. There's no scientific evidence whatsoever of anything surviving bodily death."

"What about those stories of reincarnation, you know, like on the History Channel last year or whenever?" I'd countered.

"They're interesting stories, I'll give you that, but they're not truth. They haven't been carried out under any sort of controlled conditions, and can't be disproved, so they are by definition, not scientific."

Sadness and tiredness had prevented me from finding fault with her logic. Actually, her logic seemed fine, but I knew she was wrong. Trying to beat Juliette in an argument with the line, "I just know you're wrong," doesn't work. She can always find ten good reasons why she's right. So we left things as they were.

About a fortnight later, I walked down North Road towards the Carfax in Hammerford centre. The centre of Hammerford had an island of shops and narrow passageways, with a circular road around them. Outside that road, forming a second boundary, lay a very wide pavement. This extended like a huge Polo mint of walking area and could be seen distinctly on Google Earth. Beyond that, the outer circle of main road took most of the traffic. The inner road was generally pedestrianised. I'd never thought much about it but I guess it's quite a nice feature in a small town like ours.

"Hello, Rhory!" A rich velvety voice said behind me. I turned and there stood ... oh dear, her name fled from my mind. The lady in front of me had a knitted beige coat going half way down her calves, and a multi-coloured scarf, twirled in some fancy way around her neck. Her reddish hair escaped in a wild way, and smiley creases surrounded her eyes.

"Are you feeling better, dear?"

"Yes I am thank you..." and then her name popped back, "Miranda!"

She looked at me with a lot of warmth, sort of mother like, without the need to tell you to tidy your bedroom. "I was so sorry to hear your friend died. Sofia told me about it and I meant to come round, but I've been very busy with patients over the last few weeks."

Somehow, her showing sympathy like that, brought tears to my eyes, and I didn't entirely trust my voice.

"Tell you what, dear, there's a brilliant new coffee shop just opened here by the post office. I'm desperate for my morning fix of caffeine. Why don't we nip in there and let me get you a milkshake or something." I could see no way to excuse myself, so that's what we did. I just prayed no one from school would see me with a strange woman, old enough to be my mum.

I sucked on a chocolate milkshake and demolished a huge Danish slice oozing with what mum calls 'false cream', but which tastes entirely real to me. Miranda sipped a cappuccino. We talked a bit about David. Miranda hadn't known him but listened attentively as I told some of the stories about the sort of guy he was, and how I'd benefitted from his quick thinking and courage.

"You must miss him really badly. He sounds like a good friend and someone you could admire. There are few enough of them in the world," Miranda said, "and it's hard to lose a close friend like that, so young."

"Miranda..." I started a question, and paused. She waited, her eyebrows just raised a smidgen. "Miranda, could I ask you something?"

"Of course, Rhory."

"You know you use the pendulum and all ... your owl..."

"Yes."

"And I think you can ask it anything?"

"Well, I can always ask," said Miranda, "but I don't always get answers you know."

"Yes, I know." I paused again, trying to find the right words. "But would you be able to ask if David is still ... well, if he is still somewhere."

Miranda looked towards the street, for a moment or two, and then said, "Well, I could but I wouldn't. If I did that it would become a bit like mediumship and that's not a road that I follow. I'm not saying it's wrong, but it's full of dangers, and I feel no need to use my gifts that way."

I waited, while she took a further sip of her coffee.

"I know that he's still 'somewhere' as you put it, dear," she said. "His spirit will have awakened where the spirit goes when it dies. My understanding is that he'll have had a chance to review his life and will have done so with the help of those who are 'on the other side' as it were. These will be people who love him but have already passed over.

"He will go on having experiences in this new realm. It's not the same as life here. Earth is more of a tough school for the soul. There…" she moved her hand in a graceful arc "…in the beyond, what you think of happens at once, and the quality of your surroundings is entirely dependent on the quality of your thoughts. Someone kind and courageous like your friend David, will be somewhere good, surrounded by those similar to himself. He'll be happy, dear."

At that point we both experienced something. Perhaps the angle of the cafe to the rest of the universe, shifted by a degree; or a choir just out of the range of earthly ears, started singing something beautiful; or deep, deep inside, in some hidden room, candlelight revealed a tapestry of sacred pictures. All those things, and none of those things, occurred. I knew that David had benefitted from us talking affectionately about him. His peace touched us. I could see Miranda had felt it too.

Miranda looked deep into my eyes. Normally I would've been embarrassed, but what had just happened allowed me to feel the calmest I'd felt for months.

"You really are one of those who just know, aren't you, Rhory? Hold on to that, my dear. Hold on to it, for it's worth all the tea in China. You felt David's presence and so did I. Not everyone has that gift. Indeed very few in this day and age. It allows you to know that all this materialistic nonsense is just that. Nonsense. You can run your life by a different tune. It can be a bit lonely at times, but it's really rewarding, in my experience."

I sort of got her meaning. Her words gave me confidence when I struggled to make sense of the gift I received from Aunt Bridget a little while later.

I thanked Miranda for her generosity and the great milkshake, and went off to do the errands for my mum.

Chapter 40

The Box from Quickly Lane

The following weekend, after several days of nagging, I went with Juliette and Dad to visit my Great-Aunt Bridget. The sun brought out the best in the autumn colours of the trees. "Perhaps global warming is reality after all, it's ridiculously hot," said Juliette, a sceptic on these as on most matters.

Aunt Bridget's house wasn't that hard to find, as Chorley Wood lay just outside the north-west corner of the M25 motorway. Once we exited the busyness of one of the most car-clogged roads in Great Britain, we were immediately in what felt like deepest countryside.

"It's that fact," said Dad, "that keeps house prices here mega-high. You are in a small country town only a very short distance from London, either by car or better still by train. I don't know what Aunt Bridget's house is worth but I expect you would not see much change out of a million."

Dad had phoned ahead, so when we arrived at the house in the quaintly named Quickly Lane, my venerable Aunt definitely expected us.

"It's good to see you, Angus," said Bridget, as she led the way into the house. "Now children, there's some of your favourite lemonade ready in a jug in the kitchen. You remember the way, Juliette, don't you? I just want to catch up a bit with your father, children, so why don't you get a drink and then explore the garden." *Ha, Juliette is also a child!* "Jiminy is out and about somewhere," she added.

Both of us loved the garden. I remembered it as much bigger and full of mysteries, but still wished to explore. After some lemonade, we went outside, looking for the big ginger cat.

"You know, Rhory," said Juliette, "Bridget still does all of her own gardening even the pruning of all her apple trees. And she's seventy-eight this year!"

I was impressed by that, as ten minutes of weeding in our house was enough to finish me off, with a mixture of extreme tiredness and uber-boredom. Bridget's garden must have taken her hours every week, with bushes, trees and flowerbeds all around the house.

I'd climbed up one of the trees, when Dad called us in for lunch. Great-Aunt Bridget may have been older than Methuselah's mother, but she still knew that shepherd's pie, Daddy's Sauce, and a follow up of lemon meringue pie, would go down well with children of any age. "Your favourite, Angus, if I remember rightly." Dad's big grin, and wish for second helpings of each course, indicated she had.

"Now, Angus, I've collected all those old family albums with pictures going back ... well even before my time. I thought you and Jules might like to look them over. I want to have a word with young Mr Bruce here, and to see if he is really entirely over his illness."

So a few minutes later I sat on my own, on the large settee in the front room, waiting for my aunt to get old photo albums for Jules and Dad. The piano, which she played rather well, both boring classical pieces and rather good stuff she called 'ragtime', stood by the wall opposite the bow window. On either side of the unlit fireplace opposite the settee, were bookshelves, full of books on myths, legends and fairy tales. There were also old books that showed objects dug up by archaeologists all over the world. My aunt loved India and Egypt. I remembered how even years before, when I was eight or nine, I'd spent afternoons lying on the floor looking at the amazing pictures of sphinxes and pyramids and the strange animal-headed gods and things.

Aunt Bridget came in and gave me a smile that hinted of conspiracy. "So, Rhory, your dad was just filling me in on all that's happened to you."

A pale white ring surrounded the irises of her washed-out blue eyes, and her face had papery skin, full of masses of very tiny creases and lines. Ignoring demands for correctness around children, she was smoking.

"You don't mind, dear, do you?" she'd said before lighting up. "It really is my only vice. Well that and the odd glass of wine."

She smiled. I didn't mind, and quite liked the slight tang of smoke in a room. Plus I'd always enjoyed watching the smoke climb from the end of a lit cigarette in impossible swirls and whirls.

My great-aunt asked me searching questions about my illness. She listened so well, and didn't interrupt, and soon I found myself telling her about my dreams. I also told her about the dog and the cat in the park.

"Yes, I see," she'd said, somewhat enigmatically. And she added, to herself it seemed, "Plus two makes the Nine."

She showed particular interest in the drawings I'd made in my dream diary. I'd not brought the diary with me, but I could reproduce the seven circles on a piece of paper, and even made quite a good attempt at the bird.

"I agree that looks like the Ibis, Rhory," she said, "a bird with great significance in ancient Egypt, you know."

She traced her fingers around the circles I'd just drawn. "This is the Seed of Life," she said, and paused as a noisy group of teenagers walked by, outside. She looked back at me and eased herself out of the settee.

"I am going to show you something," she said, crossing to the piano.

She took a Toby jug that sat on the piano top and up-ended it. A small key lay in the palm of her hand. She used it to unlock a door in a strange circular wooden cupboard.

"You know, Rhory, this used to be a commode. It's where the genteel stored their potties. I picked it up at an auction some years back. It makes a great little cupboard." She winked at me.

From the commode Bridget took out a leather-bound book. The

spine shifted in her hand and some of the pages had bits missing and deep brown stains. She sat down again before opening it with great care. Pages and pages were filled with flowery writing in faded brown ink.

"Copperplate," my great-aunt said, "and beautifully done. Look at this, Rhory dear." And there, amidst a finely written entry early in the book, she pointed out a picture of a bird, just like the one I'd drawn.

I went hot and cold all over.

"I know, dear," said Bridget, in a voice that was warm but quite firm. "It's a lot to take in. This is why I've sent your sister and dad away to do other things. I know they'll not understand this and for the time being it has to be your secret and mine."

Then she carefully turned two pages, and there, drawn in ink, with a precision equal to the copperplate handwriting, were the seven circles, six surrounding a central seventh, with the top circle including a tiny picture of a bird. On the next page, the jackal-headed man had been drawn with a skill that was quite beyond me. He looked just like the one I'd seen in my bedroom.

My great-aunt watched me steadily. Her eyes seemed to be seeing into and then through me, as though I'd become some transparent doorway to a world beyond. "I've waited a long time for this. You are the seventh generation you know, and I knew or at least I hoped that the Recorder would be found in the family. I thought it might be either you or Natasha, but I had to be sure. None of your other cousins showed any of the signs, and I had to wait."

I shook my head. I'd no idea what she was on about. My skin developed goose bumps. "What is that book, Aunt Bridget?" I asked.

"Well it is a diary written by one of your direct ancestors, Rhory. That is all I can tell you at the moment. I've had it and the Sphere in sacred trust from my grandfather. It was written by his grandfather. He was a Bruce like the rest of us. The diary gives clear instructions as to how to proceed and my part is clearly stated as well. However, if I were to give you the diary to read, it would affect all that may happen to you and might well mean that what should happen will not. You will just have to find your way, my dear. The test will be the Sphere and whether you can find the way in."

Before I could ask more questions, she stood up and promptly left the room. I sat on the settee feeling distinctly queasy. Everything wobbled and appeared far away.

Aunt Bridget returned with a box made of a polished wood that looked like walnut. She put the box on the settee, and looked at me. Then she left the room again to return a few moments later with some more lemonade.

"Drink this, Rhory," she said. "You look as if you might keel over."

We could hear Dad and Jules were coming back from the kitchen where they had been looking at the photos.

"Don't discuss this with anyone except Natasha. She is clearly your helpmate in this, a Guardian, even if not a fully-fledged *Companion*..." She tapped the outside of the wooden box. "Call me if you solve the riddle of the Sphere. I'd like to finally know what's inside. I've been its guardian since I was about twenty; and sixty years is a long time to wait you know, dear."

Just before Dad came back in she gave me a little brass key and said, "Put this in your pocket. Don't lose it. And mum's the word."

Neither Jules nor Dad paid much attention to the fact I left with what appeared to be an old Victorian sewing box, in a large plastic shopping bag. It's strange how some people don't really see what's in front of them when they are not interested.

Chapter 41

Shoshan Writes a Letter

When we arrived home that night, I went up to the bedroom and put the box in my wardrobe. Neither Dad nor Juliette commented on it, and Mum was more focused on getting us sat down for tea than anything else. No one seemed interested in what Aunt Bridget and I had talked about.

As usual, at tea, Dad and Juliette held forth, talking about the family photos they had looked through, and Dad filled us in, entertainingly as always, about some of his forebears. He liked to think that we were distant relations to the Bruces who had been the legitimate kings of Scotland. We were definitely distantly related to Lord Elgin (of Greek Marbles fame) through the Hershel branch of the family (whoever they were) and the current Lord Elgin was the head of Clan Bruce, so perhaps Juliette was 10,000th in line to the throne of England.

I'd be the 10,001st in line then! It was fun to think that I might be pale and a little more interesting through having a tiny peck of royal blood coursing through my veins.

That night I didn't try to open the box. The long drive had left me tired and I wanted to savour the mystery for one night longer. I suspected the box contained a puzzle that had defeated my formidable Great-Aunt Bridget, always assuming that she'd tried.

I sat on the bed to get up some energy to change for the night. I took out the diary and flipped through some of the definitions of dream symbols. I looked up what was symbolised by a park, like our Hammerford Park.

It said something about a bounded space and a mandala with four entrances. I didn't know the word 'mandala'. To be in a park, the dictionary in the book said, was to be out of normal or ordinary life. A park formed a special space. It indicated change and transcendence. There were too many words I didn't understand. Maybe if I closed my eyes for a minute I'd have the energy to go and clean my teeth and get undressed for the night.

I woke in the morning to find I'd slept in my clothes. I'd never done that before. I didn't expect to find anything in the diary, but on opening it I found a lot of writing. I checked my clock and had time to read before going to school. Shoshan had communicated using impossibly neat handwriting.

At last. I have tried several times to find you. Here I sit, Pale Boy, looking at this stone wall that glows slightly. The seat I am on is also made of stone and eventually gets uncomfortable. You know the stars have to be in exactly the right position for me to talk to you? And then if you are not there or asleep, I get cross.

I have so many questions for you, but the priest tells me that will only be possible when the link is properly forged. I don't really know what he means.

There are three priests in the Hall of Records, Pale Boy. They are funny, completely bald, with no eyebrows, painted eyes and big ears that stick out. And they are identical. They never talk. I can hear them because I am a Hearer; you know that don't you? Oh yes, I remember I told you. It's not easy talking to a wall.

When I do talk, I see the shapes of strange leaves moving over the wall. When I see those, I know you are there. Don't ask me how; I just do.

The priest has just told me he heard all of that. He's quite amused. He says the Records show that you receive this message. Makes my head spin to think what that might mean.

It should be dark down here. It isn't though. There are no rush torches. The walls have their own light. They just glow.

No, I'm not allowed to tell you any more about that. The Records show you won't learn how to do this again until... No I'm not allowed to tell you that either. Sorry.

I can tell you a bit about my training. Every day I go to the Corridors of Time. The room we use is a lovely underground temple, full of peace and soft light. In it is a stone bowl, forged by... No I'm not allowed to name him. When you look closely you can see the finest pictures are carved all over the inside. It's empty and full at the same time. That sounds silly doesn't it. It's like this. I sit, with my sisters, the other priestesses, around me. We all chant beautiful songs. As we do so, the light in the room changes and the figures in the bowl glow gently. The bowl isn't filled with anything but gradually it seems full to the brim with the purest water you could imagine. Can you imagine water mixed with light?

"Rhory, don't be late for school. Shouldn't you be going?"

"In a minute, Mum."

Because of the connection with you, Dimitris and the others...

What others? I sat back on the bed and bit down on my lower lip. *There are more of us?*

I went back to Shoshan's writing.

...I allow the waters to show what actually happens in other times. We form a sort of golden chain across the ages. It's a chain the Desert God wants to cut. Oh, I'm not allowed to tell you any more about that now. My priests say we will see that together later.

I am allowed to tell you what I heard about the future of the Plain of the Lion. In a few generations, where I am will change for ever. The Hall of Records will be hidden until the moment of Time's Choice. And that of course, is where you come in. I've heard that these Halls will be found again in the End Times, and not before. But a sign of their presence is going to be built.

The Great Bowl showed us all a truly remarkable stone structure planned by the Priests of Osiris and Ra. They will sing it into being and in years and years to come no one will know how they did it. I hope I live long enough to see that happen. I could see it in the Bowl, Pale Boy, reaching high, pointing to Ra in the heavens and connecting with all the important stars. It will be called the Pyramid, and will grow near the Lioness.

When we saw the Pyramid, I heard some words. I'm not sure if they came from my teacher or from her teacher, the one I can't name. But I am allowed to tell you the words:

"In times not yet born, people will be sure this is a tomb.

But it never will be, except the tomb of silly dreams and selfish thoughts.

No, here the children of your children's children will come and marvel.

Nothing else will ever be quite as this will be.

For here clay will become light and men will meet the Gods themselves.

If such a thing could be.

This Pyramid and others will still be standing when you help change the Course of Time."

The priest says you, Pale Boy, need to pay particular attention to those words. I have more to tell you about Time, boy from another time. But I don't have time now as the stars have moved.

The diary entry ended abruptly at that point, with what looked like a play on words across the centuries. I couldn't work out how she could be communicating to me in the present when she lived so far back in the past. I'd no idea how she could write in English. That is assuming that there is – or was – a Shoshan, from all that time ago.

Chapter 42

Shelley and the Bowl

Shelley normally didn't eat much breakfast. A quick cup of tea and yoghurt from a small plastic pot, would do the trick. Both of those she took when she arrived at work, before getting on with the day's typing. She found her appetite changed when she stayed at the house in the West Country, and did her trance work. Then she could eat a horse.

Today she'd demolished several slices of toast and a boiled egg, after a large bowl of cereal. The room where she always took breakfast alone, didn't have much of a view, just a window overlooking a rather functional courtyard. She flicked at the pages of the mini Cosmo magazine, but couldn't find anything she hadn't already read. Her watch said nine twenty-eight. *Geez, I've been here nearly an hour*. She took a sip of tea. It had turned cold in the cup.

Shelley opened the door a crack and listened. A rather large grandfather clock marked time, in the hallway down the corridor, tick by tock. Otherwise the house brooded, silently. The smell of floor polish wrestled with that of old toast. She eased her way through the door and closed it quietly behind her. Her heart beat a little more strongly as she crept down the corridor. She doubted they'd punish her for being out and about. She knew they valued her too much, to be silly about her just looking around. And anyway, maybe they'd forgotten her.

She hovered at the hallway, where the ticking clock nearly drowned out the gentle murmur of voices, coming from a distant room. Shelley turned in the opposite direction. She could always blag that she'd been seeking the toilet and become lost. A few metres down, a door stood slightly ajar. She gently pushed it open and peeked in.

She held her breath. She'd never seen a room like it. In the centre stood a huge stone bowl. *Just pour in the asses' milk and I could have a bath.* It rested on specially shaped wooden blocks, with great carved claws, and looked incredibly heavy.

The carpet had been taken out, leaving a square patch of darker floorboards, under the bowl. The floor had thin lines painted on it in various colours, radiating from the centre, with some curved lines, forming an irregular web of different angles and hues. The lines were all marked with other tiny lines about three or four centimetres long, like the edge of a ruler.

Spindly, three-legged wooden structures had been arranged around the sides of the room. A few extended only half a metre or so in height. Four stood quite a bit taller than her, and some were in-between. Each had a curved copper mirror attached to the top, slightly above and to the side of the wooden platform that completed the tripod. On the platforms, an unlit candle in a small brass candlestick sat in front of each of the mirrors.

She moved closer. The wide rim of the bowl tilted slightly inwards. She ran her hands over the inside. "Extraordinary," she murmured to herself. The whole bowl had been carved from one piece of stone. *It must weigh tons and tons.* Her fingers stroked the smooth, cool surface. *What's that?* A tingle passed up her arm.

Shelley leant over the bowl to get a better look at what her fingers had caressed. For a moment she'd the impression of looking through water. Underneath, near her fingers, she could make out carvings, the sort of fine chiselled pictures made by Egyptians long, long ago. The more she looked, the clearer the pictures became. At various places, just beyond the rim of the bowl, incised figures facing sideways. She moved her hands further along and felt the resistance of the water, except the bowl remained empty. Yet she could distinctly feel a liquid.

I'm having one of my moments.

She peered at a room reflected in the water that wasn't water. Unlike the room she stood in, this one had no windows, just tall stone walls flickering with distant torchlight. The figures around the edge of the bowl moved slowly, revolving just under the surface. *If I just leant over and slid into the bowl, I'd pass into this room.*

Shadows shifted on the stone walls. People moved about in the other room, reflected in the invisible water. Shelley stiffened as someone looked into the bowl from the other side. For less than a moment, a face looked back at her, a face so angry and vile that she snatched her hand away. Cold patches seared her arm and she rubbed them as she moved back from the bowl. Something searched for her and then vanished like a soap bubble bursting. The room became brighter and darker at the same time.

With blood thundering in her ears, Shelley slipped out into the corridor. Somewhere a door closed. She reached the hallway and could hear voices. She found the downstairs toilet and went inside. From her breakfast room, a voice that could cut through a steel door, asked the universe, "Where is that dratted girl, we need to get on?"

She knew her nerves wouldn't allow her to have a pee at this stage, so she flushed the loo, ran a tap, and splashed water on her face. Moments later she emerged all wide-eyed and innocent, ready for the work ahead.

Chapter 43

The Carved Sphere

I overslept the next day and had to rush to school without opening the box. I'd no one I could discuss it with except Natasha, and possibly Aunt Sofia. My great-aunt had made it clear I had to sort out the puzzle. My whole body ached with tiredness.

"What's up with you?" said Nick when I saw him in our maths class. "You look like you've been dragged through a hedge backwards."

"And that's how I feel, Nick. I didn't sleep well last night. Too many strange dreams." I wondered if I should tell him about the writing from Shoshan in my diary. I knew he'd be interested in the bit about the pyramids and the hidden Hall of Records.

We were interrupted by the maths teacher, and the next 40 minutes filled up with quadratic equations, which is enough to drive the weirdest dreams from your mind. I remained dozy and later Mr Hawksley actually threw a piece of chalk at me when I nodded off. He taught geography and looked eighty years old, but I guess by law, must've been younger. Most of the other classrooms had white boards and dry marker pens. He still favoured the black boards – misnamed because they were green – that revolved on a great roller, so he could reveal huge amounts of writing, with a dramatic flourish. I more or less made my way through the day without further mishap.

I cycled home and dealt with the acute pangs of hunger by eating four butter and soft brown sugar sandwiches. Just enough intake to get me through to tea at about 6.30. Delicious.

I'm as thin as the proverbial rake even though I consume more than Tweedledum and Tweedledee put together. Juliette says it's because I have my own tapeworm. However, she also has an appetite like a South Wales miner, so I guess she must have one as well.

Using superhuman willpower, I did my homework before exploring the box. Physics, more quadratic equations for the maths teacher, and an extra piece of geography, resulting from falling asleep in the lesson. I knew more about the Sheffield steel industry when I'd finished, than is considered medically safe. Just as I walked over to the wardrobe that had my great-aunt's box, Juliette shouted to say tea was ready.

Dad sat at the dining room table reading the newspaper. "Those unspeakables are still trying to get their wretched leisure centre slap bang in the middle of our park."

"I know. It's true. We had a petition at school today, to try and stop them, and save the bandstand," said Juliette.

"Christmas is coming," announced Mum. She evidently had no great interest in the park, or in local politics. "We need to go shopping and Hammerford shops are really dull when it comes to getting nice things for Christmas."

"What do you suggest?" asked Dad diplomatically. As regards shopping, the women of 3 Suffolk Road, made all the key decisions, and it was not wise to try to second guess what they wanted. Their desires changed randomly, but with utter conviction. Dad and I waited expectantly for the answer.

"Well, a trip to London is a possibility," said Mum.

"Mind you," offered Jules, "it gets really, really busy in the run up to Christmas."

"That's true," said Mum. "We need somewhere with good shops that will not be totally clogged with people."

"Yes," continued Juliette, as though the two Bruce women were operating from one stream of consciousness. "We need to avoid too many of the Great Unwashed. How about Croydon? It has a good shopping centre."

"Right," said Mum, "but who in their right mind wants to go to Croydon?"

"True," said Jules, the one brain continuing to chat with itself. "So we should go to Brighton."

"Precisely," said Mum.

"That's settled then," said Jules. "Next Saturday, Dad?" she asked, as though he had been part of the decision making.

Dad looked slightly bemused. And, as usual in matters of High Shopping, the youngest Bruce, namely moi, hadn't been consulted at all. But Brighton had excellent fish and chips, a pier with great arcade games, and several shops specialising in Xbox software, so I kept my mouth shut.

"Next Saturday it is then," said Dad.

That's how fate works, because without that trip, I'd never have solved the puzzle awaiting me upstairs. How fate intervened in the ramblings of my mother's and sister's respective minds, was beyond explanation.

As soon as I could, I made my way back to my bedroom. The wood of the box had a slight transparency, revealing golden swirls in the grain a bit below the surface. It had been polished to a mirror-like sheen. It lay on my lap, the size of a large shoebox, but much heavier. The deep lid resisted pressure from my thumbs.

Ah, a keyhole. Where there's a keyhole you need a key.

I looked for the key Aunt Bridget had given me. Shifting Jester from my artfully arranged jeans, lying on the floor, I found it in the pocket. The key fitted and with a bit of wiggling, the lock turned. I opened the lid carefully.

A fragrance filled the air. I sniffed at the aroma with a long intake of breath. *Nice. Musky but refreshing.* Inside, the box had a lot of old, red velvet. Red satin lined the lid. Nestling in the middle of the soft velvet lay a sphere of carved wood.

I eased it out. It felt heavier than solid wood. The whole sphere had been covered with intricate figures. I held it carefully, fearful that I'd somehow break it. I felt breathless and my heart thumped loud enough to hear.

The whole of its spherical surface displayed a continuous picture made up of trees, animals and the occasional building. Most were recognisable. There were elephants, monkeys and crows, following a lion. Several small dragons kept watch on a ram, and a spider. My hands shook when I saw the ibis, just like the one in my dream diary.

I had to make sense of these lifelike carvings. I knew this sphere had the answer to the way my life had changed. Great-Aunt Bridget had been unable to solve this puzzle. I didn't even know where to begin.

Most of the animals and the trees seemed to be orientated in the same direction. Their feet pointed down and their heads indicated up. Using this as a guideline I examined the top of the sphere. Right in the centre a small sun had rays extending from it. At the bottom, the artist had carved a half-moon. I gently shook the sphere in my hands and felt a slight movement. Something inside the sphere had shifted. I jiggled it some more. Nothing happened. I tapped it, but couldn't tell if it was hollow. I held it in both hands.

A bowling ball would be heavier. *A bowling ball.* In grass bowls, granddad had told me the balls have a bias. This means they'll curl in one direction when bowled straight. It literally means you can bowl around corners.

Taking great care, and moving Jester out of harm's way, I rolled the sphere across the bedroom floor. It rolled straight. I studied how I held the sphere. The elephant faced to my right and exactly at the bottom; I bowled again. Again it rolled entirely straight. Seemed like a waste of time but I tried a third experiment. This time the elephant was on the right side facing up and the stag fitted in the palm of my bowling hand. Bingo! The sphere rolled with a bias to the right. It curved each time I rolled it with the stag underneath.

Some part of sphere must be heavier than another part. *If it's not solid wood then maybe it's hollow.* In our work shed, outside the house and below where my dad has his architecture office, were his tools.

Either the axe or the saw would do the trick but they might also destroy whatever the sphere contained. Also, something nagged at me that to use force wouldn't work. I had to find the right way in.

I started at the top where the sun shone in all its wooden glory. Trickles of panic moved up my arms and legs. The wooden sunlight illumined two great stones with steps between. *Just like the steps Dimitris had been climbing when I lost sight of him in the park.* Yet the sphere had been carved a long time before. How could the artist possibly know how our bandstand appeared at the time I'd met Dimitris?

Gingerly, I put the sphere back into the box and feeling slightly disorientated, I went downstairs to watch some TV. I've no idea what I watched.

My mind went on its own dizzy course. What did the animals mean? One of the birds was a dead ringer of the bird I'd drawn in the dream diary. A jackal stared sideways, like the head of the jackal-headed man I'd seen. Were all the animals meaningful? Most were real, but not the various dragons. If my nocturnal flights would bring me into contact with dragons, then I should be making a booking to see the local psychiatrist. I didn't mind being unusual but I didn't want to be completely unhinged!

I went to bed as usual about ten o'clock. I thought I'd lie awake thinking. The next thing I knew, my alarm clock rang fit to wake the dead.

I returned to the puzzle the next evening, when tea had been completed and homework rushed through, as normal. Retrieving the box from its hiding place I took out the sphere. I'd be systematic. Not my strongest point, but I'd make a try.

I listed all the animals I could recognise. This proved to be simpler than I thought. There were two elephants and two monkeys. There was one of each of the following, a vicious looking dog, a snake, a lion, a horse, a cat, a spider, a crocodile, an owl, a hawk, a pelican, the ibis and a jackal. In addition there were four dragon-like creatures and four crow-like creatures. Two of the buildings looked like temples, one had stone pillars and steps, and the fourth building looked like a castle. All the other spaces on the sphere were filled with plants or trees. They flowed into one another and so didn't count as separate objects.

I noticed that when I pressed down on the hawk, it gave slightly. None of the other animals seemed to depress in this way although I tried them all.

I seemed a little bit further along the way to a solution but nothing of any significance. I'd have liked to show the sphere to Natasha but she had her mock exams at school which she took far too seriously. She only returned my chat message with a brief "Hi" before signing me out of her electronic universe, with the message, "Natasha is busy!"

And there I became stuck. Without doing damage to the beautiful object, I wasn't going to get closer to solving the puzzle. I couldn't find a way in. The carvings on the outside might have their own message, but I didn't have the key.

Chapter 44

Brighton Rocks

Bruce family trips had certain constants. Jules and I sat in the back, seat belts on as good citizens. Dad drove and Mum commented on Dad's driving; not too much, but just enough to occasionally lead to ructions.

"Careful, dear," and, "Is this the correct lane do you think?" and, "It's a 50 mile an hour speed limit you know," were par for the course. A sudden "Watch Out!" would make us all jump. However, Dad had not had an accident since, according to him, he backed into a road sign when learning to drive.

We sang, of course. Dad was proud of being a baritone, which apparently is a bit lower than a tenor but not as dramatic as a bass. Mum's voice was sweet and light, and the divine Juliette had the ability to harmonise with anything, usually when accompanying herself on the piano. Although not in the car. Obviously.

For us the journey to Brighton started along various main roads and back roads that Dad knew well and Mum distrusted...

"Are you sure this is right, Angus?" being a frequent refrain. Eventually he emerged triumphant on the A23 which led to the M23 and then we were on the home straight as it were, to the town of rock and the Pavilion.

"We must bring back some rock," Juliette said.

A lurid pale red on the outside and white in the middle, Brighton Rock used some sort of voodoo, to print its name in tiny red letters, all through the centre. It stuck satisfyingly to the teeth, leaving sharp splinters of sugary flavour, to be enjoyed later.

Dad refused to come anywhere near one. "I've got fillings, you know. No fluoride in my water as a child! One bite of rock and then three visits to the dentist."

"I don't know how you can eat that dreadful stuff, children," Mum said. "Now in Norway, the confectionery is really special…"

I tuned out at that point. Mum could bat on about Norwegian this and that for hours once she started. I dreamed of sticky rock. These sweet joys were yet to come, because we could only buy rock at the little shops close to the beach.

Out of the blue, Juliette turned to me and said, "Oh, I know the meaning of your name."

"Oh, yes," I said, waiting for the punch line.

"Yeah, it's part of the work Dad and I are doing, isn't it, Dad?" Dad grunted as he drove, and went on chatting to mum in the front seat. "My name means 'Jove's child' or 'youthful'. Your name is just as interesting, it means 'Red King'." An army of mice crawled all over my skin. I'd no idea my name meant anything in particular. I got teased for having it spelt with an 'h'. People usually managed to miss that out.

"Are you sure?"

"Yep," said Juliette, "you can easily check it on the internet."

I sank back into the seat. The world had taken a further step into weirdness.

Finally, we were coming down the London Road towards the Old Steine and the centre of Brighton. We found a parking space actually on the sea front. Between us and the sea stretched a mangy grassy area, at least fifty metres wide. After this some kind soul had built houses for pixies or leprechauns in extraordinary pastel shades.

"Couldn't we get one of those," Juliette said. "It would be such fun." She was pointing to the rows of fairy dwellings. Dad mentioned how much beach huts actually cost.

"That's ridiculous," said Jules. "Only an idiot would pay that much for a house that would make Munchkins feel claustrophobic." All this proved to me how Juliette could change her mind within milliseconds, and still seem ultra-rational.

Beyond these overpriced gnome houses, extended another great expanse of tarmac, used by those who like rollerblading at great speed, or doing the impossible with skateboards. Then there was an ornate metal fence followed by a huge beach entirely made up of stones. Finally, at a great distance, was the sea.

"Okay," said Juliette dismissively to Dad and me, "off you go. Us women have see-ree-us shopping to do."

So started the Great Christmas Shopping Expedition. Mum and Jules set off together. Dad and I decided to fly solo. We all agreed to meet at one of our favourite restaurants, with a view of the West Pier.

"Don't do anything I wouldn't do," shouted Jules to me, as they rounded a corner. That left me with plenty of options.

Chapter 45

The Silver Unicorn

I headed towards The Lanes, with all its little shops and coffee bars. A good place for getting presents. I'd been given funds by Mum to help with the Christmas expenses and I'd saved a little from my business of washing the neighbours' cars.

I did quite well in the first half hour and had gifts for both parents, a couple of fun things for Jules and even something for Natasha. I just had the grandparents to think of and something for Nick at school, and then I'd be done and dusted.

I wandered out of The Lanes and found myself in a street that mainly consisted of bookshops. I don't know how I got there or if I could find it again. I'd explored most of the way up one side and all the way down the other, and spent some time looking at second-hand books, with an eye out for good graphic novels. A Christmas present to myself.

A strange shop across the road, nearest The Lanes, caught my eye. *The Silver Unicorn* had a large shop front decorated in blue. The window displayed books on healing, Tibetan Bowl Chanting – whatever that is – Tai Chi, Wicca, which I don't think has anything to do with basket weaving, crystals, crop circles and such like. It also advertised a poster collection. Now I needed a good poster to brighten up my bedroom wall, so I crossed over the road again and went in.

A little bell chimed as I opened the door. Once inside, I passed under a strange structure elevated off the floor a metre or two. Stairs climbed up to a blue doorway – the dominant colour of the shop –

decorated with clouds and a rainbow. On the sales counter, a picture in a frame showed a youngish, rather pretty woman. Beneath, in neatly written letters, with the sort of gold ink Jules uses on birthday cards, it said, 'Jasmine gives Readings'.

Perhaps she reads from books? Or studies the future from used tea leaves? Brighton was full of people offering to read your fortune using different parts of your anatomy, crystal balls or Tarot cards. I wasn't interested in all that rubbish.

I moved further into the shop. The Mind, Body and Spirit section had nothing on dreams involving flying. I picked up a book by a guy who had written about ley lines. Our islands have many ancient places with a special energy, he wrote. These places connect with straight lines, linking rock formations and certain churches with old hilltops and so on. It even mentioned Hammerford in the index.

I looked it up. Our park had a node for a number of interesting lines. One originated in Stonehenge. Another started at Chanctonbury Ring. It looked really cool and I thought Nat might like it. Then I checked the price. It made my eyes water, so I put it back.

The poster collection dominated the middle of the shop, in a big rack. I was 'umming' and 'ahing' between one of Batman dispatching Catwoman, and Spiderman swinging through Metropolis, or wherever he swings. I'd buy it, and Mum would refund me; that was the agreement. I'd then pretend surprise at Christmas when Mum gave it to me. Quite a good system really. At least I'd get a present I really wanted.

"Not that one," said a voice at my elbow. I turned to see a woman, young but ageless as well. And very pretty. She had brown, wavy hair tumbling around her face. She'd flick her hair back and then it would tumble forward again. Her eyes, a deep brown colour, flecked with highlights, had large lashes. My legs began to turn to soft putty, while I grew an extra three tongues in my mouth. I didn't trust my voice not to return to its pre-broken state. At least my mouth didn't open and close like a goldfish.

She smiled, and said, "You know you've to be careful what images you surround yourself with. Now I know we sell these posters, and normally I don't mind who buys what. But not you. You must be careful."

"Why?" I managed, without squeaking or collapsing on the floor.

"Because you're not run-of-the-mill, are you, young man." Once more she smiled, and the universe seemed to have increased in brightness by at least two lumens.

"Look, I've had a cancellation. I'd like to do a reading for you." Again the smile. I felt as though I was drowning, just in sight of the mermaid of my dreams.

"A reading?" I responded, like a not-so-clever parrot.

"Yes," she said, "it'll take about half an hour. Could you manage that amount of time before meeting up with your family?"

I looked at my watch. I'd a full hour in fact. I noticed my hand shook slightly and my mouth had gone very dry. A strange sensation collected at the pit of my stomach, half way between the possibility of agony and the possibility of ecstasy. I didn't realise until later that she seemed to know more about me than was normal. I mightn't have been with my family. How did she know I was?

"Yes," I said, "I've enough time, but I really don't think I can afford it."

Again the leg-melting, mouth-drying smile. "No, this is my gift to you. Take it as an early Christmas present."

"Won't they mind in the shop if you don't charge?" I said, remembering a list of charges at the counter, depending on the type of reading done.

"That's darling," she said, as though I'd done something really marvellous. She laughed a delightful laugh. "No, they won't mind. You see it's my shop, so I guess I can bend the rules once in a while, can't I?" she said with a wink. And with that she moved off towards the eyrie above the entranceway, with a "Follow me."

Chapter 46

My Fortune is Read

I'd never been in so confined an area with so beautiful a woman in my life. The room held just two chairs and a little table. "My name is Jasmine," she said. "What's yours?"

"Rhory," I said. "Rhory Bruce."

"Rhory Bruce," she murmured, as she reached past me to close the curtains and shut us off from being seen from the street. "Lovely name, yes lovely. Courage, certainly and unusual insight I'd think."

I didn't know what she meant but could smell a delicate perfume. It reminded me of… Of what? Perhaps the wooden sphere?

"Do you mind if I close my eyes?" said Jasmine. "I can see better that way." She looked at me with another a heart-warming smile. I felt entirely at ease and smiled back. All the confusing thoughts had gone.

"No, go ahead, by all means."

So she closed her eyes. I waited. I liked studying her with her eyes closed. I could have looked at that face forever. I decided it was better manners to close my own eyes, and so I did.

She spoke quite a bit about my school and was fairly accurate about the subjects I did well at, and those where I struggled. "You haven't reached your time yet, Rhory," she said. There would come a time in my life when my ideas would be more recognised. I wasn't made for memorising book learning but for capturing sunbeams and weaving thoughts from starlight.

"Trust your mind from inside out," I remember her saying. My inner ideas had a truth against which I should measure all else. I had, she added, to explore within my own mind and find my compass and my plumb line there.

"School will not feed you, and your family are not your true family." I was about to ask what she meant, when she said, "They are truly kind and you chose them well. We choose our parents, Rhory, all of us, it is not really left to chance you know. They are just right for your emotional life. They give you love and stability, and that's a gift without price. They cannot lead you on your life path however. There are others close by. They are family but not your blood family. You've a deeper connection with each of them than you know.

"School knowledge will serve you, but it isn't the truth that will nourish you." She sat in silence for a bit. Outside a car door slammed. "Do what you have to do, Rhory, you need some of that knowledge and some of those exams to get on in this funny life of ours, but for truth, rather look to the stars in the sky, and in the summer field."

She lost me there. *Stars in a field?*

"You are never alone, Rhory. There's a woman. She's not really of this time. She watches over you. You are closest to her when you are amongst tiny flowers."

I'd always liked the sort of little wild flowers you get growing up by hedgerows and from the tumbledown bits of mossy walls, in the gardens of really old houses. Also meadow flowers that come in springtime.

"She says you must be steadfast. Keep going no matter what the odds. Her love for all of you is truly beautiful. She sees you all, but she sees you as you actually are, not as you may see yourself in a mirror." Jasmine paused and I opened my eyes. Her eyes remained closed. She smiled, and if Leonardo Da Vinci had been in this room, he'd have chosen another model for his Mona Lisa.

I closed my eyes again and waited. Jasmine remained silent once more.

"There are Seven of you but Nine must be invited." She paused again. "I am not sure what that means, Rhory. I can see it carved in stone. I am not being told this. I can read it."

A feeling of panic nestled in the depths of my guts. Hadn't my great-aunt said something like this?

"Your lady wants you to know she's not dead. I don't act as a medium, Rhory, and this is not some shade of a person who has passed over. She's as alive as you or me but just not of this time. She wants you to know that in the work you've to do…" Jasmine paused as though listening again. "…in the work you've chosen to do, you're never alone. Just look inside and you will find that she is there, standing shoulder to shoulder."

Again a long pause.

"There's one more thing. The key is in the park. More is there than you guess. She says 'Look beneath the surface.'"

Abruptly, she changed the subject and went on to say something about what I might study later if I went to university, and the sort of jobs I might do. None of this stayed in my memory.

Then Jasmine laughed. It was a gentle laugh, like a cascade of daisies or a dance of soap bubbles on a summer breeze. "Ah, there's a man. He was there before and he'll be there after. He was the start and will be the conclusion. You will meet him, Rhory, you will actually meet him because you can do no other. It has to be." And she laughed again.

I opened my eyes and found her looking at me. Her face lit up with a gentle smile. "Goodness," she said, her voice on a more normal plane. "Goodness," she repeated, "that was really beautiful, Rhory. Thank you."

"Thank you, Jasmine," I managed to say. "I'm not sure what to make of it all. There's a lot to take in."

"You'll remember just what is important, Rhory, so don't worry. You know my work is like that of a piano tuner. People come and I tighten a bit here and loosen a bit there, and put some new padding on a key or two, and then off you go, in tune. The melody that follows is up to you."

"Can I ask a question, Jasmine?" I said. She nodded and smiled.

"I'd a friend who died. He was only young, well, you know, he was my age. He was really a good, good friend, although I don't think I realised it at the time. He had so much to live for and so much to give. I don't see why God allowed him to die.

"David?" she said, with only the hint of a question mark at the end.

"Yes," I replied. "How did you know?"

"There are two ways, Rhory," Jasmine said, looking all the time deep into my eyes. "The first is that you carry the name in your mind and it just popped into mine. I've that gift of hearing other's thoughts, when they are clear, focused and have enough purity. So do we all by the way.

"And Rhory," she reached across and placed her hand lightly on the top of mine, "so do you. It's a gift you're going to have to manage, because it's not really of this time, but of a time that's being born. Those of us who are the forerunners will not always have an easy time of it. Our barriers are not as robust as most other people, and their thoughts and feelings can tumble into ours, and we have a tough job managing that. The second way is different. David was here you know, for a short time."

She stopped and continued to look at me. She became all wobbly and out of focus, as my eyes filled with tears.

"It's good to be sad at what you've lost, Rhory," Jasmine continued, "but David had done what he came to do. No ghost visited us in our little room here. He, the fullness of who he is, stood here. If you like, it was his soul, not his ghost. His work is mainly elsewhere now, and he's not really the age at which you knew him physically. But he knew you were here with me, and that I could tell you this. His work and yours will overlap a little more in this life, when the time is right."

I felt a strange sort of sensation as she said that, as though the chair no longer connected properly to the floor.

"There will be others of whom you will need to become aware.

Some were around as I spoke to you, but the lady is the one who spoke for them all, and she is your particular…" She paused, as though listening for exactly the right word. "Your particular *companion*."

Jasmine stood up. "There, that's enough for Christmas, don't you think, young man?" She smiled and turned and opened the door and led the way down. "Just wait a moment, I've something for you." She went behind the desk, and reached down to where some smaller posters were stored in cardboard rolls. "Take this, Rhory. I'd like to give this to you. I think you'll find it helpful." She smiled that smile again that was like the sun rising on a beautiful landscape.

"Don't forget your shopping bags, Rhory, we have them here." I must have left my shopping by the posters, when I went for the reading. I took the bags. She opened the door and the bell gave its celestial tinkle. She leaned over and gave me a peck on the cheek. There was a swirl of colour as she turned and her hair and skirts followed slightly later. I stood outside the shop wondering quite what I'd experienced. I could still feel the touch of her hand on the back of mine and the sensation where her lips had lightly blessed my cheek.

Chapter 47

The Poster

Feeling bemused at what had just happened I set off to find the restaurant where we were to have lunch. I knew I couldn't share Jasmine's words with Mum or Dad and certainly not with Juliette. Jules would mock, and would say, "These fortune tellers are just clever psychologists and charlatans, they say what you want to hear." Dad would be interested as he was interested in life in general, but would give what I'd been told no credibility. Mum? Well Mum was a bit of an ostrich really and not keen to explore things that upset her sense of how things are, and how things should be. So I knew I'd have to keep my peace.

After a late lunch we drove back to Hammerford. We were all tired. I went to my room and sorted out what I'd bought as Christmas presents for the family. I'd wrap them later once Dad had actually put up the Christmas tree. For the moment they went into the wardrobe, with my great-aunt's box.

As I arranged them, I noticed the present that Jasmine had given me. The poster in a cardboard roll stuck out of a shopping bag. I'd entirely forgotten it. *Should I give it to Mum to give back to me at Christmas? Then it would be a surprise. Should I open it now and see what Jasmine thought I needed that was better than Batman, Robin or Spiderman?*

The decision took little more than a millisecond. I carefully extracted the poster from the protective roll, opened it, and it immediately curled back.

I used books to pin down the corners and unfolded the poster on the floor. At the top of the picture, a shape held by two puffing angel heads was filled with spidery writing in a foreign language. The rest of the poster had a mixture of long straight thin lines, black dots, small drawings and a wavy line with heavy etching. *Why on earth has Jasmine given me this?* I sighed, as I stuck the picture on my wall with sticky blue stuff, and decided to return to the wooden puzzle.

Gingerly, I lifted the sphere out of its box and sank down on my bed. I gently pushed, shook and pushed again. None of the animals moved, except for the hawk. I stared at the carvings, and they stared back. I rubbed at the stiffness in my neck. My teeth were clamped shut. I wanted to throw the blasted sphere out the window. What was the solution? There had to be a way in even if I couldn't find a keyhole.

Through the window I could just make out distant trees running along the edge of the railway line, black cut-outs against the skyline. The dusk of the evening would soon become dark. I reached over and put on my bedside light.

In the dim light Jasmine's poster revealed a shape I recognised, the south coast of England in smudgy black and white. Surely, it had to include Hammerford, as one of the dark dots and symbols? Perhaps it provided a key to my particular mystery? Jasmine had sort of read my mind after all.

I had an idea. I took the poster down off the wall and rolled it up neatly. I'd decided what I'd do the next day and whom to speak to.

Chapter 48

Doorways of Time

I woke up at daybreak and lay in bed for a bit thinking about the poster. Jasmine at the Silver Unicorn had confirmed the reality of my experiences, with what she'd said. Maybe the poster would provide further confirmation. I hoped so. I needed to get to school early, but thought I'd just check the dream diary. Two pages were filled with neat writing.

I will tell you about where I live, Pale Boy. I am now near the biggest statue in the world. It is a lioness and she looks out towards the rising sun. According to my teacher Katesch, the First Builders carved her, at the beginning of time. That does not mean she is ageless, but Katesch told us that the doorways to time were closed when she was built and so we – that is me not you, Pale Boy – are at the beginning of time. We started in the Age of the Lion.

I don't always understand what Katesch says. I think she means I am at the start of things and you are at the end. She also suggested you and I will meet face to face before too long.

I have a new teacher now. She is a few years older than me. Her name is Hasina. She is rather strict but I think that's because she is shy. She says her job is to teach me about time.

I had not thought much about time till our lessons with Hasina. I thought my country – Hasina tells me you will know it as Egypt – had been around forever.

I do not really know what she means by the doorways of time. I once had a vision about a man who closed the doors of time. After he had done so, everyone who was alive then, and people lived for very long times in those days, gradually began to forget the times that had gone before.

Hasina says that certain priests and priestesses remembered, and so did some of the pharaohs, but ordinary people forgot. Anyway, she said it is all recorded in our Hall of Records, which is where I am now, as I think these words for you.

We had to start again. In the previous time some rulers made dreadful mistakes that offended the Gods. That is why the doors had to be closed.

I am living near the time when the Gates of Time were closed. You are living near the time when the Gates of Time will be re-opened.

In the Hall of Records, the priests can see how time will unfold. I don't understand how. Katesch says that is how we know about you and also how you know about us. The time you are living in is known as the Great Struggle or sometimes as The Last Battle. But all of us are involved in making sure that the servants of Set don't win.

Shoshan's writing just stopped at that point. I wasn't at all sure what it all meant, but sensed that the sphere and what it contained and also the visions I'd seen that night some weeks earlier, in the bandstand, were clues. I looked at my alarm clock and realised I'd have to grab a very quick breakfast if I was going to get to school early enough.

Chapter 49

Libraries Have Their Uses

The November sun warmed my back as I walked across the park. I stopped near the old oak tree. A couple of its huge lower limbs had special wooden struts sunk in the earth, to help the ancient tree bear their weight. I loved oak trees – so very British. Our kings hid in them according to the history books, and we used to build world-beating ships from their sturdy timbers.

I checked my watch. I needed to hurry. I had no free periods today and had to get to the library before school started. I took my bag off my back to make sure I had actually brought the map with me. The cardboard roll stuck out and I let out a sigh of relief. I'd not fancied running all the way home to retrieve it.

Despite the sun, my shoes were muddy when I reached the far side, near the Wild Wood. Sadness washed over me as I looked up at the conker tree and remembered Dave.

Miss Griffiths was the school librarian. She was okay in my books, as she liked me. I enjoyed listening to her talk. She'd a funny way of saying things that seemed both old fashioned and cool.

She wasn't on duty every morning, but as I walked in I could see her curly mouse coloured hair just peeping above the desk where she worked. She was reaching down to some pile of files on the floor. I went over and coughed.

"Good morning, Rhory," she said looking up by turning her head slightly. "Just give me a moment."

Librarians were born to serve. She finished inserting some

papers into the correct file and straightened up.

"What can I do for you, young sir?"

"Well, Miss, I was given something and I can't make sense of it and I wondered if you would be able to sort it out for me because it's written in some foreign language, which I'm unable to make sense of, and I think it may be important or not, I'm not really sure, but it might help me…"

"Goodness, its only eight thirty-seven, Rhory, and already I feel breathless. Why don't you just show me?"

So I did. I pulled out the rolled map and we pinned it down on her desk with paperweights. Librarians worth their salt have such things always to hand.

"Ah!" she said. I waited. She opened a drawer and took out a magnifying glass. She looked at the writing, closely printed down the left hand side. "Uh huh!" she said, smiling this time.

I shuffled from foot to foot. I waited some more, but also glanced at the clock. The fiddling with the map had eaten up some time and then two Year Sevens had come by, wanting to know where the mathematics section was, and that had taken time too. The clock said 8.53 and I had to be in assembly at 9am.

The phone rang and Miss Griffiths took the call. It was the Headmaster, who wasn't going to be kept waiting. At 8.55 I rocked back and forth on my feet, rubbing the back of my neck. Inside I wanted to scream. Miss Griffiths hung up, with a cheery, "Of course, Headmaster, that will be my pleasure." She even looked like she meant it.

"What do you reckon, Miss?" I asked, my voice almost steady.

"What I reckon is … well, more than reckon, in fact I'm pretty sure that this is a map." My heart sank. The woman was clearly simple-minded and a complete waste of space. "But not just any map, it's an old Welsh map made by those who are interested in the history of the druids. It shows the main centres of druidism before the Romans came along and closed it all down. Highly speculative of course."

"How do you know it's Welsh?" I asked.

"Because I'm Welsh, you silly billy." She gave me a big grin. "My degree was in the Welsh language before I did my diploma in librarianship. Seems I must have lost my accent with all these years in Hammerford!" At that moment the bell rang for Assembly. I started to roll up the map but Miss Griffiths laid her hand on it.

"Leave it with me, will you, Rhory, I'm interested. Come back at lunchtime."

I flew from the library, nearly ran straight into Hawk-Eye who said, "Steady, boy, the ship's not on fire is it?" I arrived at the main hall just before the staff marched in, gowns flapping, and weathering a frown from our house captain, joined others in my year.

History (bearable), Gym (great), Break (necessary), Maths (torture), Physics (worse) and then lunch time arrived. I looked for my script for the impending school play. Drat, I'd left it at home. My part involved playing a cow. It wouldn't be the end of the world if I arrived late to the lunch time rehearsal. Well, that's not true, as the play focused on Noah and the end of the world. I went to the library anyway.

I could hear the noise before I arrived. Schoolboys thronged everywhere. I had to wait while Miss Griffiths sorted out some Year Twelves who were doing a project on Rasputin. She'd explained that no one actually knew who had finally killed him. The boys disagreed with her, on the basis of a film they had seen on TV with the guy who plays Snape in Harry Potter. They left, still arguing, with books under their arms.

"Now where were we? Oh yes, I had a more careful look. Do you know it even shows Hammerford? For some reason in this Welsh map it's called Hummingfyrd, which must be an error, but it's in the right position."

"What do you think it means?"

"Means, Rhory, in what way?"

"Well, is it significant, Miss?"

"Mmm, that's an interesting question. I suggest that that is one for Mr Archer. He works at the main library, you know, the one by the park, opposite the carpet place."

"Yes, I know, Miss, I live near there."

"Oh, righty-ho, well you'll know then. Mr Archer works upstairs in the reference bit of the library. He's a history buff of sorts, and I know his interest is in pre-Roman Britain. He's a bit of an authority on that in fact, though you wouldn't know it to look at him. Say Gwyneth sent you."

"Gwyneth?" I said, feeling more than a little confused. Miss Griffiths rolled up the map without saying anything and slipped an elastic band down it. She looked up at me, over her glasses.

"Gwyneth Griffiths, silly. I've a first name as well you know, even if I do remember the time before Mrs Noah married." At that, she actually winked at me. For the first time ever, I wondered what on earth she did when she wasn't in the library. I collected the map and thanked her.

"My pleasure, Rhory, and good luck with the play."

"Thanks Mi— Oh my God, yes, the PLAY!"

I ran out of the library realising I'd get an ear bashing for being late for the animal rehearsal. I'd just remembered it was all about me and the two horses. I careered into the belly of a teacher wearing a suit and waistcoat.

"Goodness me, Bruce, are you auditioning for the running scene in Chariots of Fire?" Old Hawk-Eye. Again. I'd no idea what he meant.

"Sorry, sir, Mr Hawk Ey— Mr Hawksley, sir." He grimaced at me under his tufty white eyebrows.

"I won't say 'run along boy' because you'll take me at my word, so proceed with caution, Mr Bruce please, and remember people bruise easily."

"Yes, sir," I mumbled, and walked as fast as I dared to the rehearsal room.

The rehearsal went okay after I'd been chewed out for being late.

We animals learned our moves, and, wearing masks, we practised finding our way around stage when we couldn't see our feet. Normally this wouldn't matter, but the stage had huge platforms of wood, and the chance of tripping and falling in a clash of hooves and horse manes, remained an embarrassing risk.

Once in my bedroom for the night, I read through the account Shoshan had sent again, and wondered how all this related to the Greek boy and the druids, who'd once chanted in the oak grove of Hammerford Park. I placed the diary where I could reach it in the night, and settled down to sleep.

The next morning it lay as I'd left it, and I nearly didn't bother to look. I opened it at the entry written by me, but dictated no doubt by Shoshan from a few thousand years earlier. That whole concept made my toes curl just a little bit. I turned to the next page to discover fresh writing had appeared.

I tried to read it but failed entirely. No doubt it had been written by me, but the letters were funny. It looked like this:

Ελάτε να Κρότωνα, παρακαλώ, Δημήτρης

While some letters appeared to be in English, others looked like things I found in my science text books. I wondered about showing it to Juliette but decided I'd have to go into too much explanation. I copied the phrase as accurately as I could and decided to make use of the skills of Miss Griffiths once again.

Chapter 50

A Pool in Crotona

Miss Griffiths identified the writing as Greek and showed me how to find the right fonts on one of the library computers. I typed the words painfully slowly, into a translation programme on the internet. After a few spectacular errors, eventually the translation appeared. "Come to Croton, please, Dimitris."

Where on earth would I find ancient Croton? And if I did find it, who was to say it had not now disappeared in some earthquake or volcano. I went online and tried various searches. Eventually I found a place called Crotona. This had to be the one. It sat on the coast of Italy, a little bit above the boot, and looking at its history I found Pythagoras had his school there, a long, long time ago.

Now I knew where to go, but I didn't know how or why. I didn't think Dad would be too pleased to fund a trip to Italy and I doubted Scrivener's would see going there as more important than studying long division and the central nervous system of the earthworm.

I endured a tedious day at school with long division during Maths but no sign of earthworms in Biology.

Once home, I suffered tea with the family, listening to Jules discussing her university applications, and the value of Oxford over Edinburgh. I knew I wouldn't be likely to face a choice like that. I excused myself and carried Jester up to the bedroom, to have an in depth discussion with him about the Crotona problem. He couldn't concentrate, and after a bit of pouncing on imaginary mice, fell asleep.

Later that evening I'd negotiated the right to see the first half of

Everton versus Liverpool. Both Jules and I liked football and she supported Liverpool, so, of course, I supported Everton, when I could remember. Some quirk of fate had led to my having no homework that night. I kicked off my shoes and arranged myself on the bed, avoiding the contented bundle of fur breathing quietly in the middle. The match would start in an hour and a half. I lay there wondering about the weirdness of a boy from at least 2,000 years ago sending me messages, in Greek, via my dream diary. Even Nick might find that hard to believe.

*

The grass soaked through my socks. I'd arrived near the bandstand, in my school trousers and shirt but without any shoes. I even had on my school tie, the knot casually loose. A chilly wind gusted and dark clouds blocked out all starlight. At least I hadn't arrived in my pyjamas; then I would've been seriously cold. I could just make out the bandstand a short distance ahead. Light from faraway buildings and street lamps, provided weak illumination. A dark mass on my left showed the distant swimming pool, and behind me, a gloomy, cold darkness had swallowed the old oak. The faint noise of cars suggested I hadn't slipped back to the time of the druids. I swung around at a slight sound nearby but could see nothing. I eased my way forward, until my soggy socks registered the tarmac surrounding the bandstand. The wind cut right through my shirt and I shivered. As I reached the top of the bandstand steps, warm air swirled around me. Seriously strange.

Bright light dazzled me as I stepped into the bandstand. I could see nothing at all, my eyes struggling to adjust. I closed them, while raising my hands to shield the brilliance. Hot sunlight warmed my skin.

Squinting between my fingers, I could just make out trees sparkling in bright sunlight. I could smell something aromatic. My eyes eventually adjusted. A new doorway had appeared nearly opposite the bandstand entrance I'd come through. I walked closer. The ground fell away sharply. Ahead of me lay a valley with huge trees, rustling in the gentle warm breeze. The air had reached oven temperature, just like when Juliette made biscuits. Steps descended made of smooth white stone. I walked down a couple, and looking back, could still make out the entrance to the bandstand and the total darkness beyond.

A bird flew close by, and birdsong filled the air. In the light blue sky, a few impossibly white clouds drifted past. I took a deep breath of the fragrant, warm air and walked down a few more steps. My eyes adjusted to the intense light and I looked back. I'd walked through a wooden door, with huge brass studs, constructed in the wall of a low cliff. The bandstand had almost vanished entirely, although I could make out slight details from the sunlight reflecting onto the roof. I knew that if I walked much further away I might get lost and had no idea if I'd be able to get back to Hammerford once again. I looked up at a bird perched on a branch nearby and it twittered, flew off, did a circle above me in the clearing, and flew down the path on my right. I took this as a sign and followed.

The path meandered through dry grass and prickly bushes. I stubbed my toe on a protruding rock, and had to pick my way with care. Socks were not ideal for this goat track. The path curved back close to the cliff wall, now towering above me, and I noticed a small object in a nook in the rock. I lifted it up. It wasn't a tiny teapot, but it certainly looked like one, with a small spout and handle. I tipped it to see if it had any tea inside but only dislodged a spider. I dropped the object and shook the spider off my hand. Unfortunately the lamp, or pot or whatever, now had a chip on the spout. It fitted easily into the palm of my hand and I slipped it into my pocket.

The path split shortly after, one branch following the cliff face and the other descending between more tall trees. I looked around to see if the bird would act as my guide but couldn't see it anywhere. I checked back behind me to make sure I could find my way to the doorway again, and nearly jumped out of my skin.

A tall boy, chewing a long stem of grass, leaned on a rock that had hidden him as I walked past. It was the boy from the oak grove, the boy called Dimitris. He looked down at my feet, and then at my tie and finally at my face. He shrugged and took the grass out of his mouth. He spoke, saying something like, *"pa may ek hee."* Now, I shrugged. I searched around for some Latin, but the one year I'd done of that language, gave me nothing useful. The one verb I could remember, *'amo'*, meant 'I love you', and I didn't want to risk misunderstanding.

"Is this Crotona?" I said, and immediately a fuzz of embarrassment passed through me. It didn't really matter, did it? I'd found Dimitris. He frowned and then his face lit up with a grin, "Croton!" He then launched into more Greek, gesticulating as he spoke and pointing towards the path that descended between the trees. I used my fingers to make a mime of walking and pointed down the path. He moved his head back slightly and raised his eyebrows. I took this for a 'yes'.

"We need to meet my Teacher."

"All right."

"He will find us in Aphrodite's Grove."

"And that's this way?" I looked over at Dimitris and realised we were communicating just by thought. Cool. Really, really cool. That dealt with the language issue anyway.

"He told me to call you. I didn't know how to do that. He said I'd find the way. I could remember your face and your … your clothes, and I just imagined you here. Today, Teacher told me to wait for you on this path. He knew you would arrive."

I didn't know how to respond to that and we walked on in silence. The path descended quite steeply for a bit and I had to pay attention to where I placed my feet. Sharp stones had already wreaked havoc with my socks, and I had a slight limp.

"My sister is marrying him."

"Who?"

"Pythagoras. That's why I am here still. My sister is going to marry the Great Master." Dimitris looked across at me, his face blank.

"Is that good news?"

He walked on in silence for a bit, and then nodded slowly. "Theano, my sister, is happier than she has ever been. She says they have worked together before, in the times ... the times long past. It's strange. Pythagoras is older, much older than my father. But yes, it is good news, for me and for the world." I didn't know what he meant by that last shared thought, and we made our way down the path keeping our thoughts to ourselves.

I heard the sound of running water. The path turned to the right and passed under the dense foliage of trees, reaching up high above our heads. Shadows surrounded us and my eyes had to adjust to the dimmer illumination. Water gurgled into a roughly hewn rock basin. From there it cascaded over the edge into a dark pool, the bubbles dancing below the surface, reflecting the light of the sky. I walked over to the pool and looked in. Apart from the bubbles and a few reeds near the edge, I could see no bottom. Fragments of sky were reflected back from the ruffled surface. I wanted to drink. My thirst had crept up on me. I wondered if pool water would be safe, or if goats had peed into the spring, further up the mountain.

"It's safe and you should bathe." The voice, quite different to Dimitris's, rumbled warmly somewhere inside of me. I swung round and found two old men watching. One had curly white hair and a stocky build. He had the sort of tan you see on a fisherman, and his face crinkled with laughter lines. The other, taller and much paler, with long straight grey hair, kept his unsmiling eyes on mine. I recognised him, and for a moment I thought he'd been in some fantasy film or other. Then, I remembered the name of the druid – Abaris – the one from the oak grove. He bowed slightly at that, and words formed inside me, clear and precise like stones dropped into the pool near my feet.

"Welcome, Red King. It is good that you are here and that we meet up once again. Last time you had a trial to pass through and you did. No one could walk that path for you and you proved your strength. Today, you and your companion," he pointed with a golden stick towards Dimitris, "will forge a deeper bond, one which the powers of Typhon will not pull asunder."

"First," said the shorter man, "you should refresh yourself. Your journey has been further than you might imagine." He walked over to where the water tumbled into the basin, and filled two clay beakers. I took one and Dimitris took the other. We drank and both of us drained every last drop. No water had ever tasted so good. The energy of the mountain and the sunlight quivered through my limbs.

"It is well," said the shorter man with white curly hair, and wrinkled his nose. "Now you must bathe."

Dimitris looked over at me but I couldn't read his expression. I'm not very shy but didn't want to make a wally of myself. I assumed I had to strip off. I loosened my tie, wondering just how far I should go, and whether keeping my underpants on would be acceptable. A loud splash told me Dimitris had jumped in and I looked over to see him in the pool, his body swathed in bubbles. He had stripped off. I followed suit, feeling slightly absurd, as I sat on leaves and dry twigs, and pulled my damp socks from my feet.

The chill of the water drove my breath away, and I surfaced spluttering. I thought when I jumped in I'd touch the muddy bottom, but my feet found nothing at all. After the initial shock, all my aches and pains gradually washed away. I trod water for a bit, enjoying the sensation of the small cascade, pouring near my head, from the rock basin above.

"Come," said Dimitris's voice within me. I looked up to see his tanned, muscular body climbing out by steps, carved into the rock, at the far side of the pool. As I emerged, Abaris handed me a linen towel, and I dried myself. He gave me a tunic of soft white material, and some surprisingly comfortable leather sandals.

We stood under the limbs of the great tree, and the wind rustled the leaves above my head. The two men were behind us and one gently rested his hands on my shoulders. I closed my eyes and soft colours flowed around me. I thought the sunlight coming through the leaves must be causing this and opened my eyes. Every colour had a brilliance I'd never seen before and the birdsong sounded thrilling. I could almost understand what the birds sang.

The men walked in front of us, leading us into a clearing near the pool. They said something in Greek. Dimitris immediately kneeled and I copied him. Abaris walked over to a stone table, in front of a group of trees. He came back with a small pottery vial. First he placed his thumb on Dimitris's forehead and then he came and stood in front of me. He upended the vial over his hand and placed his thumb against my forehead.

The cool stickiness gradually melted and I passed through the aperture created by the oil. Surrounded by stars, I could hear the voice of the shorter of the two men. As he spoke in a language without words, the stars drew closer, moving around me. I could see in all directions at once. One sphere lit up around my heart, one below my feet and one above my head. The meaning of each flowed through me, as four more lights gathered on either side of me, and behind and in front. Illumined by these humming lights, I drifted towards three more spheres, softly pulsing, forming a triangle. Gradually, all the lights collected in front of me, a giant triangle made of ten globes. I could hear the wordless voice, as the globes changed colour and revealed countless patterns.

How long I drifted amongst these moving spheres of light I couldn't tell. While I watched I understood all I heard; and peace, softer and more gentle than anything I'd ever known, filled me. A deeper singing started, and I found myself back under the trees, with the leaves sighing overhead and the two men chanting.

"Come," said a voice inside me. "Follow." I opened my eyes and swayed a little. The colour had drained from Dimitris's face, and his eyes were watering. We walked over to the table and drank some more water.

The older of the two men sat down opposite us. His nose wrinkled as he fished inside his robe and drew out a small leather pouch. He unfastened the strings with slow deliberate movements, and emptied its contents into his hand. He arranged the smooth stones from his hands on the table. Ten stones formed a triangle with one at the top and four at the bottom. "This," he said, within my mind, "is the Tetractys. By this, and in the presence of the Gods, I swear." He looked over at the two of us, seated opposite him, with Abaris standing behind us. "All and everything is contained within this Decad. I give this, as a reminder to you, of all you've been shown this day. Each of you will, for a time, guard these stones, and the wisdom they contain. Now stand once more and receive the blessing of the Most High and the blessing of Pythagoras and Abaris."

He led us once more over to the edge of the pool. Kneeling somewhat stiffly, Pythagoras dipped his fingers into the water. He stood and flicked water over each of our heads. The water drops trickled slowly down my cheeks.

Abaris came and stood in front of me. "Close your eyes, Red King." I felt his hand on the centre of my chest. A warmth radiated from my heart right to the edge of my body. He pushed hard and I cried out.

I startled myself awake, to find tears trickling down my cheeks and Jester sleeping on my chest. Moments later a voice shouted, "Come on, Rhory, the kick-off is in two minutes." I splashed some water on my face and went downstairs.

I sat down as the commentator finished explaining the line-up of the two teams. I felt something in my right pocket. The lamp! I had to stand up, as my trousers were rather tight, and fished the object out of my pocket. Not the lamp, just my watch – I had put it there when the strap broke earlier in the day.

The sounds of the crowd and the commentator passed me by as I wondered about my experience. If I'd actually had the lamp it couldn't have been a dream. But I didn't. I touched my forehead between my eyebrows and felt a slight stickiness. I knew, just minutes before, I'd been in a pool in ancient Greece and had seen the mystery of the ten spheres of light. I could almost remember all I'd heard.

"Yes, yes!" shouted Juliette. Liverpool had just scored.

Chapter 51

Mr Archer and the Druids

I found it hard to concentrate the day after my visit to ancient Crotona. I received a serious wigging in maths, for not paying attention.

I had to get some answers and decided to follow up the information Miss Griffiths had given me about the town library. The library was only a few minutes' walk from our house, on the way to the park. Dad described the building as "Sixties brutalism," by which I think he meant the square shape, brick construction and flickering fluorescent lighting. To me it had always been a haven of delights, as the children's section had great books. I'd recently found the adult section worth exploring also, just that the books were longer and ruder.

I went to the desk and asked the man there if he was Mr Archer. He gave me an odd look. "No, I'm not. He's usually to be found upstairs."

"Upstairs?" I echoed. I don't think I'd really taken on board that the library had an upstairs.

"Yes, in the reference section." He helpfully indicated where the stairs started, somewhere between books on cooking and books on travel. No wonder I'd never noticed them before.

The washed out blue linoleum on the stairs revealed the scuff marks of a thousand shoes. I'd entered a different world. An empty corridor had offices on one side and a room with wooden bookshelves on the other. I went in.

I could only see two people in the room. One man, in a threadbare overcoat, sat hunched over a table. He had a pile of newspapers nearby and one open in front of him. The other sat at a desk on the far side of the room. Somewhere a light hummed.

As I approached the man at the desk didn't look up. His green jacket with leather patches at the elbows had certainly seen better days. It sat awkwardly on his rounded shoulders. His thinning dark hair had gunk on it, to slick it down.

I said, "Excuse me," and he held up his hand but didn't raise his head. Clearly, he'd something important to complete. The large book in front of him contained lots of tiny print, divided into columns; some sort of reference work.

Finally, he looked at me over the top of rather thick glasses and said a peremptory, "Yes?"

I fumbled in my bag for the map but it snagged on something. He tapped a pencil on the book, which only added to my discomfort. I finally retrieved the map without tearing it.

"Miss said I was to ask for you," I said.

"Who?"

"Er, Miss Griffiths..." I struggled to remember her first name, and then, "Gwyneth from Scrivener's." His face lit up and he looked quite human and friendly.

"I see," he said. "So what can I do for you?" It dawned on me that even though he probably arrived in the library when Julius Caesar came to pay his overdue fines, he just might be shy. I showed him the map and he immediately leant over it, tracing lines with his delicate fingers. He didn't seem to need a magnifying glass, and apparently could read the old Welsh script.

He looked up after a minute or so and said, "This is really interesting."

"Is it?"

"Yes, it is, if you know how to look and what to look for."

"Oh!"

"What's your name, young man?" I told him. "Well, Rhory, there are some who claim we don't know much about the druids." He paused and steepled his fingers. "That isn't really true. I've made a special study of pre-Christian religious movements in Albion."

"Albion, sir?" I asked.

"Oh, you don't have to call me sir," he said with a slight, nervous smile. "Just plain Thomas or Mr Archer will do."

'Thomas', that's also a Welsh name isn't it?

"So what does the map show, Mr Archer?" I asked, not using Thomas, as my toes would have curled. He didn't answer me directly, but pointed to the bottom right-hand corner. Although the map was printed, at this bottom part someone had hand written, "Checked by A.B. A.S.T.S." The date had become slightly smudged and lost in the copying process.

"A.B. is the person who checked the veracity of the map, and A.S.T.S. are the abbreviation of a semi-secret society founded, we believe, sometime in the eighteenth century. It persisted for at least one hundred years and may even exist now." He looked up at me again. "But we mightn't know if it's still secret." He gave me a conspiratorial smile.

"So what do the letters stand for?" I asked.

He crinkled his eyes and glanced over towards the other man, before leaning towards me. "We can't be absolutely sure," he said, with all the characteristic caution of a librarian, "but I'm pretty sure it stands for the Ancient Scottish Truth Society."

I'd no idea what on earth he meant and scratched my head.

"Why don't you take a seat, Rhory. There is much to explain here." And he did, at some length. I heard the occasional rustle from the decrepit man as he turned the pages of his newspapers, but mainly I just listened to Mr Archer.

He started his narrative with the sort of question the deputy head, Mr Wilson might throw out, to catch the unwary.

"Can you tell me any of the original names of the *English* Celtic tribes?" He emphasised the word 'English'.

I wasn't sure I knew the names of any of the tribes, but tried, "Mycenae?" He looked very perplexed for a moment and then actually laughed.

"Well, almost," he said. "You're thinking of Queen Boudicca's tribe, the Iceni. The fact is, Rhory, it's one of those questions no one can answer. The Romans comprehensively over-wrote the history of the English part of Albion, and we only have the Roman names of the tribes. It's different in Scotland and Wales of course. But in my view, the whole of Albion deserves to claim a Celtic heritage."

He went on to explain that the same was true of the real history of the druids. They were pretty much rubbished by the Romans, who stated, wrongly in Mr Archer's opinion, that our English druids had indulged in human sacrifice.

"The druids were deeply spiritual, or at least that's what groups like the Scottish Ancient Truth Society appear to believe." His eyes took on a faraway look for a moment.

"I like it here," he said.

I frowned.

Thomas Archer looked across at me as though appraising what level of intelligence and good will he was dealing with. He gave a slight sigh and I assumed that perhaps I'd passed whatever the test was.

"Yes," he repeated. "I like it here, because our little Hammerford Park is undoubtedly the site of one of the centres of druid learning. I believe this is where the apprentices, if we may call them that, came to learn the druidic wisdom. Much of the park once held a large oak wood you know."

I did. I nearly started babbling about my vision thing and Abaris and all, but thought better of it. I also realised why the far side of the park from where we lived had a road called 'Oakwood Lane'. I'd cycle up that road when going to visit Midlea.

"So that tree…?'"

"Yes," he responded to my incomplete question, "that is the last remaining tree of what was once probably a considerable forest. We believe…" He cleared his throat. "That is I think that the venerable tree was one of the twelve that would have made up their sacred grove. Look..."

He pointed back to the map, which I'd nearly forgotten.

"These bits down the right hand side..." He traced them with a long finger, with a perfectly manicured nail. "They are details of the druid sites drawn on the main map. Now, look at this one, labelled Hummingfyrd – Middlelea. If I'm not very much mistaken that's a detail of our park. Here's the old manor house, which is now part of the council offices, see? And these tiny drawings represent the trees that were still here in the middle of the eighteenth century. The dots represent the missing trees. If you add them up, you get to twelve."

"But it's not to scale. At that size it would cover an area greater than all of Hammerford and beyond, because it includes the edge of Midlea."

"True," he said. "Yes, you are right, but then this isn't meant to be an accurate map, it's a map for those who are interested in the work of the ASTS and the hidden spirituality of Albion. You'll see all over that they increase the size of the druid and Mithraic sites."

"Mythy whaty?" I said. His frown indicated he didn't appreciate that much levity for such a serious topic.

"Mithraic, Rhory, the places where the Roman soldiers worshipped Mithras. They often chose sites that were holy for the old religion and adapted them to their own use. If we find remains of a temple to Mithras, it often indicates that it was a holy site already, for the local Celts, if we can call them that."

"Is there a temple hereabouts?" I asked, a frisson of excitement giving me goose bumps all of a sudden. I wondered if it might begin to explain my own experiences in the park.

"Some believe so," he said, checking his watch. "Now, Rhory, I have to go to a meeting with the head librarian, in fact I should've gone a full five minutes ago. The ASTS published papers in the nineteenth century, in periodicals called 'The Quest Journal'. Some years ago a private benefactor, who had taken particular interest in the deeper history of Hammerford, gave the museum certain papers. You know where the museum is, don't you?"

I said I did, and he scribbled a quick note for the curator. Then, with a brief "Good luck," from him as he left, and, "Thank you very much, Mr…" from me, I found myself briefly alone in the upper room. Well, not alone of course, because the man with the newspapers now stared straight at me. I decided to go home.

At home, I remembered some aunt or other had given me a book that mentioned Mithras. I found the one, with a picture of Stonehenge on the front; it was from Aunt Sofia. Yes, Mr Archer was right. I lived in an area that the writer of the book claimed was both important to the druids and those Romans who followed the pre-Christian religion of Mithras. The author believed that at least one important temple must have existed in the Hammerford region. Perhaps the man at the museum would be able to tell me more.

Chapter 52

The Scarab Necklace

Egypt – the dawn of time

"Come, Shoshan, all is prepared."

Shoshan followed the young priestess down the stone corridor. The sloping floor gently glowed, as did the walls. She wondered if the direction took them under the Great Lioness statue. The corridors of time confused her and without a guide she'd have easily become lost. The walls contained beautifully carved coloured frescoes of the Gods, and she assumed this is how her guide navigated the subterranean city.

They approached the room with the great stone bowl, and found the massive wooden doors closed. Her companion knocked and the doors silently swung open. A fragrance enveloped them both; ahead of her a slight haze in the room came from the braziers, set on high tripods, producing the soft aroma.

Inside all the priestesses were seated. Katesch wore her ceremonial dark wig, as did all the other women. Shoshan once more found a fresh lotus lying in her chair, directly in front of Katesch, and across from the main wooden throne. *How did they find a fresh lotus here?* Her guide sat down in the chair on her left. Shoshan closed her eyes when instructed, and the other priestesses started chanting softly. Someone strummed a stringed instrument. After a time Katesch stood up behind her. Her words formed silently within Shoshan's heart. She opened her eyes and could see all the priestesses were listening, their eyes closed. Her companion touched her arm and Shoshan shut her eyes once more.

As Katesch sent out the words into their minds, Shoshan found pictures arising within. The images swirled around her, even as the thoughts of Katesch filled the room. Gods appeared, some with animal heads, and moved in stately procession. A huge globe rolled past, pushed by an enormous scarab beetle made of gold. Briefly a city, greater than any she'd ever imagined before, rose up, a city of crystal spires and palaces of light. No sooner had it appeared in all its glory, than it started to sink into fathomless water. Shoshan could hear, far, far away, the anguished cries of uncountable crowds as they tried to flee a terrible calamity.

This vision gradually faded, to be replaced with a simple temple built close to the fertile shores of their great river. In it sat a pharaoh and his queen on stately wooden thrones, set on a floor of shiny black stone. The man held in one fist a cloth roll, curled like a small shepherd's crook. The woman had a large gold ankh, which she grasped by the loop. Between them sat a lioness, its paws stretched out in front. This lioness had a blue pectoral of lapis lazuli around its throat.

As the doors opened, the two pharaohs looked up and greeted their Teacher. He strode in, a man unusually tall, wearing the simple linen robes of a priest. His sandals, cleaned of dust by servants in the outer courts, gleamed golden in the soft light. *Surely*, thought Shoshan, *surely he looks a bit like Captain Gruff, just a younger version.*

He knelt before the pharaohs.

"It is for us to kneel, O my Teacher."

"Come, sit." The queen's words floated through Shoshan's mind, for the woman in the vision did not open her mouth when she spoke. She started to stand.

"No," resounded from the tall man. "Of course I kneel to Ra, for you are Ra when you occupy the solar throne. So to Ra I kneel, not to his earthly representatives, whom I love." The queen sat once more and both she and her husband inclined their heads.

After kneeling for a while in silence, the tall man stood. He raised his arm slowly and as he did so the lioness also rose to her feet and lowered her head to him. “Listen.” The word radiated around the temple.

Shoshan heard a great rushing, the sound of the movement of a mighty river and a boundless ocean. The vision of the pharaohs in their palace, slowly receded, to be replaced by the tall man standing at the end of an enormous gorge. Shoshan stood with him as he looked across a plain. Before them rose beautiful cities and towns, of a mighty civilisation from long, long ago. Parts would become clearer and closer as she looked at them, and she began to drift towards a crystal palace, glowing on a low hill, near the horizon.

“No!” The man’s voice thundered within her. A force carried her back.

He raised both his arms. From either side, a great grinding noise drove all her thoughts away. Two mighty doors, of a height she couldn’t even guess, slowly began to close. The man stepped back further and Shoshan’s eyes filled with tears, as this half-remembered world gradually diminished. The view of the crystal cities and purple hills became ever thinner, until only a crack remained. Then with a sound as final as the end of days, the doors closed and fused into a solid barrier of rock reaching up to the clouds above.

Darkness enveloped her. The man had gone. She stood alone and lost. She’d no idea where or how to get back or where to return. Time stopped. Terror filled the young priestess. Even her own name had fled from her mind. She called out to the man.

A hand, gently took hers, and she found herself back in the temple with the pharaoh and his queen. The tall man stood, the lioness now by his side. He bowed to the pharaohs.

“You have seen.” His words emanated from all sides of the temple. “The Gates of Time are closed. We are now in an Age being born and you are the parents of this Age.” He bowed again to the pharaohs. “The past will gradually fade, and in years far down the river of time’s journey, will be seen as fable. If it is seen at all.” He bowed one more time, and stayed bowed for many breaths. “Build this new world wisely and build it well. I will walk with you where

I can. But I cannot do what it falls to the children of Ra to accomplish. Even with the closing of the Gates, the great division remains and must be healed."

He looked long at the pharaohs, and slowly turned. As he and the lioness walked across the dark reflective floor of the temple, the scene faded and Shoshan could once more feel the wood of her seat, in the room with the stone bowl. She opened her eyes. All around her, soft chanting continued.

In the throne opposite her sat the tall man. He looked directly at her and shards of lightning passed down her spine. His eyes had the depth of universes. *I'm sitting opposite a God. Am I dead?* Shoshan looked around to see if Osiris in his deathly shroud stood near.

"My child. You are not dead." The man raised his right arm, palm facing towards Shoshan. "Your eyes have opened for the first time this life. We welcome you. You are a bud of the Flower of Life and have been shown one of the great secrets of Time. Guard it well. It is not for all to see but much is expected of you."

His face did not change from granite stillness but his smile carried her to the outer courts of heaven. She'd never tasted such joy before.

"I am not a God, though some will claim I am in years to come. We all are Children of the Gods, as indeed are you. Your destiny touches mine, as it does all gathered here. You are the first link of a chain that must be forged and not broken. When your eyes are closed to the shimmering of this world, you will ever find my voice within, and that of your sisters. Ask when you are lost, even as you did just now, and you will hear. You are the ears for that chain of golden souls that stretches even now to the evening of time far, far away."

For a brief moment the Pale Boy stood in front of Shoshan, the one with the strange kingly name. He looked up at the great gates, even as she just had. When she opened her eyes again, the throne in front of her had no one sitting there. Gradually the voice of Katesch filled the room once more.

"We see as we see, and as the Gods decide. We have a new sister, for she has travelled, even as we, to the very borders of Time. Come, child, stand."

Shoshan stood and Katesch walked to stand between the bowl and the young priestess. The girl from her right moved forward also, carrying a tray with a blue cloth. On the cloth lay a necklace, with a pendant.

"Look well, Shoshan."

The pendant was formed from crystal, in the shape of a scarab beetle, clasped in gold. Katesch held the golden chain and placed it gently around Shoshan's neck. Her fingers rested lightly on the scarab as these words formed around Shoshan, "Wear this as a sign you serve truth and truth alone. Like truth, this crystal will pass from the birth till the ending of this age. Be its guardian, even as you will guard your words and thoughts. May the Blessed Her-Mes watch over you even as he watches over all of us, and may we prove steadfast servants of The Scribe."

Chapter 53

An Old Journal

England – about now

I took the longer route to school, by the pavement around the outside of the park, as the rain had made the grass inside the park really muddy. The wind released water drops, dangling from the trees reaching over the park wall, making my own personal shower. Cars shushed past on the wet road. Spots of rain blew in my face.

The sphere remained a locked mystery, linking somehow to druids and oak groves, and to a boy from Ancient Greece. Dimitris had led me to Pythagoras through his beautiful sister Theano. I knew her lovely face as I'd seen it when I felt seasick in my bedroom. The whole business, frankly, now had elements of serious weirdness. And to top it all, my diary held the letters from a long dead Egyptian girl, who reacted to me in real time, something dead people couldn't do, as far as I knew.

I kicked at a shiny brown conker lying on the pavement and watched it bound and bounce ahead of me. Mr Archer had proved helpful. Hopefully tonight I'd get a chance to go to the museum before it closed. I had his introductory note safely by my bed at home.

I liked Hammerford Museum. Using all the little rooms in one of Hammerford's oldest houses, it lay on my old route to and from my primary school. I'd always loved going in when I could. In the first room, various man-traps, with their vicious metal teeth that could cut halfway through a poacher's leg, grinned their metallic grins. Gruesome.

I kicked the conker again, it ricocheted off the park wall and towards the highly polished black shoes of the man Nick and I had hit with paper pellets. He looked up at me, and must have just seen a lanky schoolboy, not his blowpipe wielding nemesis. He had a scowl on his face as he walked past and his eyes caught mine.

The sensation of ice being forced into eyeballs wasn't nice. A shiver coursed straight through me. Something about this man gave me the creeps. I walked on keeping my head down and hoping the fact he'd stopped, didn't mean he'd remembered me. Then I remembered him. I'd seen him before. I recalled the eyes and the way he scowled. He'd been in the British Museum with some tarty girl when I first saw Shoshan. I desperately wanted to turn and look back, but decided that would be really unwise. If I remembered him, perhaps he'd now sussed me out.

What had Shoshan written? *The servants of Set.* I shivered again; the rain began to trickle under my shirt collar. This well-dressed man and duck shooter, was connected somehow with Set, the Egyptian desert god and all time bad guy. I didn't know how, but I knew it was so. *Another moment of high weirdness.* I quickened my pace and a few moments later turned left into Mercer Road. School now lay a little over five minutes away.

That evening, the main road shone with wetness, as I cycled down towards the museum. My lamp picked up the occasional flashes of rain, and my hands chilled as the dampness and wind whipped past them. I patted my pockets for gloves but with no success. In the distance I heard the wail of a fire engine or police car.

A car passed close by, and I nearly clipped the pavement. I glowed in the dark, with the bright yellow bands that Mum insisted I wore, so the car had no excuse. My little red light winked valiantly on my bike. A blue strobe light flashed behind me as well, accompanied by loud wailing. I glanced back to see bright headlights and pulled over to allow a police car to weave past. A few minutes later I'd arrived at the Town Hall, which dominated the top of the road leading down to the Parish Church. I'd attended primary school near here. Half way down The Causeway, lay the entrance to the museum.

Two police cars blocked my way. I could hear shouts in the distance. I turned to the right of the Town Hall where the road had not yet been cordoned off. I could only get halfway down before a fireman shouted, "Get back numbskull, it's dangerous."

Beyond the fireman, on the right hand side of The Causeway, the walls and windows wobbled and shimmered in flickering light. Something blazed opposite, hidden by the bulk of the Town Hall. At least the rain would help dampen the fire. I wouldn't be going to the museum today. I turned the bike around, and headed home.

"I know, I actually saw it."

"You were there?" asked Nick.

"Yeah, I wanted to see the museum."

"But it was the museum which burned."

"You're kidding me."

"No, really, Rhory, the local radio carried the story this morning, I heard it as my mum drove me to school. The museum's been gutted."

I stared at him. *Just a coincidence, surely? But strange it happened just before I'm about to meet the guy who might help me with the map and all.*

"Did anyone get hurt?"

"I'm not sure, mate, they didn't say. I guess not then, as they like the grizzly details if there are any. Most of the exhibits escaped, and they think the fire covered up an attempted burglary"

A cold puddle settled at the bottom of my stomach. I decided I'd go down again after school and see for myself.

The rain held off when I cycled to the Town Hall once more. I couldn't see any evidence of yesterday's fire as I walked down The Causeway. The trees swished around in the chilly wind, and the streetlights became weak strobes. I pulled my hood closer around my ears, in case the brass monkeys arrived.

Around the door to the museum, black soot smudged the brickwork. The main window to the downstairs room had been replaced by a wooden board, and this was where the fire must have done most damage. The windows of the first floor stared out in dark blankness at the street. No lights were on, and the museum remained as shut as the tomb of the Unknown Soldier.

I heard a step on the pavement behind me. My collar tightened around my neck and I struggled to catch a breath. "Come to look at your handiwork, my young friend?" I twisted, but the grip of my assailant increased. "I don't take kindly to arsonists."

I kicked backwards and shoe met bone. Now I could breathe and spun round, at the same time as stepping back. The man rubbing his shin looked at me from blazing eyes.

"*I* didn't do this. All I wanted to do was come to the museum yesterday and see the coroner," I shouted.

The man's mouth dropped open. He straightened up.

"I've a note from..." I couldn't remember the librarian's name. "I was told to come and see..." I fumbled in my pocket for the note. I found it and pulled it out.

"Here, this is for the coroner."

Still the man stared, smiled and finally laughed out loud. "Rhory! Rhory Bruce. Look I'm sorry, I'm just stressed out of my head at the moment."

When I heard his voice properly I realised that this was the ... what had I said? I knew him because he belonged to the same amateur dramatic society as Dad.

"I think you meant curator, Rhory." He chuckled. "Yes, Mr Archer told me he'd found someone with an interesting map." He reached across and took Mr Archer's note, and carried it over to the street lamp. Looking up, he continued, "Well, you'd best come inside, young man."

I still couldn't remember his name. "Thank you, Mr..."

"You can call me Cyril. And by the way, I'm the curator here. Look it even says so on the brass plate: Curator C. Stanhope." With that he opened the door and led the way inside. Using the streetlight to find his way, he picked up a large torch from a table and switched it on.

"No electricity down here though, I'm afraid. And, Rhory, I must apologise for being so rough. You see, I saw one of the yobs running away after they started the fire and he looked similar to you, in a hood."

"That's okay" I said, my face still warm from mixing up the words curator and coroner. The smell of petrol and singed wood, greeted us. We crunched over some broken glass, and I could tell that the room had been searched, with cupboards forced open. The mantraps on the wall watched us, with their metallic mouths open. I followed him up the stairs. Pictures and animal heads on the wall bobbed in and out of the beam of light and took on a life of their own. Upstairs the effects of the burglary showed in the three small displays on our left. Cabinets had been moved and a glass case broken.

A woman knitting, looked at us with flashing eyes, but didn't get up. Behind her, an equally small man held a book and his mouth moved silently. I nearly wet my trousers until I realised these were waxwork figures, appearing lifelike in the torchlight. The room in front of us reproduced life in a mid-nineteenth-century cottage, typical of Hammerford.

Cyril stepped across the velvet rope barrier, into the exhibit, and said, "Follow me, Rhory, but be careful not to knock anything over. Luckily the thieves missed what was most obvious." The curator tapped on a small door at the back that looked like part of the stage set for the diminutive knitter. "This is an actual door that no one thinks is real." He unlocked it, and we both had to duck, to enter the small landing with stairs going down steeply on the right. After a few uneven steps, they turned sharply by ninety degrees. Reaching the bottom, we found ourselves in a small kitchen, opening directly onto an office. The lights in this bit of the house still worked.

"Long ago, the society that owned these two houses, made these changes, putting in this extra space behind the house next door. It enabled the members to have meetings in a room that no one realised existed." Cyril led me past the large mahogany desk in the office, to another door that opened onto a further room. The light revealed coloured murals. The walls displayed frescoes of figures with animal heads as well as muscular men and ample women, in various states of undress. A flash of fear shot through me as I wondered if Cyril had designs on me that were not about helping me with a puzzle.

"These are over a hundred years old, Rhory, but look as fresh as the day they were painted. The society used these pictures in their teachings. You can see the main nine gods of the Egyptian Pantheon and the twelve from ancient Greece."

I looked again, my heart beating right up against my neck. The paintings probably told a story as they flowed around the four walls. A faint aroma of something musky and a little sweet, remained in the room. A smell like you get in one of those Cathedrals in France.

"It looks a bit like the prima ... prima ... prima donna?"

Once again the curator looked utterly baffled, and then cracked up laughing. "Rhory, you are priceless! Yes, I know what you mean, but I think the picture is the *Primavera*, by Botticelli."

"That's the one," I said, feeling about five centimetres tall once more. "We had a talk about it in art."

"Come back to the office. I wanted you to see this room though, as you are interested in spiritual things, and this is one of Hammerford's hidden treasures. Please don't mention it to any one, Rhory. Even today there are those who will attack people who are interested in the wisdom of the ages."

I sat down next to the great desk, and Cyril opened some glass cabinets on the far side. "This is our archive," he said, revealing several shelves of leather bound volumes. Most had a golden squiggle of some sort on the back. He pulled out four that covered the years 1832–1844. The squiggle on the back was made up the letters T,Q and J curling around one another. Inside, pages and pages of small print, all at a slight angle, challenged even my eyes. And I've never needed glasses. My heart sank, and then dropped a bit further. The thick volumes must run to hundreds of pages each. Anything of value inside them would be well hidden. I investigated the first journal. Diagrams of carvings and symbols of different kinds had been painstakingly etched, but the print still defeated me, and I couldn't see how this would help me solve the puzzle of the sphere.

"I'll fix a cup of tea," said Cyril, and went to the kitchen next door.

I put the first volume down and picked up a second at random. At the front was an introductory page that said,

The Quest Journal

Dedicated for the understanding of Ancient Truths
in the Context of Modern Society
1835–1838

Published by ASTS

And then there was an address in Aberdeen and an address in Madras, India.

"Do you take milk and sugar?"

"Just milk," I said to the disembodied voice from the kitchen.

I flipped through the pages, balking at the smudged print. I found further pictures. Various animals, perhaps copied from old woodcuts, had been drawn with considerable care. A number of birds and wild creatures, as well as various domesticated ones, stared out at me. Each included a commentary. In something called Rosicrucianism these animals had a symbolic meaning, or so the opening paragraph said.

The article had no author's name, just his initials, *A.B.* The heading stated,

Heraldic and Symbolic Animals
The cryptography of printers.

A long time before the printing of this journal, the makers of paper had hidden messages in the watermarks. Some of the watermarks displayed animals and A.B., whoever he was, explored their meaning in this article. I wondered if any of the animals were ones that appeared on the sphere.

As I thumbed through the writing I couldn't find any. My shoulders sagged, and I rubbed the sides of my head. Looking underneath the sloping columns of print, I noticed a message in a different font. I held it near to the table lamp. It said, *'Part two to be continued next Quarter'*. I looked further ahead in the fat volume. There were articles on lunar cycles, a history of the Little People of Ireland, a learned paper about the Alchemist Paracelsus, or at least that's what the title said. Then I found the part two of the article by A.B.

Here, the heading had changed to,

Symbolic Animals and the Flower of Life.
Part two of a preliminary exploration of Animals in Heraldry
By A.B.

A diagram filled a whole page. I started checking what animals had been included. It had seven of them to be precise, seven that also appeared on the sphere. I leaned back in the swivel chair and breathed out a long whoosh of air.

"You've found what you are looking for then?" said a voice behind me, to the sound of cups of tea rattling on a tray.

Chapter 54

Cracking the Sphere

Cyril put the tray of tea on the desk. He sat opposite me and passed over a cup. "I found some biscuits. I don't think they are stale."

The tea tasted great and the biscuit didn't disintegrate as I dipped it in the warm, brown liquid. "Ah, another person who likes dunking biscuits," said the curator, copying my behaviour. He ate some damp biscuit and followed it with a sip of tea. Pointing to the fat volumes between us on the desk, he said, "They are rather difficult to read I think, aren't they?" I agreed. "But I can assure you they are worth it. The people in that society certainly knew a thing or two. And at least one of the contributors used to live around here, I'm sure of it."

"Could I get a copy of this picture?" I asked, pointing to the seven animals.

Cyril went over to a photocopy machine on the far side of the room. When he returned, I showed him the same map I'd shown Mr Archer and Miss Griffiths. He moved the old journals and spread the map out on the desk. "I agree with Thomas," he said. "This does show places where the Society believed pre-Roman druid schools operated."

"Schools?"

"Not like Scrivener's, certainly," said Cyril, smiling. "But schools nonetheless. We believe people travelled from all over to attend and were trained in many mysteries. It was these mysteries that were hidden once the Romans arrived. They had more interest in power and wealth than mystery and spirituality. Which of course is true of our leaders to this very day."

As we walked back through the shambles of the main part of the museum, the curator told me about the old map room at the Town Hall. "If you can get one of your history teachers to write you a note, then you might get to look in the map archives. You may find a more detailed map of Hammerford there and that could be of use to you."

We crunched our way past the singed front door, and he held out his hand. "Good to see you, Rhory. Say hello to your mum and dad for me. It seems you've an interesting project underway. If I can be of further assistance let me know. And remember, what you saw tonight is just between the two of us. It's best that way."

He moved to go back in the door, and then turned and said, "The Society exists to help at times like this. Don't forget."

I didn't know what he meant, and went to collect my bike. I checked I had the map and also the photocopy. The wind had picked up, although the rain still held off. I unlocked my bike, and heard a soft mechanical noise. A large, expensive car pulled away on the far side of the road, driving in the direction of the town centre. It had shaded windows. Something caught my eye on the pavement, picked out by the light of the street lamp. *A pencil stub producing smoke?* Intrigued, I went over and picked it up. The cigarette glowed. I'd never seen one like it before. Black, rather than white paper, with aromatic tobacco. A thin band of gold circled the top of the filter. For a moment I had the strangest sensation that a huge eye looked at me from somewhere and I dropped the fag end as though it had burned me.

I had to rush through my homework, and expected my marks would not be all they could be, as I found it very hard to concentrate. After tea, I mumbled some excuse about needing to learn my lines for the school play and scuttled up to the bedroom. Mum gave me a strange look but said nothing. When I reached the sanctuary of my bedroom, I remembered that being the cow in the play, meant I had no lines. Oh well.

I took the walnut box from my wardrobe and unlocked it. Carefully I extracted the wooden sphere and laid it on the bed next to the photocopy of the page from 'The Quest Journal'. The original had been quite smudgy and even a good photocopy couldn't make it clearer. The picture showed seven images of animals, arranged in a formal pattern. Three were in a crescent shape on top and three in a lower crescent. In the middle position sat a pelican.

The top three animals were a horse, a hawk and a snake. The bottom three were an owl, a web-footed bird with a long beak, and a crocodile. I found each of these animals carved on the sphere. I knew the hawk moved slightly. Once more I started with that bird, and using both hands and my stomach I managed to press the owl, without dropping the sphere. The hawk moved as normal and the owl moved as well. With both depressed, I could make the wading bird move. But when I pushed the pelican, the others popped back out and I returned to square one.

I started again. When I had the first three pushed in I then pushed on the crocodile. It gave a little. My hands started to sweat and the sphere slipped a bit. After some trial and error I found I could complete the sequence with the snake and the horse. Pushing the pelican last did not do a 'reset'. Rather, I heard a satisfying 'ping' sound and the sphere opened. It now had an irregular crack that ran above and below the seven animals on the meridian of the Sphere. Carefully, I lifted the two halves apart, and found another globe inside.

For a while I just sat staring. I could hardly breathe and my heart thumped away. I wiped my hands on the coverlet of my bed. Jester stretched and produced an enormous yawn. An aroma of old fish briefly passed my nostrils.

I tapped the black globe with my nails. The slight 'ting' sound suggested metal. Close inspection revealed scratches or markings. The globe had a line running around its circumference. Perhaps it would come apart at this line. I tried. There was no movement at all. I put it down and looked back at the wood.

The two halves lay on the bedroom carpet, and resembled the irregular peel of an oversized orange. From the inside I could see an intricate system of wires and joints made of curved brass. I looked at both halves carefully.

Apart from being amazed at the brilliance of the construction, it offered no further clues to my particular mystery here. I turned back to the inner, black sphere. Again, I tried to unscrew the two halves, if that's what they were. No movement at all, my hands just slipped, slick with sweat. I walked around the room and only just resisted stamping my foot.

I'd solved the puzzle but now had a further enigma that told me nothing at all. There must be something inside this metal sphere, but I couldn't see a way in that didn't involve force.

I put the metal object down, and looked out the window. In the near darkness, the huge skeletons of the trees swayed and shook in the winter wind. Their spindly branches, illumined by the glaring yellow of North Road's streetlights, offered a sinister dance of shapes and shadows.

I decided to talk to Dad, and draw on his practical skills. I heard him going past my room with his customary breathy whistle, a sort of tuneless tune that accompanied him as he went about the house.

"Dad?" I called, and he stopped. "If I had a tin lid that was screw top and stuck, what should I use to open it?"

"There's two answers to that, Rhory," he said. "The first is elbow grease and the second is magic fluid."

"No, don't mess around, Dad, this is important."

"I'm not messing about, Rhory, I wish I'd the patent on the formula. You need WD40. It really is magical. If you don't have the strength then this will usually work, unless the screw top is damaged or rusted."

Now that rang a bell with me. The next crucial question was, "Do we have any?" The answer was in the affirmative, and in the stable.

I set off to our workshop next to our garage. We call our workshop 'the stable' because it used to be one. Our house, small though it is, had had a garage where a carriage was kept and next door was the stable for the horses. The straw had been stored in the loft upstairs – now my dad's architect's office. The house had been built during Queen Victoria's reign, and was completed well before motor cars were much in evidence. We still came across bits of straw occasionally, but had never found a horse.

With the WD40 in hand I returned to my bedroom. Using the stiff, red, very narrow tube provided with the tin, I carefully squirted the dark, thin liquid along the line where the two parts might move. The smell of the liquid was really quite compelling and I enjoyed the aroma, until I realised that black drops were falling on the carpet.

A flannel from the bathroom next door and some swift rubbing and mopping, removed most of it. I rested the metal globe on an old maths notebook, and black dribbles made stains on the front. After five minutes or so, I tried to open the metal globe. It unscrewed effortlessly. WD40 is magic indeed!

Feeling immensely clever, and with my heart about to burst through my ribs, I opened the two halves, my sweaty hands squeaking on the metal.

Chapter 55

Opening the Way

A very distinctive smell arose from the open globe, camphor or something like that; like the smell in your granny's wardrobe, where her unused dresses hang. The kind of smell insects fly away from, with good reason.

Inside the globe lay silky material, with a crackly feel about it that suggested it might crumble if handled too roughly. I gently eased it out and discovered spidery writing in faded black ink. It reminded me of the copperplate style I'd seen in Great-Aunt Bridget's leather notebook, the one she hid in the commode. I put it gently to one side. *One hundred years old, two hundred?* I'd no idea.

The objects cocooned in the fragile material each had a silk bag of their own. I unwrapped them one at a time, and laid them in a line on the bedroom carpet. Jester thought this was a game, and started to pounce on the objects as I revealed them. Saying "Jester," sternly, didn't work, so I put him out and closed the bedroom door.

I had in front of me:

two black halves of a metal globe;
some grains of what looked like rice;
a large square of old silk with writing on it;
a coin of some sort, bigger and thicker even than an old penny, with Greek letters on either side;
a small silver thimble;
a small pendant with a transparent stone in it;
a silver sphere that looked like the end off of something, and

a very worn leather bag, with a drawstring.

I opened the leather bag and found it had tiny round black beads or polished stones. I placed it carefully back on the bed and hugged my arms. I'd seen this bag and these stones when I met Pythagoras in Croton. I rubbed my temples with my hands and could feel the sweatiness. I took a few deep breaths but the feeling of totally unreality still swamped me.

I had the answer to what the wooden sphere contained, but I seemed to have replaced one puzzle with six or seven more. After all that had happened today I suddenly felt very, very tired. I decided to let Morpheus do his work and get some sleep. Perhaps the further answers would come in a dream. *Well I can wish can't I?*

I carefully packed the metal globe up again and put it, and the two halves of carved wood, back in the wooden box, and stowed everything safely in the wardrobe.

A bowl of cereal and a glass of milk later and I was ready for bed. I put the dream diary and a pen or two, strategically on my bedside table. I fell into a deep sleep.

Waking but not waking is a nightmare. I could hear nothing in the room. I couldn't move. The zombie state had struck again. A sick terror tightened all my muscles. I tried to move my arms but to no effect. I tried to open my eyes but couldn't even flutter an eyelash. Before I could send a neural message to my toes, where salvation lay, I just knew that the jackal-headed man had arrived once more in my bedroom. Even with my eyes closed I could almost see him. I could certainly smell him; the room filled with incense. I just knew he'd a grey dog-like face and – a strange detail – a wide necklace of gold.

I sensed he stood in the middle of the room at the end of my bed, looking both at me and sort of through me. I willed myself awake, forcing myself to move, and sat up while sucking in a yelping kind of breath. I looked to where the jackal-man had been.

There he stood, not a picture this time, a 3D man, with an animal's head. How come I didn't scream or wet the bed, I don't know.

He didn't fade away. His arms, a dark tan colour, had golden bracelets, set with stones of various colours. He held a wand or rod and pointed it towards my bedside table. I plucked up courage to ask him a question and as I did, he just vanished. One moment an ancient Egyptian god, skilled at embalming corpses, stood in my bedroom, and the next, I was staring open-mouthed at an empty carpet. I sniffed. The aroma of incense lingered, a smell quite distinct from the camphor in the sphere. My heart rattled away inside, threatening to come off its moorings.

I don't know how long I sat like this. Gradually the rest of the room – those bits not taken up with this all-too-real apparition – came back into focus. The branch shadows shifted slightly on the wall, next to the whitish blur of the new poster. Opening the sphere had clearly let some sort of genie out of the bottle, or out of the silver globe in this case. He had taken up brief residence in my bedroom

I put on my bedside light. I thought I ought to write some notes in case this had all faded like a really bad dream when I awoke again in the morning. I turned to the next clean page and found instead of blank paper, a detailed picture of the dog-headed man, drawn from the side, with one foot slightly in front of the other. In his right hand he had a staff with a sort of head on it. In his left hand was something I recognised, an ankh. Underneath, written in very bold but neat handwriting, were the words,

The Way is Open

Chapter 56

A Visit to Midlea

Thinking about the all too real apparition in my bedroom the previous night brought my heart to my mouth. Dreams becoming reality left many possibilities and none of them attractive. And the words in the diary saying, 'The Way is Open', hardly proved comforting. If the way had been opened, then things could come in. I could be nervous enough in the dark in my bedroom anyway, without the possibility of a High Road to other times and dimensions ending up by my wardrobe. I had to do something, but what? And how did it all connect with the sphere? I texted Natasha and she suggested I came over on Sunday when her exams would be over, and the school play out of the way.

I collected my books for school and searched frantically for my copy of the school play. Not that I really needed it but it showed where I moved on stage and when I had to say 'moo'. Tonight was the full dress rehearsal.

I had to wander on and off stage in a generally bovine way. I wore a cow headpiece, made of rubber, in which I sweated – a cheap, local sauna for my head. However, no words meant no stage nerves. I suppose it is the equivalent of having a brown paper bag on your head to give you security? By twisting the mask, I could appear to be listening to Noah or Mrs Noah, while secretly observing the audience. I enjoyed having no lines and less stress! Perhaps I'd graduate to a speaking part next year.

On Sunday, breakfast and homework done and dusted, I set off for

Midlea. Getting out of bed had been a real struggle as I'd been up late the night before, enjoying the post play party. I had not hit the sack until after midnight.

It was a typical December day, a bit drizzly, a bit chilly, and a bit windy. Gusts came from directly in front of me, especially when climbing hills. I carried the precious metal globe in my small backpack, carefully wrapped in a small towel. The stiff, wet breeze meant I had to walk most of the way up Lucky Dog Hill. The wind carried the rainwater inside my sensible, bright yellow, cycling jacket.

I arrived, chilly and damp, at Nat's house, to be greeted by both her dogs and synchronised barking. They leapt up and down, raced in circles, and put their paws in particularly vulnerable places.

"Moo, moo…" said a voice from the top of the stairs.

"Thank you, Nat, I shouted back."

"Well at least you didn't forget your lines, Rhory." Nat sniggered. "You were moo perfect. Is it true that the director had you doing method acting?" I didn't miss the insult, with its suggestion of really getting into a cow's personality.

"Ho, ho, ho, Nat," I replied.

"Oh, is it Christmas already? I thought I heard Santa." With that she reached the bottom of the stairs and the dogs had another target for their paws and enthusiasm. Her mum came into the hall.

"Do you want something to drink," said Aunt Sofia. I said no and Aunt Sofia continued, "I think it was a really good play, Rhory, and we enjoyed seeing you tower over the other animals on the stage!"

"I agree," said a voice from the kitchen. It was my uncle, Dad's older brother.

"Hi, Uncle Arthur" I said back. "Are you home from your travels?"

"Yes, Rhory, I'm back for Christmas now, and won't be travelling again till mid-January. Of course I'll have to go to my office in London quite a bit, but at least I will see more of Sofia and Nat than I usually do!"

"That's not necessarily an advantage, Dad," said Nat. But I knew she didn't mean it as she was close to her dad and missed him when he was in Prague or wherever. She gestured to me to follow her upstairs, and I did, climbing them in my damp socks, having taken off my sodden shoes.

Chapter 57

"Theano existed!"

"Goodness," she said, looking at me, "you are a damp squib aren't you!" She threw me a towel to dry my hair. "I'll turn up the heating," she continued. "We don't want you to expire before Christmas." She did just that and then said, "So, what on earth's been happening? I haven't really been able to make sense of your messages. What was it you found? You opened the sphere, didn't you?"

"Just a min, Nat," I replied, "I'll show you. It will be quickest." I took the bundle from the backpack and unwrapped the metal globe. I straightened out the cover on her bed, so we had a flat surface, and carefully unscrewed the two hemispheres, revealing their contents.

"Goodness," said Nat. "Goodness," she repeated, "I feel all sort of fizzy. These things look simple but also very important, don't you think? What do they mean?"

"I don't know, Nat, but I think it also relates to what happened to me in the park, or my dream of the park, or whatever."

"With the dog and the cat, you mean?"

"No, I'd another visit, one that seemed even more significant."

"Why didn't you tell me, Roaring Boy?" she said, giving me a poke in the ribs.

"I tried to, several times, but you were tied up with your exams. And also I'd an amazing experience in Brighton with a fortune teller or something."

"Okay, cousin. So start at the beginning and tell me all. Perhaps we will get some clues as to what is going on."

I started with the visit I'd made to Great-Aunt Bridget. ("Oh, she is a real sweetie," Nat had said, "and just a little mysterious don't you think?") I explained where the wooden sphere had come from and also mentioned the ancestor seven generations back who was a Bruce like us. I mentioned the journal that he'd kept, that Aunt Bridget hid in her commode ("That's sooo Great-Aunt Bridget," Nat had commented, before saying, "Go on, get to the meaty bits.")

I explained how I'd had no success opening the sphere without doing it serious damage. ("But you did open it," Nat had said. "Come on, Rhory the suspense has killed me twice already!") I told Nat about the visit to Brighton and how I'd come across the lady at The Silver Unicorn who had read my fortune or whatever she'd done. ("Wow, that's really nang," Nat had commented, with a peremptory, "Go on Rhory") I was not sure what 'nang' meant, but went on anyway, explaining how I'd been given the poster, and how it was Welsh and the man at the library had helped as had the man at the museum, and the old journals with their animal diagram.

"Wait a minute," said Nat. "Just hold on to your wild horses there, pardner," she continued with a bad rendition of an American cowboy accent. "I'm getting lost here."

"Okay, it's a bit confusing but it seems that where we live is a really spiritual-type place. There have been druids and temples and things and they centre on Hammerford or more particularly on its park." Nat looked a bit sceptical but said nothing.

"Apparently there's a sort of secret society that has studied these things. It had to be secret because the official church wouldn't have approved and tended to burn people with interests like this."

"Call them witches and stuff."

"That's right, Nat, at least that's what I believe."

"So this Secret Truth Society in Scotland took an interest in our neck of the woods and did maps and things…"

"Which were in Welsh, and would be a good way of keeping them secret!"

"You've a point there," said Nat, though she looked as unconvinced as I felt.

"Well the librarian guy suggested I went to our Hammerford Museum and it was there I discovered the diagram that was the key to the sphere."

"Are you seriously saying that an old magazine written over a hundred and fifty years ago has a picture that just happens to have the same animals on it that were carved by our ancestor onto a wooden sphere maybe two hundred years ago?"

"It's not so much that I am saying it, Nat, it's that it happened that way. And there's more."

Natasha sat cross-legged on the bed with the various objects spread out in front of her. "Keep going."

So I told her about the vision I had of meeting Dimitris, and the pool and Abaris and Pythagoras. Natasha was particularly interested in the bit about his sister, Theano, and the fact she'd soon marry Pythagoras.

She hopped off the bed, and collected her laptop. A bit of speedy typing later, she said, "This is seriously strange, cousin. Theano is a name that exists. She was the daughter of a dude called Brontinus and some believe she became a priestess in Delphi..."

"She didn't..."

"Hold on, it says that other accounts have her becoming the wife of Pythagoras and also the leader of his school after he died. He was much older than her apparently."

"Yes, he is," I said, "or rather was." I frowned. I'd only met him the other day.

She read on in silence for a bit longer.

"Seems that she was important enough to be remembered over 2,500 years later. Pythagoras met her when he was really old. They think he spent at least thirty of his adult years in Egypt. So he must have been, what, in his late fifties when he met Theano. And now you've kind of linked up with her family."

"And I saw both Abaris and Pythagoras. I think Abaris used to have his grove of trees where our park now is."

"So that great big oak tree goes back to druid times?"

"Yes, I think it must."

Chapter 58

Anubis

Natasha sat crossed legged on the bed. She pointed at the dark hemisphere.

"Can we take these out?"

I laid the objects in a row on the coverlet.

"What do they mean?" asked Natasha.

"I don't know. There are five of them, six if you count this bit of silk. They seem fairly random. I'm not even sure what they all are."

"So what does it say on the silk?" said Nat. "Have you read it?"

"Well I looked at it but couldn't make any sense of what was written."

"Can I look?" said Nat. With great care, I opened up the fragile silk square and showed her the writing. It looked so neat it would surely be easy to read, but it had strange letters and I could not recognise a single word.

"Oh – my – God! No wonder you couldn't read this. I am sure it is in Greek. We did some of the Greek letters in our comparative religion class. Yes, look, this is 'delta' and this is 'omega'. I bet Mum could read this you know. She did Greek at school and I think she learned some from her family when she was in Macedonia. She speaks a little when we go on holiday to Greece."

She used both hands to pass the cloth to me, and I looked at the writing. It had been written in really small letters, and I'd missed the similarity with the phrase Dimitris had written or caused me to write in the diary. I put it back in half of the sphere.

"I'm not sure I want to bring Aunt Sofia into this yet. If I do, she'll tell my dad or mum and I don't know what they'd do. I think this is a mystery I have to solve." I paused. Natasha looked at me and raised her eyebrows by a couple of hairs' breadths.

"Aunt Bridget said I should share this with you, and you could help."

Natasha gave me a funny look, and her eyes watered up.

"I don't know what to say, Rhory. But I must tell you I'm frightened. I know you're not mad, I just know that. If you tell me you've experienced these things, then I believe you. And these objects are undoubtedly real, and Great-Aunt Bridget is seriously cool, for someone of a hundred and two or whatever she is, but it's a little bit creepy, don't you think?"

"I agree, Nat, but let me finish what happened, and then let's see if we can make sense of anything." So I told her about how, a few days earlier, I'd awoken in a zombie state again, unable to move. When I described the figure in the bedroom, Nat took in a sharp breath.

"I know that one," she said. "It's an Egyptian monster, or god or something, and it's to do with the underworld." Nat got up and went to her bookshelf.

"I've got a book here on mythology, I think there is a picture here and that's why I recognise your description." She thumbed through the pages.

"Yes, look, here it is. It's called the Judgement of the Soul. I'll read to you." She did just that.

"Anubis leads the soul to the Hall of Maat (she is the goddess of truth, Rho) *and the heart is weighed on a scales against the feather of Maat. Anubis checks the scales and Thoth* (that's a bird-brained god with a pen. Goodness these Egyptians were strange in their beliefs), *Thoth records the result. If the heart was heavier than the feather, then the deceased is eaten by the Devourer of the Dead."*

Natasha came back and sat on the edge of the bed, and showed me a picture of the creature. "This devourer really is a monster, part crocodile, part lion and part hippo. Just as well he didn't show up in your bedroom, don't you think?"

"It was scary enough with the jackal man." I knew Nat had named the figure correctly. I'd found something similar when I researched in the school library.

"There is another thing Nat..." I showed her my dream diary and the entry that said *The Way is Open*. "I found I'd written this before I saw Anubis, or whatever his name is."

Natasha was still looking at her mythology book. "Look here, Rhory," she said, and her voice had a slightly husky edge as though her throat wasn't quite functioning as it should. "Look, here is a name for Anubis..." Again she read, *"Anubis is also called the Opener of the Way."*

She put the book down and leant back on her hands.

"There is clearly more of a link with Egypt here. You get messages from Shoshan, you see the sacred bird, the ibis. Perhaps you are an Egyptian re-incarnated! Maybe you were a pharaoh and maybe I was..." And she stopped and blushed, and then coughed to cover it up.

In a more matter of fact voice, she continued. "I think we should look carefully at these objects."

Chapter 59

The Silver Sphere

Natasha remained silent for a time, the objects from the sphere spread out in front of her. "We have some real clues here, I think. You know it was funny, well not funny, sort of scary actually, but as you told your stories about Greece and all, I could see them. The pictures were really clear to me. Especially the pool and the two old men. It was almost, not quite, but almost like watching a film. The scenes you saw were so vivid weren't they, like you were actually there."

I nodded and again she paused. Natasha, when she is thinking deeply wrinkles her brow and chews a bit on her teeth. I waited some more.

She tapped her fingers on each object on the bed in front of her. "I think each object comes from a different time. This one," she picked up the pendant, "this looks Egyptian. And this," she now picked up the bag with ten polished stones, "is what you and Dimitris were given."

Natasha stood up and walked over to the window, looking out onto the windswept garden. A flurry of rain pattered on the glass in front of her, and we both watched as drops eased their way down the windowpane. She turned and looked at me.

"There are five objects that we have to make sense of and the square of silk." I nodded. "So I bet the pendant has to do with Shoshan. And we know that ... even though it's spooky, we know that the bag of little stones is yours and Dimitris's. You were given it together, right?" I nodded again. "So that leaves these four objects."

She walked back over to the bed. "I think there are six ... no, seven of you."

"What do you mean?"

"Well, you were contacted by the earliest one, Shoshan. She comes from sooo, so long ago, right?"

"Yes. From a time before the Great Pyramid I think."

"Hmm, interesting. And then we know the second one is from about 500 BC. And there will be four more, perhaps including the person who made this sphere, and the wooden puzzle it came in."

I did my nodding dog in the back of a car impression.

"You're all on the same team?"

"What do you mean?" I said.

"Well Aunt Bridget spoke of the Companions, didn't she?"

"Yes," I said.

"Then the seven of you are the Companions – sort of reaching out to each other over time."

"Yes, she did say that. In fact," I smiled at my cousin, "she said you were a sort of Guardian."

Natasha nodded gravely at that, as though it was an entirely normal and proper thing to be.

"But I've only been in touch with two people," I continued. "We have no idea who the others are."

"True, but now you've solved the puzzle, who knows what will happen." Natasha walked back over to the window and breathed on it, and drew squeaky nonsense swirls on the foggy glass. She spun round.

"The Unicorn lady, in Brighton, didn't she say, "There are seven of you but nine must be invited?"

I thought for a moment. "Yes, yes, she did."

"Then that's confirmation. All we have to do is to work out who are the two that must be invited. Oh, and also find out who are the other four." She grinned at me and pulled off her turban. Her hair had nearly grown back about an inch all over. "Oh, by the way, I'm all clear at my last three tests."

I grinned back.

"Children, I need you to lay the table." Aunt Sofia's voice floated up from the room below.

After lunch, we went once more back into Nat's room, and rescued the objects from where we'd hastily put them in a clothes drawer. Once more we laid them out on the bed. There were five, not counting the globe itself or the silk with writing on it; a silver thimble; a bag with the ten small black stones, like tiny marbles; a pendant made of clear crystal carved with various markings; a round silver object a little smaller than a Ping-Pong ball; and a large coin.

"Look," said Natasha, "this coin has Greek writing on it as well. On the front it has an 'alpha' (like our English 'a') and on the back, an 'omega', which is Greek for big 'O'." She smiled the sort of self-satisfied smile that comes to English girls who can demonstrate command of Greek, however slim. "And around the edge on this side, aren't those zodiacal signs?"

I must admit that I hadn't studied it closely, it just looked like an old coin to me, and some of the other objects had been more interesting.

"Well that's five objects and the piece of silk. Unless the silk is the sixth object, then we are missing one for your theory to work, Nat," I said.

"True …" she said and paused, again wrinkling her forehead. "Let's see what we can be sure of. First, the silk material cannot be too old, or it would have disintegrated over time wouldn't it? So that is probably something written by our ancestor, who seems to have put this sphere together."

"Yes," I said. "Yes that makes sense." I remembered Great-Aunt Bridget had the note book written by my ancestor. It would follow that he had assembled these objects. I had no idea how, but someone had and they were in our family.

We both sat in silence for a bit, and heard one of the dogs

scraping at Nat's bedroom door. "Not now, Tennyson," Nat shouted. Both Natasha's dogs have the names of poets, the other being called Wordsworth.

"How do you know it's Tennyson?" I said.

"Simple, he is the thick one who can only scratch. Wordsworth has actually learned to knock the handle of the door. He taps three times distinctly."

"Weird!"

"I don't think the sixth object is the silk square. I think our ancestor chose that because he could write on it, it was light and durable, and would act as packing for the other objects. You are sure there was nothing else? Something really small that you missed as you undid the globe?"

"No, Nat," I said, feeling a trifle irritated. "Or rather, yes, Natasha, I am sure. I was really careful, and had to chase Jester away, he was so interested."

"Okay, don't get stressy, Rho, I am just thinking aloud here." Natasha leaned over the bed and picked up the two halves of the metal globe. "What about this?"

"But it's just a container, it's black and dirty. I thought it was just to keep the other things safe. Anyway, there's nothing special about it is there?"

Natasha put the globe back together and placed in on her desk. She gave it a slight flick with her fingernail. That produced a satisfying ping sound, like a small bell. "I don't think this is crap metal. I think this may be silver." And on that note she went across the room and disappeared through the door.

A moment later she returned with a cloth, a small blue and white tin and an old newspaper. One of the dogs followed her in, and nearly jumped on the bed. He was quickly dismissed, and the door firmly closed.

She spread the paper on her bedroom floor, and knelt down placing the globe carefully in the middle. The tin, called Silvo, delivered a light brown gunk which she proceeded to wipe on the outside of the globe. The cloth immediately went a grimy black where she wiped. She carried on, her fingers and her hands getting blacker and blacker.

At first the metal became covered with black, slimy smudges. Where the cleaning liquid had begun to dry, it turned a lighter brown colour. Gradually, when Natasha rubbed with a fresh bit of the cloth, the metal became streaky with black and dull silver. She worked at one bit, and rubbed and rubbed. This came up a bright silver.

"There," she said triumphantly. "I've done the real dirty work, you can do the rest." I took over while she went off to get another cloth. The globe was beginning to reveal its glory. It had been made of solid silver or high quality silver plate and began to shine with a glorious lustre. I polished hard, and could see that what I thought were scratches were clearly etchings of some sort, right into the metal.

"Look, Nat, it's amazing," I said when she returned. "It's got more of that Greek writing, and then, see, it seems to be covered in points and dotted lines."

"Mmm, let me see," said Natasha. She took the globe to the window, where it shimmered in the light, even in the dull light of an overcast day. "These are not just random dots, my dear, these are stars," she said with a note of real triumph in her voice. "And this is over two hundred years old, this must be worth an absolute fortune, surely!"

"I suppose it is," I said, feeling a bit perplexed. "You are not saying we should sell it are you?"

"Heaven forfend," said Natasha, quoting some play or other she'd read in class. "No, I'm not saying we should sell it, tho' thanks for including me on any potential deal." She smiled a sly smile. Then looking serious again, she said, "No, not sell it, but you better make sure no one steals it. Who knows what it's worth."

"I get you," I responded. "Well only you and Aunt Bridget know that I have this, so I think it is safe for the moment. People are unlikely to break into my bedroom looking for broken transformers and old Xbox games now, are they?"

"No, you're right. But can I suggest you don't tell any of your mates at school, or even Jules. She might chat to her friends and then who can tell what would happen. Let's keep it just entre-nous."

"In train who?" I said, but my French could actually cope. "It's our little secret for the time being. We have to find out where the other objects might have come from though."

"Yes," said Natasha. "And I've an idea about what to do next." She told me, and we laid our plans.

Chapter 60

"If it's Surrey, it's quiche"

The final half week at Scrivener's had crawled past. We were breaking up for the Christmas Holidays on the Thursday and both teachers and students had seemed to lose the will to work. I felt knackered and so did everyone else. I'd still not caught up on all the late nights being a cow in the play. At lunchtime on Thursday, grasping a few envelopes with Christmas cards, from Nick and others, and feeling guilty that I'd entirely forgotten to bring any myself, I headed home.

The next day Natasha and I had permission to visit our cousins in deepest Surrey. It was Natasha's idea because she reminded me that our Uncle Adam, my dad's youngest brother, had married a Copt.

"What on earth is a Copt?" I'd said.

"An Egyptian silly, she is a Christian Egyptian, or perhaps she is Muslim, I'm not quite sure. And of course Uncle Adam met her in Egypt. He works at the Egyptian department of the British Museum." So he did. I'd completely forgotten. Uncle Adam and my dad were not so very close. There was some history there and my mum would get a little tense at the mention of his name. Auntie Aida I quite liked, although apart from my birthday, I hadn't seen much of her for a year or two.

Aida, and the terrible twins, Jason and Pericles, picked us up at Godalming station, in an impressive 4 by 4. Her accent sounded almost French, with just a hint of Eastern mystery. She lived in a smallish house that had an amazing view across the Surrey countryside.

We arrived and dashed through the rain to the front door, with cries of "Wipe your feet, kids," ringing in our ears. It had taken Nat and me so long to get there that lunch came before anything else.

I suspect it is a by-law in Surrey that lunch must be quiche, even if you do not have a single green wellington boot in the hallway. Aida's quiche tasted great and she served it with a delicious salad, full of Eastern promise and strange tastes.

"This is lovely," said Natasha, never one to be slow to curry favour. We all agreed, even the terrible twins.

We could see Chanctonbury Ring from where we sat, an impressive dark smudge on a hilltop on the South Downs. Apparently some young lad, a century or more back, had come to the hill fort and planted little trees each time he visited. Gradually these became the impressive ring of trees we could see. This had been one of the places connected to Hammerford Park by those ley line thingies.

"What do you want to do in afternoon, children?" Aida asked us. "Dad won't be back till quite late, she has something to do at the museum this afternoon. Will Playstation do it for you, or is there a DVD you want to watch. You know we have a 3D TV now, and we've got *The Avengers* if you want."

"Ooh, yes, *Avengers*," said the twins in spooky unison.

Neither Natasha or I commented on our aunt apparently changing her husband's gender. "Actually, Auntie," said Natasha at her smoothest, "we were rather hoping to talk to you for a bit."

"That's fine with us," said Jason, or possibly Pete – as Pericles is wisely called – I couldn't identify who was who when they were dashing around, which they were now.

"Of course, if you would like to. Do you mind if I make myself coffee? Egyptians cannot survive without coffee every couple of hours or so, it's in our genes."

So she did and we started to tell her the story.

Chapter 61

Aida

Aida sat on the sofa in the lounge, I perched on an armchair and Natasha sat cross-legged on the floor. I tried to tell the story logically and Nat would come in saying, "Don't forget such and such, Rhory," or, "Show Auntie the page in the dream diary." I hadn't been sure how much I could tell my aunt, but she listened very carefully, only asking questions if confused or if she didn't understand a particular word. I gradually found Aida easy to talk to, and the slight tension I always seem to get when invited to talk at length, had evaporated.

Aida had a sort of rounded body, neither too thin or too fat. Nat had described her features as rather fine, on the journey down, and said she liked her 'Nefertiti Eyes'.

"Can I look at the bits where you've written in the diary?" Aida said. "I won't if you don't want me to, but I'd like to see the pictures if you don't mind."

I immediately said, "That's fine, Auntie, that's why I brought it." She studied the pictures for a while and then asked if she could see the pendant. I took the silver sphere from my backpack, opened it and took the silk bag that held the green pendant. I passed it to her, still hidden it its silky container.

She took it out very carefully, and sharply took in her breath. Without saying anything, she put it carefully on the coffee table, the crystal and gold object resting on the silk, and left the room with "I'll just be second," floating back after her.

In a moment she'd returned with a magnifying glass, the sort watch makers or jewellers hold in one eye, in old films. She placed it in her left eye and held it there by screwing up the left side of her face. She carefully lifted up the silk, and not touching the pendant, studied it for a long time.

Jason or Pete rushed into the room, being chased by Pete or Jason, doing a respectable imitation of a World War II aerial dogfight complete with machine gun fire noises. A "NOT NOW, children," from their mother sent them out again where they strafed two cats, who took no notice of them at all.

Aida got up again, and placing the pendant back in its silk bag, went across to a bookcase. She pulled out several issues of a magazine and having consulted an index, carried two across to her seat.

"Look at this," she said. She showed us a rather dull black and white photograph of a pendant now in some museum in America. It appeared very similar to the one I had. Aida held up a colour picture. "The French ran Egypt for a while, as well as the British, and many of our most beautiful objects were taken to French museums. Here is a scarab like yours, Rhory."

The crystal lay on a black velvet background and looked nearly identical to mine. Underneath the picture it said, 'Found in a Temple that is tentatively attributed to the Goddess Neith, in the 19th Century'.

"You mean it's quite modern?"

"No, Rhory," my aunt replied, with just a slight tinge of impatience. "This was dug up in the nineteenth century but see what it says underneath, the bit about the temple. The museum now believes this came from one of the very early dynasties, or maybe is pre-dynastic. It must be at least 5,000 years old, but I suspect it may be even more. However, I'm a minority voice and even Adam wouldn't agree with me."

She stopped and looked towards the garden where the twins had gone out in coats and wellington boots. "You know it's odd you've brought me this. It is a little, how should I say, upsetting. No, that's not right word ... perplexing. This is an object that relates or rather is related to my specialty at the museum in Cairo. Did you know I used to be researcher into artefacts of ancient Egypt?"

Our blank expressions showed that we'd no idea she'd been anything of the sort.

She continued, "Well I lost my job, a little bit before I met Adam. We met through a mutual friend. My specialty was jewellery from the earliest times in Egypt. I had a theory that these jewels had a particular significance and marked stages in ritual and initiation ceremonies. Someone who had a scarab had, if you like, reached the stage of the scarab. Other stages followed, relating to Isis and the Djed or backbone of Osiris and then the eye of Horus. Now that mystical eye is cheapened by being on sale to anyone in a bazaar, but I think before the deep wisdom was obscured or hidden, having the eye indicated a high initiate and a winged sun marked a higher stage still."

"How did you lose your job, Auntie?" asked Natasha, polite as ever.

"It was to do with the Great Pyramid, the so called Pyramid of Khufu. Some years ago a German researcher investigated one of the shafts going up from the King's Chamber. They found a stone door and had a robot go up to see what was beyond the door." Aida sipped her coffee. The cup rattled as she put it back on the table.

"What they found was never fully published. The powers that be in Egyptology, made sure the research stopped there. There are two reasons I think. The first is that it showed the Egyptian technology was far in advance of what is generally believed, especially in terms of work with metals. The second is that I think further work would show the Pyramid wasn't a glorified mausoleum for a grandiose pharaoh called Khufu, but a sacred Temple of Initiation." She looked at Natasha and then across at me.

"I was one of those who wanted the research to continue because it fitted with my theories that the Egyptian civilisation is much older and was also far more advanced, than most so called experts believe. Too many things are covered up and not published, because no one can really fit these facts into their all-too-narrow theories. I was quite unorthodox in my approach and had started using a local sensitive to gather information. Not many people knew, but I lost my job anyway."

"How do you mean, a sensitive?" I asked.

"You might call them psychics. Some I worked with, and Egypt has a number who are good, just have to hold an object in their hands to tell you all sorts of possibilities. I was making real progress in dating jewellery, when one of my so-called colleagues made a complaint about me, and used the term 'necromancy'. In a Muslim community, when you are the daughter of a Christian mother, it's enough to have you lose your job. That's what happened, but Adam sort of rescued me, and now I quietly help, from the Surrey countryside, with some of his work."

We all sat in silence for a bit. Upstairs we could hear that the twins had come back in and put on a DVD in their bedroom. Distant film music and the slow ticking of the grandfather clock took over the room.

Aida cleared her throat, and turned to Natasha and then to me. "You young people have given me quite a shock you know. I thought I'd put certain things behind me, but I see that I cannot escape my kismet, my fate. I suspect you cannot now escape yours either." She made a sound halfway between a laugh and a sigh. "I think I should tell you a bit more about me. Even Adam doesn't know my full story, but now is the time for someone in ... what does Adam call it ... 'dear old Blighty' to know. I think I'll get another cup of coffee first though. Do you want something to drink, you two?"

Chapter 62

Copts and Robbers

Fortified with lemonade, we waited for Aida to begin. She now sat cross-legged on the settee, still looking sort of glam, with her chin resting on the interlinked fingers of her hands. She had lit a cigarette with the words, "Another Egyptian habit I'm afraid, but only two or three a day."

Aida nodded slowly, a faint smile struggling with the sadness in her eyes.

"We are Baladi. We are everywhere in Egypt and we remember our roots." She drew hard on the cigarette, and the end glowed bright red.

Natasha and I waited, not having the least idea what she meant.

"We have been conquered by so many people since the days of our pharaohs. Greeks, Romans, Arabs, Turks, French, and the English. Now when we are so-called independent, we can still do little without an 'okay' from some power outside Egypt."

"The true Egyptians, those who think of themselves as Egyptian first and Muslim, Christian, Arab or what have you second, are the Baladi. We know … we just passionately know that we are direct descendants of the ancients, who knew so much and generally ruled so wisely. When we look at the statues of Rameses II or Tutankhamen, we think of them as our old rulers, our great rulers. We Baladi, don't talk of the ancient Egyptians as 'them', we think of them as 'us' and we are proud to be their children's children."

She stood up and released her hair from the large hairgrip that held it in place. She pulled her hair forwards and leant her head down, so her face was hidden in a cascade of dark locks. She asked, "What can you see?" When we were not sure how to reply, she said, "Look at the shape of my skull."

Then we saw. The back part of her skull extended further out from her neck than a standard English skull.

Aida let her hair swing back into place, and immediately looked several years younger. She took a book from the bookcase and showed us some pictures of some ancient Egyptians in side view. They had the same shaped head.

"Wow, Auntie, you look like you could be descended from Nefertiti or something," said Natasha.

"Well that's kind of you, Natasha, because I think she was a great beauty. But you are right. We both have same shaped head."

She stopped at the sound of the front door opening. Uncle Adam came in in his wet overcoat.

"Don't walk your rainwater into our carpet," Aida said, but she was smiling, and Adam apologised and popped out to hang up his wet coat and take off his shoes.

"It's raining Anubises and Bastets," he called. This was apparently the sort of joke Egyptologists make to each other. I remembered Bastet as a big cat goddess, from my visit to the British Museum.

Aida quickly picked up the pendant and gave it to me, saying, "Put this away, Rhory, and be a dear…" She looked me in the eyes. "Don't mention it."

We had tea with Adam and the twins and then Aida took us back to the station. We arrived fifteen minutes before the train was due. Aida talked to us in the car, with the rain hammering down on the roof.

"Thanks for coming to me the two of you," she said. "I've been around long enough, and seen enough strange things to know that nothing like this happens by chance. I'm one of a handful of people in the whole world who could both accurately describe the purpose of this pendant and accurately date it. And you, Rhory, my niece … sorry, nephew," she flicked her eyebrows up and smiled slightly, "bring it to show me. Amazing, really, you know."

"What do you think it all means, Auntie?" asked Natasha, from the back seat of the car. "Have you any explanation about what's happening to Rhory?"

"I can only spectate, darling … no, sorry … speculate. You must excuse my English, even after all these years I still get little lost."

She let down her window a little, and lit a cigarette. The smell of tobacco filled the car, and fine drops of water splashed in from outside.

"I've told you there are things that the orthodox Egyptologists wish to cover up. They don't want to admit that the ancient Egyptians, the very early rulers, may have known more about certain things than we do today. It doesn't fit with their view of what progress is."

She paused for another boost of nicotine, blew the smoke out of the window, and turned to look at us both.

"One last thing I want to say, Rhory dear, and Natasha, I believe the ancient Egyptians were so wise they saw how history would go. They could see that they were the first people, with the fullest knowledge, and those following them would lose the vision they had. They foresaw that the temples and graves would be robbed and they went to enormous lengths to prevent that happening, but it happened anyway. As long as the graves were in place, and the mummies were untouched, the deep, deep wisdom remained effective across the land and the Kingdoms were safe." Again she stopped, and sighed. "The time came when the graves, even those best hidden, were robbed, and pendants like yours, Rhory, were stolen. It's known as the age of Set or the time of Typhon."

"Yes," I said, "who exactly is that?"

"Well you might say he is evil personified. But really it's chaos, when human selfishness is given full reign, and the vision of the gods is lost. We all have to fight Typhon. Once he ruled, the innocence of the first of times was lost and the gradual sinking away from the stars and into the ignorance of the earth, began.

"Knowledge vanished little by little. The vision of the whole, the vision of Thoth, as we say, was shattered. Like the eye of Horus smashed to pieces by his wicked uncle, Seth. It's because of some robber in antique times that your pendant became separated from its initiate, a woman I believe from the time of ancient wisdom, as we like to call it."

With that she got out the car and we dashed through the rain to the shelter of the station forecourt.

"Keep in touch with me, my dears. This is a real adventure isn't it?"

She kissed each of us and promptly turned and left. We had found another ally.

Chapter 63

The Town Hall

"She's super, isn't she?" said Natasha.

"Who?"

"Auntie Aida! We were just talking about her."

"Oh, yes." We stopped at the main road, waiting to cross over and trying to avoid being splashed by passing cars. "I was thinking about the map, and whether we will actually find anything. No, you're right. I really liked her. She loved the pendant, didn't she. And that bit about initiation sounded wicked."

Natasha and I crossed over and walked briskly through Hammerford Carfax heading for the Town Hall. The warm alluring smell of fish and chips greeted us from one of the alleys, as we cut through. Little gift shops tempted us with music about red-nosed Rudolph, Little Drummer Boys and people who gave their heart unwisely the previous Christmas. Hammerford centre didn't have a shopping mall as such, so we had cold rain blowing in our faces. I opened the umbrella but it immediately turned inside out.

"Never mind," said Natasha. "We'll just get damp. A little rain never harmed anyone."

"I could just do with some chips," I said as the last whiff of chip fat and vinegar got whisked away in a wet squall.

"Me too, Rho, but we must catch the Town Hall before it closes."

We'd asked Dad and Mum if they'd drive us down to the Town Hall, given the weather, but they had more important things to do. Strange how the idea, 'The walk will do you good, dear,' only applies to us teenagers and never to those who have their own car keys.

We arrived at the entrance to the Town Hall, therefore, somewhat damp and cold. Something nudged me to look behind, and I saw headlights moving slowly down the road. We were in a dark spot across the pavement from the large Georgian building, and I pulled Natasha more into the shadows of the doorway to Finch Bros. and Sons, Solicitors.

"What!"

"There, Nat, that car. The one just going past now. It's the same car I saw when I visited the museum a few days back. I think we're being followed."

The car went past slowly, its tinted windows hiding whoever travelled inside. Did I imagine I could see a glowing cigarette as someone took a drag in the back seat? Probably. But I could feel the ice in my veins again. Surely they couldn't see us on a dark night like this.

"It's just a car. Looks bulletproof, mark you, but it's just a car."

"It's unusual and it's the one I saw after coming out of the museum, after it had been fire bombed." I told her about seeing the unusual cigarette on the pavement and the feeling I had when I picked it up that some malevolent eye or presence was looking at me.

Natasha frowned her deep thinking frown. "Sounds like Aida is right," she said.

"How d'ya mean?" I asked.

"We're dealing with this Typhon bloke, who's a bit like Darth Vader apparently, only worse."

"I hope you're wrong, Nat," I said. But I had a horrible feeling she might be right. I had no idea in this day and age, how we were meant to deal with bloodthirsty, murderous gods from ancient times.

"Let's go map hunting," I said with more enthusiasm than I felt. It seemed like Aunt Bridget's box was becoming more trouble than it was worth.

The letter from Mr Wilson at Scrivener's, worked its magic. It appeared that the crusty old dude was actually a man of some influence in this town. We were taken down to the basement by a youth on work experience, whose strongest personality point was his acne.

He showed us where the maps were stored, told us to be "really, really careful, 'cos they're precious," and went back to his desk upstairs. The strip lighting hummed and produced barely adequate light. The bluish flickering didn't fully penetrate to the racks, where the old maps were stored in deep pigeon holes. Actually, they were so deep they would be better described as python holes. Each hole was filled with what looked like black wood disks. "Ebony," declared Natasha. "Wouldn't be allowed today."

When you pulled at a disk, what came out was a long, white roll, up to two or more metres in length. The wooden spindles, with the maps, had a disk at each end. The huge maps wrapped around the spindle. We carried one over to the wide purpose made table, and carefully opened it. It unrolled so quickly I had to dash round the table, to prevent the moving part crashing to the floor.

At first we could make out nothing that made any sense. Faint long straight lines had been drawn on the map, leaving most of it white and blank. Closer inspection showed that these were boundary lines and that there were also individual trees and houses marked.

We struck lucky with our second map. "This is part of Midlea," Natasha said. "Look, here's Cuckoo Farm, and Lucky Dog Hill. And there's the ruined abbey."

As the map had been drawn in the 1850s, very few of the current houses were shown. It took us a while to work out how the maps were stored. The further you went in to the racks, the older the maps became. Faded labels, written in copperplate by some work experience person in the 1930s, said things like,

'"*Hammerford South, 1900–1920*'

and

'*Hammerford Causeway Region, 1850–1885*'

This last one showed the Town Hall, the Museum and even where I'd gone to primary school. In fact nearly all the buildings were unchanged. It even showed where 'Finch Bros. Solicitors' had set up their business.

"Are you finished yet?" asked the spotty youth. We said we wouldn't be long and he vanished upstairs again.

"We best divide up and search," said Natasha. We went deep into the darker regions of the storage racks, and using our mobiles, illumined the fading labels. After some dusty minutes I found something promising.

"There's a label here that says Hammerford Estate, Trethowan House."

"There's a coffee shop called Trethowan's, isn't there," said Natasha, "in West Street."

"Yes, there is, so I suppose they're an old Hammerford family."

I pulled out the map – one a lot shorter than the others – being a little over a metre long. It showed what was now the park, the bandstand, some of the boundary walls of the time, Trethowan House (now the council offices) and two large oak trees (where now only one survived).

There didn't seem to be much else. "What's this?" asked Natasha, pointing to a little circle with some spidery writing near to it, in the middle of a field.

"That has to be quite near Scrivener's," I said, and squinted to try to read it. The flickering of the strip lighting didn't help and I added my mobile as a source of illumination. I'd have done better with Miss Griffiths's magnifying glass.

"It says, 'Well'," I said. "And underneath..." I squinted "...'potable water'. Do you think they meant portable?"

Natasha looked at me to see if I was joking. I wasn't. "Potable, you dumb-cluck, means drinkable."

"Oh," I said, feeling just a bit daft, "of course it does."

I returned the map to its holder at the end of the rack. It looked like we'd learn nothing of real value on this visit. I pushed the map home into its hole with rather too much force, born of frustration. It hit something and bounced out about 30 centimetres.

"Hey, Nat, there's something hidden here." We pulled out the map again and peered into the gloom. Even with our mobiles it was impossible to see what lay back there.

Nat went back into the illumined part of the room and returned with the brolly. It proved just long enough to use as a hook. With Natasha's slim arms she was able to reach in and hook whatever blocked the hole further down. She pulled out another map. This one was similar to the others, but had ivory disks at the end. They were a yellowy white colour and had tiny cracks.

We opened the map with great care, spreading the ancient paper on the table bit by bit. We had in front of us a map of the Trethowan Estate. It displayed a coat of arms and a lot of very fancy writing in the centre, at the bottom.

"We are closing up now," said a disembodied voice from the stairs.

"Stop him," hissed Nat. I went out and did auto verbal that ranged from how grateful we were, to his favourite football team (West Ham, apparently, for no discernible reason).

He jangled keys in his hand, and after telling me that he'd seen every West Ham match for the last five years, indicated that he'd now really have to lock up. At that point Natasha emerged carrying the umbrella, her coat done up against the elements outside. We thanked our football enthusiast for his help and left.

"Boy, these are good!" said Natasha.

We were in the chippy, sitting at a red-topped table that had seen better days. The wind drove cold air around our legs but the chips we shared warmed us up, in a salty, dripping with vinegar, sort of way. Totally delicious. "Do you know," said Natasha, "when I was back in Macedonia, people thought I was crazy asking for vinegar for my chips. They just don't do that there."

"Let's see the pictures, Nat," I said, not willing to explore

Macedonian eating habits at this point in time.

She took out her rather expensive iPhone, and showed me the pictures she'd taken. Even on the tiny screen we could make out all the details on the map. In fact we could enlarge any portion of it.

Gradually we explored the estate. We became oblivious to people coming in and out of the shop ordering 'rock salmon and chips', and those who wanted pickled onions. We even forgot the cold dampness. We'd found exactly what we were looking for. Hammerford Park had many surprises, and these went a long way to explaining my various experiences.

The next day, Natasha sent me the photos through the wonders of the Internet, and I looked at them on Dad's laptop. Whoever had done this map hadn't intended it for general use. It provided a guide to those who wanted to find what had been artfully hidden, a long way below the site of the current bandstand. Three objects enabled Natasha and me to orientate ourselves: Trethowan House, now incorporated into the council offices, the old oak tree that might or might not date back to the time of Abaris, and finally the well. I recognised it as the well I'd found with David Milford, a little while before he'd died so tragically from his accident.

I spoke to Natasha on the phone and we agreed that *The Small Palladium* had to mark the position of the current bandstand. Actually it said 'fmall', which made it even more quaint. "Have you noticed, Nat," I said, "there are some dotted lines that run from the well right up to the palladium. What do you think they represent?"

She paused at the other end of the line. "I think it's obvious. Just look under where the palladium is shown. Written very small are the words Templum Occultus."

"Yes, I'd noticed that. Occult means secret, doesn't it, and often relates to witchcraft and things, like people with occult powers?"

"In Latin it just means hidden. And Templum is the Latin for temple. I think the map is showing us something obvious. It's not that the palladium is a hidden temple, rather it's that the temple is hidden under the palladium."

"And the dotted lines..."

"...show an underground passage."

"The way in is from the well and that's the purpose of the map."

"Exactly!" Natasha concluded.

We agreed that I should see if I had any more flying dreams, and whether I could then get into the temple that way. If not, we'd have to see if it was possible to get to the temple the old fashioned way, using the well.

Maybe there would be a chance in the Christmas holidays.

Chapter 64

Sherlock Takes the Tube

This year Christmas would be manic. Granny and Grandpa had come over from Norway, which was a bit odd when you think about it. We should've gone there for this festive occasion. When I was very young I believed that's where Santa Claus actually lived. Mum and Dad confirmed that, until Juliette put me right.

We had gone to Norway to celebrate Christmas in Stavanger. I'd planned to keep a lookout for Father Christmas and his reindeer.

"You don't *still* believe in Father Christmas, do you, Rhory?" Well of course I did because he was REAL!

"It's just a story, for very, very young children," Juliette had continued, witheringly, from the authority of her nine years. She shattered my dreams. She'd only just found out herself but made sure I joined her in this infinitely less magical universe, without silliness or mystery.

This Christmas, with the presents opened and wrapping paper all over the floor, Mum made an announcement.

"We're going to see The Nutcracker, two days after Boxing Day."

Faces lit up around the room. Apparently this is considered good news. A Christmas treat.

"It's a great ballet," said Dad, "where toys come to life and mice turn vicious."

Who in their right mind would want to see a lot of people prancing around in tights and silly skirts?

"Oh," I said, "that'll be interesting." Juliette smirked at me, a sort of 'glad you'll suffer if I've to suffer smirk'.

"Apparently the staging is fantastic. Mum has gone to a lot of trouble to order tickets. It's a sell out and we're lucky to be going," said Dad

And then I remembered that Mum had bought the tickets on the day I'd been dropped off at the British Museum; the day I'd first seen Shoshan. And that day had followed from when I'd seen the funny man at the door. How strange. I'd not thought much about him since. Really it all started with him. And he'd mentioned the Bandstand too. A fist tightened inside my stomach. Now I just knew this Nutcracker thing would be significant in some way.

Three days later, all the cold turkey had been consumed in endless sandwiches and cold collations. We'd taken the train to London. Now we were heading for entirely different food, namely Sushi. Definitely not my choice. The women had had a conspiracy and I sensed Juliette's hand in all of this, Sushi being 'cool' with her friends. For me, it's just sticky rice and dubious fish with a weird green sauce that's far too hot.

"But, it's quick, Rhory," Mum had said, "and we mustn't be late at the Coliseum."

"The Coliseum?" I'd said. "You mean we're going to watch gladiators?"

"Don't be silly, dear," was Mum's response. We travelled by tube from Victoria Station to the mysteriously named West End.

"Shall we play our usual game, Rho?" said Juliette.

"Yes," I responded. "We'll take whoever is sitting exactly opposite me from the next station."

We played 'Sherlock Holmes'. We would choose someone we could both see on a train journey, and do a sleuth job on him or her, seeing what we could deduce just from what we observed. At the next stop an enormous African man sat opposite me, with a bright green turban on his head and a voluminous robe down to his ankles. Silky trousers of the same dramatic colour reached down to his rather fancy leather shoes. Jules sat next to him and I sat across the aisle. He got up as the train jerked to a halt, and headed for the door.

Jules hissed across the gap between us, "Clearly a guy going to a party, who likes to be noticed."

Even Doctor Watson could've done better than that. He disembarked, as did about ten other people. A noisy group of men entered and clustered around the door, holding beer cans and all speaking at once. Next to Jules, a rather attractive girl now sat where the African guy had been. No lines on her face, so aged mid-to-late twenties. Black hair, held with various clips. Eyes with sparkly make-up. Long eyelashes that surely would need to be attached with superglue.

Her black winter coat, suited the near zero temperatures outside, as did the brown boots. The coat was undone. I glanced down at her surprisingly short skirt and wondered how she didn't freeze. She carried a large brown handbag, with buckles and pockets and zips, a space full of mystery and lipsticks.

What do girls carry in bags like that?

She opened one of its compartments and took out a notebook. She searched for something in it and her face puckered a bit with concentration. I nearly leaned across and said 'careful' because of the lines that will soon occur if she did too much thinking like this. I didn't of course.

I thought I'd seen her somewhere before. Perhaps she'd starred in a TV soap?

Later she investigated another pocket in the bag and got out a couple of letters, which she read, again with a puzzled expression on her face. One was written in a girly, twirly script. That one was the one that puzzled her the most. She thrust the letters away with just a hint of irritation, got out a small music player, closed her eyes, and disappeared into her own musical world.

Now I could look at her even more carefully. Her cheeks sparkled slightly with that fairy dust stuff girls use. So maybe she acted. But I couldn't back that up with evidence. I couldn't see mud on her boots or anything that the real Sherlock would use to draw conclusions. I looked back at her face.

Fit, definitely fit.

Just before we got to our stop, Charing Cross, she opened her eyes. She looked straight at me. Even with all the foundation and make up I could see her go pale. She looked away and then back again. I looked down, feeling my cheeks go red. Normally, hot girls with slightly OTT make-up, didn't find me an object of interest.

When we arrived at Charing Cross she stood up as well. The crowds prevented me seeing if she got off or just changed her seat. From there we braved the chilly air until we reached the Sushi Restaurant near to where we'd see the ballet.

Chapter 65

Food with Attitude

It's not easy to have a conversation when you sit in a long line in a restaurant. We were perched on high plastic seats, and a moving conveyor belt passed by in front of us with sticky rice and fish dishes in different coloured plastic pots. On my left two Hooray Henry's talked in Eton accents about the Boxing Day hunt. I thought foxhunting had been banned but they had chased one a couple of days earlier. Juliette perched on my right, explaining the dishes to Granny sitting on her right.

Jules looked quite the thing in a dress. Normally she was a trouser sort of girl, but today she'd made a real effort in the loveliness department, and succeeded. Not that I'd tell her so. I wore a jacket, present from Dad, and a tie with a grinning Homer Simpson, a present from Jules. My hair, all spikes and attitude, held more or less in place by gel, a present from Mum. Christmas present boy, me.

I took a sip of Coke through a straw and the bubbles went right up to the back of my nose. I snorted and Juliette turned to me.

"What did you make of her?" she asked. I wondered if she meant our Japanese waitress on the other side of the conveyor belt.

"Who?" I asked.

"The girl on the tube."

"Oh, right, her." I supposed the answer 'not much' wouldn't suffice, and 'drop dead gorgeous' would've earned me a kick on the shins.

"Well, she looked sort of Irish."

"Yes, I agree," said Juliette. "What else?"

"I don't think she is married, and I don't think she has a boyfriend."

"Mmm, interesting," said my sister. "There wasn't a ring, I agree, but why no boyfriend?"

"Well, it's a surmise, Doctor Watson," I said, keeping in the spirit of the game. "It's a special night, just before Christmas. She's going out somewhere nice I'd assume, with that amount of warpaint on her face."

Juliette nodded, not being one to overdo things at all in the make-up department. "And," I continued, "any boyfriend worth his salt would travel with her, wouldn't he?"

"Maybe she was going to meet him?" offered Juliette.

"Could be," I said. "But I could see she took interest in more than one young man who passed down the aisle. She'd sneak glances at them."

"Not definitive," said Juliette. "Did you get her name?"

"Don't be silly, Jules," I said, and then I saw a look of triumph in her eyes. "Okay, but you had the advantage of sitting next to her. You must have read one of her letters."

"No," said Juliette, "that would be improper and rude." Her arched eyebrows told a different message as we both knew she would've read them if she could. "I did read the address on the pinkish envelope, sent by one of her girlfriends I assume. It was Shelley Prendergast."

"That sounds like it could be Irish," I said.

"Agreed," said Juliette. "And I could see what was written irritated her."

"I noticed that."

"And it was in code."

"What?" I said.

"Well, I can't be sure," said Juliette," but she was counting the letters and tracing words with her finger. It seemed to me that she was working out certain letters and these were making new words.

The letter was handwritten in a rather immature writing that made it difficult for me to read, but I could see our Shelley was counting after some markings or clues that she could recognise, and working something out. I think she needed help."

"What on earth do you mean?"

"Well, you saw her open her diary, it was just before we got off."

"I saw her do something with her bag, but people had come and stood between us, so I missed that."

"Yes, true, I got a much better look, didn't I," conceded my sister with uncharacteristic fairness. "She took out her diary, and wrote something in it for later this month. What she wrote looked like 'S.O.S', though I couldn't see it entirely clearly. 'S.O.S', Rho Boyo," she said, assuming a sudden Welsh accent, for no reason I could fathom, "is the international distress signal." She gave me her dazzling super-detective smile.

"It is," I agreed. "But that's not something you would write down as a date, is it?" We both paused for a moment. "No, I think it is an assignation she doesn't want, and she is writing it in code of some sort."

"A sort of Secret Society," Juliette said for no apparent reason, and then went on, "I say this, Rhory, because she had a book in her huge handbag, and it was called *Secret Societies from Ancient Egypt to the Current Day.* That's an oxymoron if you think about it. It had a subtitle, *The True Story of the Illuminati.*

"What on earth is that?" I said.

"We had a talk about this at school. Some teacher did a thing on conspiracy theories. This is one of the biggest and most absurd," Juliette continued. "It suggests that this secret group has controlled the banks and governments of Europe and America for about three hundred or more years. Of course there is no evidence at all. D'y know, Rhory, some people believe Mozart was one."

"One what?"

"An Illuminatus," said my sister.

"So what does that tell us about our Shelley, Sherlock?"

"Our Shelley is into something beyond her depth," said Juliette. "I picked up fear and something else I can't quite put my hand on."

"All right, children, we've paid and must go now," said a voice from the world of adults, and Juliette's consideration of Shelley Prendergast came to an end. I'd a strange uneasy feeling in the pit of my stomach. Something about the woman on the train disturbed me. I didn't know what or why she seemed familiar. I felt that once again the finger of fate had poked fun at me.

Chapter 66

Shelley Prendergast

Shelley should have left the London Underground at Tottenham Court Road to go to a party at a club being thrown by one of her friends. Instead she'd followed the tall boy and his family off the tube at Charing Cross Road.

She'd nearly had a seizure when, on the tube, she'd looked up to catch the boy sitting opposite staring right at her. She'd recognised him at once from her vision in the druid circle, when he showed up in his pyjamas with his hair all askew, like today. The Stones wanted him, and here he sat on a London Tube train, looking at her boots or maybe her boobs. For a moment or two she'd felt a bit giddy and wondered if he'd turned up in a vision. He stood up with his family and she decided to see where they went.

The wind blew freezing rain into her face. She walked quite fast to keep up with the family; not because they walked fast, but the crowds of theatregoers and friends intent on a good night out, made movement in a straight line difficult. The boy's height helped keep him in sight.

At her last visit to the house in the West Country, she'd had the uncomfortable experience with the bowl. The trance session that followed, had revealed new information to the Stones. Of course, they didn't tell her what she'd said in the trance state. But they couldn't hide their desperation to track down the boy. Either he had, or would, move through time soon. Actually time travel. They ignored her as they talked, mentioning the 'jump room' on the west coast. Shelley concluded someone had the ability to hunt her poor

Red King, in his striped pyjamas, through time. They said, in hushed tones, that Diamond had found where he lived and may even have seen him. Once more she resolved to warn the lad.

She saw him enter a Sushi bar with his family. She waited in a coffee bar across the busy London road, where she could watch them through the restaurant window.

If the wretched Stones got hold of him she'd no doubt they'd harm him. Her psychic gifts were greater than any of theirs, but she knew that Fatty Haemorrhoid, with her malevolent green brooch, would doubtless get a fix on him soon. The woman had the gift but grossly misused it.

After the time it took to drink two cups of coffee but not to get properly warmed through, she saw the boy and his girlfriend or sister emerge, followed by assorted adults. *His sister, she's clearly older than him*. She realised this girl had been sitting next to her on the train.

Shelley left money on the table, said, "Happy New Year" to the Pakistani couple who ran the cafe, and ducked out into the cold, wet street. Through the sleet she could see the family heading towards St Martin's Lane.

Shelley guessed they were going to theatre land. She just knew she had to talk to … to Rhory. The name just popped in. It must be because he'd been studying her so closely on the tube train. Shelley wondered if he'd recognised her the way she'd recognised him.

She became aware of one of the Stones nearby. Shelley looked around quickly but could see none of them behind her. She continued to follow Rhory and his family but extended her awareness. Yes, one of the blooming Stones lurking in the vicinity. *Maybe they are following pyjama boy.* She made an invocation her mother had taught her, to protect herself. A picture arose inside her. The Stone she liked least. 'Haemorrhoid'.

At that same moment a taxi passed by on the far side of the road. Shelley recognised the large woman sitting in the back, checking a text message on her mobile. The heavy traffic ensured the taxi moved no faster than Shelley. She reached into her handbag and pulled out a woolly hat and sunglasses. The glasses would make her more conspicuous in the dark and snow, so she just put on the hat. Now she could be anyone.

The boy and his family stopped in front of a well-lit theatre, with pictures of manic mice on huge posters outside. The taxi arrived a few moments later. Shelley smiled and remembered her mum's favourite saying, 'You can't buck fate'. So they all had tickets for the ballet.

They all went in.

Chapter 67

The Coliseum

"Gosh that was a wet walk," said Granny, as we made it to the steps of the Coliseum. "Let's hope it's warm inside."

A welcome blanket of warmth wrapped around us. So did masses of people, all smiling and talking and looking like they might actually enjoy two hours of ballet. I liked the theatre though. The atrium or whatever had all sorts of posters from previous shows, with no mad mice in sight. Why couldn't we have gone to one of those? Grand staircases swept up on each side of the crowded reception area.

"You did well to get us the best seats, dear," said Dad to Mum. "I know we don't have front row stalls, but the front of the dress circle is even better, I reckon. You get the best view."

I'd spotted a sign, written in gold that said, 'To the Boxes'.

"What are the boxes, Dad?"

"What?" The feet shuffling, doors opening and umbrellas being shaken out made a racket all around us.

"The boxes," I said pointing.

"I'll show you inside, Rhory," he said. "We need to get out of this wet draught or we'll all get pneumonia."

A boy with acne, a stud in his nose and a spiky haircut, checked our tickets. His thin white shirt and black dicky bow didn't seem much protection against the chilly blasts of air when the doors opened to let in the theatre goers.

"Up the stairs and on your right," he said, with an accent that would put a Harrow schoolboy to shame. "The circle bar is on your left at the top."

Mum said, "Let's leave our wet coats on our seats and get to the bar."

"Good idea, Kyrsten," said Granny. "We can also order drinks for the interval?"

"Yes, Mum," said my mum.

How odd it is for my mum to have a mum, who's a granny. I suppose one day my mum will look as old as granny, and I… I didn't continue that thought. After all, who really wants to be an adult?

As we went up the stairs, something prompted me to look back towards the doors, and their chilly draughts. A man with silvery hair was coming in. He held a furled umbrella, and his expensive looking coat had a few drops of rainwater glinting on it. Clearly, he'd just emerged from a taxi. No tube train journey for him then. Behind him were two young adults, a rather large and plain girl, and a man who looked like he could be an all-in wrestler. He had bronze coloured hair and a heavy-set face, with slightly mean looking eyes, too small for the rest of his bulk. The young man turned to greet someone behind him, but at that point Mum said, "Hurry up, Rhory, don't dawdle so." We continued on into the theatre.

Our seats were right at the front of the circle, not quite in the middle but with an excellent view of the stage. Luckily I don't suffer from vertigo, because we could lean forward and see right down into the rows of seats below. I resisted the urge to jump or let out a little blob of spit. Lots of empty seats remained below but we were quite early.

I had a fantasy about shooting paper pellets at the heads of people. I checked my jacket pocket, but my blowpipe remained at home tucked in my school clothes. Oh well. Voices floated up with cut-glass accents, speaking with that sort of loud authority which Jules says comes naturally to the Range Rover class.

Leaving our coats, we progressed to the circle bar. The room sat above the entrance and the bar ran its full width, with the window behind peppered with sleety rain.

Dad bought two programmes and received no change from a ten-pound note. They were full of coloured pictures of oversized wooden soldiers, or, I suppose, people dressed as wooden soldiers. For some reason, more big mice with guns featured. What sort of a story was this? I admitted, in the privacy of my own brain that maybe, just maybe, there might be a tiny bit of fun in store, in-between the endless boring parts of course.

We all chose drinks and following Granny's suggestion, Grandpa ordered some for the interval as well.

"Saves us queuing," said Mum, which seemed a good idea. Grandpa insisted on paying, and seemed slightly bemused when he had to hand over two twenty-pound notes."

Goodness," he said, and then added something in Norwegian.

"What name shall I put," said the bar girl, or woman, because she looked a good deal older than Mum. Grandpa started to say, "Gudmundson," which is my mother's maiden name, but thought better of it, and said, "Bruce."

The woman scribbled something on a slip of paper, and also gave Grandpa a receipt, which I saw had changed our name to 'Bryce'. I helped carry drinks to where the rest of the family were dutifully reading the programme notes.

Chapter 68

"Any Returns?"

Shelley waited as Emerald eased herself out of the taxi. The frightful woman looked neither to left nor right, and hurried through the sleet into the foyer. Her voice carried above the general racket, greeting the rest of her family. Shelley walked further down and entered by one of the doors at the far end of the foyer, mingling with the crowds until the Haemorrhoid family had left.

Emerald had continued talking loud enough for Shelley to hear they were headed for a box. She wondered what that meant. Emerald's husband had said, "Shall we get a drink in the bar, Georgina?" as he threw the ticket envelope into a stylish litterbin. A few moments later Shelley walked past and retrieved it from where it had caught in the small gap below the sand, used to stub out cigarette butts. The envelope was addressed to Mrs G. Rillington. *Knowledge is power.*

Tickets & Returns, announced the sign in gold letters, at a kiosk at the far end of the foyer. Anyone unable to see whatever the show was tonight, would bring tickets back for resale here. Shelley edged her way past groups in wet overcoats, buzzing with post-Christmas enthusiasm and joined the small queue. She closed her eyes for a moment and did one of her little tricks, learned from her nan.

"Are you all right, dear?"

Shelley opened her eyes to see a woman with prematurely grey hair and a pale, expensive green mackintosh. She'd a paisley scarf around her neck, beaded with tiny rain drops. "Fine actually," said Shelley, "really, just fine, thanks." She thought the woman looked kind. She also knew now that if she waited, a ticket would arrive.

Bells rang out all over the theatre five minutes later. In front of her, three couples waited expectantly, as a man had returned five tickets. The first two couples took two seats each. The final couple wanted to see the show together and decided to return later in the season.

"Any returns?" said Shelley to the woman the other side of the Tickets & Returns window.

"Yes, dear, you're lucky," said the woman. "There is only one left and it just came in."

Luck didn't come into it. She mounted the stairs to her right and continued up to her seat in the balcony. She looked down on the upper circle and could just make out the dress circle below. Putting a pound in the slot on the seat in front of her, she took out the red plastic opera glasses. She quickly discovered where Emerald presided in her box. Being so much higher than her sometime employer, she doubted the spook would see where Shelley was sitting. Shelley did another trick her nan had taught her. She sat back, confident that Haemorrhoid wouldn't look her way.

Shelley scanned the theatre with her glasses. People were moving along aisles and between seats. The theatre hummed with chatter and the orchestra had begun to file in. She spotted Rhory easily, just settling himself into his front row seat, and leaning over the edge to look at the people below. A cold ripple passed through her stomach. *Mrs Rillington will find Rhory tonight. He is in more danger than he can imagine.* How odd they'd all ended up in the same theatre.

The orchestra started tuning up. *These things are not set in stone. There must be something I can do.*

Chapter 69

Georgina Rillington

"Why do they do that?" I asked Juliette, as the orchestra made a sound like twenty-five cats being put through a meat blender.

"They are tuning up," she replied.

"Surely they could do that at home couldn't they?"

"Yes, they do, but their strings go out of tune as they move from the cold outside to the warmth of the theatre."

"Oh, right," I said, feeling a bit silly at so obvious an explanation. I read the programme notes, while the cats died again and again. The programme had come to me last, a reverse perk of being the youngest.

Tchaikovsky wrote the Nutcracker, based on a rather dark Russian fairy tale, or so it said in the programme. (He was the sort of composer you hope doesn't feature in a dictation in an English class at school!) Some lost little girl was given a wooden nutcracker by a peddler. She unwisely fell asleep with it, and her dream put her in the power of an evil Mouse King. *Not a great problem. Just buy a cat.* But either the room with toys under the Christmas tree had grown, or she'd shrunk. Whichever, she needed the help of the toy soldiers.

I turned the page to see arty pics of girls dressed in truly bizarre clothes, in sparkling snow. The Kingdom of Sweets included the Sugar Plum Fairy. *I think I know that one.* I wanted the Mouse to succeed but I guessed it would be the girl that won in the end. They always do. All the really magical changes took place once the midnight hour struck.

I bobbed up and down as people filed past to reach their seats. I preferred Dad's opera glasses to the rubbish red plastic ones. They even had the cheek to charge one pound after all the money Mum had forked out for the tickets. I used Dad's glasses to reconnoitre the orchestra and the posh people in the expensive boxes.

The all-in wrestler guy and his dumpy sister sat in a box virtually above the stage on my right. I'd seen them when we climbed the stairs from the atrium place. They sat with their parents. The mother poured herself some champagne and eased her bulk into her seat. A green splinter of light shot towards me, reflected from some brooch she wore. *She must be wealthy if that stone's real.* The woman never stopped talking, directing most remarks to her husband sitting behind her, who nodded, and then to her son sitting next to her, who didn't.

I came out in goose bumps and shuddered slightly. The eye I'd seen outside the burnt door of Hammerford museum hovered at the edge of things. I knew I should look away but couldn't. The eye searched. I didn't like this fat woman with her noisy manner but couldn't look away. She stopped talking and started to look systematically around the theatre. The eye looked with her. Her brooch flashed again as it caught a spotlight. She looked straight up towards me.

"Excuse us," said the couple, as they came past Juliette and then me.

"Sorry … sorry," they murmured, as we had to half stand and juggle to retrieve our coats that were on the floor by our feet. By the time they had gone past, the lights dimmed in the auditorium and the music proper began.

*

Shelley watched the misty eye shape hover around Emerald. The woman had forgotten to cloak her activities, and had relaxed with the champagne she clearly enjoyed. The flashes from her brooch illumined parts of the theatre and the eye focused where the spikes of light had hit. *Astral rubbish. This woman is not nice at all.* The eye filled the box where her family, completely subordinate to her, sat and listened as she talked. The pupil of the eye centred on the brooch. Shelley murmured some words of protection and drew a circle of light around herself.

The pyjama boy, Rhory, had started looking around the theatre and now looked straight at Mrs G. Rillington and family. *That's how she'll find him. She doesn't know he is here yet, but the eye will, if he catches its attention.* Shelley didn't want to draw attention to herself but needed to warn the lad about the very real danger he faced. *Look away, Rhory.* It did no good he just continued staring.

The lights in the theatre began to go down as the eye burned a deep green colour. Some people passed by Rhory and his family. Perhaps Haemorrhoid hadn't actually seen him and what he looked like. Darkness settled and the ballet began. Shelley changed her way of seeing so she'd not be distracted by the auras of the dancers. She'd plan what to do next as the dancers spun on the stage far down below her.

Chapter 70

Sweets at the Nutcracker

Mum passed me the box of mints, my favourite. Unfortunately, everyone's favourite. The opening music had finished and so had all the chatter. Feet slapped and bumped on the stage in the silence. I'd have to wait before taking off the cellophane. The music picked up again and I released the box from its shiny wrapper, with a loud, crinkling hiss. My toes curled and Jules giggled.

Each sweet opened with a sound of a crisp packet being scrunched. Someone behind us went "tch tch" to indicate Hammerford children hadn't been raised properly. Jules giggled more.

The minty tang filled my mouth and I admitted to myself that this Nutcracker thing might be okay. The girl dancing the part of Clara had looks to die for. Mum had said the staging would be amazing, and I had to agree.

Midnight approached – the hour of magic – when the action goes from the everyday to something fantastical. I thought seriously about running away with Clara after the show, to walk hand in hand forever through country houses and around fabulous Christmas trees.

I also felt sick. When had that started? The answer arose immediately in my mind. How very strange. A voice in me, but not mine, said, "Careful." I briefly had the image of the druids in the circle, and a woman behind me somewhere.

The dancers leaped and spun on the glittering stage. At the same time, in slow motion, the woman with champagne and that odd green brooch, searched and searched. A pool of dirty grey light surrounded her sending foggy strands in all directions, but mainly towards where I sat.

"These things are possible," said a voice within me, and once more the circle of druids I'd seen in Hammerford Park gathered around me. As long as they did then I knew the grey smog wouldn't find me.

The clock on the stage struck twelve, and the set changed dramatically, with the Christmas tree growing truly huge. I absolutely had to go to the loo. My bladder had just reached bursting point. It would *not* be ignored. I tried to ignore it and realised any time now there would be an accident. Luckily, only three seats separated me from the aisle on my left, and one had Juliette in it.

"I must squeeze past," I whispered. Juliette frowned and then ignored me.

"I must *go,*" I said.

"Shh," said some insensitive idiot behind me.

"I must," I said and Juliette gave way, still scowling. I manoeuvred past the two other people and headed towards the place where only gentlemen can enter. *Oh the relief.*

The girl who'd sold us programmes sat texting on her mobile. No doubt she'd seen the Mad Mouse leaping about the stage behind me, many times already. I left the auditorium and letting the heavy door swish behind me. I looked for the Relief of Mafeking as dad called it, for reasons known only to him.

A doorway, painted white with gold edgings, might be the toilet. I hadn't noticed it on the way in and thought the men's room would be further away. I opened the door to discover stairs possibly used by staff. They rose steeply. I thought the toilet must be this way and started climbing.

I looked for doorways on my right or left, but at each landing just gave on to a further staircase. I concluded I must have found the fire escape for the highest seats. I thought of going back but that would be silly, so I pressed on. The walls were no longer the flock paper with red velvet designs that were pretty much everywhere. I ran my hands over them and felt the slight rough coolness of stone. My feet rang out on stone steps. I stopped. I couldn't hear anything, not even faint strains of music. The walls looked more like those I'd seen in a castle in Wales rather than a theatre in London. I arrived at a sharp turn and a small landing entirely made of large stone blocks. A long flight of stairs ascended to the open sky. I could see the stars. That didn't begin to make sense, given it had been sleeting with heavy cloud cover only half an hour ago. I carried on climbing.

I emerged onto a great flat plain. The London skyline I expected had vanished. The sky above held more stars than I'd ever seen, except perhaps in northern Norway on a clear winter night. I could recognise various constellations but others were bright and unfamiliar. The plain, made of dark stone, extended as far as I could see in all directions, grooves and fissures criss-crossed the surface. I couldn't tell if they were close and a few centimetres wide or far off and significant crevasses.

A voice spoke behind me, a mature woman's voice, but I didn't understand. I froze, and waited. I didn't wish to meet the fat woman with her ghastly eye up here. The voice sounded again, deep and kindly speaking in a language I could almost, but not quite, understand. I drew a deep breath and spun round, my arms up like a bare-knuckle fighter. I couldn't see anyone, just the top of the staircase. I turned back and looked once more over the landscape. The voice arose again, calming my nerves. A melody of spoken sounds. I listened as deeply as I could to the echo and heard, "Trust me, I will not harm you."

"Okay," I thought, "I trust you."

At once the melodious voice sounded once more, the words drifting featherlike into my mind. I waited for the echo translation. "Reach out your left hand, child." *Child!* I reached out and nearly wet myself when a hand took mine. The soft dry skin of her hand squeezed mine. I squeezed back. The echo voice inside me said, "Whatever you do now, don't let go."

That seemed sensible, so, following her lead, we set off.

Chapter 71

I Meet a Goddess

"What is your name?" I asked the empty space in front of me.

I felt the hand holding mine give another squeeze. A sound arose a long, way away that gradually became clear in my mind. "Hah-See-Na."

I said, "Your name is Ha Seenaa?" Well I didn't say it, I thought it. I received further squeeze to my hand. We now stood at an opening in the surface of this great plain of stone, with steps going down.

Hah-See-Na led the way in. Although we left the bright starlight behind, light emerged from the walls from thousands of tiny glowing crystals, embedded in them. Amazing. This was how Shoshan had described the Hall of Records. I could see my hand clearly in front of me, but my guide remained invisible.

She said, "Stand here, child." I did. I had a moment of pure terror when she let go of my hand. I could be here forever in a nook in the time-space continuum. *I'm being buried alive.* "Turn around, child," the sweet melody of the voice sounded inside me.

I did. The woman towered above me, taller than most male basketball players. Her eyes, dark hazel-green, picked out with strong lines of mascara or whatever girls wear. They looked far into me and I could sense both their strength and compassion. Her dark, wavy hair, framed her face with its oval shape and olive skin. I'd never stood this close to such a tall, beautiful woman before. Her light whitish garments did little to hide the shape of her body. Blood warmed my face and my neck burned.

If I could hear her thoughts, she could hear mine. I reddened more and swallowed.

"I have brought you as close to my time as is safe for you. I am from Kemet, which you call…" She searched for the right word. "Which you now call Egypt."

Her smile spread light all through me. *Is she a goddess or an angel?*

"No," she said inwardly, "I am only a priestess." Her smile would melt a glacier. "I'm dedicated to Anubis, the jackal-headed God, for I'm a guide to those who must find their way through time."

"Have we travelled through time then?" I thought.

"We are close to my time now, which is why you can see me, and not just feel my hand. Your time has seen the Lion look at three different midsummer constellations beyond where we are now."

I didn't know what she meant, but guessed that would be an awful long time, maybe 5,000 or 6,000 years. *Wow.* The deep dark pools of her eyes held mine, and I felt tears starting to form. I framed the thought, "Did you visit me before?"

"I helped awaken you to your task, Raw-Ree." She made an attempt at my name, which sounded really sweet.

That's what I am in ancient Egyptian.

"I worked with Shoshan to remind you of your destiny."

My destiny?

"We could draw close to you when you hovered between sleep and wakefulness. Then the knot of time is looser and you could see with your inner eyes. You will become better at this as we all work more closely together."

The idea of working with the most stunning woman in the cosmos had its appeal. Before I could wonder what the work might be, she sent the thought, "Come," she said. "It is important you trust me, which is why I have shown you my face, child."

I still couldn't get used to the child bit, but being 6,000 years younger than her, justified the description, I supposed.

"You have a long journey ahead."

We started to climb the stairs again, towards the surface of the plain and the sparkling stars. One moment I could see her climbing just in front of me and the next I could only feel the warmth of her hand. We came out on the plain, and I cringed at the thought of my sweat against the dryness of her palm.

"Watch the stars, Raw-Ree, and remember." I looked up and gazed at the pattern of the stars above me. Some pulsed, highlighting a complex pattern. I remembered the orbs of light surrounding me when I'd been with Dimitris and the two wise men. This pattern settled deep within me.

The tall invisible woman held my hand tightly while we walked. The stars tilted and moved, like a planetarium controlled by a drunk operator who wants to get home early.

The stars completely shifted in their orientation. Again, a slight warm pressure on my hands. "I will leave you here." She let go of my hand. "Farewell, Raw-Ree, till we meet again."

I couldn't breathe as panic swept over me. I stood completely still, my hand held out in front of me, the slight memory of the tall woman's grasp sliding away. Utter silence pressed in on all sides. Finally, I took a breath.

"So you've made it to the conker competition then?" said a voice.

Chapter 72

Special Conker Competition

I swung round to see a young man sitting on a stone bench near an open doorway, also made of stone. A gold box glinted next to him. He wore jeans, with dark shoes, and a T-shirt with words on it. The upper word stated "PSYCHO" separated from the lower word "POMP" next to one of those Egyptian god pictures, seen sideways on.

"Yes," said the familiar voice. "It's Anubis the Jackal god, I thought you would enjoy the joke."

"Milford?" I said, my voice quivering.

"Yes, Rhory." He smiled.

"Sorry," I corrected myself. "Dave." Then the realisation hit me. "But you're dead." He shrugged. "Does that mean that I'm dead?" My extreme panic moved up a notch.

"Depends what you mean by dead," he replied. "I feel more alive now than I ever did in Hammerford. And from my perspective you, and nearly everyone else 'alive' on earth," he did air quotes, "is more dead that I am."

"I don't follow," I said.

"Well, you're not dead in the sense you've a flesh and blood body. And I'm not dead, in the sense that I'm even more fully conscious than I was when on earth. The trick to get your mind round Rhory, is that in reality death is an illusion. It's a cat and dog trick as you will see."

"It's a what?"

"Indulge me," said Dave, avoiding giving an explanation, "I

thought we'd have the competition that my accident prevented." He opened the gold box and inside, nestling on rather fine red velvet lay half a dozen shiny conkers, with holes drilled through them. There were two waxed shoelaces.

"You choose your three conkers first and I will use what you leave. Fair?" He raised his eyebrows.

"You can't say fairer than that," I said, feeling completely bemused. I took the box and closed the lid. On the top it said,

All Time
Special Conker Competition
between
David Milford and Rhory Bruce

I opened up the box again and chose my three conkers, and proceeded to thread the first one on a lace. David did the same, but, before we started, I said, "Dave, what are you doing here, and don't say, 'playing conkers'!"

"I'm not sure I can explain it all, Rhory, as it involves all sorts of things that you don't know, about how reality actually works. I've been chosen to show you something now that's important for you to see and think about. It explains in part the experiences you've been having. You need to be able to experience something of the mystery of time, and it's very hard for someone immersed in time to see time for what it is. Once you are 'dead' as you call it, then you are freed from the suffocating anchor of Earth time and its ticking clocks. I can move more freely than you can move."

"Do you know what I've been experiencing, Dave?" I asked, thinking I might now get an explanation of what's been going on.

"I've been around a bit more than you think," said David. "I was there when you met Justine in Brighton. From that point on I could move back and forth and keep a bit of a weather eye on you! I'm not able to go back to when I lived in Midlea. I don't fully know why. Since I left though, I've moved out of ordinary time and you could say I've had many, many years of experience."

"You mean over the last month or two?"

"Yes. That time limitation has no real meaning for me anymore. I've learned many things it's not really possible to know on earth. But I cannot, and would not, be able to share those things with you. It breaks some natural law and those laws are strictly enforced."

"I see," I said, but I didn't really.

"But after the conker competition I can show you certain things that you are allowed to see. I may not answer all your questions but what you make of what you see is yours to keep."

"Fine," I said. "When do we go to look at these things?"

"After we have had our competition," said David, smiling.

"But you must know already who wins," I said.

"Actually, I don't," said David, and then added, "I told you it was complex."

We played, and the fact I challenged a dead boy at conkers, on a rocky plain below glowing stars, appeared normal for a while. In the end Dave won, but only just. We gathered up the bits of broken conker and put them back in his gold box.

"We will need to hold hands," said David. "I hope you don't mind."

So like friends at a primary school, we walked along holding hands. David glanced above him once in a while, to check the positions of stars, as they span high above our heads. We walked for a long time and talked about all sorts of things, who headed the charts, and how Everton were doing, and whether Elvis had actually died. I can't remember now whether David said he had or hadn't. It didn't seem to matter much as we strolled along the by-ways of time.

"Where are we actually?" I asked David.

"We are at the edges of time as it relates to Earth".

"You mean Earth time and other times are different?"

"They are, indeed, but it is virtually impossible to demonstrate that experimentally, while embodied on earth. However, the ancients knew it. We, people living now on Earth that is, have forgotten those things."

"Did the druids know about time being not what it appears?" I asked, thinking of Abaris.

David looked at me with his eyebrows slightly raised.

"I think you know the answer to that question better than most, Rhory my friend. The druids, the ancient Egyptians and the ancient Greeks had a much more sophisticated grasp of what time is and is not than many of our best scientific minds today. You've seen that for yourself haven't you?"

"Yes, I suppose I have."

"We are nearly there, Rhory, we are going to look at where time started and then we are going to look at where time will end. End that is, until it starts again."

"You've lost me now, Dave," I said.

"No," he said. "I don't think so." He squeezed my hand. "Just look at what's in front of us."

Chapter 73

Portals of Time

The flat plain extended behind us and in front, a sheer cliff of immense size rose high above our heads. This barrier of dark rock extended miles and miles upwards. The starlight glinted off its smooth surface. I rubbed my hands along it, feeling the slight curves and bumps. Bubbles were trapped beneath the diamond hard skin of the glassy rock. Beneath these bubbles, reflecting the starlight, it became impenetrable black. I craned my neck and looked up. I stepped back a pace or two and could see no way to get to the top, a black edge obscuring the twinkle of the stars.

"It's actually harder than diamond," said David. "There's no climbing it and no one could fly over it either. This is the time barrier, the finishing point, the deadest of dead ends."

"What's on the other side?" I asked.

"That's both a possible and impossible question and the answer is nothing and the improbable past."

"The improbable past?"

"Like I said, Rhory, our concept of time is too limited to get to grips with how things actually are. It rests on the idea that the things that are most real are atoms and caesium clocks and other parts of the material world. It also rests on the idea that time travels constantly in a straight line from what we think of as past to what we think of as future."

The conversation with our friend Nick, far, far away and long, long ago, returned. He had described time as a spiral.

"Have you heard of the Kali Yuga?" asked David.

"No."

"It is an incredibly long period of time, when the world is in darkness, *Kali* meaning dark or black in the Hindu language."

"Is that why this cliff face is black."

"An interesting point, Rhory, but next time you are here, it might appear differently. Even I don't necessarily see it as you do. We are at a barrier that our ordinary minds cannot really fathom. So it appears as it does, as we try and make sense of the nonsensical. No, the Indian wise men and women were describing the time we live in now, a time when true spiritual values and deeper wisdom would inevitably be lost. The Egyptians and the ancient Greeks both foresaw this collapse."

"Couldn't they do anything about it, if they were so clever?"

"Come, let me show you something rather than answer that question just with words."

I followed Dave as he walked beside the wall. We travelled a considerable distance until we reached a huge column, partly buried in the glass like surface. This post, supporting a door of vast proportions, rose to a dizzying height above us, and took us about a minute to walk its width. We moved a long way back from the wall to get a better view. I couldn't tell how high the doors were. There were two of them meeting in the middle between the vast doorposts. They were of a dullish green metallic colour, like very old copper and must have been a mile or two wide.

"Can they be opened?"

"They can and will," said David, but only when the age we, or especially you, live in now, has resolved into the next age."

"You are losing me again, Dave," I said, feeling really confused now.

"These doors give on to the past that existed before about 11,000 BC. You will know that there are all sorts of theories about Atlantis and things like that…?" He looked at me raising his eyebrows again.

"Yes, but I thought that was entirely a myth."

"It became a myth when these doors were closed. Until that time the very early dwellers in Egypt, Greece and India could remember directly what had gone before. These great doors to that past were definitively closed so that the errors in that past should not be repeated."

"Who closed them?"

"There are some questions I cannot answer because I don't know, and some that I cannot answer because you couldn't understand at this stage, and some because there are many answers and no single one is adequate. The best I can do is to say that the Egyptian that is known as Thoth closed them."

"A god?" I said, screwing up my face in disbelief.

"A man, expressing the divine necessity that certain knowledge be hidden for a time."

I thought again of the man with the white gloves and shiny shoes who'd come to my door months ago, before all this craziness started. I wondered if he'd a part to play in some way.

"You will understand better when we go to the other end of time."

I just looked at Dave and shrugged. He knew best, clearly.

We left the wall and walked purposefully away. After a little while I glanced back and the barrier was a tiny shadow at the very edge of the horizon. We had apparently covered hundreds of miles in just a few minutes.

David had firm hold of my hand.

"You are beginning to see how things work at Time's Edge," he said. "I wouldn't want to have to search for you if I let go of your hand. That could prove to be almost an eternal quest."

"But I'm worth it," I said.

"That's as may be. Now we must stop here because if you go through that arch, neither I nor any of your friends and helpers could get you out again. That's the definitive future."

Chapter 74

The Black Dog and the Silver Cat Return

Ahead of me a path made of huge, irregular blocks of stone led towards to an enormous archway. To our right, a massive ravine ran past and continued beyond the arch. The ground fell away so rapidly that when I looked over, keeping a tight grip on David's hand, I couldn't see the bottom. Far below, mists swirled, reflecting back in a pallid haze, the starlight above. The archway, perched on the edge of this abyss, could have had a cathedral tucked inside and still had room for more. The top of the arch, high above us, curved like a vast church window.

The archway connected to a vast dome. Dark lines extended from the arch and curved far above our heads. London railway stations look a bit like this with all their huge metal struts. A cosmic engineer must have been behind this structure, as the glass roof extended miles over our heads. The pillars and struts connected in lines both straight and curved, dividing the night sky into geometric sectors. I moved round looking above. The stars gradually shifted, and the whole dome gave the impression of being mobile.

"Really, it's like a giant sundial," said David, "only this one measures the passage of the stars. The dome is never still, all its parts move, even if ever so slowly."

"Who on earth made it?"

"Wrong question, mate," said David. "No one on earth could have made it. It goes beyond what your current computers could do, or could ever do. I like to think of this place as the Now Point. It calculates by a wisdom far beyond my ability to comprehend, all the outcomes of all the intentions in the world."

I pondered that for a moment. A pattern of struts far above me glowed electric blue for a few moments and then returned to darkness.

"When it's done its calculations," I asked, "what happens?"

"It determines how time will flow."

"Time flows?"

"Like a river. But our thoughts, hopes and prayers, as well as everything we do on and off our world, affects how it flows. That is what the Great Battle is about."

"What great battle?"

"The one between the two brothers: Cain and Abel, Set and Osiris, Typhon and Zeus, Loki and Balder. Since the great doors we saw just now have been closed, we have lived in the Age of Struggle. The time when for want of a better way of putting it, good and evil have battled it out."

"You mean that battle has raged for, what, thousands of years?"

"Maybe for all time. But it has really heated up in the last few hundred years, and the crisis point is now."

"Oh," I said, feeling that perhaps this might have something to do with what was happening to me.

"Things are balanced on a knife edge now, Rhory. Those who can read this Star Dial where we are standing, see the next few weeks, months and years as crucial. Do we go through that arch ahead, or do we cross the little bridge there."

I followed where he was pointing, and saw a slim bridge extending across the ravine.

The far side of the ravine had brighter illumination than what I could glimpse though the arch. Small misty clouds, rising from the ravine, hid and revealed parts of the bridge, so I couldn't get a clear view all the way over. On the far side stood a building. I'd seen nothing like it since ascending to this strange timeless zone.

"What's that?" I asked, pointing towards the building, with its huge columns and pediments, swathed in misty clouds. Like the bridge, only parts of this grand building stood revealed at any one time.

David turned and looked at me, but didn't speak for a moment. The building continued to appear and disappear as hazy, light filled clouds, drifted around it. "Where you see mist and cloud, Rhory, is where the future is uncertain. It depends on what people do and what they wish for. That building is known as The Temple on the Plain of Time."

"Can we go to it?"

"If we could, then all would be simple. Getting over that bridge is what it's all about. First, though, you need to understand this archway."

He let go of my hand and walked towards the arch. I followed him.

"You are entirely safe as long as you stay within this dome. If you go through that arch you are lost. Perhaps you can see why?"

Standing closer to the arch I studied the detailed carvings highlighted in bright colours. On the left hand of the arch stunted faces and bodies writhed in a mixture of terror and utter sadness. Group after group of enormous dwarf-like beings, struggled with the pressure of being crushed by the paw of a gigantic dog. The beast, bigger than any statue I'd ever seen, snarled high above, just short of where the arch started to bend over to the right. It shared the colour of night, and even its teeth were dark.

I stared at the statue and memories of the horrid dog I'd seen in the park all those nights ago flooded back. I shuddered. Perched at the top of the arch, its back up and fur on end, the silver cat spat at the dog. Its tail extended down the right hand column of the arch. Faces of ordinary people looked at the cat adoringly with the squeals of delight you see when someone wins a TV game show. The cat's tail had become a snake, binding the people to the pillar. They loved the cat too much to notice. When I looked back at the huge stone dwarves, they had moved. All the figures remained still when my eyes rested on them but had changed position when I looked again.

"Jeez … it's alive, Dave."

"Yes, that makes it all the more horrible. Those are the forces that bind people to earth, in this dark age of fratricide. The people of the Cat seek to dominate the people of the Dog, and the people of the Dog try to control the people of the Cat. Both types seek to mislead everyone else."

"Fratricide?" I asked.

"Brother against brother. All the wars, all the strife, all the hatred, belong to these two, one way or another. The followers of the two beasts know that their time is running out. They are doing everything they can to have time flow through this arch and to prevent people crossing over that bridge."

"So how do we get over the bridge?"

"By doing your best, as Hawk-Eye would say," said David, grinning. "Your part is important, Rhory, because you are connecting distant past with the present and making crossing the bridge more likely. If you – and others – succeed, then these dark millennia will begin to fade from memory and the wonders hidden behind the doors, far, far in the past, can be revealed once again. By then mankind will be wise enough to use that knowledge."

I rubbed my temple with my free hand. Discomfort spread all over me. "And if I fail?"

"I'd hope you won't old chum. None of us want to go through that arch. As I said before, there is absolutely no way back." David turned and squeezed my hand.

"Come, we must go, because even here, nothing remains static for long. There has been a development, something unexpected. You've an ally we didn't know about. One of those happy chance things that occur to keep us on our toes. When you go back to the theatre you will find someone you've seen but not spoken to. Trust her. Learn from her. And if time turns the way it may, protect her when she needs it. Oh and Rhory…"

"Yes?"

"Whatever you do, avoid the lady with the Green Eye."

"Yes, of course." I'd pretty much forgotten the theatre and even my sister and parents might have come from a fairy tale long ago and far away. Everything about this starry dome zinged with reality. We walked in a straight line for a while and crossed over a band of wide smooth rocks with points and dotted lines carved in them. I hadn't seen these on the way into the dome. Looking up I could see we'd left the dome behind, the sky stretched undivided above my head, the stars bright enough to touch.

I reflected on what David had just said and turned to him to ask about the green eye. He stopped before I could speak and slowly looked around. He checked at the stars above our heads and then faced me.

"I cannot come further with you for to do so is to enter the domain of the living, the blood and guts living as we call it. I'm not allowed to do that and anyway have no wish to. I'm having far too much fun up in these realms! You'll find your guide down..." He hesitated for a moment. "Down this one. Go now." He pointed to a descending stairway, like a big version of an entrance to the London Underground.

I looked at David and bit my lip. I didn't know what to say.

"I'll certainly see you on the other side of the bridge." His outline became fainter and I could just about see stars shining through him.

"I'll just have to get there then, Dave." A great sadness welled up in my chest. He had gone.

I descended the stairs slowly, expecting any moment to meet the lovely Egyptian lady, embodied or disembodied. I didn't find her but instead received a sharp dig in my left side.

Chapter 75

The Green-eyed Girl

The stairway vanished as another poke in my ribs arrived from nowhere. I opened my eyes.

"Flipping heck, Rhory," Juliette hissed in my ear. I glanced right at her scowling face. *What had I done now?*

It took me some moments to focus. In front of me a snowstorm swept across a stage and music swirled along with the snowflakes. The melody rose to a crescendo threatening to damage my eardrums. Where I'd just walked, had been totally and beautifully silent, except for … already the starry place seemed far away. Had I really just been talking to David? And the beautiful Egyptian lady who had been my invisible guide?

On the stage, silly people in silly costumes, leapt around, and the music became even louder. I nearly covered my ears. A clash of cymbals, a roll of drums and the audience roared their approval. The First Act was over.

"I cannot believe you snored in the middle of that," hissed Juliette. She leaned close to me so I could hear over the sound of the applause. "I was so embarrassed when I couldn't wake you up and you just kept on like a clapped out motor cycle."

I looked at Juliette and could see the anger in her eyes. I opened my mouth but couldn't find any words. Juliette shrugged and looked at the stage, clapping manically. I could hardly explain that I'd just been on a journey through time with a dead friend of mine. Even Juliette's quick mind might balk at that explanation.

"Come on, you two, let's get to the bar before the rush," said Dad easing past Jules and me. Mum followed close behind.

"Great, isn't it, children?" She smiled at us both. "Just like Norway, don't you think?" We followed them as they mounted the steep dress circle stairs. We climbed fast to be ahead of the rush. At the top, Juliette paused. "I'll just wait for Grandpa and Grandma. We don't want to lose them." I glanced back to see them caught in a clump of people about ten steps below the top.

"Okay," I said. "I'll make sure your drink is safe."

Our drinks were in the huge bar area on one of the small tables by the side. I collected my Coke and decided I wouldn't embarrass myself commenting on a ballet that I'd missed most of. I wove across throngs of people heading for the bar, so I could look at a picture on the far side of the room. It showed a map of the Coliseum and the various fire exits. I wondered if it showed the doorway I'd gone through earlier in the evening, the one that had led me all the way up to…

"Psst." I looked round but couldn't see anyone I knew. "Hey, psst." Just outside the door a young woman leaned against the wall, so I could only see her face and shoulder. She looked right at me, frowned, and then beckoned to me.

Pretty women didn't do that to me. Generally they didn't look at me at all, even though I was tall for my age. This woman beckoned again. I recognised her face but had no idea why. She gestured once more, nodded and looked intensely at me.

My chest constricted and legs became rubbery as I eased past the chattering theatregoers and slipped out of the bar. Her long dark hair and large green eyes nearly overwhelmed me as I came closer. I had little experience of being this close to drop-dead gorgeous girls, but tonight it was becoming a pattern. I swallowed.

She took my hand and said, "Hurry!" My heart now thumped away for all sorts of reasons. I didn't know what I'd do or say if I bumped into Juliette or my grandparents. Her brown boots were at my eye level as we climbed the stairs. That jogged my memory. I had studied her as she sat opposite me on the tube earlier in the evening.

Why on earth had she suddenly appeared here?

As I followed her, I looked in vain for the doorway I'd found earlier that evening. All the corridors and stairs had so many people moving through them that I couldn't see any doors at all. For the second time in an hour I had my sweaty hand in the grasp of a young woman. She glanced back and gave me a radiant smile. *Is she real? Can other people see her? What is a femme fatale, anyway? Am I having a breakdown?* We slipped back into the auditorium, much higher in the theatre. The stage set had shrunk and small snow laden trees moved around of their own accord. I blinked, and spotted the ant-like stagehands manoeuvring them.

"Let's sit here, shall we?" said the girl, her green eyes fixed on mine. The fluffy texture of her pink cardigan brushed against my sleeve, and I battled with the realisation that her black skirt, somewhat short, revealed metres of leg. I kept my eyes sensibly on her face. My stomach constricted at the notion that this woman might actually be dangerous. *She'll hardly attack me, next to a queue full of children buying tubs of ice cream.*

"Thank you," she said. "Thank you for trusting me. I know you've been having extraordinary experiences." She looked at me and smiled again, as if awaiting confirmation. Before I could confirm or deny, she looked away towards the boxes near the stage area. "I don't think she can see us here, so we're safe for a bit. There's a lot I must tell you." I heard her slight Irish accent clearly for the first time.

"Who can't see us?" I asked, finally trusting my voice enough not to squeak like an excited puppy.

"The woman from MI5, the one I know as Emerald. She's here with her family, in that box down there, and I know for sure she's a fully paid up spook. She's also nasty and dangerous."

"Oh," I said, not at all sure how to respond to this information. A memory of the stout woman drinking champagne with her family, before The Nutcracker started, came back to me. So much had happened since seeing her that I'd almost forgotten how I'd felt compelled to study her, like a fly watching a fascinating spider. My dark haired acquaintance was now looking steadily at me.

"Um, sorry, um, but who are you?" I asked.

She let go of my hand, and kindly did not wipe her palm on her hairy cardigan. "I'm silly aren't I? I recognised you on the tube. And I followed you here. I'd seen you before, remember? You should. You were wearing your pyjamas when you … how should I say … when you turned up so unexpectedly amongst the oak trees. I feel I know you really quite well!"

My brain went into overdrive. "Oh," I said again, hardly improving on my fluency. "Ah, oh I see … yes. You were with the druids?"

She looked at me for a long moment, as a young boy next to me complained his sister had taken the last tub of strawberry ice cream. Her eyes narrowed slightly and her lips pursed.

"This is complex isn't it, Rhory? You are Rhory aren't you?" I nodded as the unreality index went through the roof. "That meeting took place over two thousand years ago, you know that, don't you?" I nodded again, although the urge to burst into tears hovered somewhere nearby. "Either I took part in the ceremony, or I looked out through the eyes of someone who did."

"Oh." I offered a weak smile. "Are you a dead druid priestess then?"

She frowned at me, and something flashed behind her green eyes. Then she laughed.

"Yes, I probably am aren't I. But not in this life. My friends know me as Shelley." She held out her hand. I wiped mine on the edge of my jacket and shook hers.

"I'm Rhory Bruce."

Shelley took my hand in both of hers. "Well, Rhory Bruce, you've to take these people seriously. They know about you and the others. They don't exactly know who you are but they're getting closer. They know you live in or visit Hammerford. They also know more than a little about the special qualities of the Hammerford Park and they believe something important is hidden there."

She reached into her handbag and took out a piece of paper. "We don't have very long. Here, I wrote down my mobile. Well it's not mine, it's my mate Laila's. I'm sure that my phone is bugged, so I use this one for special occasions. Don't call me from your home, just in case. Call me using a friend's phone. I'll tell you all I know about the Society and what they are up to. I'll help you as best I can."

"Society?

"Yes, the Society of Secrets. Emerald, the fat lady from the box down there, is one. She's not the worst of them, though I think she's a horrid bully. No, a worse one actually lives in Hammerford."

A chill passed down my neck and across my shoulders. Shelley looked at me as though deciding what to say next. I helped her out.

"You know what's been happening to me, Shelley?" I asked.

"Not everything, not in detail, but you are on one side of the fence, and the Stones ... the people I work with, Emerald and her friends, are on the other side. They are playing with time in some way, Rhory. You, and that other boy, are able to do something and they want to stop you. He comes from another time I think, doesn't he?"

"Yes, I think so."

Shelley stood up and gave my hand a squeeze. "You're not alone, Rhory, not now. I'll help as I can. I've an inside track. And I've the Gift ... more than they realise." She nodded in the direction of the empty box where Emerald and her family had been sitting. I could see coats draped over chairs.

"I'll explain when you call me. You better get back to your family now before they miss you." She smiled her glacier-melting smile once more, touched my cheek and was gone. I made my way down towards the dress circle bar. My dry mouth needed refreshment, but I'd left my Coke by the seat where I'd been talking to Shelley. I hadn't even had a sip.

Chapter 76

"We are both in danger"

I reached the bar, just as the first bell calling us back to our seats rang out its warning. Jules spotted me and came across carrying her drink. She looked cross.

"Don't be mad at me, Sis," I said.

"Where have you been?"

"I went through the door and got a bit lost," I said, keeping as close to the truth as I dared. "By the way, how does this diagram work?"

If in doubt, I'd always found Juliette's need to explain everything trumped almost anything else. She pointed to where we stood and how we could use various ways to get out of the building in the event of a fire.

"Let's go out a different way, Jules," I suggested, "when the ballet is over, so as to avoid the crush in the main entrance."

She agreed and at that point the bell rang again for us to return to our seats. I noticed an abandoned Coke, drank straight from the bottle and burped surreptitiously as we left the bar.

I really did need to go to the loo. Surely I'd been before hadn't I? I looked for the extra door I'd used before but couldn't see it, and after joining the queue of desperate men, I did what I had to do. As I returned, the orchestra was enjoying the flaying of more cats and the second act began. I burped a little more as I sat down.

*

When Shelley left Rhory, she slipped out into the corridor and put her woolly hat back on her head, tucking her hair in. The disguise would have to do. The tall boy emerged into the corridor a moment later and walked slowly back down the stairs. *Poor love, he doesn't know what he's got himself into. But then neither do I.*

The lad talked to his sister and Shelley kept an eye on them both until they waved across the room to their parents and grandparents. The girl headed for her seat and the boy followed a moment or two later. At the far end of the corridor, outside the bar, Emerald stood with her back towards Shelley. *That's rich. The spook is spying.*

Sure enough, when the rest of Rhory's family left, Emerald moved with some grace past the last few patrons finishing their drinks and picked up a scrap of paper from the table where the Bruce family had been drinking. She read it and replaced it. The crowds still gave Shelley cover and once Emerald had disappeared from the bar area, she ducked in and crossed to the table. The paper lay there in a puddle of water. Shelley read it. "Bryce."

Shelley smiled to herself as she returned to her seat high up in the theatre. *The good powers watch over our Rhory. Lucky boy.*

Shelley enjoyed the rest of the ballet. Not that ballet did much for her, but she knew many of the tunes and the story became exciting as it moved towards the climax. Shelley slipped out of her seat just before the final curtain and made her way down to the main foyer. She stood by the stairs, on the side far away from Emerald's box, and where the Bruce family had sat, and waited. Tucked in next to the handrail, wearing her woolly hat, she doubted anyone would recognise her. Moments later, the chattering hordes came out, all smiles and enthusiasm. As Shelley expected, Emerald and her massive son soon took up a position watching the other stairs to the dress circle.

Shelley waited for a good ten minutes but the Bruce family did not come out of the theatre by the normal route and Emerald had waited in vain. Shelley slipped out with the last of those from the stalls area. *Well he lives to fight another day, our brave boy from Hammerford.*

Chapter 77

Return to the Park

"Jumping Jelly Beans, but it is mighty parky."

"Yep," I agreed with Nick, "it would freeze the proverbials off a brass monkey." I blew on my hands and hitched my sports bag onto my shoulder. We were heading towards the tennis courts.

Two nights ago, I'd been at the theatre in London, and walking over the plain of time, with a dead boy we both knew. I'd also travelled close enough to ancient Egypt to see a priestess of Amazon proportions and stunning looks. I couldn't share any of this with Nick. Not yet at least.

The weak sun offered little warmth and any that made it through the stratosphere blew away with the biting wind.

"Oh, I love that smell," said Nick. I breathed in, the smell of warm tar.

"Hmm, me too," I said as we rounded the corner to where the eight tennis courts stood in a row. No nets, no lines, just a lot of workmen laying a new surface. "No tennis today then."

We walked over to the machine producing the liquid tar, and shared its free warmth for a bit. Watching the men pour the tar and scrape it smooth proved compelling. One man drove a small, motorised, heavy roller, to push the tar down.

"I'd love that job," said Nick, breathing the tarry fumes deep into his lungs.

I wanted to share with Nick that Dave, our good, good friend, still lived on somewhere near and far away, but couldn't find the right words to begin. Instead fate intervened when I suggested, "We can't play tennis, so let's go and pick off a few passing dog owners. The wall will be in sunshine and the leaves have fallen from the trees."

"Okay, Field Marshal," said Nick.

We had our empty ballpoint pen tubes and a supply of paper just in case. The walk from the tennis courts took three or four minutes and we ducked in through the bushes, which screened us from prying secretaries in the council offices behind us.

I looked over the wall and read, 'Best Value Carpets in Hammerford' on the huge billboard across the road. I looked left towards the station and quickly ducked my head back in. "Nick, it's blooming Hacker."

"Great, let's zap the S.O.B."

"Oh, I don't think so, he's with Gary. They won't be fooled for an instant and I don't want to give them an excuse to pulverise me, thanks very much."

We stayed ducked down behind the wall, to wait until they'd gone past. A moment later we heard voices about one metre away from where we were crouching. Hacker had been joined by another of his mates just on the other side of the wall. He lit up a cigarette.

"We've got a job." Smoke curled up and vanished in the breeze.

"Not more fruit picking, Hack, that did my head and my hands in last time."

"No, Mike, this is real money. For old rope."

"Old rope?"

"Oh never mind, Gary, it's an expression me dad uses. Money for doing nothing very much."

"So what we gotta do?" said a fourth voice I didn't recognise. They must have met with two of their mates coming the other way, Mike and someone else.

"Just burn down the bandstand."

"But that's arson, Hack," said Mike. "They put you away a long time for arson."

"No, it's community service, mate, we're getting help and

backing from very high places indeed."

"Who?" This from the mystery voice.

"Never mind who, but let's just say he doesn't work a million miles from where we are standing."

"When we got to do this?" said Gary. "If we've got to do this?"

"No one's got to do nothin'," said Hacker. "But if you want shares of the hundreds we'll be paid, it has to be this week.

"This week!" said Mike.

"Yeah, as soon as possible, like you're a deaf parrot or somethin', Mike. Okay, I need to know who's in and who's out on this."

A few moments chat established they were all in. Hacker told them he'd phone with the exact details. They walked off in their various directions.

"We should tell the police," said Nick.

"I suppose we should, but I'm not sure it'd do any good."

"Why?"

"Well," I thought aloud, "if it's true they have support from someone high up in the Hammerford Mafia—"

"The what?"

"You know, not literally, but the tough nuts who tried to get the road right through Hammerford, and who run the town from that building there." I nodded towards the council offices. "I think you'll find," I continued, "that the police won't take it seriously. And at a senior level, they may be in on it."

I was thinking of some of the things Shelley had confided to me, about how powerful the Stones were, and the link to MI5. A few minutes later, Nick headed off for home and I went back for lunch.

"So, are you gay?" said Natasha with a wicked smile on her face.

"What on earth are you on, Nats?"

"Well, one ballet is usually enough to make straight men gay, I'm told!"

"Don't be daft, g-Nat," I said, emphasising her status as the small irritating flying insect.

"At the very least you are now an aesthete!"

Now I was genuinely perplexed.

"An *east feet*, Nat, what are you burbling about?"

Natasha had come round to our house. Term would start in a few days and Mum had agreed she could stay over. She'd be sleeping on the pull-out bed in Juliette's room, built by my dad. One bed fitted under the other and it rolled out on castors. He'd made the headboards and everything without using a single screw or nail. Clever Dad.

"So tell me about this Irish girl. The one at the ballet. She just called to you and you followed?"

"Well, sort of. I'd seen her earlier on the tube, like sink, sinko…"

"Synchronicity."

"Yes, like that," I said. I told Natasha that Shelley had somehow seen me once before, when I arrived back in time in Hammerford Park. ("Cool.") And that a group called the Society of Secrets wanted to find me. ("Not cool.") But Shelley would help me if she could, given that she worked with them as a psychic.

"So she's either incredibly brave or incredibly stupid then."

"I got the impression she didn't have all that much choice. They use her to gather information and they need her to find me."

Natasha looked up at me from where she sat cross-legged on the floor. "Do you trust her?"

"I think so. I know it could have been a set up, but bumping into her on the tube really did seem to be chance, and she knew about my meeting the druids and all."

"Well, that's true, Rhory, if we're to believe you that is, and you've not eaten too many Christmas liqueur chocolates."

Natasha gave me a crooked smile. I knew she believed me. At least I didn't have to deal with all this on my own. I rubbed my temples, hoping to clear my mind by the direct route.

"She gave me a phone number by the way." Natasha arched her eyebrows and puckered her lips. "No, Nat, blimey, she's nearly old enough to be my mum for goodness sake. Actually she gave me a friend's mobile number as she thinks my phone and hers will be bugged."

"You're kidding, right?

"No, really." I explained the connection with Emerald, the spook.

"Did you call her yet?"

"No. She only gave me the number a few days ago, I haven't felt the need."

"So she doesn't have a number for you?"

I thought about that, and rubbed my temples harder. Natasha went over to her backpack, dropped in a corner of the room. "Here, use this one."

"You've more than one?"

"It's my emergency phone, quite old."

I looked at the chunky clamshell design and agreed with her on the age. I retrieved Shelley's note from the back of my dream diary, and texted her, to make a link.

"There, now she can contact me if she wants."

While I used her phone, Natasha used mine to check on the scores of several Premier League matches taking place that night. I sat watching her expert thumbs navigate around my phone, a lot quicker than I ever managed.

The phone in my hand buzzed and vibrated. "Here, Nat," I said, holding it out to her.

"No one ever calls me on that number, Rhory. Look and see who is calling."

I did, it said 'unknown'.

"So it's your Irish girlfriend then. Answer it."

I pulled a face but pressed the little green phone symbol. I listened with care as a voice with a much stronger Irish accent than I remembered talked to me solidly for a minute and then hung up.

Natasha leaned forward and opened her arms. "Well…?"

I swallowed. "It has to be tonight. She sounded desperate actually, spoke with hardly taking a breath, very quietly into the phone. The Society thingy, you know, the secret one, is meeting tonight. They are going to try to stop the work me and Dimitris and Shoshan are doing, at least that's what she guessed. She's going to be involved in some ceremony or other. She didn't sound too pleased about that."

"What will you do?"

"I have to find that temple, the one on the map. I have to dream myself into the well..." I tailed off. I'd never dreamed a night flight to order, and Natasha and I both knew it.

"Look, numbskull," she said, "if you can't dream your way to fly to the park, you could just walk!"

"I guess."

"So, take me with you, Rho, I might be able to help. I'm not sure you want to go climbing down a well on your own."

"There are complications, Nat, real complications."

"Such as...?"

I told her how Nick and I'd heard Hacker and his gang talking about burning down the bandstand.

"Well, we just have to stop them," announced Natasha.

We talked about what we'd need to take with us, and made some quick preparations.

"All right, Natasha, I'll scratch on the bedroom door late tonight, once everyone is asleep. Jester does that all the time. You'll have to creep out of Jules's room quietly though. It'll be okay, because she'd sleep through an earthquake."

I sat on my bed listening to the noises in the house. The branches of the winter trees projected their silent dance on the wall. Mum and Dad went to bed and I heard their bedroom door click shut. I peeked out onto the landing ten minutes later, to see a strip of light under their bedroom door and also next to me, where Jules and Nat must still be reading, or more likely, gabbing.

I'd changed for bed earlier, to prevent Mum from being suspicious when she insisted on kissing me goodnight. Moving stealthily around my room, to avoid tell-tale creaking, I pulled on jeans over my jim-jams and slipped on a pullover. My leather jacket hung on its hook near the back door. I sank back onto my bed as tiredness swept over me. My bones ached with the tension of the last few days. I hadn't really begun to sort out what had happened with seeing David, and that weird archway, and the bridge to the Temple of Time or whatever. I kept sitting upright and stared at the skeleton branches doing their dance.

I jerked myself awake, my head having dropped forward. Jeez, I could have just fallen asleep. Disastrous.

I opened my door really quietly, crept the two metres down the corridor and listened at the door to Juliette's room. I could hear the sound of steady deep breathing, so I scratched on the door. Light from the street lamps illumined the corridor.

Moments later, Natasha slipped out fully dressed, her finger to her lips. Coats on, with a torch in my pocket, we eased our way out of the back door. I'd used the amazing WD40 earlier in that evening to ensure the lock moved silently. It had. We breathed in the damp night air. Natasha had her small backpack with its vital supplies.

We tiptoed down to the end of Suffolk Road and crossed the wide expanse of street at the major junction of the various roads. We turned right in the direction of the station. The library watched us through its dark blank windows. When we reached the first park gate and pushed it, it didn't budge. We hoped for better luck with the north gate but this also proved to be locked.

The wall on this side of the park rose more than two metres, much too high for us both to climb. We tried and proved the point. I kicked the wall, and hurt my foot. Nat blew on her hands to counter the cold. Neither of us had gloves.

"What about the tunnel?" What was the girl talking about? "Rhory, are you deaf," she whispered, even though there was no one anywhere near. "What about the flipping tunnel?"

"Oh, the tunnel!" I said, my neurones beginning to fire again. Of course there is a way in that does not involve flying, or climbing, or keys to gates, just a lot of nerve on a dark, damp night.

"Yes, Nat, good idea," I said.

We headed up the road and crossed over again, because the tunnel entrance was on the far side. We walked down the slope away from the road, and turned sharp left. The metal gate here proved dead easy to climb. The mouth of the tunnel, like an opening to the underworld, glowed faintly in front of us, lit by a couple of weak lights.

Chapter 78

The Well

The meeting room on the top floor of Trethowan House afforded a panoramic view of Hammerford Park. All the features briefly stood out in the silvery sheen of the moon. The man looked across the formal garden that graced the back of the council building. Beyond the yew hedge he could just see the dark smudge of the old oak in the distance to the left and the top of the bandstand to the right. This useless structure would finally be destroyed tonight. This would have two benefits; it would open the way for the construction of the leisure centre and that would add handsomely to his private bank account. More importantly, it would destroy the portal, crack or glitch in time that was playing havoc with the long-term plans of the Stones.

The man checked his watch by the light of a small torch. He picked up his mobile phone and slipped on his dark overcoat. As he emerged from a side door of the council offices, into the light of the moon, the amethyst ring on his finger sparkled in the cold, blue light.

He kept to the shadows and then walked purposefully to the bandstand. He put on gloves and slotted a slightly rusty iron key into the door of the storage room, below the raised floor of the bandstand. The door was stiff and creaked a bit as he opened it. The musty smell of old chairs and decaying canvas wafted past. He closed the door once more but didn't lock it. Petrol, canvas and the wood of nearly 100 deck chairs would make a fine blaze.

He straightened up and listened to the deep silence in the park.

He could just make out the noise of the occasional car as it made its way up North Road. Taking the slight risk of being seen, he swiftly walked from the bandstand towards the protective shadows of the old oak. A few minutes later, in the deep gloom under the ancient boughs, he chose a position where he could wait. The bandstand vanished temporarily, as a large cloud passed in front of the moon. Raindrops pattered on the branches overhead and he wondered if the yobs would be put off by a shower. Surely not. Not with the money they thought they were getting. From here, he'd quietly control the night's events.

*

Beyond the tunnel under the road, we could see the path ascending once more, briefly picked out in moonlight. Moments later it vanished into darkness.

"Bother," said Natasha, looking up, "there are clouds."

"And rain," I added, having felt a couple of drops land on my head.

"There's no one in the tunnel, let's get through," said Natasha.

At that moment we caught the murmur of voices behind us. The sound came from the second tunnel that went under the railway tracks. That tunnel had no lights at all. I'd no idea if someone standing in it could see us.

"Quickly," I said, and we walked swiftly through the mossy underground entrance to the park. As we cleared the tunnel, the moon came out once more, lighting up the path ahead. Someone behind us shouted, "Stop."

We had at least fifty metres on whoever had shouted and pelted up the tarmac pathway into the park. Both of us had sneakers on and we ran in almost complete silence. We veered right, passing my old nursery school on the left, and turning right again to take the path circling the whole park. Whoever had been behind us had made different choices and we could hear no sounds of pursuit. We jogged until we reached the Wild Wood, with its great conker tree, close to the hidden well.

I cupped my hands, "Come on, Nat, put your foot here."

I stood on the far side of the metal railings, and above my head the horse chestnut tree swayed in the increasing wind. I'd pulled myself over but the railings proved just too high for Natasha to climb without help. She landed in a heap.

"Drat," said Natasha. "I've dropped my torch."

I felt around in the dry leaves and soon found it. Natasha switched it on briefly to locate her small backpack with its essential supplies.

"Careful, Nat, we can be seen," I whispered. Navigating once more just by the dappled light of the moon, we crossed to the hawthorn bush. Natasha pushed its sharp branches aside and I cleared the top of the old well that I'd found with David.

Natasha reached into her bag and took out the screwdriver and the WD40. She gave the screwdriver to me and sprayed the area around the three large screws that held on the iron bands fixing the wooden lid securely to the well. At first none of the old screws would budge.

"Shall I try?" said Natasha.

"Give it a moment, Nat," I said feeling a bit irritated, "the oil has to have time to work." The screwdriver twisted in my hands and switching on the torch I could see that the screw head had partially sheared.

"Now what?" said Natasha.

"Let's wait a moment or two. We're completely stumped if another screw breaks."

I moved on to the next screw, applied pressure gingerly and it turned. I loosened it and moved on to the third screw. This also turned and soon I removed both of them. The fourth screw hole had no screw. Using our combined strength, we forced the cover up; the rusted iron band held in place by the broken screw, first bent and then broke. We eased the top off and looked in. As expected, I could see the metal rungs of a ladder extending down the side of the well. The depth of the well remained a mystery in the darkness.

"I think I can see a tunnel down there," said Natasha, shining her torch down into the gloom below. "It's about five metres down."

I put on the backpack and swung my legs over the edge of the well and leaned in to take a firm grip on the first metal rung. The rusty metal scraped against my palm as I reached out with my foot to find a lower foothold. The end of my shoe slid on the slime of the wall and then engaged with the metal support.

"Point the torch down so I can see where I'm going." Natasha did so, and I began my descent. "I'll go down as far as I can and see if the tunnel is there."

"I'll follow you when you shout," said Natasha. "Only shout quietly!"

A few steps down and a rung wobbled under my foot. I didn't trust it with my weight. The light danced around me, showing the curved bricks of the old well. They still held a slight glaze in places but dampness had hidden most of them behind moss and slime. A cold stillness surrounded me the moment my head went below the top of the well. I looked up and grinned at Natasha.

"I can see water below and I think I can also see something dark that may be the tunnel." I eased my hands past the loose rung and found my foot reaching into space. I stretched my right leg down further and just made contact with a metal support that held. Two rungs must have fallen out.

A greater coldness came alongside a deeper darkness next to me. I reached out and my hand waved in space. The tunnel. I looked up to shout to Natasha, when her torchlight zigged around and then vanished. I held my breath and looked up into the gloom above me.

A pale face looked over.

"Gotcha, you creep." A scraping noise announced the replacement of the cover and moments later I could hear the screw being turned. A faint muffled cry suggested Natasha had shouted or fought back. I hung onto the rung a metre or two above the water, my heart pounding in my ears and sick fear tightening my stomach. I fiddled with my pocket and, hanging on with one hand, located the torch. It slipped in my hand and splashed into the darkness below.

Chapter 79

The Old Temple

I clung on to the cold metal in the pitch darkness, wishing I'd brought some gloves, and struggling to hear the voices above me. They faded, and after a minute or so I knew for sure they'd gone. If I climbed up I wouldn't be able to budge the lid. For a moment fear surged right through me, and I had to clasp the rung tighter so as not to fall. I pressed my forehead against the cold damp wall. *I must find the temple.* I reached out with my left foot and touched a flat surface. Pivoting, I pushed with my right hand on the rung and reaching inside the tunnel with my left. A moment later I stood on a level surface in the total darkness. Now what?

The ground beneath my feet felt so soggy I didn't want to sit down. A still, damp mustiness of undisturbed old air stuck in my nostrils. I eased the backpack over my shoulders, my fingers shaking so much I could hardly manage the buckles. I held the bag between my knees and rubbed my hands together, to stop myself shivering quite so much. I loosened the cord at the top of the pack and reached inside.

I could feel various cloth containers and I knew that Natasha had packed the small sack of stones and the scarab pendant. We both thought they'd be needed tonight if we found the temple. I reached around but couldn't find the candle and the matches. Perhaps she had those on her for easy access. Finally my hand closed around something round, metal and hard. The spare torch. I withdrew it carefully, not wishing to spill anything on the wet ground beneath my feet.

The beam dazzled my eyes and I waited until I could cope with the light. Behind me, an oval space showed the entrance from the well. Ahead, the tunnel sloped down slightly, into a distant total blackness. The sides of the tunnel had brickwork similar to the well. I could see no point in waiting so moved cautiously forward, my feet sliding a little on the slick ground.

After several metres, the tunnel levelled out and the floor felt less damp. I stopped and shone the torch around. The tunnel no longer had brickwork, and in this part had been constructed of stone blocks similar to those used for Hammerford Town Hall. The roof arched. I ran the beam of light along it, and saw that in places stones had fallen out leaving black gashes. *Hope my walking down here doesn't collapse it on my head.*

Walking had moved my blood around a bit and my teeth no longer chattered. The air remained moist and a little fetid, but the tunnel became much drier as I worked my way forward. On the walls, higher than my head, occasional twisted metal shapes stuck out. They had almost rusted away and would have held torches in some past era. The tunnel seemed to go on forever and my footfalls echoed both behind and in front of me. I whistled once and regretted it, as the sound lasted for several seconds, the piping of a mournful ghost. I moved on as silently as I could manage, my heart banging away inside my chest. I desperately needed a drink but didn't want to stop in this tube of darkness and fiddle with the backpack again. *What has happened to Natasha? What will they do to her?*

I'd keep Natasha safest by pressing on. My powerful friends might have lived a few thousand years ago, but they remained powerful in a way beyond easy explanation.

The torchlight highlighted the old stonework of an archway. It resembled the side entrance to a gothic church. After the archway, broad worn steps descended. A small beetle scuttled by. As I descended, my footsteps echoed on each stone slab. A moment or two later I stood in a small chamber. *How far had I walked? I should be near or under the bandstand by now.* I couldn't be sure, but I guessed I'd walked far enough.

The small room had the tunnel entrance on one side and on the adjoining wall, a square doorway. Metal pegs in the stonework had once held a heavy door. The door itself had mainly vanished, but some rotten planks had been propped against the wall. I entered a small passageway, about a metre and a half long.

Shining the light ahead I could see very little. When I passed through the next doorway, the echo from my shoes changed and reverberated. I'd come into a big room. Circular markings had been carved into the stone floor. I couldn't see any moss or puddles, and the room smelled entirely dry. Vents must have existed to let in fresh air. I breathed in deeply and felt calmness beginning to return. The roof above my head must have been several metres high. I said, "hello," and it echoed back to me.

I shone the torch beam ahead revealing the face of a huge bull. That did nothing for my nerves. As I moved the torch some more, it revealed parts of a large carving filling one wall, showing a man with a pointy hat wrestling with a bull and pushing its head down towards the ground. The moving torchlight caused the man and bull to bob around in an alarming way.

I stood for a while wondering what to do next. I knew I'd found the old temple. It dated back centuries. On one side stood a thick, stone table like an altar; it reminded me of the one at which Pythagoras and Abaris had sat when I found myself in Croton.

Once more I let the light beam play on the floor. The deeply engraved circles could have easily contained one of Juliette's dance hoops. I moved from one circle to the next and counted six around a central seventh. I went back two circles. *Yes. Not my imagination. A warmth.* I knelt down and felt the stone. It had the profound cold of a deserted temple deep underground, and felt no different from the circles on either side. When I stood again, I could distinctly feel the warmth. More to the point, I felt safe standing there.

I knew what to do, and quickly unpacked the backpack, taking out the pendant and the bag with ten stones. I walked around the outer six circles and felt a shift in the atmosphere, not warmth, this time, but a texture in the air. I placed the pendant in one circle, missed out the next and then put down the stones. I returned to the warm circle and stood. Checking with my torch I could see I now had a position at the point of a triangle with the pendant and the stones forming the other two points. *Just right. Now breathe slowly and wait.*

So I switched off the torch and waited. The silence pressed in around me. Where I stood gradually became warmer. The illumination, when it arose, poured through the walls of the temple and a triangle of white light formed between my feet and the other two circles. The stone walls all around me changed, becoming more and more like one of those ice-sculptures they do in Norway at Christmas-time. I could see through the walls and through the bull and the man. Beyond stood a larger temple, lit by many torches. A voice sounded inside me. "Welcome, brother. We have awaited your arrival."

Chapter 80

Shelley in the Hot Seat

Shelley

Shelley's emergency phone hummed a quiet tune in her handbag. She moved her lipsticks, compact and keys aside to fish out the pink handset, borrowed from Laila. This one she guessed would not be bugged, even here in the West Country. She pressed a few buttons and found Rhory's text. Now she had his number. She phoned, and the lad had answered almost at once. Shelley had urgently shared with him what she knew and described the slight panic in the house.

"They are doing something big tonight. You do what you can at your end, and I'll do my best here." She disconnected.

She'd had the summons to the house late the previous night. The caller – she guessed Emerald, but couldn't be sure – had said a car would be sent to her flat. A step up in the world then, chauffeur service.

Killer Joe had duly arrived earlier this afternoon, and even talked a bit on the way as they drove down the A4. Nothing consequential and nothing that revealed anything about Joe or the Society of Stony hearts. She chatted brightly about the charts, the latest excitement over Manchester United, skiing in Austria – they had both done that apparently – and the most recent Batman film. Afterwards they'd fallen silent, but not the awkward silence of earlier lifts.

Something had changed. Shelley went into search mode but could pick up little about the man driving her. He couldn't screen himself as well as the Stones, but he had an emptiness inside that she found eerie. *He fancies me though.* She shuddered slightly.

"You cold? I could put the heating higher if you want," he said.

Once she arrived, they gave her a hot meal in the breakfast room she used. She loved the food: Onyx brought her chicken in some fancy sauce, after a starter with seafood and a small Italian dessert with whipped cream. *I'm getting the same fare as the Stones. They must be in a rush. No time to send to Lidl to sort out my meal.*

After she finished, Sardius walked into the room.

"We'll be working in a different way tonight. Have a rest if you need one, Miss..."

"Prendergast..."

"Yes, indeed, silly of me, of course," he purred.

Shelley had wondered what he called her when she'd left the room. The Irish tart probably.

Shortly after returning to the bedroom, feeling pleasantly full, Rhory's text message had arrived.

Now she'd spoken to him, she put up her feet and began to read one of her magazines.

At quarter to eleven, with the house hushed for the night, a soft knock on her door announced they were ready. For the first time ever, Sardius took her down the main stairs, and turned right instead of left at the bottom. *He's heading for the room with the bowl.*

Shelley's mouth went dry and she took a few deep breaths, imagining herself surrounded by an egg of white light with a silvery sheen. *Usually works, but with these guys, you never know.*

The door opened onto a wonderland. All the wooden tripods had been moved around, with their candles and reflectors at different heights. The huge stone bowl glimmered and shimmered in the candlelight. Shelley flicked her eyes around the room. Most of the usual suspects were there, with a couple of new faces. A tall man with Asiatic features stood on the far side of the room talking quietly to Emerald. All of them wore robes of deep hues: dark blues, maroons and deep sea greens.

"Wear this," said Sardius, with more than a little edge to his voice. *He's nervous. What are they up to?*

He handed her a white robe to put on. It slipped easily over her head and she found two armholes. *I'm a cross between a sacrifice and a choir boy.*

"We're gathered, at somewhat short notice, for this important ritual," said the tall man with Asian looks. His broad shoulders and height gave an impressive air, and he alone wore a black robe. "We represent a noble and important tradition stretching back to antiquity. And that tradition is threatened." He spoke softly, with the authority of one used to others obeying him. All eyes were on him.

Shelley's brother, back in Ireland, loved Samurai films, and she occasionally watched with him. Looking at this man, with his dark, straight hair, swept back from his forehand, and hard, high cheekbones, she could imagine him wielding the sword that lopped off the heads of those who displeased him. He didn't bother to shield his aura, unlike the others in the room. A silvery blue predominated, with deep reds below the surface and dark streaks. *This dude is one heck of a powerful man.* Shelley tried to swallow but found her mouth entirely dry. *Will I actually get out of here alive?*

"Today is a time node," the man said, and the others in the room nodded. "What happens today will set the course for years to come. Until recently we were entirely on track and our plans, laid over centuries, were unfolding impeccably. An unexpected disturbance set in some months back, and across the whole time chain. We've traced it in local time, to one person living in Southern England. This is the reason Amethyst isn't with us this evening, as emergency action has to be taken. The portal we've known about for several years has to be blocked, and will be, as we do our work tonight."

Shelley carefully avoided saying Rhory's name in her head. She could shield her thoughts from others better than most, but this guy in black had a presence she'd never come across before, and she doubted she could hide much from him. *I hope the boy remains safe.*

His work tonight may stop these jokers in their tracks.

The man in black looked across at her. "Thank you for joining us tonight, Shelley. Your part is simple and we are grateful for all you've done so far. We couldn't have arranged this star chamber in the way we have, without the calibrations you've provided over the months."

So that's what I've been doing. Shelley managed a toothy smile, while her innards continued to contract.

"You will work seated tonight," announced the man, continuing to drill into Shelley's soul with his eyes, hooded in the candlelight. "Will that be a problem for you?"

Shelley shook her head. Going into a trance wouldn't be a problem. Getting away from this dark corner of the universe might be.

The man swept his eyes over the others. "Two of us will physically return to the dawn of our era. We've never travelled so far before and to do so safely has taken some years of preparation, as you all know."

Onyx, her honey blonde hair gathered into a tight bun for once, and her face with hardly any make-up, nodded. Her eyes held Shelley's for a moment. She wore a dark robe in smudgy blue. *Not her best colour.* The ice cubes at the bottom of Shelley's stomach rearranged themselves.

"The honour falls, of course, to Emerald. We all know of her links to the foundation time. Now is the moment to use these links to our advantage. I will accompany her. Please take your positions."

Sardius touched Shelley's shoulder and indicated the seat she should take. She had her back to the door, and her seat matched three others at the cardinal points. Onyx glided over to the chair on her left – no high heels for once – and Jasper took the chair on her right. Both wore deep grey-blue. Opposite her Emerald sat down, her robe a lustrous sea green. Alone, of all those gathered in the room, she wore her stone prominently, high on her robe, just below her neck. The candles reflected from it in dark green pulses. Shelley mentally did a sign of the cross and then added more power to the shiny eggshell of light she'd gathered around her.

The tall man in the black robe stood behind Emerald and chanted softly in a language Shelley didn't recognise at all. The others bowed their heads. Shelley closed her eyes and immediately found herself at the steps of a temple made of reddish stone, with stumpy round pillars, much fatter at the bottom than the top. Something snorted behind her and she turned to see a huge hairy pig in a stone enclosure. She opened her eyes and for a moment had the impression the whole room, in the west of England, floated in space, with the candles twinkling – a cosmos of local stars.

Sardius had knelt down beside her, a booklet in his hand, full of words and symbols. She kept her eyes forward, towards the bowl, as he whispered words she didn't recognise. Smokey light rose in the bowl and the figures incised on the inside surface began to move. Shelley blinked and they became still. Within moments the smoky light increased once more and the figures followed a slow dance of their own.

She looked up to see Emerald's eyes had turned up in their sockets. *She'll have eye ache tomorrow. That's so unnecessary.* Her stout body now a floaty nature quite different to how she normally appeared. Sardius's voice crooned on and on and Shelley's eyes fell closed once more.

The temple steps had filled with people. All the men had shaven heads. They mounted the steps in pairs, and when a priest stood on each step they turned to look back at the beast in the enclosure. It stared back with piercing black eyes that glinted in its hairy face. Its tusks looked vicious.

Two palanquins arrived. The priests all bowed their heads, their long robes of deep green and blue flapping slightly in the warm breeze. From the first, a man emerged. He wore a black wig. At his throat a gem stone glittered in the final light of the setting sun. Sparks of icy light flashed as he walked up the steps between the two lines of priests. Inside, Shelley could hear women chanting. The priests on the steps turned transparent, wobbled, vanished and reappeared.

"We are losing contact," said the familiar voice, purring in her ear. Shelley's awareness centred at the top right of the temple steps but her viewpoint bobbed around.

"Move those two candles," the voice murmured on, somewhere far, far away. For just a moment the steps emptied entirely and the sun vanished. Three children appeared at the bottom of the steps, a girl and two boys. She recognised the boys, and through the foggy mist in her mind, looked for their names.

"That's it," said the soft voice in her right ear, and the steps once more turned pink in the evening sun. The children vanished and a woman stepped out of the second palanquin. She had a powerful build, a wig of dark red hair, with green beads. At her throat a green stone shone, held in place by a silver necklet. *I know her too … Emma … Hemma?*

All the priests raised their right arms in a salute and placed their left hands over their hearts. The woman swept into the temple as though she owned the place. Shelley swept in behind her, dragged like a child's balloon on a long, elastic string.

Chapter 81

The Golden Arrow

Rhory

The deep black sky above my head twinkled with starlight. The empty temple had no roof and the smooth stone floor showed six circles, in different coloured stone, gathered around a central circle picked out in white marble. I looked around for the speaker, the one who had greeted me as a brother. Light shimmered and gathered in the circles and something clicked. I jerked as electricity jabbed through my nerves. Opposite me Pythagoras appeared, dressed in a long, woollen white robe. On his right, Dimitris now had his feet planted like a wrestler, ready for anything. To his left lay an empty circle. Theano, whose face I'd once seen in my bedroom, stood to the right of me and Abaris completed the circle to my left. They all looked at me and smiled.

"Ah, you're here. Praise the Gods, who've guided you safely." This thought emanated from Pythagoras. His nose crinkled as he raised his eyebrows in my direction.

"Today you passed your second initiation." This thought came from Abaris. He wore a blue pectoral around his neck. Pythagoras had one of a golden colour. Theano, also clad in white thick robes, had a broad pectoral of copper, nestling below her neck. Dimitris wore a tunic of dark blue wool, with a cloak of grey edged with rectangular designs. He had leggings and small leather boots. I stood in my jeans and stained leather jacket, my shoes slightly scuffed. Theano, her dark wavy hair loose apart from a simple band tied around her brow, smiled at me once more. Her eyes remained calm and serious. Her inner voice, when it came, the sound of distant waves.

"You and my brother hold in your hands, time now and time yet to come. We honour you and the one who works with you." She indicated the empty circle opposite her. "We'll be here for as long as you need – to offer protection as best we are able. No one else can make this journey with the two of you." As these words formed inside me, Theano stretched out both her hands, touching my shoulder and her brother's. A warmth spread through me at that touch and the chill of the underground tunnel and temple finally vanished.

Theano reached into the folds of her tunic and crossed the central circle. Bending forward, she placed something in the circle opposite. It caught the light of the torches fixed around the temple walls. I recognised it. Shoshan's pendant, the clear crystal scarab of initiation. Moving with small, graceful steps, Theano walked around the outside of the group, past Pythagoras and Dimitris and returned to her place next to me.

Abaris then moved to the central circle.

"The Arrow of Gold, protection of the sacred lore of the Ancient Ones, is the power of the Northern wisdom. You," he pointed the golden rod at my chest, "come from those Sacred Isles and bear their impress. Today, this is yours to have and use. When you strike, strike sure, Rhory." He walked two steps towards me and held out the rod. I took it and could feel it vibrate softly in my hand. He indicated I should place it safely. "Only reveal the arrow when the moment demands."

I slipped it into a deep pocket inside my jacket. Abaris returned to his place, again passing round the outside of the circle. When back in position, he nodded across to Theano.

In her real voice, she started singing. The notes, plaintive and simple, filled the temple. Both the men joined in. Pythagoras had a deep bass, and Abaris had a voice surprisingly light for a man of his stature. The words and song intensified in the temple. From outside, stringed instruments joined in and the soft rhythm of a drum. I closed my eyes for a bit and let the music sweep over and through me. Every cell in my body vibrated gently and a calm light rose from the floor and surrounded us. I opened my eyes and looked at Dimitris. He swayed as his sister and two teachers continued to sing. His body clarified, becoming sharper and more clearly lit. I swayed in time with him and found the music passing far, far away.

Also swaying on my left stood a tall girl, with thick dark hair cut at shoulder length. Shimmering in and out of view, a circle of people now encompassed us. They danced, slowly and deliberately, a repetitive pattern of complicated steps, never moving much in any one moment and gradually revolving around us. The three older Greeks had vanished, leaving only Dimitris. The girl, appearing in the circle that moments before had held the pendant, now wore the scarab necklace at her throat. Her eyes remained closed and she moved gently back and forth in time to the music and the dancing. A fragrance of something exotic wafted by me as a woman, quite extraordinarily tall, passed my right shoulder and stood in the central circle. Her hair, or wig, added to her great height, and her robes flowed with her as she turned slowly, looking at each of us in turn.

"Welcome, Red King." Her words rolled into my mind carrying the power of a great thunderstorm. She turned to Dimitris. "Welcome servant of the Goddess of Life." She moved once more until she faced the young girl, who'd now opened her eyes. "And welcome, my lotus flower. Your bravery and hard work has drawn the three Companions of the Golden Chain of Time together, just as it is needed."

She walked to the edge of the circle, standing where Pythagoras had been, and raised her arms as though calling down light from somewhere high above.

"The Holy High Gods have allowed this moment to be, and their seal is upon this endeavour. The war of the servants of Set on the followers of Osiris never ends until we return to Sothis, from whence we came. But victory need not come to the followers of the

Boar, and will not come if we each fulfil the destiny allotted us by the Scribe Himself."

The tall lady paused and held up her hand. The music and dancing stopped and everyone stood silent and still.

For a moment she spoke to another tall priestess, using her actual voice. The power in that voice reverberated around the room, even though she spoke in soft tones. The other priestess looked across at me and smiled. I'd met her before, on the night of the ballet. Hasina, my tall guide across the Plain of Time.

"Follow." This came from Hasina. The three of us did and passed by the circle of priests and priestesses who had been dancing around us. We left the room and entered a courtyard. I could see the dark sky, pricked with bright starlight, above our heads. A simple trestle table held a jug and a few clay beakers.

We stood around the table, looking like teenagers at our first party. I caught Shoshan's eye and swallowed. My smile must have betrayed my nervousness.

"You're still pale, Red King. Don't they have any sunlight left in the time you live in?" Then her face broke into a grin, and all three of us giggled. I'd no idea what we were drinking. It wasn't sweet and it wasn't water. It smelt a bit musty but was cool and refreshed my dry mouth.

I glanced over at the building we'd just left. Inside, I could see the priests and priestesses moving about. The walls were built of grey bricks. Mud. Auntie Aida told us the palaces of nobles in Egypt were made of mud bricks. Only the temples had the honour of being permanent and made of stone. So we were in a private house.

I nearly fainted when Aunt Bridget walked out of the door. My mouth dropped open and I spilled my drink. The moonlight caught her white robes. I put down my beaker and rubbed my temples, scrunching up my eyes. *Far too weird.* When I opened my eyes the amazingly tall priestess stood where my ancient auntie had just been. She walked over to us.

"Time is not as you think it is, my Red King." Her words rolled majestically through my mind. "Past is not so far away and future closer than anyone believes. We are each a note, precious to the Gods and that note is always sounded no matter in which age our body is born. The three of you are more closely related than you think. How else could it be that you can so easily pass through the veils of time?"

She directed us to sit. "I am Katesch, leader of the priestesses of Maat. We guard the sacred truth as it passes down through the ages. We are all servants of the Scribe and He is but the mouthpiece of the splendour of the Gods." She looked up at the stars above us, and the torchlight played on her face. Her eyes, large and almond shaped, held a light of their own. Seated, she looked normal and not the giantess she became when standing. She regarded at each of us in turn.

"No one can take your place tonight. The servants of the desert God meet close by and weave their dangerous spells. I cannot penetrate them on my own and were I to enter where they hold sway, I'd doubtless be destroyed. My duty is to Truth. Yours," and here she looked again at the three of us, "is to the mystery of Time. Your ability to dance at the edges of time means you can enter the dark spaces of the Boar and disrupt their plans. This moment, now, here and everywhere, they seek to disrupt time's natural flow for their own selfish ends."

Once more she looked towards the stars. A tall stone structure rose in two parts next to the house, framing, with a serrated silhouette, this bit of the sparkling sky. Stars moved into view, crossed the space and disappeared. A sidereal clock! Neat.

"We are ready," Katesch announced and once more towered over me. I followed her back to the room in the palace, with Shoshan at my side and Dimitris behind us. Shoshan stood several inches taller than Juliette. It wasn't often I felt small, but these two ladies from ancient Egypt had that effect on me all right. Shoshan smiled, and gave my arm a squeeze. Electricity sparked through me once again, and blood rose up my face.

"I feel much safer with you around." The words from the young

Egyptian priestess bubbled inside me.

"I'm pleased to meet you." I responded, sending the lame thoughts through the ether. She glanced over and smiled again.

"Yes, finally, it's good to meet in you one time and one place. Maybe someday I will arrive at your palace." I grinned at the thought of Suffolk Road having a palace.

We took our places in our respective circles and the priests and priestesses on the outside started to dance and chant once more. *Hang on. What are we meant to do? We're going against murderous time travelling priests and I've no idea what to expect.*

My words sounded in everyone's minds because I heard an echo from all round the room. Katesch came through most clearly. "Act as a king, Red King, use the power given only to you. You will know in the moment what that moment requires. That is how the great Her-Mes works. Protect Shoshan."

The room and its priests gradually faded as her words rolled through my mind. I looked for both Dimitris and Shoshan, but darkness had swallowed all three of us.

After a timeless moment, the three of us stood near a huge river looking up the steps to a squat temple. The setting sun painted it blood red. Where had night gone?

"We are just near the edge of time, Raw-Rhee."

"Oh," I thought.

"We have moved a little through space and a little through time, but stand several moments ahead of what is occurring in this temple." Shoshan's thoughts left me none the wiser.

"Because we are just ahead of their time, they cannot see us. We three can do this because you are both from a time ahead of my time. Hasina explained it all to me once." Shoshan reached into her robe and took out a small pouch. "When I say…" she shook the pouch "…eat this salt. Swallow it all and we will be in their time. Then do what the Gods direct."

She placed a pinch of salt into Dimitris's palm and into mine.

Chapter 82

The Temple of Set

Shelley

Incense rose from the many braziers in the gloomy interior of the temple. Shelley hovered – a disembodied presence – high up near an inner pillar. Below her, dominating the centre of the vast room in which hundreds had gathered, stood a huge basin of stone, several times bigger than the one in that house, somewhere far in the future.

Priests and priestesses danced in procession, using the bowl as a centrepiece and moving anticlockwise. To the side, just out of Shelley's vision, musicians made a pulsing racket with cymbals, tambours, drums and some wind instruments that sounded like oxen in labour. The man from the palanquin stood near the entrance door and anointed Emerald with red liquid from a small bowl as she came in. The blood trickled down her brow as she walked around the bowl and took her place on the side farthest away from the temple door. Each move Emerald made tugged on invisible strands connected to Shelley.

The light of the setting sun poured through the temple door and all the dancers and celebrants took on a bloody hue. The music rose to a crescendo. The tall man with angular features walked across to a central brazier, between the door and the great stone bowl, and threw something in. The light flared. Sharp pains passed through Shelley, the ache of extreme flu, hurting her spirit more than her body, far, far away.

Everyone stopped. A further flame leapt from the brazier right up towards the roof, a flash of green. Emerald's head snapped back and the green stone at her throat emitted deadly cold fire all of its own. The silence of pure hatred filled the whole temple, squeezing in on Shelley. The sun had set. Into the temple ran a single girl, tall, very young. She looked swiftly over her shoulder, but no one had followed her in.

*

Shoshan

Shoshan looked at the two boys, standing on the first step bathed in the light of the setting sun. Utter silence surrounded them. Occupying a fold of time meant no sound, except that of their thoughts, could disturb them. Once they ate the salt it would be different. They would have the advantage of surprise. Katesch had told Shoshan that only the Pale Boy could break the web being woven in this temple of Set. He would know what to do when the moment arrived. Her-Mes worked with his servants that way, offering insight just when needed.

Her teacher had stood, for some moments, with her hands resting on Shoshan's shoulders, her eyes bathing Shoshan's with love and support. "You will face Set. That is your task, as it is the task of every Soul. The protection of all of us will be with you, but no one can know, my beautiful lotus flower, how such confrontation will work out."

Shoshan had quivered then as she quivered now, on hearing those words. She had to play her part in this drama of the murder of Osiris and his resurrection and rebirth as Horus. She didn't wish to die but knew absolutely that her death in this cause would ensure the eternal blessing of Maat Herself, the Lady of the Feather.

At the moment of the sunset, as instructed, Shoshan said, "Eat the salt, and then follow me into the temple." She raised her hand to her own mouth and shuddered as the salt bit into her tongue. Running up the steps, she strode into the temple.

At first all she could sense in the empty temple, were swirling shapes, like currents in the Nile. She avoided these and moved towards the Great Eye. The huge stone bowl came from the time before time. The time forever sealed behind great doors by The Scribe. Stolen by the priests of Set on their rebellion, the bowl had been turned to the direst of purposes and provided this dark Order with an opening to many futures through which they learned of times to be. The shapes of the priests, the false Children of Set, gradually coalesced around her. She waited, poised on the balls of her feet by a great brazier, looking for the woman with the green stone. This woman was the key to the dark twist in time.

As the smoky shapes of moving people formed around her, she looked back to see Dimitris and Raw-Rhee, but neither had followed her. Panic swept through her body. Had she spoken out loud? Did they know to eat the salt? Neither of the boys would have understood her. Now their moment in time had become separate from her own. She jumped as a green flame leaped up from the brazier.

The tall man reached out and held her arms easily, his powerful hands biting into her skin. His eyes, black coals radiating a dark light, held her own. All her strength ebbed away. At his throat, a clear white stone throbbed, sending shards of icy light into her body. She reached up and touched the pendant at her neck but the man jerked her hands away before she could draw on its protection. "Praise be to Set," he murmured. He raised his head and looked around. "Our sacrifice has delivered itself." His voice filled the whole temple.

Figures surrounded her, their dark eyes cold, calculating, deadly. "Praise be. Praise be," they said in unison. A shriek filled the air as the huge priestess from the far side of the bowl stood. She spread both hands wide and pointed into the bowl. Images, shapes, cries, screams, swirled around, a torrent of torment yet to come in the world.

"She is one who hears!" shouted the priestess, her face lit from the green stone glowing at her throat. "Bring her bloody corpse to the bowl and we shall hear also, right till the end of time."

"Praise be. Praise be," chanted the voices around her. Shoshan took a slow breath and sought out the voice of Katesch within herself. A blow from the big man holding her arms knocked all the wind out of her and tears blinded her eyes.

"Take her," said the man. "Take her now and show her Set."

Two priests, one male and one female, took her arms. Their grip, like pincers of ice, drained Shoshan's courage. One moment the gloomy darkness of the temple surrounded her, the next, the cold of the desert night chilled the sweat on her skin. She looked desperately for the two boys but couldn't see them. Torchlight bobbed around the priests pouring out of the temple. Loud discordant music assaulted her ears. She resisted being pulled down the steps but they jerked her forward and she scraped her knee, stumbling onto the grainy sand at the bottom. The tall dark-eyed priest now stood by a gate. The icy stone at his neck caught strands of light from the passing torches and needled them into her eyes.

One moment, sound swamped her senses. Then a collective sigh, and she stood alone beyond the gate, rubbing her bruised arms. The pale moon offered little more than a silvery wash, hardly illuminating the great space in which she now stood. All around, torches flared, held high by priestly hands. A snuffling and a scraping came from the darkness ahead. She peered into the deep gloom. A blackness deeper than the surrounding darkness separated itself and, with a chilling squeal, charged towards her. Shoshan reached for her pendant at her neck and fell to her knees. "May my death be quick," she prayed, as the ground trembled and the beast hurtled straight at her.

Chapter 83

Sacrifice to Set

Dimitris

The sun's final rays transformed the temple steps and the robes worn by Shoshan, into a gentle pink. Even the tall boy, Rhory, with his funny clothes, radiated health in that light. The boy looked across at Dimitris and nodded. Dimitris smiled back as Shoshan turned and said something. The idea behind what she said didn't come through. Her hand moved to her mouth as she coughed and moments later, vanished.

Dimitris looked at the space where she'd stood seconds before, his mouth wide open. He turned round to see what the other boy made of this, but Rhory was looking at something in an enclosure between the temple and the river. Rhory also spoke, but fear had clouded his ideas and Dimitris saw inwardly a small wild pig and then a bull, and didn't understand the message.

"The salt, we must eat the salt," Dimitris shouted, realising finally what had happened, and licked the crystals off the palm of his hand. The sudden arrival of darkness startled him. He looked around wildly, but no one stood near. Rhory had completely disappeared. "Fool, fool, fool," he said to himself, "I spoke out loud, of course he didn't understand." He climbed the steps of the temple, two at a time.

A great shriek came from within followed by a crashing of music. Dimitris darted to the side of the steps and pushed himself flat against a pillar. Priests swarmed near him, and then two passed by, dragging Shoshan between them. Panic rose through his chest to his mouth and he had to work hard not to scream. He forced himself not to form clear words. Shoshan mustn't look at him, and he mustn't signal his presence to priests who could hear thoughts. No one glanced his way. *Perhaps I'm still invisible.*

A female priest stopped, turned and stared. Dimitris gaped, pointing towards where the man and woman dragged Shoshan towards the enclosure. The priestess followed where he pointed just as a tall dark haired priest opened the gate. Torchlight and the weak moon faintly revealed a moving shadow on the far side. *A bull? No, not a bull. A huge wild boar.* The biggest Dimitris had ever seen.

Then the words of Pythagoras made sense to him. "Typhon must be slain, Dimitris, and slain again, for he never dies but must be beaten each step of the path home. Take the sling from Sophis and this one stone. Use it wisely."

Sophis had been happy to give Dimitris his sling earlier in the day, and had asked no questions. The stone, smooth and white, had come from near the Spring of Aphrodite, where he and the boy from the future had bathed.

He placed the stone in the sling, and waited. The moonlight picked out the lustre of Shoshan's white robes. Her tall, slight figure stood alone in the vast space. *I must get closer.*

Everyone stared at the girl, soon to be sacrificed to the incarnation of Set. Dimitris had eased his way down the steps, and moved slightly to the side when the great pig charged. He prayed to Zeus to make his aim true and drew back his arm to spin the sling. A hand grabbed him and someone shouted, "An enemy." Dimitris spun round to see the priestess who had spotted him earlier. Behind her, at the top of the steps, a massive woman stood pointing straight at him, with green fire sparkling from a stone at her throat.

*

Rhory

The Nile flowed past, blood red in the setting sun. A large stone enclosure, nearly the size of a football pitch lay between the river and me. Something lumbered around at the far side. I scrunched my eyes against the sunlight and shaded them with my hand. A bull? No, not a bull. A huge hairy pig. *Do they have wild boars in ancient Egypt? Apparently they do.* I turned to Shoshan and Dimitris to warn them about this beast but couldn't see Shoshan anywhere.

Where could she have gone? She'd said something just moments before, in her own tongue. I moved past Dimitris to get a better look at the temple steps. They remained entirely empty. She couldn't have run into the temple, could she? I turned back to Dimitris to carefully form that thought, so he could hear it inwardly, but he'd disappeared.

I bit down on my lip and spun round quickly. I felt sick and didn't trust my muscles to support me. Blood thundered in my ears. I'd been left alone in ancient Egypt with no way of getting home, and a temple full of manic devil worshipping priests. *The salt, of course, the salt.* I quickly raised my hand to my mouth and projected the damp salt onto my tongue, plunging myself into chaotic darkness.

A tall man, his back to me, shouted orders in a deep bass voice to priests standing everywhere, torches held high. I couldn't understand a word, but had an image of someone drowning in blood. A shudder passed right through me. Two priests, dressed in robes of dark green, dragged Shoshan down the crowded temple steps, none too gently. Everyone pouring out of the temple had their eyes on her, and I slipped to the side of the steps, far from the range of the torch-bearers. Everywhere priests were chanting and musicians made enough racket to wake the dead. I scanned the steps and faces to pick out Dimitris. *Has he been caught too?*

Priests and wild-eyed priestesses ran down the steps watching Shoshan, pointing at her and shouting to each other. I moved further back as the torchlight licked over my leather jacket. *I'm a walking anachronism.* In no time at all Shoshan had been dragged to the stone enclosure. I could no longer see the monster inside, but knew she wouldn't have a hope of surviving an attack from that huge beast.

When the tall priest pushed her in, a strange quiet descended, with everyone, including me, holding their breath. Priests grasping torches circled the outside walls, and the rising moon added its sickly light. Shoshan stood all alone, a few metres from the closed gate behind her. She fell to her knees. The hundreds of priests sighed, as the animal pawed the ground and squawked loud enough for everyone to hear. A cry from hell. A green light played on the backs of the robes of some priests, and I turned to see a tall, stocky priestess, with thick reddish hair, cut in the Egyptian style. Standing at the top of the temple steps, her mouth open and her eyes blazing, she could have been a double for that Greek monster with snakes in her hair.

Emerald. It's that dreadful woman, Emerald. I don't know how I knew, but I did. She stood much taller and she'd less flab, but inwardly I just knew this priestess and the woman from the Nutcracker were one and the same.

I reached for the golden arrow. My hands closed around my mobile at the same moment that some priests broke the hush and shouted, pointing right at me. I pulled the mobile out and touching a button, it lit up. The priests and priestesses walking towards me, stopped. Several made signs. *Protection against the evil mobile.*

I spotted Dimitris standing further up the steps. He had something in his hand and looked out towards Shoshan. A priestess grabbed his arm. I pushed another button and the flash went off. All those close enough to see me cowered back. Some screamed. I ran up the steps two at a time and barrelled into the priestess, who stumbled and let go of Dimitris's arm. He nodded at me and started to rotate the sling he held in his hand. I jumped back to avoid being struck and heard the crowd roar as the boar charged. The stone flew in a smooth arc, passing just over Shoshan's kneeling form, and cracked the big pig on its giant head. Its legs splayed and its vast body crashed over on its side, skidding in a cloud of dust and grit towards Shoshan. She rolled out of the way as I turned to confront the Green She-devil.

I bounded up the stairs towards the Emerald priestess, waving Abaris's golden rod. The green light at her throat throbbed and fear joined the anger in her eyes. Surprisingly nimble, she turned and ran back into the temple.

Inside, the smell of sweat and pungent incense filled the smoky air. Braziers gave quivering light to the rows of pillars. Emerald's feet slapped on the stone floor. Once she reached a huge stone discus in the middle of the temple, she turned and faced me, a maniacal grin on her face. Vapours rose behind her, with shapes writhing in the mistiness. The spook or priestess or whatever, stood tall and full of confidence.

"You fell right into our trap, you brat," she shouted in English. "And now you and that meddling girl can go to damnation."

She pointed to something behind me, and I glanced back to see a crowd of furious priests and priestesses advancing, carrying vicious looking staves. *In for a penny, in for a pound.* I charged at the woman, shouting goodness knows what, my anger colouring her and everything else, red. Yelling, snarling and the clatter of feet sounded behind me. Something high in the temple spoke my name but I ran on regardless, the golden rod held before me. Emerald, wig and all, disappeared entirely as I jumped at her.

*

Shelley, minutes earlier

Emerald remained seated, unseeing, as violent priests dragged the young girl outside. Shelley's whole consciousness ached with joyless sickness. Behind the stout priestess, taller and more frightening than her English counterpart, Shelley watched as the vapours in the vast stone bowl coagulated into shapes and scenes. Battles with great slaughter, cities sacked, tyrants ruling through terror, acts of horror and meanness tumbling and rumbling over each other to appear and vanish, leaving a sick pall before the next scene arose. Human sacrifice, burnings, hangings and things so terrible Shelley couldn't comprehend their awfulness, swirled around in a never-ending whirlpool of hate.

Emerald slowly rose, a woman fully powerful, terrible, and determined. She touched the stone at her throat, and everything around Shelley constricted, as her awareness jerked towards the temple doorway. The massive priestess stood still in the doorway, as shrieking sounds poured into the temple, followed by a deathlike lull.

A single shout. Emerald pointing. A scream, followed by a tumult of shouting, and Emerald turned and half strode, half ran, towards the bowl. Shelley, wrenched along, metres above her head, saw in the bowl cities burning and planes crashing. Emerald, her back to the bowl, hands gripping its edge, triumphantly faced … faced Rhory, who was dressed in a leather jacket and carrying a small brass curtain rail. *Why would he have a curtain rail? Maybe it's a…* Rhory shouted something unrepeatable in English and rushed at the woman, who laughed in his face. Behind the boy, hordes chased into the temple carrying long flaming sticks.

Shelley's leg buzzed. *I don't have a leg here, I'm an airy spirit.* The buzz repeated, and the temple wobbled and melted away, just as Rhory launched himself at the dreadful Emerald priestess.

Emerald screamed. Shelley opened her physical eyes to see Emerald clutching her face and tumbling forward from her chair, in the house in the West Country. Shelley felt the vibration in her leg and realised Laila's phone was ringing, on silent vibrator mode.

Onyx moved swiftly towards Emerald and received a vicious kick for her pains. The tall Samurai man, stood holding his head, his eyes clenched shut. Shelley could see right through him as he gradually faded.

Everyone clustered around Emerald as the great stone bowl cracked right down the middle. An audible sigh from the contents in the bowl, washed around the walls. The mournful cry of lost souls. Shelley used the confusion to stand up and slip out the room. The raised voices in the bowl room became muffled as the door swung shut behind her. She retrieved her handbag from the hall table where she'd left it after coming down with Sardius. She ran down the corridor and towards the kitchen area where there should be a back door. Bursting into the kitchen, she saw a game show on the TV, the sound turned low. Killer Joe stood in the centre of the kitchen, twirling car keys in his hand.

"Well, well, Miss Prendergast," he said, advancing towards her.

*

Rhory

I couldn't stop and leaped as I reached the bowl. I'd never been much of a hurdler, but did better at high jump. One foot caught the rim and I spun in, sliding down the smooth sides. Howling faces, destroyed buildings, burning trees, dead oceans all shot past me, and twirled into a tight tornado of spiky mist. I struck the centre of the bowl with the golden arrow and the mist crackled and vanished. The whole bowl filled with tiny cracks and started to fall apart. The centre just about held and I stood there looking at the horrified expression of priests and priestesses, struck dumb, like extras from a silent movie, as I waved Abaris's Arrow above my head. Adrenaline surged through me.

I leapt down scattering the priests. *Moses parting the Red Sea.* I raced through them to the door and took the steps down three at a time. Dimitris and Shoshan stood inside the enclosure. She leaned on his arm, and rubbed her leg.

"Come on, we must go," I shouted.

They both looked up at me. Dimitris had a bruise near his eye. Shoshan had blood on her leg, a dark streak in the moonlight.

Shoshan held my eyes with hers. "How ... do ... we ... return?"

"I don't know..." I stopped and framed the thought, "You don't know how we will return?"

Shoshan shook her head, and the words arose inside me: "Katesch said we would just be back with her when our task had been completed."

"She lied," said a voice in English. I twisted round to see the tall priest with dark shoulder length hair, the one who had thrown Shoshan in the enclosure. He strode towards me. I stepped back too slowly to avoid his right hand as he struck me backhanded across my face. I felt my skin tear, and saw his ring sparkle white ice, in the moonlight. I'm normally polite but I'd had enough and kicked him hard between his legs. He doubled over.

"Make a triangle."

The words came from within but with Dimitris's signature. *A triangle, we are going to form a percussion band?*

"Stand as we stood in the temple." Dimitris again.

We understood and formed up at the three points of an isosceles with the dead boar in the middle.

"Hold something from where you are from."

I could see the tall priest struggling to get up from his knees. *My kick must have hit the jackpot then.* I threw the arrow to Dimitris, which he caught easily, and pulled out my mobile. Shoshan looked at each of us and smiled as she reached for the pendant at her throat. The man stumbled towards me, holding his head and shouting, "Oh no you don't, you…"

I didn't hear the rest as the chilly air of an English winter surrounded me. My torch lay on its side, illumining the nostrils of a bull, wrestled to the ground by some hero or other. I'd escaped from mad priests in Egypt, only to wake up metres of earth below a bandstand, with no way out.

Chapter 84

Finding Natasha

My heart thundered away inside me and my ears couldn't believe the sudden, total silence. Faint echoes of screaming priests bobbed around my mind. How come one Egyptian priest could speak English? I would need to think about that later. Now I just wanted to get home. I used the phone to illumine the floor, and picked up Shoshan's scarab pendant and Dimitris's ten stones. Tiredness washed all through me, as I put the precious objects back in the backpack. Fuzziness filled my head. Natasha. Natasha had to be rescued. I must get out. I raised my hands up to my temples, setting off the phone flash once more and revealing all the sacred room, in a brief blaze of light.

The image of the flash remained in my eyes. A layer of pallid light surrounded the darkened relief of the bull and man. I held my breath, my eyes tight shut, watching the after-image change, light to dark and dark to light. If the carving threw a shadow, it had to have a space behind it. I picked up the backpack, my heart thumping with excitement rather than fear. As I retrieved the torch, it went out. I shook it, and it came on again. Loose bulb.

I walked to the end of the carving and shone the torch into the gap. The stone extended back about a third of a metre and didn't fuse with the wall. I had to take the backpack off again to squeeze in sideways. A cool breeze passed my face. This air had to come from behind the enormous carving. I eased my way down the gap and emerged into a narrow corridor. At the end, stairs rose, twisting out of sight. I climbed up the spiral staircase, placing my feet carefully on well-worn steps. I'd no idea how old these were, but doubted they could be much younger than the Norman church, at the other end of Hammerford.

Eventually, I emerged into a small circular room. Faces looked at me from all sides as I shone the torch around. The circular walls had paintings, just like the ones in the hidden room at the museum. Once more, Egyptian gods merged with those of Greece and Rome. These might make a good school project, but the ladder opposite, had more immediate use. I crossed over and felt the solid wooden rungs. I climbed and reached up to the trap door above my head. The oiled wood looked in good repair. *Who on earth does that?*

I pushed and it didn't budge. I climbed another rung, and pushed with both hands. Still no movement and the rung my feet rested on cracked ominously. Cold sweat sprang onto my forehead and dribbled down. I rubbed the back of my hand across my eyes. The wet came from tears and sweat, but also from blood. My cheek throbbed from a blow some five thousand years earlier.

I climbed a further rung, put my back against the trap door and pushed up with my legs. It sprang open with a clatter and a shower of dust. Putting my head through I found myself within a carefully constructed pile of old deckchairs. One had fallen against the trap door, and pinned it closed. I'd snapped its rotten wood when I pushed harder.

I eased myself through and carefully closed the trap door, rearranging the broken chair to keep it hidden. I found just enough room by the walls to squeeze past the piles of wood and canvas, and a moment or two later had reached a little door. It had a handle on the inside and this had been oiled. It opened easily.

The thunder rolled across the park as I peeked out. The flickering blue light played on the distant bushes, which shimmered and danced. I couldn't see the cause. Blue flashes on the tarmac revealed large raindrops splashing down and lightening and a thunder crash suggested a storm on its way. Dark clouds raced across the sky.

*

Natasha, thirty minutes earlier

Natasha dropped the big torch by the well in the Wild Wood, as she turned round to see her attacker. His face hooded, he hissed, "You want to join your boyfriend in the well, bitch?" She bit the hand that held her and jumped free. The lad grabbed her again and put his hand to her throat. Someone the other side of the well said, "Cool it, Gary." She watched horrified while they tightly screwed the well cover back in place.

"You, stupid pigs, he'll die if left in there."

"Should've thought about that then, shouldn't he," said Gary.

"You're an ocean going twit, Gary Stratford," said Natasha. "That would be murder and you would spend your whole life in prison.

"Not if we put you— Hey, how'd'ya know my name?"

"Never mind," said Natasha, whose close friend from school had endured a couple of pointless dates with a Gary from Scrivener's. She guessed it must be the same gormless, rugby playing git, especially after all Rhory had told her about Hacker's gang.

"Okay, okay," said the other voice coming out of the gloom nearby. "We haven't got all night. Work to do, and you, you useless piece of skirt, can help us."

Gary jostled her over to the fence, and the other boy squeezed her arms painfully as Gary swung himself over. "Okay then, climb up on my hands. Gary, grab her on the other side. I don't want her falling and leaving herself crippled."

He cupped his hands and Natasha climbed, placing one foot on a curved metal hoop at the top of the fence. She quickly moved the other one up, and swayed for a moment, balancing on the thin metal supports, before leaping right over Gary's head and tumbling behind him onto the path. Both boys shouted as Natasha rolled over on her side, jumped up and ran straight through the thin bushes and tall grass, out onto the flat grass beyond.

"Get her," shouted the boy as he struggled to get over the fence. She could hear Gary stumble through the bushes and swear as he tripped. Natasha, fit from all her football training, raced straight ahead. She could make out very little detail, as the moon had disappeared behind a cloud. Feet pounded behind her and she hoped she could outrace them. She swerved to the left but heard the boy behind move his position too to cut her off from the park tunnel, so she veered to the right hoping to get to the large duck pond about three hundred metres away. A sharp pain in her side reminded her that she sometimes developed a stitch. She rubbed at it, and still ran flat out.

The thumping of the feet behind moved closer. The stitch became worse. In front, the darker smudge across the grey of the grass, suggested the duck pond and possible sanctuary. The footsteps drummed close by and she could hear the boy panting. A moment later his arms closed around her knees and Natasha went down in a classic rugby tackle.

He swiftly crawled up and grabbed her arms, pinning her on the ground. "I should smash your face in, you stupid slag," he snarled and panted at her. The boy, larger and meaner than Gary, drew back a fist for a moment but decided in the end to spit right in her face. "Don't do anything like that again, or I'll break your freakin' nose."

He pulled her up, jerking her arms nearly out of their sockets, and holding one arm behind her back, pushed her in the direction of the swimming pool. Natasha used her free hand to wipe the spittle from her face. They both panted hard as they recovered their wind, and stumbled along in hostile silence. Gradually the darker shape of the high hedge around the swimming pool appeared. Grey wraiths moved about ahead of them and Natasha could hear whispered conversation.

"Look, Hacker," she took a stab at his name, "if anything happens to Rhory it'll be a murder charge and you won't possibly get away with it."

"Shut up, you dumb calf," said Hacker, a note of exasperation in his voice. "Of course we'll let him out. He'll just chill for a bit that's all."

"He'll freeze to death in there, you moron."

"She gave you a run for your money," said a fresh voice from the gloom. The moon revealed Gary and two other boys, all with hoodies, carrying some square red metal tins.

"Shut it," said Hacker, "we're late now because of this little distraction." He wrenched Natasha's arm further up her back.

"Ow, that really hurts, you gormless cretin."

One of the boys sniggered at that. "She's got you to a tee, Hack."

"Shut it right now," said Hacker, with such venom that the other boy just muttered,

"Only sayin' y'know. Only a joke, man."

Gary walked over and pulled the hood from Natasha's head. Her turban twisted as he did so.

"What's this crap on your head," he said, pulling off the silk turban. "God, you've got a crew cut or somethin'. You're a bloomin' freakshow."

"I lost all my hair," shouted Natasha, "because I had cancer, you brainless weasel."

"Leave her alone," muttered one of the other boys, "my mum died of cancer and she lost all her hair too. It's not something to joke about."

"Don't shout and don't run again, and I'll let go of your arm, okay?" This from Hacker.

"Okay," said Natasha, determined to run any chance she got. She could smell the petrol in the cans, and had a fair idea what Hacker's gang intended to do. Her hands in her pockets felt the box of matches and the single squat candle she'd put there for emergencies. She wondered if a plan might form.

Hacker checked his watch. "Jeez, we're seriously late now. Come on, let's head over to the freakin' bandstand and get this job done. And keep your bloomin' voices down, we don't want to be heard on the far side of Hammerford."

They all moved off together and skirted around the edge of the pool enclosure. Thunder cracked loudly out of nowhere and huge boulders rumbled slowly across the sky.

"That's all we need, a storm," muttered Gary.

"What's that?" said one of the other boys.

"What?" said Hacker.

"That!" said the boy, pointing, his voice having risen several notches. He waved his arm towards the bandstand. Blue light played all around the building, running up the struts and over the roof. Natasha thought it looked like the flames on a Christmas pudding, when her mum lit the brandy.

"It's been hit by lightning," said Gary.

"No it hasn't," said Hacker. "It's an atmospheric anomaly that's all, St Vitus's fire or whatever it is."

"St Elmo," muttered Natasha, wondering if Rhory had made it to the temple after all.

"Come on," said Hacker. "Let's get the job done properly." They moved a bit closer and the lights continued to dance around the whole structure, sending blue tongues up high above the roof.

"Never seen anything like it," said one of the boys.

"Get the top off those cans" said Hacker. "We're going to start pouring here and go right up to the deckchair store. Gary, you're going to light the trail when I signal, then we run like hell. And you, you stupid waste of space, can just go home and forget you ever saw this, otherwise we'll leave your boyfriend to his watery grave."

Natasha nodded, clear now what she intended to do. A drop of rain splashed on her head. She looked up at the hazy the moon cloaked behind a wisp of cloud. Another more distant rumble of thunder, followed by lights flickering across the clouds. The boys were all kneeling down taking the caps off the petrol cans.

"Wait for my signal, Gary."

"Oh, fracking bumming hell, what the frickin frack is that?"

Natasha looked where Gary pointed and saw a white figure float across the grass behind the bandstand. The rain began to splash down on her head as her heart raced.

"Frack, frick, frackin hell," said Gary. "It's a ghost."

"Don't be daft," said Hacker, but the bravado had gone out of his voice. The shape had stopped and looked towards them. It glided forwards slowly, glowing blue and white.

A 'bong' as from a muffled bell, made them all jump. Gary had dropped his can of petrol and started running back towards the swimming pool. Natasha seized her chance and pulled out the matches. Hacker shouted to Gary to come back, then glanced back at the ghostly shape approaching them at a run.

The match caught first time, and the petrol ignited with a whoosh, a small rolling ball of bright light, racing across the grass towards the petrol can. Natasha bounded towards the white shape. The great flash that followed synchronised with a huge clap of thunder. She looked back to see a wall of fire, with the boys on the far side. She ran on towards the glowing blue shape near the bandstand.

*

Rhory, two minutes earlier

I didn't want to get soaked. I shone the torch around the store and it highlighted a white dustsheet covering the musicians' chairs. *I'll use that to keep the worst of the rain off.* I pulled it from the chairs and wrapped it quickly around my shoulders, making a cowl for my head. As I passed through the door, the blue light intensified and I could see electric flames dancing over the whole of the bandstand. I walked further back to get a better view, just as a light sparked up from the centre of the roof. The sheet glowed blue as well. Something to do with time travelling from the temple below. Nothing burned in the flames as they licked everything around me. *Wait till I tell Natasha.*

I heard a shout and could see a group of boys, a pale clump in the moonlight, between the bandstand and the swimming pool. The steady drops of rain splashed on the sheet above my head. This must be Hacker about to torch the bandstand. Ha, more difficult in the rain. After what I'd been through, Hacker and his team of gits didn't bother me much. What about Natasha?

I moved towards them, relaxed and detached. The blue light shimmered around me. Someone had started running down the slope towards the swimming pool. A ball of fire exploded up from the ground, silhouetting a person moving towards me. I recognised the way of running. Natasha!

The lightning flash picked out everything for a moment, the blazing petrol, and the three boys turning and running just beyond it. A further figure was standing near the pool, mouth wide open. The thunder clattered and smashed into my ears, the loudest I'd ever heard, as Natasha raced over to me.

"Rhory?"

"Yes, Natasha. You all right?"

"Think so, but let's-get-out-of-here before they realise the ghost is just you!" She stopped and stared at me.

"You're glowing blue, Rhory, and you're cheek's badly cut."

"Oh, am I, never mind." I turned back up the slope and started jogging towards the tunnel. Natasha came up by my side.

"I thought you might have drowned."

"Naw. Not really. It's been amazing, Nat."

"What's that?" said Natasha, stopping dead. We could see a blue flashing light in the distance and torches coming in our direction from the tunnel. More appeared over near the library. A car drove in the distance, crossing a far off football pitch and approaching the old oak tree.

"Heck, the old tree's on fire I think."

*

Amethyst, ten minutes earlier

Amethyst stood in the lee of the old oak. He pulled his coat closer around him. The wind had carried the sound of distant shouts but nothing he could understand. He checked his watch. They're late, seriously late. He stamped his feet to keep warm.

The blue flames around the bandstand didn't look like a petrol fire. He wondered if the local boy had partially succeeded in his time travel. The S.O.S. had wanted him to, to destroy the whole blasted chain, using the Egyptian bitch. He knew something of the strange physical effects that occurred when bending and weaving time. Shelley had delivered lots of information about that in several trance sessions. Something about 'Zero Point Energy' that could potentially give free energy to all households. Well that wasn't ever going to happen. Not if he had his way. The destruction of the bandstand couldn't come quick enough.

He could just make out Hacker and his fellow louts gesticulating. Then they went forward again, as the light display decreased. Amethyst took out the mobile, the one with the untraceable sim card. He punched in a memorised number. The voice in his ear said, "Hammerford Police, how can I help you?" He told the helpful lady exactly how she could assist. He slipped the mobile into his pocket. He'd need to throw it away as soon as he could.

Still the yobs didn't set the building ablaze. He punched one gloved hand into the other. The distant wail of police sirens confirmed his message had led to an instant response. You just have to know how to jerk the puppet strings.

He jumped when the plume of fire rose about 50 metres from the bandstand and felt rather than saw the lightning strike the tree behind him.

*

Rhory

"Follow me," I said, as the rain hammered down in earnest, and Natasha joined me under the slight protection of the sheet. We doubled around the tennis court side of the nursery school and crept past the edge of the council building.

"Where are we going?" asked Natasha. "The tunnel is cut off and there are police cars down there by the other gate."

"It's okay," I said, "there's an escape route I've used before. We need to leave the sheet here though, too noticeable."

"Just as well you've stopped glowing with blue light," said Natasha. "That stood out as well. Must be the rain."

We dashed across the small internal road, as more lightning flashed in the distance. Ducking through the familiar bushes, we received an impromptu shower.

"Through here," I said. "We can easily get over at this spot." I led the way, through the wet bushes, to the wall. Getting onto the top proved very simple. I eased myself around and hung on with my hands, before dropping the last half-metre onto the pavement.

Natasha sat on the wall, water dripping off her short hair and running down her face. The streetlights completely lit us up. She dropped down into my arms and I lowered her onto the pavement.

"Quick, across the road."

We ran over the road, the lights above us reflected back as crazy patterns in the water, as we splashed through. Thunder rolled past above us. A police car with flashing lights drove up towards the station.

"Hold my hand," said Natasha. "Make like we are boy and girlfriend."

I did, feeling twizzly and strange, her hand cold and small in mine. She nestled against my shoulder and water bounced off her head. The car braked, skidding slightly, and stopped some metres up the road from us.

A copper shouted from the window. "Hey, you two, where you going? Come over here."

"Run," said Natasha, doing so.

I had no choice, and ran also as the car door opened.

Feet pounded behind us.

*

Sergeant Munnery

Sergeant Jason Munnery enjoyed his great girth. Policing gave him the chance to throw his weight around, both literally and meta … meta… He couldn't remember the word, but he relished the power that came with being known as Hammerford's toughest cop.

As he had jumped out of the car near the old oak, he looked across to the bandstand, surprised he couldn't see any flames. The phone call to the station had said the bandstand had been set alight. Clearly it hadn't. He could see fire certainly, two fires in fact. One roared away between the bandstand and the swimming pool. The other, nearer at hand, sprang from the old oak which had taken a direct hit. *Must have been that lightning strike as we drove into the park.*

He could see figures running in the distance, making for the tunnel. *Just as well we've blocked that off.* He had his hand on his two-way radio when the man crawled out just from in front of his car. The light from the flaming tree revealed the burn on one side of his face. *I nearly drove right over him.* Not that it bothered him; the man had no right being here after the park had been closed for hours.

The man looked up at Munnery and burbled about a lost ring "Very important… Must be found… NOW!"

He's clearly delirious, thought Munnery, stopping the injured man from going back towards the burning tree. Munnery, not a man given to puzzling overmuch, puzzled now. *I know this man from somewhere, but where?*

Policewoman Sonia Blenkinsop spotted something lying on the ground. She rescued the burnt man's briefcase; that would make interesting reading later on. She also found a mobile phone lying on the wet grass. She didn't find a ring. No one did.

*

Rhory

"Quick," I said, grabbing Natasha's hand. "Up here!" We swerved up the path by the Carpet Emporium and heard the policeman shout back to a colleague, before charging after us. I took Natasha into the darkness under the tall trees, now thrashing about in the wind. My house was only a few metres away.

"Climb here," I said, helping her get a leg up. The shadows hid us and the policeman ran straight past. I followed her, using some broken bricks in the wall as hand and footholds, just as Juliette and I had done many times before. We dropped into my garden and moved quietly down towards the back door.

Somewhere close by a police whistle sounded. We slipped inside, panting and giggling. I went to the kitchen and picked up a dishcloth. "Here Nat, dry your face." She did so, and then used the soaking cloth to dab my cheek.

"You need antiseptic on this, Rhory, it goes quite deep. What on earth happened?"

"Yes, I'd like to know that too," said Juliette standing in her dressing gown at the door to the dining room. "What on earth have you two been up to?" She kept her voice low, and closed the door quietly behind her.

Natasha and I looked at each other then back at Juliette, and shrugged.

"It's a bit of a long story, Jules," I said.

"I've plenty of time," said Juliette at her most imperious.

"In a nutshell, we stopped some crazy hoodies from destroying the bandstand," said Natasha. "Rhory really bravely fought boys much bigger than him, and rescued me, and the bandstand is safe and the police are everywhere, and…"

"Okay, okay," said Juliette holding up her hands. "I'll put the kettle on. You get out of your wet things and tell me all about it. I don't want you both with pneumonia tomorrow."

When I reached my bedroom my shivering reached epic proportions. I used a towel to dry off most of the water, and noted the red stain when I touched my cheek, which now blazed with pain. I hadn't felt it until that point. I slipped on my dressing gown and crept downstairs, avoiding the creaks.

Natasha and Juliette had made three mugs of steaming tea, and Natasha's eyes were sparkling with excitement. Juliette patched up my cheek with something that stung a lot but reduced the pain. I took some painkillers and sipped the hot tea.

Natasha's explanation stayed close enough to the truth, as she described the fight by the well. ("We thought it might be a secret entrance to the space below the bandstand.") The flight from the boys. ("Rhory went one way and I ran the other, until Hacker tackled me like I was playing rugby or something.") The sheet subterfuge. ("Rhory had reached the bandstand and brilliantly did this ghost thing and scared the sh – the guts out of them and they ran.") The petrol cans. ("They were so careless, Jules, they allowed the petrol to light before getting to the bandstand.") And finally, she explained about the lightning and the arrival of the police.

"Hmm, well, you two have been very, very stupid and I've a good mind—" The doorbell rang before Juliette could finish. She looked at her watch. "Who on earth is it at this time? It's well after midnight."

"The police," I said. "It'll be the police."

"Okay," said Juliette. "Leave them to me."

She made a slight adjustment in how her dressing gown looked, put out the light and left the door slightly ajar. We heard her responding quietly to the policeman, and explaining everyone was in and no one had gone out, and her parents worked in the morning, and would he be so kind as to speak softly, and yes, she'd watch out for arsonists, but no, there weren't any in this house. The squawk box on the policeman's shoulder went off and a distant parrot voice said something we couldn't quite hear.

"That's okay," said Juliette coming back in and resuming drinking her tea. "They caught the youths apparently, four of them and also some man. The other policeman sounded quite excited, said something about a bigwig. Okay, Rhory, I'm going to put a plaster on your face. I think you'd better tell Mum and Dad you tripped in the night, came to me, and I patched you up. All true," she said, winking. "But maybe not the whole truth."

Natasha and I looked at each other, and shared a weak smile.

*

Shelley, half an hour earlier

"Ah, I'm glad you're here," said Shelley, offering Joe her most winning smile. "They've asked for you in the other room. There's been an accident."

"Has there now," said the driver, his unsmiling eyes on Shelley's. "And what would that be then?"

"Something to do with … to do with … excuse me." Shelley sneezed, and held up her hand, her eyes watering. "Must be something in the kitchen." She rummaged in her handbag, slipping her fingers around the red goo spray. "Bother, no hanky." She sniffed loudly. "The big bowl thing, it broke and a lady's hurt," she said looking up from her bag and seeing a moment's uncertainty cross his eyes.

"Ah," he said as a kettle, no doubt for a cup of his tea, reached the boil. He glanced across towards the sound of the boiling water, and Shelley took out the aerosol and sprayed it directly into his face, a long satisfying jet of red gunk.

He howled and jumped back, dropping the car keys, his hands rubbing his eyes. He flailed out at her, but with his eyes closed, he tripped and crashed into the table. Shelley glanced at the boiling water but decided against it, and ducked down to grab the car keys. He still couldn't see and struggled to get to the sink. She stamped her high-heeled shoe down on his foot, just as she'd learned in self-defence classes, four years earlier. He jumped blindly at her, struck a chair and ended up splayed on the floor. Shelley quietly opened the back door and slipped into the back garden.

The sigh of the trees and a chill wind greeted her. Lights in a couple of upstairs windows gave just enough illumination to make her way around towards the garages. Pale white shapes of statues in the garden watched her progress with sightless eyes. The garage door stood open. No Mercedes. Drat. Distant voices rose in the house. Shelley jogged as best she could around the side of the house, a curious tiptoed run in her high heels.

The Mercedes had been parked close to the front door. *I wonder why? Just as well.* The proximity of the car key allowed the door to open and Shelley slipped inside on the driver's side, kicking off her shoes. She looked for the key slot and pushed the key home. Light flooded over the car as the front door opened. The engine started to order and Shelley pulled away in a hail of gravel. She glanced in the mirror. The back window had filled with a tell-tale spider web of cracks. *Jesus, Mary and Joseph, they shot at me!*

The car hurtled down the long curving drive, as Shelley desperately searched for the headlight switch. They burst on, showing the wrought iron gate approaching rapidly. She screeched to a halt half a metre from the closed gate and opened a small compartment to take out the electronic key. She'd seen Killer Joe use this on the way in. The headlights illumined a hoe with a long ash handle leaning against one of the pillars. *Just right.*

The iron gate crept open and, glancing in her mirror, Shelley could see lights coming on all over the house with headlights catching trees nearby. Before the gates completely opened she drove through, scraping the offside door on a pillar. She braked, put the car in neutral and jumped out, the gravel biting through her stocking soles. Walking with huge fairy steps she reached for the hoe and started the gate on its closure programme. A car had reached the top of the drive near the house and its lights flashed over bushes and tree trunks quite close to her.

The metal gate edged closed, and Shelley waited, holding the hoe horizontally. Once the iron gate clicked home she jammed the ash pole against a low piece of ironwork and the hoe end against the pillar. It would be invisible from the far side at night, but would jam the gate. She jumped back into the car and headed for the main road.

Hardly any other traffic drove past and heavy rain had begun to fall. She shot through Warminster, none too worried if a speed camera caught the car breaking the law. A problem for Killer Joe and the Stony Hearts. At the sign for London, to the right, she turned left. Signs for Bristol and then the Severn Bridge came and went, and in a couple of hours Shelley had reached far into Wales.

Grabbing a coffee at a late night petrol station, she saw another web of splintered glass in a side window and two indentations near the boot. *Just as well the limo is bullet proof.* Before the dawn had arrived, Shelley had parked in Holyhead, near the Ferry Terminal, bought a ticket for Ireland and had eaten a stale croissant in a cafe.

She always carried her passport. Shelley O'Keefe said the name in the little green book. Her uncle had influence and an interest in republicanism, and the fictitious Prendergast had suited them both a few years earlier. An hour after sunrise, the boat pulled out and sailed for Dublin.

*

"I don't know what got into you three yesterday," said my mum, as she served us our supper two days later. "Anyone would think you were out all the other night, the way you sat there yawning all day. Glad to see you're more awake today."

Natasha developed a sudden coughing fit to cover up her giggles. Dad laid down the local paper he'd been scanning. "Seems the Chairman of the Council has resigned," he said. "Wants to spend more time with his family apparently. Can't think why." He winked at Mum. She frowned back at him. "There's a picture of him with his arm in a sling."

I took the paper. The injured Chair of the Council ducked in the paparazzi snap, hiding his face as he entered his own home.

"He orchestrated an attempt to set fire to the bandstand," Dad continued, "and has been dissed by the youths he employed. The police say they have clear evidence linking him to the crime. Something about a mobile phone."

"It's a bad day for bigwigs, Dad," said Juliette. "Did you see that high up spook from MI5, has had to leave also to spend more time with *her* family. It's in *The Times*. I wonder what's behind that story."

Natasha, who had heard all that had happened in ancient Egypt and the temple from me earlier in the afternoon, sputtered into her milk.

"You alright, dear?" asked Mum.

"Her name's Georgina Rillington," Juliette continued. "Unfortunate name I reckon, being as that's the road Crippen lived in – isn't it?"

"No, wrong murderer," said Dad. "10 Rillington Place, the infamous home of the bent copper, John Christie."

I recognised the man in the paper. I'd hit him with a paper pellet so very long ago, and then with a conker! The story underneath said he claimed to have been in the park searching for an amethyst ring he'd lost earlier. The reporter thought that excuse to be both lame and bizarre.

Underneath the snap of the councillor, the paper had a picture of the Save Our Bandstand Committee. They had been photographed in front of the unharmed structure, saying no one would allow it to be taken from Hammerford residents now. The reporter stated that the project for a new leisure centre in our great park was now dead in the water.

I studied the photo carefully. The museum curator and Mr Archer from the library stood alongside half a dozen others, pointing proudly at the bandstand. Slightly apart from them and the only one staring straight at the camera, stood a young man with dark, spiky hair, white gloves and a formal black jacket. I'd the weird impression he smiled at me, right out of the newspaper.

Chapter 85

Epilogue

The old lady climbed up the stairs, stopping half way to catch her breath. Jiminy, her faithful cat, mewed plaintively at the bottom of the stairs, but didn't follow her.

Bridget entered her bedroom. She sat on the bed for some time, resting her long aching limbs. Something had shifted, something had changed. A deep peace spread over her body. Of course neither Rhory nor Natasha had been in touch with her. She hadn't really expected them to. At thirteen years of age, their lives lay ahead of them. She knew much of what they had been through. She knew something of what awaited them.

Her powers of hearing seemed to have returned a little. Not her physical hearing. Her left ear remained obstinately deaf and her right no longer worked as it used to. No, the inner hearing, a skill that she'd learned so very long ago, had returned more distinctly. She had 'heard' that the connection between the Companions had been made, across time, just as it should. This evening she'd sat in the front room and read the old diary, the one from India over two hundred years earlier. Would Rhory find it? She thought he would, although she did not know how he'd cope with the Greek. She'd put the key just where she always did, confident he'd remember.

Night had fallen and a little light from the moon filtered into her bedroom. She stood up and moved to the window. Her knees ached.

The winter had transformed her beloved garden and she knew she would miss its spring glory this year. Above, the winter sky revealed a liberal sprinkling of stars. There was Orion, always so easy to identify. Once again she followed his belt downwards and to the left, to find Sothis, or Sirius as it is known today, the star, sacred to Isis and sacred to the Scribe himself.

Its light beguiled her. The star appeared to move gently in the sky, adding brightness as it did so. Her whole body gradually filled with this clear illumination.

The light eased her away from the house and the stars slowly revolved above her head. The landscape in front of her no longer held her garden. Ahead rested the familiar outline of the massive lioness. Bridget looked down at her arms, and smiled. Her hands were an olive brown and smooth, the skin of a woman in fullness of life. Her soft linen robes felt gentle and light against her body and took the sting out of the winter's chill. She came closer to the lion.

Its massive shape blocked out the stars. She moved round to where its paws pointed towards the great river. "Come child," said the voice, at once so familiar and also the voice she had sought for time's whole duration.

The man, neither young nor old, gazed out over the river Nile. He turned to face her, and there was the face she knew so well, the face of the Scribe.

He smiled and held out his hand.

Lodestone Books is a new imprint, which offers a broad spectrum of subjects in YA/NA literature. Compelling reading, the Teen/Young/New Adult reader is sure to find something edgy, enticing and innovative. From dystopian societies, through a whole range of fantasy, horror, science fiction and paranormal fiction, all the way to the other end of the sphere, historical drama, steam-punk adventure, and everything in between. You'll find stories of crime, coming of age and contemporary romance. Whatever your preference you will discover it here.